STEALING SACRED FIRE

BY

STORM CONSTANTINE

Meisha Merlin Publishing, Inc
Atlanta, GA

STEALING SACRED FIRE

An MM Publishing Book
Published by Meisha Merlin Publishing, Inc.
PO Box 7
Decatur, GA   30031

Editing & interior layout by Stephen Pagel
Copyediting & proofreading by Teddi Stransky

ISBN: 0-9658345-6-5

http://www.MeishaMerlin.com

First MM Publishing edition: January 2001

Printed in the United States of America
0 9 8 7 6 5 4 3 2 1

Library of Congress Cataloging-in-Publication Data

Constantine, Storm.
    Stealing sacred fire / by Storm Constantine.
        p. cm.
    ISBN 0-9658345-6-5 (pbk. : alk. paper)
    1. Millennialism—Fiction. I. Title.
    PR6053.O5134 S74 2000
    823'.914—dc21
                                                    00-010452

A few words from Storm on writing
Stealing Sacred Fire

This book was first published in 1997, two and a half years before the Millennium. I wanted the story to end with the Millennium, the dawn of a new age. People asked why I considered that date important. It was a celebration of two thousand years of Christianity, after all, and as I am distinctly not Christian, surely it made no sense for me to give it any credence.

I understood their point, but for me the most important aspect of the event was the fact that all over the world people would be focusing upon it. All that energy. It defies belief in itself. It did not matter what people were celebrating. For an ephemeral moment, humanity was in accord, as that hour of midnight swept across the world like a scythe. To any practitioner of magic, the life energy inherent in that event had to be at least interesting, if not a direct source of power.

Another aspect of the Millennium also intrigued me greatly. At the turn of nearly every century, magical groups and societies, through ritual, have attempted to initiate a new Golden Age for humanity, an age of freedom. I was interested in the symbolic and spiritual implications of this supposed New Age of Man.

Also, after two thousand years of patriarchal religion, it was interesting to reflect on where we are now, spiritually and politically. Although I am not Christian, I have no grudge against Christ, who, if we are to believe his story is historical rather than mythical, imparted sound teaching. It was what happened after he died that I condemn, how warped individuals twisted his message into an ascetic, repressive misogyny, almost a hatred and denial of life itself. Now, in the year 2000, we can see that Western people have far greater freedom to express themselves spiritually in the manner they choose, without being tortured, burned or hung for it. This might not be the case the whole world over, but it is a progression.

The total eclipse of the sun on August 11th, 1999, was also regarded as an exceptionally powerful magical event. Some people thought that what happened on that day would set the pattern for the rest of the year, the build up to the New Year.

As I was writing this book, the eclipse was two years in the future, and I had to speculate about what would happen. In this edition, I have slightly revised that section to be more realistic. The best place to view the eclipse in England was predicted by psychics to be The Lizard in Cornwall, which featured heavily in the second book of this trilogy, *Scenting Hallowed Blood*. Although I was unable to go down there myself, some of my friends braved the hordes and hired a cottage on The Lizard for a few days. On the day of the eclipse, which was due to occur at 11.00 a.m., the sky was smothered in clouds. My friends went to sit on the lion simulacre in the cliffs, (named Azumi in *Scenting Hallowed Blood*), and thought they wouldn't be able to see much. However, for just a few minutes, the clouds opened, and they were able to view the entire eclipse. Only ten miles north in Falmouth, where all the scientist and astronomers had set up their equipment, nothing was visible except the darkness at the moment of the eclipse.

When my friends came home, they barely had the words to describe the feelings that had swept through the crowd during those brief minutes. Several of them told of how before it happened, they had felt depressed or even physically ill, and people around them complained of similar conditions. The moments of blackness were entirely surreal and some primitive instinct within them had been terrified, as if it really had been the end of the world, the death of the sun. But when the sun came back, and radiant rays of diamond brilliance shone forth around the black centre, hope and joy surged through the crowd. People yelled, sang, clapped and wept. Any sense of depression or nausea lifted instantly. The last two thousand years of civilisation might never have happened. For just a short time, people were united in a pagan conjunction with nature.

Those of us who hadn't been able to go to Cornwall went up to Cannock Chase, miles of ancient heathland near our town, which before the advance of towns and roads had been joined to Sherwood Forest in Nottinghamshire, legendary home of Robin Hood. Many other people had the same idea, so it was quite a festival atmosphere. One of my friends suffered a depression similar to the ailment that had assailed people in Cornwall. While the eclipse was actually happening, she couldn't even bring herself to look at it. Everyone was offering her their smoked glasses, saying, 'Go on, you can't miss it.' But she just *refused*. Afterwards, escaping the crowds who were still engaged in picnics around us, we went to an ancient oak grove a short distance away, where we often meet to meditate. Here, we performed a short visualisation about the birth of the Child of the Aeon. Everyone felt extremely strange or disorientated. Something magical was certainly happening that day.

Prior to this, in 1998, I attended a Kurdish rally in Trafalgar Square in London. As I was writing about the Kurds in 'Stealing', I wanted to meet some of them first-hand. My friend and colleague, Andy Collins, whose research has always inspired me, had made contact with Kurdish organisations while writing his book *From the Ashes of Angels*. Andy believed that Kurdish factions, such as the Yezidi and Yaresan, are direct descendants from the race who'd once lived in their country. He'd found evidence to suggest that Kurdistan was Eden, and the Kurds' ancestors were the Anannage. Although the majority of Kurds are dark-haired and skinned, astonishing red-heads and blondes are sometimes born, who have blue or green eyes. The Yezidi practice an unusual form of angel worship and have been called devil worshippers, because they see the serpent of Eden as a good guy, who brought knowledge and enlightenment to humankind. In their religion, he is called Azazil. Shemyaza.

You need to read *From the Ashes of Angels* to learn the complete justification for Andy's well-researched claims. There is simply not the room here for me to do so.

The Kurds invited Andy to speak at the rally, after all the politicians, actors, and celebrities who supported their cause had had their say. I wasn't quite sure how the people would react to Andy's ideas. He would follow worthy speakers, who were working towards political aid for the Kurds. I knew what he was going to say, and I could barely bring myself to watch, sure he'd get lynched. I glanced around the crowd and saw men in wheel-chairs with missing limbs, and other obvious casualties of the conflict in Kurdistan, who had come to England for treatment. How would *they* view Andy's ideas? It seemed almost insulting. But Andy knew no such temerity. He got on stage and told these people, most of them exiles, many of them combat veterans, that they were descended from angels and that their country was the cradle of civilisation. Well, he didn't get lynched, and the applause was enthusiastic, but I suspect the truth was that few people there really understood what was being said to them. This day, however, provided great inspiration for one of the chapters near the beginning of this book, when Shemyaza first comes into contact with the Yarasadi, who are a fictional Kurdish faction.

In this novel, Shemyaza, from one viewpoint, is the Anti-Christ, he who comes to break down the rigours of patriarchy and asceticism. But from another viewpoint, he is the true Christ, shorn of millennia of dogma and misunderstanding. This is why there is one scene in the book where he is shown as both Christ and the Devil, two sides of the same coin: Ahura Mazda and Ahriman; Horus and Set. I found a passage in *The Genealogy of Morality* by the philosopher Friedrich Nietzsche, which seemed to describe Shemyaza, a being who is beyond good and evil and could raise humanity from its degenerative state to a new freedom and power:

'But some time, in a stronger age than this mouldy, self-doubting present day, he will have to come to us, the *redeeming* man of great love and contempt, the creative spirit who is pushed out of any position 'outside' or 'beyond' by his surging strength again and again, whose solitude will be misunderstood by the people as though it were flight *from* reality: whereas it is just his way of being absorbed, buried and immersed in reality so that from it, when he emerges into the light again, he can return with the *redemption* of this reality: redeem it from the curse which its ideal has placed on it up till now. This man of the future will redeem us not just from the ideal held up till now, but also from the things *which will have to arise from it*, from the great nausea, the will to nothingness, from nihilism, that stroke of midday and of great decision which makes the will free again, which gives earth its purpose and man his hope again, this Antichrist and anti-nihilist, this conqueror of God and of nothingness—*he must come one day...*'

Writing this book affected me greatly. It was as if I was tapping into some primal vein of archetypes, using symbols that have great meaning for the human race. The scene involving the well in St Menas (I won't say more to avoid plot-spoiling) made me feel physically sick. It was one of the most difficult scenes I have ever written.

Some of the scenes were inspired by dreams that I had during the writing process. The episode in the mountains of Kurdistan, when Daniel has a vision of the holy twins, was lifted directly from a dream I had a couple of days before. The appearance of the Crystal Chambers and their history was inspired by the visions of a psychic called Bernard, who worked with Andy Collins on this subject in 1985.

The time when I was writing this novel is long past, the Millennium spent, and we have returned to mundane routine. The sky did not open at mid-night on December 31st, no angels flew against the stars, and humanity did not change miraculously for the better. At this point in time, I cannot emulate the introduction to 'Scenting Hallowed Blood' and give directions to readers who might want to investigate the areas I've written about, because war and political regimes have made them inaccessible to Western travellers. We cannot seek the valley of Kharsag and soak ourselves in its history. But in fiction, we can dream better futures, better worlds. We can dream of living there.

Storm Constantine
June 27th, 2000

STEALING

SACRED

FIRE

Prologue

Iraq

The mound reared up incongruously from the rubbled hot-plate of the desert. It did not look like a city at all. Around it, the plains of scorching rocks were flat, like the dun, shattered terrain of some hostile planet, where only parched lizards blinked at the sun. The mound, or *tell*, had lain dead for many thousands of years. Here, at the hot girdle of earth, ancient secrets smouldered beneath miles of dust and memories. Shunned and feared, remembered only as the lost dwelling-place of demons, who had no place in the world of more recent, jealous gods, the *tell* had lain untouched by human hand for millennia. But now men had come here, religious taboos broken in the crack of stone, the opening of the earth. On the side of the *tell* a wound had been made, a simple, black hole that oozed cold. Carrion birds wheeled over the excavation; dark angels against the intense blue sky. Their cry was an echo of forgotten calls to buried gods.

An old man, squatting near the opened earth, glanced up at the ragged shapes and said to himself, "Death is here. The eyes of the ancient ones have come." He made a protective sign with his fingers and shivered as the cold breath that came out of the ground touched his cheek. Some hours earlier he had heard shouts below, and felt deep in his ancient fibres a tingling. The hot ground seemed fragile beneath him, as if it could open up like a hungry mouth, or a cut made in flesh by a blade, and swallow him into itself. They had found something momentous in the forgotten city below; something that should not have been found. Nothing would induce him to enter the tunnels of the excavation, not even the generous pay offered by the king to those who would work there.

Presently, having been advised of the new discovery, the king arrived at the site, his jeep throwing up a spray of desert grit. He alighted with dignity, trod purposefully up the slope in his shiny boots; a tall man in the prime of life. Like many dictators before him, he was dressed in khaki, his dark-skinned face half hidden by a neatly trimmed moustache. But, unlike his predecessors in this turbulent land, his hair was long and oiled into coils and on the second finger of his left hand, over his leather glove, he wore a large, golden ring, which bore an ancient seal. All creatures would kneel before him and did. He had named himself Nimnezzar, having been taught in a dream his true origins. He believed that royal, unearthly blood ran in his veins.

As the king strode up the side of the *tell*, scattering stones, the old man made an obeisance. "Do not enter, great one. The secrets of the ages must remain in darkness."

The king paused. His expression was unreadable as he peered down at the old man, although the fingers of his right hand tapped his khaki-clad thigh. "Why is that?" he demanded. "You know why we are here."

The old man ducked his head in deference. "Yes, oh great one." He pointed to the sky. "But the eyes of the Old Ones behold your subjects desecrating the ancient domain. I speak only to warn you."

The king stood motionless for a moment. His eyes seemed empty of feeling. They were eyes that could watch death in all its forms without flinching. He could snuff out a life with a twitch of his fingers. Yet he did not call for his guard to punish the old man for his outspoken words. He smiled. "Hassan, I am of the ancient line. The eyes of the Old Ones are my eyes. They are here to attend this great moment, like serpents drawn to the birth of a divine king. Do not fear for me."

Again, the old man ducked his head. "I have served your family long, great one. I know that your blood is sacred, yet the shadows of those carrion wings hang over me...Once you have beheld what lies within the darkness, there is no going back."

The king reached down and touched the old man lightly on his shoulder. "This is a new age," he said, with a tenderness that seemed inappropriate from his lips. "The world is different now."

He climbed over the rubble and then on, into the darkness. His personal guard followed him, casting cold glances at the old man as they passed. He did not look at their faces, only their guns.

Within, the tunnel sloped downwards steeply. Temporary lighting hung from the walls, trailing ropes of cable and emitting an electrical hum. The air smelled musty, but also sweet, and it was hot upon the lungs. This was unexpected, for the king had been told by experts that in the underground cities temperatures remained constant. The bright lighting must be heating the air.

The chambers in the levels nearest the surface were empty, and had been constructed at a later date than those beneath them. They were crude in design and had perhaps been storehouses, or else barracks for military, but who could really tell how the inhabitants of this alien place had run their community?

Markers had been placed to show the way through the labyrinth to the lower levels. The king and his entourage emerged from a twisting corridor onto the lip of what first appeared to be a ledge. The king paused. He made no outward sign, but there was no doubt the scene before him surprised and awed him.

He and his officers stood at the brink of a great circular shaft; their heads nearly brushed the ceiling. Dark openings punctuated the walls of the shaft, visible in the sporadic glares of yellow light. Further below, there was darkness.

A curl of worn, spiralling steps led down from where the king stood to the lower levels. It could be seen that before each doorway in the circular face of the rock, there was a narrow platform. The shaft was crawling with workers, their voices shrill yet strangely muffled. Wooden carriers, some empty, some full of rubble and broken artefacts, glided up and down the sheer stone face, via pulleys and ropes.

A short man dressed in dusty khaki appeared over the ledge. His moustache was rimed in white powder, like snow, and also his black hair. He bowed to the king. "It is an honour to welcome you, great one." He brushed at his moustache self-consciously.

The king nodded, looking past the man. He pointed. "This is impressive, Rashid. You have worked hard."

The man, who was the chief archaeologist of the dig, made a self-deprecating shrug. "All we needed to do was clear the upper levels. It was all waiting for us."

"Good, good," said the king, sticking out his lower lip. He waved his hand at the yawning chasm. "All the little openings down there. Where do they lead? Tombs?"

The archaeologist smiled, but not too broadly. "No, great one. What you perceive as small openings are in fact very large. Twenty feet high, perhaps. They lead out into the city, which has lain hidden beneath the *tell* above for thousands of years."

"So what have you found?"

The archaeologist gestured towards the steps. "If you would allow me to precede you, great one, I shall take you to it. Take care. We have set ropes into the wall for support, but the steps are still shallow and very worn." He did not mention the six workers who had already fallen to their deaths from the steps. As yet, the team had not penetrated to the bottom of the shaft.

Slowly, the royal entourage made its way down the steps. Occasionally, the archaeologist would pause to indicate features of interest to the king. "At one time the whole of the walls would have been painted, but most of it has gone now. At least in this place. There are treasures to be found further within." They looked into some of the openings, but Rashid did not lead them inside.

As they descended Nimnezzar noticed that the air changed. It was no longer humid, but almost of blood heat. It smelled dry and faintly electric. He had expected mustiness, the stench of corpse-dust, perhaps a trace of ancient incense.

"Here, great one." The archaeologist had paused on one of the ledges.

The king joined him. Within, he sensed the bustle of industry. "In here?"

"Yes. Please lead us. It is quite safe."

The king entered the opening, and as he did so, a strange, fleeting feeling gripped his body and an echo of a sound—a deep, resonating tone—vibrated through him. He was aware of the antiquity of the stone walls around him, aware of their memories. He belonged in this place. It knew him.

The walls here were painted with figures; winged men, goat-headed guardians, serpent women. The king had never seen art like it anywhere else in his kingdom, and he examined every excavation personally. He paused and touched one of the walls. It felt warm beneath his fingers. These are the faces of my ancestors, he thought.

His party waited for him to enjoy this private moment, their breath stilled.

Then, he exhaled through his nose and continued to walk down the corridor. Everyone followed.

Open doorways appeared on both sides of the tunnel. The king stopped to look into each chamber. All were furnished, with long tables and shelves.

"We think this was a market quarter," said the archaeologist. "Remains have been found of cloth, jewelery, coin, even dried food. It is amazing that so much of it remains given the age of the place. It has never been plundered. No-one has found it before." Rashid frowned, clearly remembering he was perhaps touching upon the volatile politics of earlier regimes. In those days, all interest in the pagan past had been seen as heresy and men such as Rashid, who had a keen, academic interest in antiquities, had known it prudent not to talk about their obsessions. Rashid had resigned himself to a life working behind a desk, but since Nimnezzar had seized power, things had changed dramatically. There were now whispers that previous rulers had known all about the forbidden legacy of their land, but had kept quiet about it, no doubt believing it was the work of Iblis. Still, for Rashid, it meant that a life of bureaucratic dullness, with no prospects, had been changed to that of limitless possibilities. The king thought well of his archaeologists and rewarded them highly. Rashid could smell the exciting perfume of his land's ancient heritage; he could taste its dust in his mouth.

Nimnezzar was not thinking about the recent past. It meant nothing to him now, for he had changed the course of the history of his people. He considered that perhaps no-one had *dared* venture here before, and then remembered the warning of the old man, Hassan.

"Who lived here?" asked one of the king's guard, a senior officer.

The archaeologist smiled widely. "Why, sir, the ancestors of our beloved king. The Arallu lived here, demon lords, the sons of angels."

"Yes." Nimnezzar nodded. "They were here." He spoke with authority, and no-one doubted that he could hear the voice of the past welcoming him home.

"Have you found...any bodies?" asked the officer.

The king flicked him an admonishing glance. The question lacked propriety.

The officer made an apologetic gesture. "I mean, is there any physical evidence remaining of the Revered Ancients?"

The archaeologist steepled his fingers beneath his chin. Otherwise, his body was perfectly still. "No-one was left here. The city was clearly abandoned. They left belongings, but nothing else. No animals, no birds. There are no catacombs. But..." He flapped his hands. "Come, come. See for yourselves."

Now he preceded the king down the corridor. They came across a huddle of workers outside a doorway. All dropped their tools and panniers, and fell to their knees at the king's approach, placing their foreheads carefully against the stone floor. The king ignored them. "Ah," he said. "And this?"

"You sense its significance, great one," said Rashid. He bustled through the prostrate crowd.

They entered a circular chamber. The walls were painted with sentinel figures, their attenuated, ophidian faces grave and watchful. They wore long robes of dark red, over which lay cloaks of feathers. There was another opening opposite the entrance, but it did not appear to be a natural doorway, rather that it had been hacked out from the stone walls. Rubble lay to either side. The king frowned at the sight. "What has happened here?"

The archaeologist bowed rapidly a few times. "It was a sealed doorway, great one," he explained, "but the glyphs upon it indicated that something momentous lay beyond. It has taken my people six weeks to cut their way through, but the effort has brought great reward." He scurried forward and laid a hand upon the jagged lip of the entrance. "It is a pity that some minor destruction was involved, but we have saved the plaster that bore the glyphs. It was extracted most carefully from the wall. You may examine the fragments later, if you wish."

The king made a dismissive sound. "My translators will be presented with this material. What lies within this place?" He approached the opening, but felt oddly reluctant to proceed. His ancestors had sealed this chamber tightly. Was even he meant to ignore their efforts to keep people out?

The archaeologist seemed unconcerned by such thoughts. He stepped into the dark tunnel beyond. "Come, come," he said, apparently forgetting protocol in his excitement.

The king cast his eyes around the edge of the opening, then took a single step through. Another vibration coursed through his flesh; stronger this time, like the echo of a great booming deep within the earth. He shuddered, and sensed a wind against his skin, flying fragments of dust. He blinked.

There was no wind now, and it seemed no-one else had felt its passage. The archaeologist was hurrying ahead. Nimnezzar followed, his flesh numb.

The short tunnel, which once had been solidly filled in with stone blocks, led into a larger chamber. Concentric rings were cut into the otherwise unadorned basalt floor, and plain columns surrounded its perimeter. In its centre stood what appeared to be an Egyptian sarcophagus, placed on a raised dais. That, of course, could not be so. The shadowy culture who had built this city had predated the earliest pharaonic dynasties by perhaps thousands of years. The dais was covered in rubble, its origin not immediately apparent. The lid of the sarcophagus had been removed and now stood propped up between two of the columns. Upon it was carved the representation of a winged man, curving pinions arranged over his body. He had the long, serpent face, the slanting eyes. It looked like a stylised mask.

"You said there were no tombs," said the king. He could feel his heart beating strongly. He felt breathless.

"We are not sure whether this is a tomb," answered the archaeologist cautiously. "When we first opened the sarcophagus, we thought it was full of rocks." He indicated the rubble. "These that you see here. It seemed likely that the artefact had once contained remains, which at some stage had been removed and replaced with the rocks. We took them out, hoping to find some clue as to had what been contained in the sarcophagus. We found more than we hoped for."

Slowly, the king approached the open sarcophagus. He realised he was afraid of what he would see within it. The case was at least six feet high. He had to go right up to it to look inside, and he was a tall man.

"It is lined with obsidian," babbled Rashid, "the ancients believed that the black glass had magical properties, and would act as a containment…"

Nimnezzar's guard waited anxiously, sensitive, like hounds, to their king's mood. They saw him peer over the lip of the stone. For a moment, he stood wide-eyed in apparent shock, then he uttered, "Mighty Allah!" the name of a god he had forsaken years before. He stepped back, staggering as his heels met the rubble. He had seen someone—no desiccated mummy, but a man lying as if asleep within the tomb.

The guards all gripped their weapons more firmly, their bodies stooped into postures of alertness.

The archaeologist hurried up to the dais. "I know it is a shock to first behold it. Perfectly preserved. Not even the rocks have crushed it."

The king turned to him, his eyes holes of dark fire. "It?" he shouted. "Don't you realise who this is?"

The archaeologist cowered. "We are presently engaged in translating the inscriptions found around the edge of the casing."

"Look at him!" roared the king. He grabbed Rashid by his shirt collar and lifted him up bodily so he could see into the sarcophagus. The king shook the smaller man as if he were a child. "That is the noble countenance of a Watcher lord," he said. "Be humble in his presence."

He let go of the archaeologist, who staggered back off the dais. The king summoned the senior officer of his guard. "Come, Nerim."

The officer stepped up beside him and together they gazed down into the tomb.

The figure within lay as if asleep, shrouded in a layer of rock dust. Through the dust, it could be seen that he was robed in costly if rotted fabrics that were adorned with jewels. A cloak of vulture feathers surrounded him. His red hair was braided over his chest, glinting still like bronze, even beneath the patina of crumbled stone.

"He looks as if he could wake at any moment," said the officer in a low voice.

Nimnezzar hunkered down and ran his fingers over the inscriptions on the stone walls of the casing. "I know this sigil," he said.

"Who?" Nerim knelt down beside him, and the king took his hand and pressed it against the stone. His eyes looked feverish. "I know."

He stood up once more and looked over the side. "Penemue," he said, "who gave knowledge of the bitter and the sweet."

"Penemue," repeated Nerim, his brow creased.

Nimnezzar shook his head in wonderment. "If it is he who lies within this tomb, he was one of the original rebel Watchers who fell from grace. For five thousand years, he has endured the punishment of internment."

The officer looked sceptical. "But how could the body remain preserved this long? It looks as if it...he...was entombed recently. But that cannot be possible."

"No." The king looked at his officer with feverish eyes. "Presuming, of course, that he is dead."

For a moment, all was silent, but for the humming of the bare electric lights.

The officer leaned away from the king; his knees cracked. "Not dead?"

The king stood up. He had been waiting for this moment a long time, since the vision that had come to him as a young man. In the vision, an angel lord had appeared before him and told him of his sacred destiny. He was to reinstate the line of divine kings, strengthen the blood-line that ran so faintly within him. In his blood: a memory of ancient days, when the rebel angels had ruled the land and built their hidden cities beneath it. Nimnezzar had seized power, but still he lacked knowledge. There had been no more visions.

"Penemue," he said, and put his hands against the edge of the sarcophagus. His voice was a low, respectful whisper. "You, who are the father of Sargon, grandfather of Naram-Sin, ancestor of Sennacherib, Ashurbanipal, and the guardian protector of my family: hear me, Nimnezzar, spiritual son of Nimrod and Nebuchadnezzar. Honour the ancient contract…"

And there was movement in the tomb. Dust stirred in eddies as if wind had somehow invaded the sarcophagus. The dais began to vibrate, and some of the light-bulbs in the room popped out into darkness. Several people in the chamber uttered gasps of fear. The king gripped the stone, although his officer retreated hastily.

"Penemue!" cried Nimnezzar. "The time of your sacrifice is ended. May your spirit come forth from the furthest reaches of the universe and return unto your body!"

A weird, eerie shriek sped through the labyrinthine tunnels and vaults of the ancient city. Stones fell from the ceiling of the chamber onto the heads of the king and his followers. Fear gripped Nimnezzar's soul. He wanted to retreat, order his people to pile the rocks back into the sarcophagus, but it was too late now. He had to continue and fulfil his destiny. "Penemue," he said again; it sounded like a sob.

Below him, the eye-lids of the Watcher opened slowly, revealing reddened, desiccated orbs within. Nimnezzar saw an expression of terror cross the long, inhuman face. Lips cracked open, eyes widened. And the city reverberated to the silent vibrations of a voiceless scream of pain and despair.

Chapter One
Two Suns Rise

The Midlands, England

His eyes opened and, for a moment, the screams of carrion birds echoed around his mind; fragments of a dream. He lay still for some minutes, his body tingling with discomfort. Then an urge to move stabbed through him, and he sat up abruptly in the bed, unsure of where he was. It felt as if he'd been sleeping for millennia.

A figure moved into his line of sight. His sight was unclear for he could see no more than a shining outline. "Who's there?"

The figure came forward, swam into focus. "Shem. You are awake." The statement was almost a question, as if the sleeper had made false awakenings many times before, only to deceive those who watched him.

"Salamiel." He held out his left hand, and once Salamiel's fingers curled around his own, he realised how cold he was. "How long have I slept?" He felt drugged, unable to recall how he'd come to this place, and when.

Salamiel sat down on the edge of the bed. He seemed reluctant to answer. "How much do you remember, Shem?"

Shemyaza pressed a hand against his eyes. "Enough."

Salamiel stood up. "Let me fetch you something to drink. Are you hungry?"

Shem nodded. "Whatever."

After Salamiel had left the room, Shemyaza lay back down on the bed, blinking at the ceiling. Warmth was flooding back into his system. He was aware of the summer afternoon beyond the window. The room did not face the sun, and in fact was very dark, but the air beyond was full of

summer sounds; children crying out, the clear sound of traffic, birds. He knew who he was, what he was: Shemyaza,
spiritual king of the Grigori, the descendants of angels. Many
life-times seemed to tumble through his mind. He had lived
for thousands of years, yet had not. He had been reborn,
reshaped, remembered. Fallen angel.

His history was the fabric of legends, most forgotten now,
and some so fragmented in the dreaming mind of the world
that the truth was lost or obscured.

Many thousands of years before, in the most ancient of
days, the race remembered as angels had openly walked the earth,
and were worshipped as gods by humanity. They were known
as the Anannage, the Sons of God, who harboured dangerous
and terrible secrets concerning the nature of the universe and
how to manipulate its subtle forces. Humanity, whom they regarded as a lesser species, was often used as labour for their
clandestine work projects, forever excluded from the light of
the Anannage's great knowledge. Their secrets were not for
sharing with children. Inevitably, change had devastated their
closed world. Shemyaza and a number of his colleagues had
scorned the laws of their people, which forbade intimate inter-
action with the lesser race and, having been bewitched by the
beauty of human women, had taken them as lovers, revealing
to them the forbidden knowledge of the Anannage. The fruit
of this doomed union was a long and bloody conflict between
different factions of the Anannage. Shemyaza and his co-con-
spirators had been captured and punished. Some had been buried alive beneath the earth, while Shemyaza himself had been
burned, his soul cast into the constellation of Orion where it
had been imprisoned for millennia.

The time of the Anannage's glory had passed, and they
disappeared from the world. Their great achievements were
forgotten, their superior knowledge remembered only as myths.
In their wake, they left the surviving members of a hybrid race
spawned from the union of Anannage and human: the Grigori.
Shunned as demons, the Grigori went into hiding, but continued to govern human affairs from afar. Now, they wielded
enormous power in the world, having great influence over both
commerce and government.

The end of the millennium approached, heralding a time of great changes. The soul of Shemyaza had returned to the earth, his consciousness thrust into the body of a Grigori maverick named Peverel Othman. Shemyaza could not remember much of Othman's life, but enough to know he had committed atrocities against human beings and Grigori alike. He had wandered into a village named Little Moor, and there had discovered the hybrid Winter twins, in whose veins ran Grigori blood, although they had not known it. Their father, Kashday Murkaster, had been driven from Little Moor nearly twenty years previously by the Parzupheim, who were the governing body of the Grigori. Kashday had been a rebel, and had used a human woman—the twins' mother Helen—to enact forbidden rituals. Othman, discovering this rotting nest of past Grigori activity in the village, had sought to reproduce Kashday's dark work. He had coerced the Winters into helping him and had rejuvenated one of Kashday's elderly, human helpers—Emma Manden—so that she could assist him. Then there was Daniel, a boy unaware of his psychic powers. Othman had been prepared to sacrifice him to achieve his aims. Othman's schemes, however, had failed. The only result of his activities in Little Moor was that he remembered who and what he really was. Shemyaza had awoken after a sleep of millennia among the silence of the stars. Daniel had become his vizier.

Daniel, where was Daniel? Shemyaza blinked at the ceiling, watched a single fly circle the electric light. What had happened after Little Moor? What was he doing here in this house?

Reconstituting fragments of memory, he recalled being discovered by the Grigori. He had been taken to Cornwall. He remembered how resentful he'd been of the role that had been thrust upon him there. The Grigori had wanted him to be their Divine King, who would lead them into the new millennium and help reclaim their lost heritage. In the distant past, Shemyaza had dared to rebel against his superiors, had tried to initiate change in the world. But it had been so long ago. Shemyaza had no interest now in the power struggles of his people. However, the events that had taken place in Cornwall had changed him. Almost against his instincts, he had re-claimed his kingship, if not his kingdom. He had entered the underworld of Albion's soul, and there had awoken a slumbering serpent power, emplaced thousands of years before by the first Grigori who'd made land-fall in England. Soon after he'd emerged from the underworld, his mind had retreated in upon itself; perhaps to recuperate or else to forget. Why had he slept for so long?

Salamiel return broke his reverie. Shem studied him as he approached the bed, carrying a tray. Salamiel too was a survivor of the ancient conflict. Like Shem, he had transgressed the laws of his people and taken a human lover. For thousands of years, he'd lain buried in a tomb, only to be resuscitated by the Grigori adept, Sofia, who had sought to gain control of Shem's power in Cornwall. Sofia's plans had failed, but her greed had reunited the erstwhile Watcher rebels. Shem knew that others must also have survived, or still lay sleeping somewhere. They must be found.

Shem's mouth filled with saliva at the sight of thick white sandwiches, heaped on a plate on Salamiel's tray. He realised how hungry he was.

Salamiel sat down on the bed again to watch him eat. His dark orange eyes were shadowed with concern, almost as if he feared Shemyaza might lapse back into a waking sleep at any moment. "So, what exactly *do* you remember, Shem?"

"The beach," he said, biting into the soft bread. "Cornwall." He looked up at Salamiel again. "Where are we?"

"Nowhere very exotic, I'm afraid. This is a house in the Midlands. A friend of Enniel Prussoe's owns it."

Enniel Prussoe. The name conjured more recollections. Enniel was a Grigori patriarch, a member of the Parzupheim, an organisation that governed Grigori affairs. The Prussoe house, High Crag, had been both Shem's prison and refuge during the time he'd been in Cornwall. He remembered the wildness of the dark winter sea-scape of the Lizard: the cry of buzzards, the lashing of raging waves against wet serpentine rock. It had been so cold there. Now, it was summertime. "How long?" Shem repeated. "Months?"

Salamiel stood up. "You haven't been asleep exactly. You've been able to feed yourself, bathe yourself, but..." He turned to the window. "You haven't been with us, Shem. Not for a long time."

"Why?"

Salamiel shook his head. "We're not sure. Your experiences in Cornwall exhausted you, clearly. Perhaps you needed time to recover, and to assimilate what happened to you there."

Shem swung his legs over the side of the bed, wondering whether he'd feel dizzy, but it seemed his body, if not his mind, was used to movement.

Salamiel handed him a towelling robe. "You haven't been with us for over five years," he said.

Shem thrust his arms into the robe. It took a few moments for the information to hit him. Then he had to sit down again. "Five years? Unconscious?"

Salamiel nodded. "Well, in a way."

"They did something to me. Enniel and his cronies."

"No, Shem. Shortly after you woke the Serpent, you became listless. Enniel had physicians look you over, but there was no explanation. We came here, for you to recuperate. We knew you would be back with us soon. It is nearly time."

"For what?"

"The new millennium. This is August, Shem. August 1999."

"Where's Daniel?"

"In Cornwall with the Prussoes. He's gone to observe the solar eclipse with them." Salamiel glanced out of the window. "It must have begun some minutes ago. The best place to view it is The Lizard."

"Bring him back," Shem said. "I need my vizier by me."

Cornwall

Daniel Cranton had wandered away from High Crag, seeking solitude. It had been five years since he'd walked this cliff path, high above the beach. The last time he'd been there had been as Shemyaza's vizier, his eyes in the unseen, spiritual world. It all seemed so unreal now. Since Shem's collapse, Daniel had lived a fairly mundane life with Salamiel up in the

Midlands, watching and waiting for Shemyaza to look at him once more with intelligence in his eyes. A couple of times a year, Daniel had come down to Cornwall, to stay with Lily and Owen Winter, in the cottage that Enniel Prussoe had given to them, but the holidays had not been easy. Too much had changed between them all. Once, they'd been three teenagers leading aimless existences in a small, English village. Then Peverel Othman had invaded their lives, turned them upside down. The twins and Daniel had been instrumental in awakening Shemyaza's true being. Like many human dependants of the Grigori, Daniel had been granted an extended life-span, but that miraculous gift had not changed his essential humanity. Lily and Owen had eagerly embraced the Grigori half of their ancestry; a gulf had opened up between Daniel and the twins. At one time, Daniel and Owen had been lovers, but now because of past rancours, all engendered by Othman, they tended to avoid one another. As for Lily, the carefree and rather wild young woman Daniel had loved seemed to have vanished for ever. Since she'd become a mother, she was too engrossed in her daughter to be much of a confidante to Daniel.

All along the coast, people were gathering to watch the impending solar eclipse, which had been heralded madly in the press for months. The best place to view in the UK would be the Lizard, so it seemed that every New Ager and astronomy buff in the country had gathered there, as well as hordes of ordinary people who just wanted to see an unusual astronomical event. Throughout the county, hotels and guest-houses were charging up to five times normal rates for the week and some roads had been closed off. Anticipation buzzed in the air. Sad that the sky was so overcast. It was doubtful there'd be much to see.

Daniel had had to negotiate the buzzing crowds to find an empty path. So far, among the ordinary people, he had identified gatherings of UFO enthusiasts, Japanese Shinto devotees, Wiccans and Christians, as well as more obscure groups he could not name. Mixed in with the colourful clothes of casual sight-seers were the saffron robes of the followers of Krishna, who were handing out leaflets. Evangelist types in semi-military uniforms sang bright, marching songs, eyeing

other groups present with jittery distaste. It seemed every belief system, religious and otherwise, was represented, all convinced the eclipse was some kind of significant, if not spiritual, event. It was a build up to the New Year. Some people
believed that whatever circumstances you were in this day
would be fixed until 1999 rolled over into 2000. For that reason, perhaps, the crowds were determined to have a good time,
whatever the weather. Daniel knew this was an important
event, but was cynically amused by the millennium madness
he sensed around him. This would be but a feeble foretaste
for the hysteria that would erupt on New Year's Eve.

In a field, some yards back from the cliff edge, a group of
eminent astronomers had set up complex equipment amid a
sea of tents. The large outside broadcast vans of TV companies clustered like beetles around them. Anchor men and
women were thrusting themselves upon anyone who was prepared to talk about what the coming event meant to them, but
not one of them had approached Daniel. He had made sure
he projected an aura that would discourage forced introductions. A faint skirl of music shivered through the air—violins
and hand-drums—as New Agers danced to greet the darkening of the sun. Daniel felt remote from it all.

When Shem had awoken the serpent, Daniel had been convinced the world as he knew it would change. He'd expected
new levels of tolerance and compassion, some kind of human
epiphany. Where was it? The news was still full of the abominations of juvenile crime, international corruption, senseless
massacres and rising despair. Had Shem's spiritual journey
been for nothing? Daniel felt depressed by the scene around
him. Who were these people kidding? Just themselves.

The Prussoes, and probably his old friend, Emma Manden's
coven of Pelleth witches, would undoubtedly already be gathering on the cliff above Mermaid's Cove, which was the private beach to High Crag, Enniel's home. Daniel knew he should
try and muster some energy, plaster a smile across his face and
go back to the house. He should make an effort to greet his
friends and join in with the party spirit, but his mood was too
melancholy for festivities. Shem should be here. Things should
be different.

Daniel sat down on the grass and closed his eyes. *Do I really want him to come back?* He shivered in the humid air. Life was quiet now. Perhaps it would be better to keep it that way.

A noise behind him made him open his eyes and glance round in irritation. A new crowd of sight-seers was strolling towards him, and he could see many more approaching. Clearly, they'd spotted the unpopulated area of cliff top and aimed to change the situation. The slam of car doors and the shriek of children offended Daniel's ears. Before anyone could touch the periphery of his aura, he was on his feet and heading back to High Crag.

The Prussoes, an extended family in the literal sense of the word, were still wandering out from the house to gather at the cliff edge, above their private cove. High Crag loomed above them, its tall chimneys stark against the summer sky. As well as the Prussoes, prominent members of other Grigori families had gathered to watch the event. Quite a crowd was milling around on the cliff top, sampling the refreshments being handed out by Enniel's household staff.

Daniel found Enniel, standing apart from the main group, examining the sight-seers further down the cliff through a pair of high power binoculars. Dark red hair blew free around his head and his clothes, for Enniel, were casual. Somehow he didn't look right in T-shirt and jeans. His long, handsome face was set in a disapproving expression. Daniel smiled privately as he approached.

"Tch!" Enniel complained. "Just look at them. Sheep!" Enniel was not known for his tolerance of humankind.

"The flotsam of humanity gather on your sacred ground," Daniel said, unable to keep a sharp tone from his voice.

Enniel lowered the binoculars, cast an unreadable eye over Daniel. "A predictable turn of events."

Daniel shrugged, hands in pockets. He felt that Enniel still disapproved of his position as Shemyaza's vizier. Even though he had been granted the privilege of an extended life-span, he was still, to most Grigori, an upstart human aspiring above his station in life.

One of the Prussoe aunts was distributing smoked glass screens to the family—obviously in the hope that the sky would clear—and swooped up with a sycophantic smile for Enniel. Her name was Kharael, a tall, spindly woman dressed in the faded garments of an earlier age. She seemed to notice Daniel as an afterthought. "You haven't been down here for a while, Daniel." She pushed a glass into his hands.

He smiled wanly. "No."

"Daniel's kept busy up north," Enniel remarked dryly, a reference to Daniel's day job in a supermarket. "Aren't you?"

"Yeah, very," Daniel answered. To end the embarrassing discussion, he raised the glass to his eyes. While they'd been talking the eclipse had begun. The thick clouds had moved apart, to provide a brief glimpse of the phenomenon. Already the sun was being eaten away, gobbled up by a segment of dark. The sight conjured a roar from the crowd. Strange feelings conflicted within Daniel's heart. Would something unusual happen? His body and mind felt taut, uneasy. The clouds slid back, hiding everything, but it was getting colder wasn't it?

A hand touched Daniel's shoulder, fingers curling around him. For a moment, his flesh crawled with dread.

"Daniel, hi! I didn't know you were here!"

He turned round to the smile of a tall young woman, who wore a long ethnic-print dress. Her red hair fell in thick waves over her shoulders. Relief. He had expected it to be Owen. "Hello, Lily. How are you?" He glanced over her shoulder to see if her brother was around and was glad to see he was not. She was accompanied by her young daughter, Helen.

"We're fine," Lily said. "Hel, say hello to Daniel."

The child murmured a greeting. Daniel narrowed his eyes. Helen had grown up quite a lot since the last time he'd seen her. She was very dark-skinned, a trait she had inherited from her dead father, Israel. Her dark eyes fixed on Daniel in a peculiarly adult expression. He did not warm to the knowing slant of her smile. Mentally, he shook himself. This was a Grigori child, and was bound to appear different from other children he'd met.

"So," Lily began in a firm yet humorous tone, "why haven't you come to the cottage?"

Daniel smiled uneasily. "Didn't get down till late last night."

Lily wrinkled her nose. "I suppose that will do as an excuse." She paused. "How's Shem?"

"The same."

Lily pantomimed an exaggerated grin. "I feel like I shouldn't ask." Her brow creased. "Are you OK, Dan?"

He forced a smile. "Sorry. I feel a bit weird today. Not very sociable."

Lily nodded. They both watched Helen for a while, who had dropped her mother's hand to squat down on the grass. At first, it looked as if she was innocently picking flowers, then Daniel noticed she was actually examining some kind of beetle.

"I suppose being here brings back memories for you," Lily said. "And I doubt they're good ones."

"Well, a little."

Lily squeezed his shoulder. "I'm sorry, Dan. Listen, you will come over later, won't you?"

He nodded. "Yes. OK."

The clouds had drawn back again like theatre curtains to reveal another poignant image of the sun being devoured by darkness. As far as Daniel could see, light glimmered off the smoked glasses people held to their eyes. The light around the cliff-tops was altogether surreal. It felt like the end of the world. Daniel fought an urge to run back to High Crag and seek sanctuary in the shadows of the house. It was almost as if he might suddenly blip back in time and find himself waiting to discover whether Shem had survived his ordeal in the underworld or not: this time, the outcome might be different.

"My God!" Lily exclaimed beside him. "What's that?"

A corona had now appeared around the sun, but something moved against it, a heaving, cloudy tide. Daniel squinted through his glass. "It's moving…looks like…"

"Birds!" Lily cried. "Thousands and thousands of little birds!"

They seemed to fly directly out of the dark sun, billowing down towards the earth as if caught in a solar wind. The air was filled with an eerie cheeping. "That's incredible!" Lily said. "Has the eclipse attracted them or something?"

Daniel shuddered. He could not help but look for omens in the phenomenon. Perhaps only he and Lily could see it. Then, shouts from further along cliff advertised that at least some people in the waiting crowds of devotees and sight-seers were also witnessing the event. Daniel turned his head to observe their reaction. Even from here, he could see that certain huddles of people were moving excitedly, pointing at the sky. One group stood apart, in a circle. They all held up what appeared to be short swords towards the eclipse. It was clear, however, that not everyone could see the birds.

"What is it, Daniel?" Lily asked. "What does it mean?"

The birds danced across the sky before them. Daniel searched for patterns in their curling formation, but saw none. "I don't know. Could be a natural phenomenon."

"But it's so *weird.*"

Daniel shrugged. "Should be just what people want, then." He didn't want to look at the birds now; their cheeping sounded cruel, hysterical, and echoed through his head. Would they attack those who could see them on the cliff-top? He thought of pecked eyes and raised, bleeding arms. He felt sick, and had to drop the glass from his eyes, press the fingers of one hand against them. The sky had gone black, and a chill like that of the land of the dead gripped the world. Light had died. It was terrible, all wrong. Daniel could not bear to look up at the black disk, which would be like proof of the triumph of death.

"Daniel!" Lily cried.

Daniel dropped his hand. "It's OK. I felt a bit…" But Lily's sharp word was not an indication of concern. She was gazing through her smoked glass at the eastern sky. "What the hell is that?"

A globe of radiant light had lifted above the horizon.

"A second sun…' Daniel said bleakly.

"A UFO!" Lily's voice was more excited.

At first, Daniel thought that the great cry that emanated from the crowd along the cliff-top was their response to this apparition. Everyone was cheering, clapping, singing, weeping, hugging one another. The arms of the new-agers were raised to the sky in adoration, while other people reacted by falling to their knees, hands clasped beneath their chins. From the group of sword-wielders, a taller man stepped forth, holding a black blade up to the sky.

This is their sign, Daniel thought, the summons for their madness. Then he realised that again only a select few could see the phenomenon in the east. Everyone else reacted to the radiant diamond of light that had appeared at the edge of the blackened sun high overhead. It presaged the return of light. People's spirits soared as any mood of depression was lifted instantly. Daniel could sense this, but it did not affect him.

Lily was still examining the light in the east. "Daniel, it's unreal!" she breathed. "So beautiful."

"It's an earth-light," Daniel said. He lowered his glass. "Truly a natural phenomenon, Lil. It's probably been triggered by the eclipse."

Lily dropped her glass. "It's gone now. What's an earth-light?"

"A manifestation of natural energy."

She grinned. "Oh, did Shem teach you that?"

He shook his head uncomfortably. "No, but I haven't been idle while I've been in the Midlands. Let's say I've been continuing my studies."

Lily frowned. "No one else seemed to be looking at it."

"No," Daniel said dryly.

"But what does it matter?" Lily said. "The sun looks incredible. It's like a cosmic birth or something."

Daniel noticed that Enniel was loping towards them, grinning widely, his binoculars still in his hands. "Well, isn't this something!" Enniel said, his voice full of pleasure. "Just look at them! Fatima revisited! I wonder how many of them are seeing the Virgin Mary floating in the sky?"

Daniel jerked his head in the direction of the crowds. "Some are seeing something more than that, I think. Have you noticed the group with the swords?"

Enniel trained his binoculars on them, and uttered a sound of surprise. "Hmm. Perhaps I should send someone to look into that."

Daniel shook his head in exasperation. "I suppose this has made a memorable day out. Did you notice the other phenomenon, the earthlight?"

"Yes. It was there for those with eyes to see, which does not include the sheep, of course."

Daniel put his head to one side quizzically. "And what do you see in the sky, Enniel? Computer print-outs?"

Enniel uttered a chuckle devoid of amusement and lowered his binoculars. "I see the future, Daniel. There'll be more phenomena like that earth light as the year progresses."

"You hope."

"Hope has nothing to do with it. It's fact."

Daniel uttered a small sound of annoyance and put the smoked glass to his eyes again. Enniel never failed to irritate him in some way. He stared at the eclipse merely to find an excuse not to talk or listen to Enniel, but the gradually brightening sun seemed to draw his attention. He wanted to tear his eyes away, but could not. Even as he looked at it, three concentric rings of light appeared within it, and at their centre a shape manifested; a cone of what looked like crystal that emitted rays of multi-coloured light. A series of high-pitched tones suddenly assaulted Daniel's ears. He blinked, and felt a constriction in his head.

The next moment he was lying on the ground, looking up at Lily's face. He could see Enniel behind her, his expression that of interest rather than concern.

"Dan!" Lily cried. "What happened? You fainted!"

Embarrassed, Daniel pushed her hands away and started to get to his feet. "I'm fine. It's OK." He didn't feel disoriented or muzzy-headed, as he'd expect to if he'd simply passed out. It was almost as if someone, or something, had punched him in the head and sent him flying. The weird tones still rang in his ears. As he stood up, his eyes met Helen's on the same level.

"He didn't faint, Mummy," she said. "He saw the light."

"What did you see?" Lily asked sharply.

Daniel pressed a hand to his eyes, shook his head.

"Daniel!" Enniel snapped. "What did you see?"

"All right, all right. Rings in the eclipse. A cone of light. That's all."

"And that means?"

Daniel shrugged. "You tell me. I just see the stuff. Other people can interpret it."

Presently, warmth returned to the land and the sun shone down benignly as normal. While parties raged along the beach, the Grigori started drifting back towards High Crag.

"I'm coming back to High Crag for a while," Lily said, and linked her free arm through Daniel's. "Are you coming? I mean, yes, you *are* coming. I'm not leaving you out here, moping."

"I'm not moping," Daniel said, managing a smile. He let her begin to lead him back towards the house, keeping half an eye on Helen, who was walking straight-backed and sombre beside her mother. Lily chatted amiably of inconsequential things and Daniel felt himself begin to relax. Then, Helen pulled away sharply from Lily's hand and ran backwards in front of them, laughing. "He's awake!" she cried. "Awake!"

Daniel glanced at Lily, then back at the child, who fixed him with bright eyes. She pointed at him stiffly and, when she spoke, her voice sounded weirdly adult. "He wants you," she said. "He wants you now."

Daniel pulled away from Lily's arm and began to run towards High Crag.

"Daniel, wait!" Lily cried, but he ignored her.

Chapter Two
The Children of Lamech

New York

Smoking was forbidden in the building, which loomed high and shining behind her, its summit resplendent in the afternoon sun, its side-walk root bathed in shadow. Hectic city traffic surged past at street level, horns blared. The aromas of coffee, cinnamon, fried dough and vanilla smoked from a nearby café and hung on the hot, chemical-filled air like incense.

Melandra Maynard stood just beyond the entrance to the building, smoking a final cigarette before her meeting. She had been to Lamech House many times before, even worked on some of the floors, which housed the offices of various industries owned by the corporation. But today she would be granted admission to the inner sanctum. Some part of her, childish in its fears, worried that she might not come out again. She did not fear death, but change. Melandra as she was now might cease to exist.

She had lived a normal life in New England until the age of five, brought up by god-fearing parents who were members of a secretive Christian sect called the Children of Lamech. Then, her cousin Isaac had died, carried off by leukaemia at the age of ten. At the funeral, Melandra had noticed how some people—who weren't relatives—had looked at her strangely. She could tell they were talking about her. At first, she had thought she'd done something wrong. Then, one Sunday, soon afterwards, a man and a woman whom she'd never met before came to her parents' house.

It had been an autumn day, the air full of soft rain and smoke, the trees hanging onto the last of their gaudy finery. Melandra had been playing on her bicycle in the yard and had watched the big, black car slide up to the house, and the strangers get out of it. The couple had been very tanned, full of smiles, their smart, city clothes so stiff it seemed they would creak. They had gone into the house, and after a while, Melandra had been called indoors. The strangers sat with china teacups in tooth-thin saucers resting on their laps. Their bright teeth were like china. Melandra looked at her mother and father. They looked odd, strained.

"You're going to school," Melandra's mother had told her. "Away."

"Be a good girl, Melly," said her father.

Melandra hadn't wanted to go with the strangers, but because she'd never been a troublesome child, she had kept her bewilderment and shock to herself. It had all happened so quickly. Her mother had packed a suit-case for her daughter, and with suppressed emotion, kissed the child on her head and offered her into the hands of the strangers. There had been no explanations as to why this unexpected fate had fallen upon her. Perhaps it had been planned for a long time. Melandra never saw her parents again.

The child had sat in the back of big, black car and had watched her familiar life retreat through the rear window. The strangers gave her sweets to suck, and a colour comic of stories about Jesus. The leather smell of the car had made her head ache. They had driven for a long time.

Melandra had been taken to a big, grey house at the end of a gravel driveway surrounded by trees. The house was a school, but there were no children there. Just Melandra. She had six teachers, who were all mousy spinsters. The headmistress at least had the distinction of being widowed, but seemed hardly marked by the past experience of marriage. It had been a house of dry, genderless women, who smelled of moth-balls and lavender, and who all wore cardigans of colourless wool. Melandra had been absorbed into this cloister-like environment, and it had seemed as if the gates to the outside world had sealed behind her like flesh over a wound. Her teachers had been kind, and because she was naturally an obedient child, rarely had to be strict. Melandra had learned she was different from other children. She had a purpose in life; a very special one. But no-one would tell her what it was. Once, she had wondered whether the death of her cousin had been instrumental in changing her life, but had never voiced the thought. In her isolation, she learned to create a secret life for herself. She was imaginative and naturally wild, but no-one who met the demure, tidy child would ever have guessed that.

Once she turned sixteen, she had been removed to another grey house; this one a college rather than a school. There had been other girls and boys there, which made Melandra feel uneasy for she was unused to mixing with people her own age. In this place, she had been told she was one of God's special warriors, and the skills she had learned there had no place in the mind of a young girl.

Now, she was twenty-four years old, living rent-free in an apartment owned by the Children of Lamech. She did not work, but received a payment from the church into her bank account every month. It was sufficient to live on. She'd always been aware that her life had been on hold, and that eventually it would be turned on by someone else's finger on a secret switch. Today it would happen.

Grinding out her stub on the side-walk Melandra turned to the main entrance, caught sight of her reflection in the eternally revolving doors, and paused for a moment to inspect herself for flaws. Dark suit, severe in cut; long, dark hair cut in a bob that was equally severe. A light summer coat hung over her arm. She held a briefcase. Her make-up was precise; pale foundation, dark eye-shadow, a perfect slash of red lipstick. Her perfume was salty-citric, a mere suggestion of a scent. All was in order. She was ready. At last. She would learn why she'd been trained to kill.

Inside, the lobby was spacious, like a shopping mall. Enormous escalators swept up to and down from a mezzanine floor above. Security guards, stationed behind a desk by the door, equipped Melandra with an identification tag; then one of them made a murmured call, not through the main switch-board but from another, independent phone.

"Go right on up, Ms Maynard." He spoke in a Brooklyn drawl.

She nodded curtly, did not smile, and walked to the elevators. The guards did not know where she was going. It was doubtful operatives employed on the ground were even aware of the secret floor high above their heads. There were so many stories to the building, each a squirming hive of labour and commerce, that one so near the clouds could easily be missed.

There was a line of elevator doors—like the portals to temples, vaguely art-deco—and Melandra halted before the one farthest from the entrance. She did not have to summon the elevator herself. Presently, its polished doors slid open of their own accord and she entered it alone. The doors whispered shut and encased her in a micro-world of darkened mirrors, lustrous brass and soft, almost sinister, music. She pressed the button for the top floor. Her mouth was dry. She wanted to reach into her pocket for a mint candy, but felt it would not be approved of if she arrived at her destination with something in her mouth. Breathing shallow, she watched the indicator above the door as the floor numbers lit up in succession. Twelfth: Lamech Communications; fourteenth: Lamech Hydro-Power; twenty: Lamech Investments. She had forgotten all but a few of the companies housed within the building. They did not concern her.

Up, up and up. She felt as if she was flying towards the stratosphere.

The intercom emitted a chime to indicate she had reached the top floor. All was quiet for a moment, but for the low intrusion of the piped music. Then, without a shudder, and only the faintest of mechanical hums, the elevator began to move again, obeying the injunctions of a primed receptionist on the restricted floor above all the others.

The doors slid open onto muted splendour. The light was greenish and people moved slowly within it. Melandra stepped onto the thick teal carpet. It was as if she'd entered the lobby of a high class hotel. The people around her did not look like office personnel, but guests. They sat round low tables, on plush sofas, reading sheaves of papers or talking softly together, elegant coffee cups and cafetieres on designer trays beside them. Others strolled languidly across the expanse of carpet as if going nowhere. They inclined their heads politely to Melandra, and she returned the gesture.

She approached the reception desk—vast and greenish marble—behind which sat three women, all of them groomed to perfection. They looked like models or actresses and perhaps were. Behind them, on the wall, was a huge carved banner in gold and green: it proclaimed 'The Children of Lamech'. This was the heart of the corporation; its ruling cabal was hidden here. Melandra knew it must have little to do with commerce, for all that was attended to lower down in the building. Lamech House was like a representation of heaven; angels worked on the lower levels; seraphim and thrones as the sidewalk diminished in perspective; but here the splendour of God, incomprehensible and remote, reigned supreme.

"Good afternoon," Melandra said, putting down her briefcase. "Melandra Maynard. I'm expected."

The nearest receptionist smiled widely. She wore an identification tag that named her as Natasha. "Hi there. Good to see you." She stood up. "I'm to take you right in. Just sign here first."

She pushed a thick, leather-bound book towards her.

Melandra was conscious of her damp palms as she lifted the gold-nibbed fountain pen and signed her name in the space on the creamy page next to where the receptionist's long, ochre-lacquered fingernail rested.

"Great!" said the receptionist and came out from behind the desk. She indicated Melandra's briefcase. "Allow me?"

Melandra nodded. "Yes. Thanks."

The receptionist picked up the brief-case, plucked Melandra's coat from her arm and sashayed across the room. "This way, ma'am."

Melandra felt as if she'd stepped into a different reality as she followed the receptionist through gliding double doors into a vast room. A reception or party was going on. The room was panelled in dark, lustrous wood and ponderous classical music played, louder than in the elevator. People milled around; some in evening dress, others in what appeared to be traditional costume from far lands. Green-and-gold liveried waiters hovered among them, bearing trays of drinks and canapés. In a corner of the room, next to a palm tree, a photographer was taking carefully posed pictures of some of the participants. Surreal.

Melandra wanted to smile, but she felt unnerved. All through her childhood and her teenage years, even beyond it during her training, she'd been unable to dismiss the anxiety that her purpose in life would also be her curse. She did not want to discover it, for then it might be that her remaining life-time would be measurable, like visiting a fortune-teller and learning the day of your death. Yet she'd been told how important she was, how special and how needed.

She had never disobeyed anyone openly, ever, but she had thought about doing so, and they had known.

Now, she stood at the threshold, fearing the unknown. The receptionist had glided over to a tall, handsome man with steel grey hair, who looked to be in his fifties. He stood within a group of people, all of whom were smaller than he, and he held a glass in his hand. As he leaned down to listen to the receptionist, his eyes flicked upwards in their sockets and fixed upon Melandra. Grey eyes. Metal eyes. Unyielding. Melandra did not smile. He would not approve of that. Not yet.

She watched him excuse himself from his companions and then saunter across the room towards her. He wore an immaculate tuxedo and gold glinted at his wrist. "Hello, Melandra Maynard," he said, and held out a large, tanned hand. "I'm Nathaniel Fox. Pleased you could make it."

She took the hand, felt its dry heat engulf her. "Glad to be here." As if she'd had a choice.

"Drink?" He put proprietorial fingers beneath her elbow and began to lead her into the crowd.

"Yeah, thanks. The driest white wine you have."

Fox smiled. "A white drink, a glacier drink. Of course."

She knew she had passed a test and, absurdly, relaxed. The receptionist had disappeared—with her briefcase and coat.

They paused at a vast, linen-snowed table while Fox ordered her drink. Accepting it, Melandra risked a brittle laugh. "This wasn't quite what I was expecting." She put the glass to her lips, tongued the cold liquor.

Nathaniel Fox ignored her remark. "The meeting will take place in seven minutes. There are a couple of people who want to be introduced to you first."

She downed her drink. "OK."

They were just faces, people who seemed to be impressed by her. A couple of them were senators, she knew, but they failed to make an impression on her. In no time at all, Fox was ushering her through another set of doors, and the soft babble of the party was cut off as if it had never existed.

The room before her now was long, silent and dimly-lit. A slim, gleaming road of executive table lay before her. Around it sat a group of formally-dressed, middle-aged men. No women: she was the only one. The walls were swathed in dark-grey curtains, and if there were any windows, they were obscured.

Fox came into the room behind her and put his hands upon her shoulders. "Gentlemen, this is the young lady we've been waiting to meet."

All eyes were upon her. She both hated and feared them. They were rigid, merciless beings. She wanted to please them. It was instinctive. They were her masters. "Good afternoon." She inclined her head.

"Here, sit down, sit down." Fox pressed her into a vacant seat next to the head of the table, where he himself sat down. Beside his right hand was a console covered in numbered pressure pads that looked like an enormous remote control. Fox drew in a great breath, then threw his head backwards, exhaling. "Let us pray, brothers."

Around the table, the delegates of the cabal bowed their heads. Melandra did likewise, although she could not close her eyes.

"Dear Lord!" cried Nathaniel Fox. "We are your humble servants, bound to do your duty and honour your causes. We meet here today to discuss a matter of grave importance, for the time has come. Your bond-woman, Melandra, awaits the touch of your spirit. Grant her this, oh Lord: your strength and your purpose. May she be our tool to accomplish your great design, for she herself is willing to sacrifice her very being upon the altar of this holy conflict."

Am I? thought Melandra. She remained silent, conscious of the slight pull of a frown across her forehead.

"The evil ones mass in the filthiest corners of the earth," Fox continued, his voice filling out with a greedy relish for the words. "Even now, they speak their blasphemies and call upon He Who Walks the Deserts. The Scapegoat shall come forth from the bowels of the earth, shaking curses from his hair. His breath shall be poisonous fire, his words the foul stink of hell!"

Fox uttered a shuddering sigh. "Prepare us, oh Lord, for what is to come. Arm us with your spiritual weapons." He reached out blindly and placed his hand heavily on Melandra's head. Her neck jerked. "Bless your bond-woman, and protect her from the ancient, blaspheming memories of the weaker sex. It is by your will that the Scapegoat shall be purged by the hand of a woman, one of the creatures whom he corrupted in sin. Amen."

"Amen," echoed the assembly.

Nathaniel took his hand from Melandra's head and she felt dizzy from the sudden lifting of the weight.

Fox laced his hands before him on the table. "Shall we begin, gentlemen?" He touched a pad on the console beside him.

The curtains that covered the left hand wall glided open. Banks of television screens or monitors were revealed. There must have been over a hundred of them. At another command from Fox, the screens flickered into life; they showed news reports from around the world: war, famine, political summits.

"What do you see, Melandra Maynard?" Fox enquired.

Melandra shrugged. "Reality. Not a pretty sight."

Fox sucked his upper lip, nodding. "Yes. But reality as you see it is the work of devils. This, if you like, is the entr'acte before their grand performance, and the finale will be the end of the world."

"Devils," said Melandra. She presumed he meant some rival cartel, who dealt in arms or drugs.

"That is one word for them. Others are Nephilim, Watchers and Grigori. Fallen angels. Just look upon their filthy work, my sister."

Melandra glanced at him sharply, then back at the screens. She knew what Fox was talking about. Once, when she was very young, she had found a book on her Sunday school teacher's desk. It had been old and frayed; well thumbed. Her teacher had come into the room and had snatched the book from her hands with a sharp rebuke. "You mustn't look at that," she had been told. "You are not old enough." Like any child, Melandra had been curious about knowledge that was forbidden and had asked awkward questions. Patiently, the teacher had explained that the book contained stories about the Fallen Ones, the rebel Sons of God, who in the distant past, before the Great Flood, had come down from heaven and corrupted human women. Her teacher had refrained from explaining in detail the fallen angels' unholy behaviour. Melandra had been told it was sinful even to think of them now. They were God's enemies, for they had disobeyed him and revelled in sin. For that, they had been punished, utterly destroyed, but their spirits might live on to tempt the weak. Good girls would certainly not want to read about them.

Over the years, in her isolated boarding school and college, Melandra had learned to regard the Grigori as a spiritual evil, like having bad thoughts about a friend or a teacher. Now, the suspicion stirred within her that Fox and his colleagues believed they might be something more.

Fox turned in his seat. His voice was laconic. "The ancient leader of the Grigori, Azazel, walks the earth again, Melandra. He is the anti-Christ, the Satan, the Adversary. He gathers his people beneath a banner of blood. When the millennium turns, he plans to cast a pestilence of war and ravagement upon the earth. Only his debased followers will survive it, into the darkest centuries mankind will ever know. He must be stopped. He must be destroyed. All your life, you, Melandra, have been trained for this divine purpose. God has deemed it shall be you who will destroy Azazel."

Melandra's mouth dropped open involuntarily, and she had to shut it again quickly. "Excuse me? I...*how?*"

Fox smiled. "You are horrified, and no-one could blame you for that! How will you do it? Well, that is simple. You have your gender on your side. All women have ever been followers of the Scapegoat. He is the great seducer, after all. In the days before Abraham, the wife of our founder, Lamech,

gave birth to a monstrous child, spawned of a fallen angel.
Although she denied it, Lamech knew the truth and began the
holy war to root out and destroy the tainted blood of these
unholy unions."

"Where is this written?" Melandra asked. She could not
help but take his remarks about women personally.

"In the Book of Enoch," Fox replied. "It was a book that
was excluded from the Old Testament, for the terrible history
it contained was not for the eyes and ears of common Christians. The time has come for you to learn its contents. I will
give you a copy to read while you journey to your appointed
duty. Azazel will not expect the fatal thrust to come from a
woman. Remember your Bible history, Melandra. Remember
Judith. "Praise God, for he hath not taken away his mercy
from the house of Israel, but hath destroyed our enemies by
mine hands this night.""

"You want me to be Judith?" Melandra was well aware of
the story. Judith had cut the head from her enemy, Holofernes,
while he slept. Did that mean she'd have to get close enough
to this Azazel to sleep with him?

"Sacrifices may have to be made," Fox said carefully, "but
may not be necessary, in the event." He smiled. "You are an
excellent shot, after all. Perhaps you won't need to get that
close."

"Who is it?" she asked, expecting to hear a name she had
heard before.

Fox pulled a quizzical face. "I told you. Azazel, leader of
the Grigori."

Melandra smiled. "Yes, but…I mean, it isn't *really* him. It
can't be. He died thousands of years ago. And the
Grigori…fallen angels…" She shook her head. "Do they *really* still walk the earth?"

Fox shook his head and spoke gently. "Believe me, the
Grigori have never left this world. Like maggots they have
feasted on its flesh, and it is the holy duty of our order to root
them out wherever they hide. God is with us, my child. We
are his arms in this world; we mete out his vengeance to the
miscreants and their spawn. We bring down fire upon their
vile heads."

Melandra swallowed. She didn't want to offend Nathaniel Fox, but even after all her training, this information was hard to take in. Why hadn't they told her before, prepared her? For a few moments, her faith wavered. Were the Children of Lamech all mad? It could not be true that the Grigori still lived.

Fox was eyeing her steadily, and a hard light had come into his eyes. "Let not the devil's doubt assail you, my child. Disbelief in their existence is the Grigori's greatest defence."

Melandra touched her lips briefly with cold fingers. So this was the answer she'd been waiting for. Since her early days at the college, she had known she would eventually be sent out into the world to destroy God's enemies, but she'd had no idea her targets would be angels, fallen or otherwise. It didn't seem real to her. "They never told me," she said. "Not once. Is it the same for everyone at the college?"

Fox looked slightly uncomfortable. "Everyone has their duty," he said. "All of our warriors hunt down the children of the Fallen Ones. There have been many before you, who have efficiently and discreetly removed identified Grigori and their supporters."

"But why weren't we told about this?"

Fox sucked his upper lip, nodding distractedly. "I understand your surprise. All of your college friends have now gone on to destroy Grigori that we uncover, but you—you have this special purpose. You were not born to it, no, but when your cousin Isaac died, his fate fell upon you. The Scourge of Azazel. We knew that when the eve of the millennium was upon us, the Evil One would rise up from the earth to glory in destruction. We had to protect you, Melandra, keep you in ignorance. A child with such knowledge would be a dangerous thing. The Grigori might have sniffed you out, contaminated you."

Melandra shivered, remembering all the hours she had spent alone as a young girl, and the tall, sinister shadows that might have waited for her in the tangled corners of her garden playgrounds.

Fox touched her hand. "Have no doubt that the man you must kill *is* Azazel. In the flesh. He has been reborn, not

under another name, but his own. At least..." He paused.
"He uses another form of his name: Shemyaza."

At the sound of the word, a strange charge volted through
Melandra's body. She felt both revolted and thrilled, and then
sickened by the response. Perhaps Nathaniel was right about
this fallen angel's influence over womankind. It was important to remember her purpose; she was an assassin, an expert.
She swallowed. "What do you know of him?"

"He is at present in England. God willing, you might accomplish your mission there. In London."

"How do you know of him?"

"That is not for you to know, my child." Nathaniel grinned.
"Our sources of information must necessarily remain secret,
but rest assured that the data has been verified."

"Is he in hiding?"

"Not totally. He walks among humanity. Only those
with eyes to see could tell he is not a man. You will go to
London tonight, and will be given instructions on how to
find him. Then, you must do your work as cleanly and discreetly as possible."

Melandra desperately needed a cigarette. "It seems...too
easy."

"He might become aware of you and flee. You may have
to follow him."

"I see." This seemed more likely, and also the unspoken
possibility that he might kill her first. "How dangerous is he?"

Nathaniel laughed. "More than you can ever imagine. You
must be clever, but remember that the spirit of the Lord is
ever within you and will shield you with the wings of holy
angels. Azazel's aim is to return to the sacred lands of his
ancestors. Eden. That is where he will want to build his vile
empire. His followers are already preparing the way. You
have only to examine the situation in the Middle East to appreciate that."

"They are Islamic countries," Melandra said. "Are you im-
plying that Islam follows the Scapegoat?"

Fox shook his head. "Not at all. It is the secret societies
concealed in those lands. A dark star has arisen in the east, a
dictator who wishes to restore the glory of the Grigori. He

worships fire and is undoubtedly one of Azazel's creatures. The situation there is very precarious. The pagan aspect of the Scapegoat has encouraged the belief that the land of the idolaters, Egypt, is the site of the New Age. Foolish followers of this creed, unaware of the seductive evil behind their beliefs, wish to flock there and reclaim what they see as their lost heritage. Naturally, this has caused some concern among the native population, and fundamentalists are prepared to take extreme measures. Already the West is talking in terms of sending in peace-keeping forces. We do not wish that to happen. Ridding the world of the figure-head of this movement will stem the rising tide of devil-worship that grips the minds of the impressionable. You must appreciate, Melandra, how vital your task is."

Melandra again found it hard to take in what she was being told. It all seemed too unreal. Surely Fox was blaming Middle Eastern political troubles on what was essentially a fantasy? She could not believe that the Scapegoat, literally the Devil, was incarnated in the world. It seemed like paranoia to her. Yet, if they wanted her to kill a man for them, she would do it. He was undoubtedly just some little tin-pot New Age guru, spouting heresies to impress the young.

"Do not under-estimate your adversary," Fox said in a silky voice, as if he could read her mind.

"I…" Melandra began to speak, but before she could muster any words, the lights in the room began to flicker on and off. All the TV screens sputtered, their images reduced to grey fuzz.

Fox frowned and silenced Melandra with a wave of his hand. He began to press buttons on his console. "What the…"

The other delegates had begun speaking to one another in soft, urgent tones, and Melandra became aware that a strange atmosphere had come into the room. Her skin tingled with what felt like static electricity. The hair had lifted on her head. "What is it?" she asked.

Fox did not answer her. Beneath his hands, the long table began to shake. Evincing only slight unease, he pressed the intercom button. "Kimberley? Can you hear me? We got problems with the systems in here…" The intercom expelled a high-pitched whine. Fox cursed beneath his breath.

Abruptly, one of the other delegates sprang to his feet. He wore glasses, and all Melandra could fix her eyes upon was the reflection of the fuzzy TV screens in the lenses.

"Abraham?" Fox snapped. "Sit down. I'll get this fixed."

The man, an overweight, grandfatherly figure, opened and shut his mouth with a fish-like popping sound. His body was shaking, as if he was about to go into convulsion.

Fox made an impatient sound. "Someone help him out." He pointed at another man. "Mordecai, go to my secretary's office and call the technicians."

Mordecai nodded shortly and went to the door. Melandra saw him try to open it, and fail. He turned to Fox. "Somethin's wrong with this here door…"

Fox uttered a snort of irritation and jumped to his feet, but activity from further down the table took his attention. Two men were trying to ease Abraham back into his seat, but he suddenly uttered a distressed cry and pushed the helping hands away violently. Strange sounds began to issue from his distended mouth. It sounded like a language, but none that Melandra had ever heard.

"Get him out of here!" roared Fox.

"How? The door's jammed!" someone yelled.

"Then break down the goddam door!"

For a moment, chaotic activity erupted around the table as the men jumped to their feet to obey their leader's command. Then, a brilliant flash of blue light threw everybody back into their seats. Melandra yelped and shielded her eyes. When she dared open them again, she saw a dozen or so baseball-sized globes of blue-white light whizzing around the room, just above the heads of all present. The men cowered beneath them.

"Lord, protect us!" gasped Fox.

After what appeared to be a few light-hearted circuits of the room, the light balls converged to form a single, hovering globe of radiance above the centre of the table. It emitted an electric hum.

"What is it?" Melandra asked in a high voice. "Mr Fox…what *is* it?"

"Abomination!" Fox could not take his eyes from the light.

Melandra glanced around herself. Her limbs were tense to the point of paralysis, and it seemed no-one else could move either. The room was held in stasis. Power, confidence, and a certain mordant humour, seemed to ooze from the globe of radiance. It pulsed before them, gradually increasing in size. Then Melandra became aware that a tall shape was forming within it. "My God!"

Abomination? Surely not. An alien creature now hung above the table, its hands extended in a gesture of welcome. It was beautiful. An angel. Its face was utter benevolence, its body clad in a long, shifting robe of coloured light. White-gold hair floated around its head and shoulders like a halo of wind-blown feather-down.

Beside her, Fox uttered a choked cry. Melandra thought he didn't know whether to pray or scream. Beneath his breath, he murmured lines from Luke: absurdly inappropriate, or perhaps not. "And the angel said unto her, fear not: for thou hast found favour with God."

Had this being manifested for Melandra's benefit: one of God's angels sent to offer His support to her mission?

Then, the radiance around the angel began to change. The blue light became darker, slowly mutating into indigo, then growing gradually more purple. Finally, dark red light surrounded the ethereal figure, as if it was splashed with blood. Scarlet sparks spat out from the pulsing effulgence and the beatific face of the angel twisted into an expression of contempt. Its robes fell away, revealing a body of corded muscle, with huge, jutting genitals. Its hands became clawed, and a long, black tongue shot out from its mouth, flicking the shuddering cheeks of Abraham, who still stood rigid against the table.

Then, with a silent explosion, the apparition vanished.

All was silent in the room, but for the crackle of the TV screens. Then, somebody whimpered, and Melandra heard the sound of a chair scraping against the carpet. Abraham made a gurgling sound in his throat and slumped forward, face-first, onto the table.

Nathaniel's face was ashen beneath his tan. He looked very old. "Do you see now, Melandra Maynard? Do you see what you are up against?"

After the meeting, Nathaniel Fox led Melandra from the board-room, leaving his shocked colleagues to discuss the significance of what had occurred. In the privacy of Fox's spacious, private office, he subjected Melandra to another lecture upon the holy work of The Children of Lamech. He spoke passionately, loudly and with evangelistic colour.

Even after the inexplicable phenomenon in the board room, Melandra was unsettled by Fox's zeal, sure his claims were fired only by paranoia. She found herself vacillating between unquestioning belief in the Grigori and scepticism. Fox sensed this, but was patient with her indecision. He pointed out that surely she had been given more evidence than she needed to know that his words were true. A demon had manifested before them, mocking their mission. Melandra was still unsure what she had seen. It could have been some kind of group hallucination, invoked by their heightened emotion. And yet, as Fox talked to her persistently, passing her folder after folder of classified documents that he told her contained hard evidence, she found her pessimism fraying. She read reports, examined photographs. Before and after death. Tall, handsome people gunned down, poisoned, but who in life had controlled industries and communities through dark magic and deception. The most damning evidence to prove Fox's words was the fact that none of these deaths had been reported in the press.

"They are clever," Fox said, "and powerful. They know what we are planning and no doubt intruded into our meeting to make us aware of that. They want us to fear them, and are not afraid of us, which might be their weakness. Arrogance. But you must be careful, Melandra. Very careful."

Melandra was not cheered by this information. "So, what exactly are we dealing with? A select group? An underground movement? What numbers are involved?"

Fox closed the last folder with a snap. "Not even we know how many there are of them, or how far-reaching their influence is. Many powerful men support our work, but we suspect just as many are slaves of the Grigori. You can trust no-one, but for the select few you have met in this building."

"What I'd like to know," Melandra said carefully, "is, if these people exist, why no-one's aware of them. How have they managed to hide for so long?"

Fox raised a single eyebrow, then smiled. "But, my child, *we* are aware of them. However, you are right to ask these questions. You must be clear in your own mind about what is going on. The Grigori have hidden among us by counting on people's inability to accept they might exist. Angels?" He laughed. "Aren't they just artistic ornaments on religious paintings and Christmas cards?" He shook his head. "The fallen ones have been idolised by writers and poets, swallowed by fiction. People see them as romantic martyrs, unaware that their descendants are very real, a passionless race that seeks to take control of the world. God cast them out of heaven for their wickedness and pride, stripped them of their divinity. Now, they are jealous and greedy. They would like to enslave all humanity. That was their original intention when they divulged secret knowledge to humanity, and it still is. Control. They look almost like us, and only a trained eye can spot them. They are seducers, Melandra, and they have waited an immeasurably long time to get their revenge. The Lord knows they are cunning and deadly. Be in no doubt about that. It might be your only defence. The last two millennia have been the centuries of Christ, and the Grigori were disabled, but now the new millennium approaches and if the Son of God is to remain its king, the Grigori must be stopped."

After several hours of intensive information intake, Melandra left the House of Lamech dazed with facts. Walking out into the dusk of the city, she had seen Grigori in every shadow; tall men and women on the street seemed to pause and glance at her with suspicious eyes. She had to go into a bar and have a few drinks to get a grip on herself.

As a teenager, when she'd first tasted the forbidden luxuries of alcohol and tobacco, she'd reasoned with herself that although there was no mention in the Bible of Jesus smoking cigarettes (they weren't invented then, after all), he had certainly drunk wine. He wouldn't mind if she did too. No other liquor had ever touched her lips. Once, she had been caught sneaking into the college with a secret purchase wrapped in

brown paper. Her teachers had expressed their disappointment, and because Melandra appeared to be an obedient girl,
they had never had to chastise her again. She had become
more careful. It all seemed farcical now. She had been brought
up to be trained as an assassin, yet it offended them if she
drank alcohol. They had looked like men and women, but
their hearts had been cold and inhuman. They could kill in the
name of God, and had taught her that this was a righteous and
noble thing to do. She had learned to emulate their zeal and
had taken pride in the accuracy of her work. Still, as yet, her
skill was untried. She had killed all manner of God's creatures, except the ones created in His image. Was she up to the
task Fox had invested in her? Sometimes she felt too shaky
and vulnerable to be what they wanted her to be. Her guardians had never known the real Melandra. If she met this great
Shemyaza, the devil himself, would she be strong enough to
stand up to him?

After a bottle of good wine, the prospect seemed less chilling, although she still vacillated between belief and scepticism. Why was it so difficult to believe in the Grigori? After
all, she believed without question in God and the love of Jesus
Christ, and had felt it often during the lonely, aching years of
her insular childhood. Their holy presences had sometimes
seemed more real to her than those of the dour, devout women
who'd raised her. Alone in her room at night, she had talked to
the sorrowful man on the crucifix, which hung on her wall.
He had been her only confidant. He knew her childish hopes
and desires, even though she could not articulate them fully.
A yearning for love, perhaps, which unacknowledged bitterness had hardened into something else. Jesus loves you, she
had been told, and there had been stories of the good angels,
who crouched around the throne of God, eternally singing his
praises. The bad angels burned in hell. Because of the stories,
she could imagine angels as spiritual beings, the messengers
of God. But it was more difficult to accept Fox's theories.

She sighed, drew circles on the table-top with the wet base
of her wine glass. This great story sustained the Children of
Lamech; it was their reason for being. She had grown up with
it, without even knowing it.

Later, at home, she took down her crucifix from the wall, and touched the emaciated belly of Christ with a reverent finger. His enemies must be her enemies. "Is it real?" she asked him. He looked, as always, despairing. Perhaps, now, she knew the reason why.

Chapter Three
Reawakening

London

Shemyaza had forgotten how filthy the capital city was. Even pedestrians wore masks against the polluting air nowadays. Yet still London charmed him. He sensed its great age beneath his feet and even now, closing his eyes upon the busy street, fancied he could sense its previous incarnations, when the streets had been merely mud. Perhaps it had always been filthy.

He and Salamiel had been in the city for two days, staying at a Grigori-owned hotel hidden amongst the streets of Soho. Enniel Prussoe had arranged the accommodation for them, and had booked them in under assumed names. He assured them the hotel management was renowned for its discretion.

Daniel had been summoned, but for some reason was delaying his return. Shem was amused by this. He knew Daniel did not like having his strings tweaked too forcefully, and the phone call he'd made to Cornwall had perhaps been a little abrupt:

"What are you doing down there, Daniel? Get back here now! We have work to do."

Daniel's silence had been eloquent on the other end of the line. Shem was reminded that his vizier was five years older now; a boy no longer, and perhaps not quite as malleable as in the past. To Shem, it felt as if he'd only seen Daniel a few days before. "So, thanks for asking after my health." He couldn't help sounding sharp.

"I know how you are. Salamiel called Enniel as soon as you woke up."

"Salamiel and I are going to London. I want you to meet us there."

Daniel uttered a repressed groan. "What's the hurry? What are you planning?"

Shem noticed the reserve in Daniel's tone, a stony reticence that had not been there before. "To carry on what was started. That *is* what you want of me, isn't it?"

"I don't know what we started. I don't know how we carry on."

"You've changed, then."

Shem heard Daniel sigh down the line. "It all seems so unreal now. What you did here...what effect did it have? I can't see any. Perhaps it's pointless, and we're kidding ourselves..."

"We shouldn't be talking about this on the phone, Daniel."

"No...Shem, I'm not sure I want to come back..."

"You don't have a choice."

"Something strange happened today."

Shem listened as Daniel told him about the events surrounding the eclipse. "That just sounds like proof to me. We have to act."

"Do what though?"

Shem paused. "We need to talk. Please come to London, Daniel. I want to see you."

Again, a sigh. "OK, but we must talk, Shem, not just go haring off somewhere."

"We'll talk. I promise."

"Give me a couple of days, will you? I want to see Lily."

"Whatever you wish. Give her my regards."

Shem had fought the impulse to slam down the phone. How could Daniel become so estranged? Shem knew him as a warm, compassionate creature, and had been sure of his love. Had five years eroded that loyalty?

Attempting to banish any doubts about Daniel, Shem immersed himself in the bustle of Oxford Street, letting the crowds swirl around him like water. No-one seemed to notice him. He felt invisible.

So much activity; most of it mindless. Was Daniel right? It was difficult to see a spiritual awakening in the land. Shem gazed into shop windows, contemptuous of the siren-allure of the colourful displays. Perhaps Daniel was right. So little seemed to have changed since his ordeal in the underworld.

He wandered past an electrical goods mega-store, and the flickering banks of televisions in the display window caught his eye. What he saw depressed his spirits further. Every set was tuned to a channel showing a brutal public demonstration in the Middle East. Contorted faces yelled at the cameras, which flashed to pictures of burned bodies lying in a dusty village street, and scuffles with the armed forces. A strong emotion coursed through him. His homeland: gripped by war and mindless violence. What had happened to the people who had once lived there, the noble race of his ancestors? The invaders who'd raided the land after his people had been forced to flee had made it wholly their own, permeated it with their repressive creeds, destroyed and buried the knowledge of the Elders, the race who had existed even before the Anannage. He burned with a cold fury. It was all so wrong. The knowledge of the Elders belonged to the world. He had died for that belief, once.

While the lands of his ancestors were torn by cruelty and intolerance, there could be no evolution in the world. But how could he end it? He had been shown the possibility of ultimate power in the underworld of Cornwall, but that stage of his work was over. He had been a conductor for the force, a catalyst, but he did not feel as if any shred of it remained inside him.

Before he could continue his stroll, weighed down with melancholy, Shem's attention was attracted to an image on the screens. He did not want to see any more violence, yet could not tear his eyes away. A struggling melee was being shown; a mass of bodies. All was confusion, yet in its midst stood a lone, motionless figure. This person was taller than those around him or her. The face was concealed by a dark red scarf, only the eyes showed through, but they stared straight into the camera; challenging, fearless, *alive*.

Shem shivered in the clammy heat of the city. It felt as if the picture had crossed time as well as distance to reach him. "Come," the eyes seemed to say. "We are waiting." He put one hand flat against the window; it felt greasy and hot beneath his palm. Were his eyes blurring or had the image on the screens gone out of focus? He blinked, and the noise of the demonstration crashed through the glass to fill his ears with its clamour. He staggered backwards, and bodies thrust against him, rough hands pushing him away, further into the midst of the crowd. At first, he thought he had somehow been propelled into the image on the screens, transported across oceans and many lands to the country of his ancestors. Then, he glimpsed shop fronts through the crowd, and realised he was still on Oxford Street, but inexplicably caught up in a marching throng. Voices called out furious slogans, but he could not understand them. What were they protesting about? He saw many dark-skinned people, a few wearing Middle-Eastern head-gear. Had the demonstration been brought to him rather than the other way around?

Shem clawed and struggled his way to the edge of the crowd. Sightseers and shoppers had vanished, probably having sought sanctuary behind the doors of shops. Shem grabbed hold of the arm of an olive-skinned girl. She turned hot, brown eyes upon him; impatient and afire, and spoke to him sharply in a tongue he could not fathom.

"What's this all about?" Shem asked her.

For a moment, he thought she would pull away from him. Her lips curled into a contemptuous sneer. Then, some kind of political zeal got the better of her. "Yarasadi!" she snapped.

Shem looked at her blankly. It meant nothing. "I've been away a long time. Tell me."

"My people are being murdered!" the girl cried. "And your politicians look on, fearful and ignorant. We mean nothing to them, but our voices are loud!"

"Yarasadi? Where? Middle East?"

She nodded, then smiled coldly. "Yes. You *have* been away a long time! Don't you watch the news?"

Shem shook his head. "Who are your people?"

"We are an ancient race, and our lands have been plundered. Now, we raise our voices in protest. Now, we are not afraid to fight! It is not too late." It sounded like lines from a manifesto, learned by heart.

Shem thought the girl seemed almost crazed. She was probably nothing more than a foreign student, far removed from her roots, who was caught up in the political enthusiasms of the young, yet something about her eyes, her proud stance, touched his soul. He saw echoes of the past in her. "Tell me more. It's important I know what's happened."

She looked him up and down, probably assessing his pale skin and white-gold hair. He would not seem kin to her. Then, she shrugged. "I have to go, but you can always follow us to the meeting place. There, you will learn all you need to know, *if* you're that interested." She glanced around, probably to look for comrades who had marched on without her.

"Take me there," Shem said.

The girl looked at him with suspicion. He stared deep into her eyes, exerted his will. Then without a word, the girl jerked her head to indicate ahead of her, turned away from him and began to walk quickly alongside the crowd. Shem followed. He did not let her out of his sight.

The police were a very visible presence around the meeting hall, but here the demonstration seemed to have quietened down, most of its participants having already entered the hall. Shem caught up with his reluctant guide. She looked over her shoulder at him, clearly suspicious, although still subject to his will. She gave him a guarded half smile, and he directed the full force of his own smile upon her. "I *am* interested," he said. "You don't know how much."

They walked into the shadow of the lobby, where people were milling around makeshift stalls that were adrift with pamphlets and posters. There were even T-shirts on sale; samples pinned up on boards behind the stalls. "Where exactly do your people come from?" he asked her.

"Our land is known by many names, but never its own. It is dismembered."

Shem eyed the red, gold and green banners on the walls. "Kurdistan," he said. "Yarasadi equates with Yezidi, Yaresan, yes?"

She smiled, shrugged. "We are seen as Kurdish yes, but our blood-lines are older than the Yezidis."

"You have kept very quiet about it for a long, long time, then!"

She did not seem offended. "It is only recently that we've discovered who we really are. We were scattered, our memories taken from us, then a new prophet came. A messenger from the Ancient Ones. We learned of our divine blood..." She paused. "Now, you think we are crazy, as most of your people do. But it is true."

Shem frowned and shook his head briefly. "I don't think you're crazy. Who is your prophet?"

"Come, you will see." The girl hurried off into the crowd and Shem followed her. They came into a darkened hall, where a video was being shown on a large screen. The sound system echoed and spluttered, competing with the constant underlying hubbub of conversation. Westerners mingled with the dark-skinned crowd; photographers, journalists and those who followed causes. Children ran around, laughing and screeching, oblivious of the serious subject of the meeting.

Shem forced himself not to turn away from the scenes being shown on the screen. The introduction to the film was clearly over: images of carnage dominated the presentation; the bodies of children rotting in the streets; ruined buildings; forlorn survivors wandering like zombies amongst the remains of a community. It reminded him of times long past, when his Nephilim sons had prompted the High Lord Anu to release the Flood. Thousands of people had died then; pathetic corpses waterlogged in mud.

"Who did this?" Shem asked in clear, low voice.

The girl leaned towards him. "It is the handiwork of a man who calls himself the King of Babylon."

"There is no Babylon," Shem said. "Not any more."

"There is," the girl replied. "The king calls himself Nimnezzar."

Shem raised his eyebrows. He would need to find out about this king, but first there was other information to gather. He smiled reassuringly at the girl. "Will you tell me more about your prophet?"

The girl brushed a nervous hand through her hair. "He came to us about the same time Nimnezzar seized control of what was once Iraq. It was no coincidence. We are a threat to this false despot, for we carry the true ancient blood. He wants to eradicate us completely, but we too are strong, in a different way. As his great foot stamps down to crush us, we scatter and scamper away." She grinned, uplifted by the speech she had made. "Now, a lot of us are here in England, seeking support."

"And are you getting it?"

She pulled a wry face. "In some areas."

He reached out and with one long finger briefly touched her cheek, smooth with youth. "I think *you've* been here for a long time, young lady. Have you experienced the atrocities first hand? I don't think so."

She narrowed her eyes at him. "So, what if that is true? I know where my roots lie."

He raised his hands. "That was not a criticism…er, you did not tell me your name."

"Meenah," she answered, clearly uncomfortable with surrendering the information, but unable to stop herself.

"I am Shemyaza," he said. "Shem."

She raised her eyebrows. "An odd name for an Englishman."

"I'm not English," he replied.

More might have been said on this topic, but Meenah grabbed his arm and pointed at the screen with her free hand. "Look! There is our only hope of victory."

The scenes of brutality and death had been replaced by the image of a vast gathering, much like the one they were attending now, but this one was being held outdoors, beneath the merciless canopy of a foreign sky. Hot sunlight shone down upon sharp, grey rocks that were virtually covered by a seated crowd. Some were dressed in Western clothes, while others were adorned with colourful ethnic costumes. All were paying rapt attention to the speaker, who stood high above them; a lone figure silhouetted against the unbearable blue. But that was not the prophet. Meenah explained the great man would not communicate directly with crowds, although he always stood silently watching on as his followers relayed his words to the masses. Shem tried to discern details of the one who stood tall with folded arms behind the animated speaker. The prophet was disguised; wrapped in a black robe that flashed with metallic embroidery. His head was entirely covered by a scarlet scarf. Shem's body went utterly still as if, for a moment, his heart ceased to pump, but *listened*. He recognised that figure, and for a moment could not think from where. Then he remembered. The TV screens before he'd been caught up in the demonstration. He could discern no details about the figure on the rocks, but he just *knew* that it was the same person.

"What is the name of your prophet?" he asked Meenah.

"Gadreel," she replied with feeling.

"Gadreel," Shem echoed in barely more than a whisper. "That is the name of a fallen angel."

Meenah glanced at him sharply. "Is that so?" She shrugged. "To us, Gadreel was the name of one of the Ancient Ones with Shining Faces. I suppose you westerners would call them angels. The Yarasadi worship the Ancient Ones; we are descended from them."

Shem nodded. He knew that the people of Kurdistan were descended from those who had perhaps served the race Meenah called the Ancient Ones. Interbreeding would have taken place after the Fall. What amazed him was that this knowledge was becoming public. Perhaps it was a result of what had taken place in the underworld of Cornwall, five years before. Somehow, *he* had released the information into the unconscious mind of the world, and perhaps the person who had styled himself prophet of the Yarasadi had somehow picked up on it. England was far from Kurdistan, and the links between the two countries might seem negligible, but a faction of the Grigori had fled to this island many millennia ago and had brought their sacred knowledge with them, hidden it in the bones of the land. Since reawakening, Shem had looked for changes here in England, some sign that his experience in the underworld had been beneficial, but perhaps the seeds of his work had taken root in the homeland, the cradle of all civilisation.

Meenah took Shem's silence for scepticism. "The Ancient Ones existed as people of flesh and blood," she said. "You can believe it or not, I don't care, but it is true. They were wiped out, their knowledge lost. Perhaps the same thing happened to them that's happening to us now. There are always cycles in history."

Shem smiled at her. "I don't dispute it." He directed his attention back to the screen. Had another of his brethren reappeared as a prophet to these people? What was he trying to accomplish? The Grigori had always hidden themselves in the world, yet here was a man who used the name of one of the Fallen Ones, blatantly telling forbidden truths to the descendants of people who had once served the Anannage. Perhaps he was deluding himself and was as human as Meenah herself, yet looking at the imposing figure on the screen, Shem did not think so. He recognised the charismatic presence of another Grigori. The Parzupheims of the world must know about this. Why had they done nothing? It didn't make sense. He realised this could be another example of a Watcher undergoing a period of awakening. Perhaps, like Shem and Salamiel, Gadreel had only recently remembered who and what he was. Shem wanted a good, close-up look at the figure, but the cameraman seemed to be at the back of the crowd with limited zoom facility. Cheap camcorder perhaps.

"Do you think we'll get a closer look at Gadreel on this film?" Shem asked.

Meenah shook her head. "No. He discourages revealing his identity. Not many people have met him personally. He has an elite company around him that disseminates his word among his followers. He has to be careful, for obvious reasons."

"You have not met him yourself, then?"

She scowled at him. "Of course not. I've been studying at university over here for the last three years." She turned back to the screen. "But I'm going over there for the millennium. Nothing could keep me away, not guns, not borders, not even the threat of death."

"Why? What's going to happen?"

She glanced at him sideways. "We won't know until it does happen, but it will be…unimaginable."

The video finished and the screen went dark. Lights came on in the hall, and people began to drift to the back, where a shutter was being lifted to reveal a refreshments counter. "Coffee?" Shem asked.

Meenah looked around for a few moments, again as if searching for friends, then nodded. "OK."

Coffee purchased, they went to sit in a side room, where long tables had been set out. The room had at some time perhaps been used for religious purposes; the tall, narrow windows were arched, admitting a diluted sunlight over the heads of those seated at the tables.

Meenah frowned into her drink. "Why are you so interested in our troubles? What are you after?" Later, she would wonder at the strange influence this handsome stranger seemed to have had over her.

Shem had no doubt that generally she was far too sensible to be so open with a man she did not know, and who set alarm bells of self-preservation ringing madly within her. "I thought you wanted people to be interested."

"Of course we do, but your interest seems...different. What are our problems to you?"

He raised an eyebrow. "Is that a racist remark, Meenah?"

She smiled, in spite of herself, ducked her head. "Maybe. As I said, most people think we're crazy. Just another crackpot religion to cause trouble in the world."

"Well, they're very stupid then. The worship of angels is the most ancient of all, and it is true they are rumoured to have lived in your ancestral lands. *If* you believe they existed at all. Archaeologists and scholars are still desperately trying to prove it, although the archaeological establishment takes a dim view of innovative ideas."

Meenah rolled her eyes. "Of this we know!"

Shem folded his hands together on the table in front of him, and leaned forward. "So, what can you tell me about the King of Babylon?"

Meenah pulled a sour face. "He was originally just a nobody way down in the ranks of a repressive regime, but he clearly had ambitions and—may his name be cursed—he does have charisma. About four years ago, he instigated a revolution in his country. Publicly, he says he wanted better for his people, but we know the truth, for our prophet told us. He believes his destiny is to rebuild the great empires of the past, when human kings were guided by the knowledge of the Ancient Ones. He envies and fears my people, because we carry the blood in our veins that he covets. The West

wants to keep him sweet, and won't believe, or rather ig-
nores, the atrocities his military commit. So many of our
villages have been destroyed, women and children tortured
and killed."

"That sounds a familiar story," Shem said.

The girl sneered. "Oh, it is, but this man is different, more
dangerous. Our prophet told us that Nimnezzar believes he is
a direct descendent of the race who were known as the Arallu.
Demons. They were the spawn of the Ancient Ones who
turned away from the Light and took human wives. Nimnezzar
claims they were not evil, but somehow martyrs for a human
cause." She uttered a scornful sound. "Now can you understand why we detest him so much?"

Shem nodded encouragingly. "Yes, I understand." Privately, he considered that Meenah's people were undoubtedly
descended from the same stock as Nimnezzar, because as far
as he was aware only the rebel angels bred with humans, although it was clear the Yarasadi viewed things differently.

Meenah's hands flexed into fists involuntarily on either
side of her coffee. "He lies so well! People believe it readily!
He promises a Golden Age of prosperity, so people are flock-
ing beneath his banners. They are converting from Islam
back to the old faiths of the Magian priests. They worship
fire again in the deserts. My people see this as a great blas-
phemy, for Nimnezzar is a follower of the Lie rather than the
Truth. For thousands of years, and despite persecution, we
have practised the old beliefs, in the right and proper manner. Muslims all over the world, but particularly in Egypt
and Turkey, are incensed by Nimnezzar's effrontery. They
know he wants these countries to be part of his empire, because of their history and ancient sites. We are caught between all these opposing powers." She sighed. "We need
allies, powerful allies…"

"Hmm," Shem said. "I see." He paused. "What do you
know of Babylon itself?"

Meenah rolled her eyes. "I have heard that it is wondrous.
Nimnezzar has reconstructed the Tower of Babel there, and
other ancient monuments. It was built so quickly, Nimnezzar
must have had the help of djinn. Or so people say."

Shem smiled down at her. "A city built by fire demons! What do you believe?"

The girl narrowed her eyes a fraction. "I think there is more truth in myth than people want to admit. It's just been distorted over the centuries."

Shem nodded. "Oh, I agree with you…What else can you tell me about this king who commands demons?"

"He's summoned the world's surviving Magian priests to his court. It is said they were scattered throughout Europe and India, still practising in secret the ancient fire religion. The Magians who chose to heed the summons are now his to command. I've heard that they perform powerful rites for him, so that his soldiers become possessed by djinn, who will be used to crush Babylon's enemies." Meenah moved closer and lowered her voice. "The media speak of atrocities against my people, but they refuse to talk about the true perpetrators. Nimnezzar's warriors assault my people at night, in the deserts and in the mountains."

"A powerful and…intriguing man, this king."

"Intriguing?" Meenah sounded outraged. "He's a mad-man, who wants the Arallu to return to this world. Foolishly, he believes he will stay in control."

Shem put his head on one side, glanced up at the ceiling as if in thought. "Perhaps he knows less of the Arallu's repu-tation than he thinks. They are a particularly blood-thirsty faction of the fallen ones, whose practices are unmention-able in polite company."

"What do you know about it?" the girl interrupted in a cold voice. "The name Arallu was revealed to our prophet in trance. It is not a common term."

Shem raised his eyebrows. "Really? Forgive me, but I have an interest in the mythology of your part of the world. The term Arallu is not that unknown. They were an off-shoot of the Biblical Nephilim, known also as the Grigori."

The girl stared at him for a moment. "Nephilim, maybe. I've not heard of the other term."

"Your prophet appears well-educated in ancient beliefs."

"It is more than that!"

"I'm sure it is. Look, I'm not mocking you. Where does this Gadreel hang around?"

Meenah frowned, but with humour. "He does not *hang around* anywhere. He keeps on the move. Has to."

"So how would I find him?"

Meenah's mouth dropped open. "Why would you want to?" Her mouth closed with a snap. "Hey, just who are you? What do you want with us?" Suspicion flared in her eyes again and, more deeply, fear.

Shem raised his hands in an appeasing gesture. "Don't worry. I'm on your side."

"You're a journalist, aren't you."

"In some respects, in others a scholar."

"Half an hour ago, you claimed to know nothing about what was going on, now you're grilling me for information and asking how to find our prophet! Also, you seem to know a lot already." She stood up. "Thanks for the coffee, but I think I'd better go now. People will be waiting for me."

Shem looked up at her, conscious of the afternoon sunlight slanting in through the high windows. He knew he was bathed in it, reflecting it. If she was truly what she claimed to be, surely she would realise what he was, if only instinctively. Her eyes were wide, and she did not move away.

"Meenah..." No, he could tell her nothing. He smiled. "It's OK. I enjoyed your company. Thanks for bringing me here."

She hesitated. "Who are you?"

He raised his plastic coffee cup to her. "A friend. Now go and find your companions. They might be worrying."

Dismissed, she left in a hurry. Released from his influence, she looked as if she was desperate to get away from him. He watched her straight back retreating through the doorway, then drained his cup. Gadreel. Nimnezzar. He must speak to Salamiel and Daniel about this as soon as possible. They would have a journey to make.

Chapter Four
A Dream of the Garden

When Daniel finally arrived in London, and presented himself at Shem's hotel room, Shem was shocked by his appearance. There were now faint lines on Daniel's face, which over the years had become more angular and muscular than Shem remembered. His eyes were clearer, yet strangely haunted. He seemed much taller, his long, light-brown hair confined in a band at the back of his neck, wisps of it escaping over his shoulders. The ethereal beauty of him appeared to have solidified. He was a very attractive young man, but hardly fey. The army jacket, combat trousers, scuffed para boots and surly demeanour conveyed an entirely different image to the one Shem kept fondly in his memory. When Shem stood up to welcome him, Daniel stood unyielding in his embrace. He seemed uncomfortable, perhaps embarrassed. Perturbed, Shem held him at arm's length. "Thank you for coming."

Daniel shrugged and wriggled away. "I had no choice. You told me that."

"Didn't you want to come?" Shem smiled widely, inflected the question with innuendo.

Daniel held his eyes. "You left me, Shem. Why? I couldn't reach you. Your mind was closed to me. After all that happened, it was cruel!"

Shem didn't want to be drawn into a conversation of this type. He was impatient with it. Daniel was being peevish and too human. He wanted to say, "I didn't grant you longevity for this!" but held his tongue. Instead, he told Daniel about what had happened at the Yarasadi meeting.

"So now you want to go to the Middle East?" Daniel said sarcastically. "A holiday; great! Let's dodge bullets in the sun."

"I told you a long time ago we'd have to go there eventually. I want you to start work now, Daniel. We mustn't waste time."

"We'd never make it, Shem. The obvious route is through Turkey, and it's common knowledge the Turkish authorities discourage any westerners from making contact with the rebels. We'd end up in prison, if not dead, before we even got a sniff at this Gadreel."

Shem shook his head. "Daniel! Remember who I am. No human will bar my passage to the old land. We must leave England as soon as possible."

Daniel rolled his eyes. "You said we'd talk about this first, remember?"

Shem sighed. "Things have happened, Daniel. Stop behaving like a child. You are now a man. Once, you soared in astral flight with me. You wore my wings and took the gift of extended life. You can't just back away from our work together."

Daniel held his eyes for a moment, then relented. "OK. What do you want me to do?"

"See what you can find out about this Gadreel character. Salamiel and I are sure there must be others of our kind around. We must find them."

"Then what?"

Shem's expression became distant. "I don't know yet. There is something, and I'm driven to accomplish it, but I just don't know what it is." He flicked a direct glance at his vizier. "It's perhaps your job to find out. What have you been picking up recently?"

Daniel frowned. "Nothing to do with you, but then I haven't been trying. For the last five years, I've been learning about my psychic ability, from an academic point of view, but I sort of closed down after you shut me out."

Shem nodded. "You probably needed to recuperate as much as I did. But you must open up again now. Flex your muscles and dream for me tonight, Daniel. Dream as well as you used to. Be my eyes and my ears."

Daniel shook his head. "I hope I can."

"What do you mean?"

"Well, I'm older now. It's not so easy. I'm a different person." He sat down on a chair, sticking his legs out before him. "It's quite common, Shem. The younger a psychic is, the stronger their ability. Perhaps you need a new vizier now, another young boy, or girl, who's starry-eyed and easy to manipulate."

"I won't listen to this!" Shem snapped. "Just get on with it! I only have one vizier, and that's you. I don't believe you mean what you say. You can't have changed that much."

Daniel laughed; it altered his face considerably. Shem dared to think the Daniel he knew still hid inside this prickly exterior. "All right, all right. I'll see what I can do. Perhaps I just don't relish the thought of living dangerously again."

"But that's what makes life interesting," Shem said.

Daniel was still grinning. "If you can hang on to it."

Dreams. It had all begun with dreams. Daniel tried to compose himself for sleep, listening to the crackings in the wall of the hotel. His mind seemed to skitter away from allowing any psychic impressions to enter into it. Was he afraid? He'd put up emotional barriers, but he'd always known that, one day, he'd have to continue the work he'd begun with Shem. Give in to it, he told himself. Open up.

Gradually, he felt the old, familiar sensations creep up on him; the strange tension in his head, behind his eyes; the presence of half-heard voices whispering to him from far away.

In the past, he'd used the image of Ishtahar to help him acquire psychic information. She was Shemyaza's lost love, the woman who, a long time ago, had been the cause of his fall, and whose shade, even now, haunted the boundaries of Shem's existence. Shem might not speak about her openly, yet Daniel knew that he hoped one day to be reunited with her. Ishtahar's spirit had become Daniel's goddess. Through her advice and encouragement, she had guided him through many strange experiences, present as a shadow in his awareness.

In the darkness, Daniel whispered her name. "Ishtahar, it's me, Daniel. Are you there? Will you speak to me?"

He visualised her form; a slim, dark-haired young woman, clad in peacock blue veils. Yet the image would not come easily. Had he lost her? For years, he had not called upon her.

Perhaps she felt shut out and abandoned, as Daniel had done by Shem. Daniel regulated his breathing, tried to concentrate on Ishtahar's face, but all he could think about, bizarrely, was Lily's daughter.

His mind wandered, lost concentration. He knew he should have called Lily this evening. Before he'd set off for London, they'd managed to spend a couple of evenings together at High Crag and had discussed what Daniel should do.

On the first night, they had chatted easily together, reminiscing more than anything, but on the second night, Lily had felt confident enough to speak her mind more stridently. She thought that Daniel should start putting his foot down with Shem, to show he could no longer be pushed around. "Remember how he used to treat you, Dan," she'd said. "He drove you ahead of him all of the way, to set off any traps that might have been laid for him."

While Daniel couldn't dispute her words, neither could he explain the complexities of his relationship with Shem to her.

As they'd shared a bottle of wine, Lily's exhortations to him had grown louder. "Daniel, you must stand up for yourself!"

Tired, he'd ended up sitting before her, murmuring, "Mmm, mmm," to everything she said. It had seemed easier than trying to tell her things he couldn't even articulate to himself.

Before she'd left the house, Lily had said, "You must ring me as soon as you've spoken to Shem. You will, won't you?"

"Mmm," he'd answered.

He supposed that, even then, he hadn't intended doing so.

That night, as he'd got into bed, he'd glanced at the phone and remembered his promise, but he'd felt unable to face her demands and advice. He knew she cared about him deeply and secretly felt hurt that he'd not kept up their friendship, but she didn't seem to realise that constantly telling him things he didn't want to hear discouraged the contact.

He fell into a restless sleep, thoughts churning round his mind, until he was unsure whether he was asleep or awake.

Ishtahar stood waiting for him at the threshold of dreams. She leaned back against a closed, wooden doorway, set in a high, sun-drenched wall of mud bricks. The sky overhead was a perfect blue, and the air was filled with the scents of flowers and fragrant trees. Daniel walked towards her along a road of dust and ashes. He could not perceive what lay to either side.

Ishtahar looked about eighteen years old. She was dressed, as always, in blue; a simple dress belted at the waist with a cord. Well-worn sandals of kid leather encased her feet. Her long black hair was plaited, and the rope of it fell over one shoulder, undulating around the curve of a breast.

She smiled in welcome, reaching out with one hand to push open the gate in the wall. "Come, Daniel." She disappeared into a hazy, blue-white light.

Daniel followed her through it and they emerged into a vast, terraced garden that soared up, slope upon slope, until it disappeared into a dark haze of cedar forest. It was an enchanted place, and Daniel knew it well: Kharsag, the garden in Eden. Large white dwellings could be seen, partially screened by carefully-placed foliage. These were the houses of the Anannage lords and their households.

A host of people, whom Daniel knew to be human labourers of both sexes, worked on the terraces, baskets tied to their bent backs as they weeded and pruned among the riot of foliage. Plants from many different climates flourished together; fan-leaved ferns next to tiny desert flowers. Among the huge, obsidian glass domes of the green-houses, waterfalls flashed from terrace to terrace; rainbow light danced in the air. Once, in a far distant life, Daniel had been born in this place, nurtured to be Shemyaza's vizier. How different his role had become in comparison to the days of leisurely contemplation, when he'd scried the universe for his master, spellbound by rarefied ideas and abstract thoughts. Shemyaza and he were now firmly entrenched in the new century of their birth, as alien to their past selves as spirit forms were to humans.

Ishtahar waited for him beneath a spreading cedar, sunlight dappling her bare arms.

"Why have you brought me here?" he asked her.

Ishtahar pointed up through the spreading branches. "Look, do you see that white building up there? That is the house of Shemyaza."

Reluctantly, Daniel followed her gaze. "Yes, I remember it. Is that what I'm here to see? I need to know about Gadreel. Shem thinks he's still alive or has been reincarnated. Tell me, Ishtahar, is he right? Are there other Watchers waiting to be found?"

Ishtahar only smiled and, reaching for his hand, began to lead him through an orchard, where some trees were in fruit, others not. She chattered constantly, but Daniel could only pick up fragments of her speech. "The Watchers are in flight. The sand weighs heavily on the past. Listen to the sound of her feet."

Daniel knew better than to ask questions. Ishtahar was a dream vision; he must let her speak as she willed, and hopefully remember her words for later analysis.

As they walked, Daniel sensed a change occurring, a shift in the dream reality. He realised that he was holding the hand of a child. When he looked down at her, he recognised Ishtahar's face, but now she looked no more than seven or eight years old.

Back in time, Daniel thought. Younger selves. Ours? Is that where the answer lies?

The child chuckled and planted her feet firmly on the ground, so that Daniel had to stop walking. She tugged on his hand to make him squat down before her. "Gadreel," Daniel said to her, hoping to provoke some information.

Ishtahar wrinkled up her nose. "Hidden in cloth," she said. "Angry yet proud."

"Gadreel is?"

She nodded. "On a horse with tassels. Running hard, ahead of the smell of blood. Hot, cruel land. Don't like it."

"Who else?" Daniel asked gently. "Any more?"

"He works with knives. Unhappy. He's forgotten everything, because they made him forget."

"What's his name?"

Ishtahar pursed her lips and shook her head. "It's the key to the Chambers of Light."

"Knives?"

She giggled. "No! The key's waiting to be found. It was in the Cave of Treasures, but now it's in the sky."

"Where, Ishtahar?"

"In the place of beginning, where the Anannage held dominion."

"Here, then," Daniel said, his heart sinking. "Eden. What do we do with the key?"

"Open." She giggled again. "He's born for it. He will know." Then, she let go of his hands and went running away swiftly through the trees. Daniel watched her go, feeling the dream disintegrate in her wake, casting his consciousness back to a hotel room in London.

In the morning, Daniel discovered that Shem had already instructed Salamiel to book flights to Istanbul. "We'll fly into Turkey and take it from there," he told Daniel over breakfast. Salamiel was still in his bedroom, phoning Grigori agents in an attempt to find last minute seats. Daniel had no doubt Salamiel would be successful. Everything was developing as he'd feared.

"Shouldn't we think about this first?" he suggested. "You know, discuss it?"

"We can talk on the flight." Shem paused. "Did you sleep well?"

"Yes, thank you."

"Dreams?"

Daniel sighed. "I think you may be right about Gadreel, and also that there might be others. The only other information I picked up was that we have to find the key to the Chambers of Light. Does that mean anything to you?"

Shem shrugged. "Anything else?"

"Apparently, it was in a place called the Cave of Treasures, but the information I received was a bit fragmented. Something about it being in the sky now. Doesn't make much sense. I picked up that you should know about the key. You were born for it."

Shem leaned back in his chair to think, then spoke slowly. "I think we should make contact with Gadreel and then concentrate on locating this cave. You can work on it psychically while we're in Turkey."

"What is the key for though? What are these Chambers of Light that you have to open?"

Shem stood up and began to pace around the table. "It could be a reference the Hall of Records, where the Anannage allegedly hid the store of their knowledge before withdrawing from the world." He stopped pacing. "I'm not sure. You work it out. All I want to do is get to Gadreel and find Eden."

Daniel was unnerved by the feverish gleam in Shem's eyes. "It will be dangerous though. We might be killed before we find him."

Shem shook his head in amusement. "Daniel, what has happened to you? Where's your sense of wonder? What we began in Cornwall was only the small, first step. A trial run, if you like."

"There's one thing you haven't considered," Daniel said. "What about this self-styled King of Babylon? Doesn't he believe he's a descendent of the Anannage too? How will that affect us? Remember we will have to cross his lands to find Gadreel."

Shem nodded thoughtfully. "I have a feeling I will meet this man."

"Shem, he's a dangerous mad-man! Is that wise?"

Shem grinned. "Daniel, many people think I'm a dangerous mad-man too. I'm intrigued by King Nimnezzar. I want to find out if he's authentic or not."

Daniel shook his head in disbelief. "Are you mad? Authentic? He's a murdering dictator! Do you really think he has Grigori blood?"

"Daniel, I'm surprised to hear you say that. The fact that he's a murdering dictator makes it more likely he's the genuine article! Remember Peverel Othman."

Daniel groaned. "This trip will be hell. I know it."

Chapter Five
The Assassin

London

Melandra Maynard watched television as she carefully cleaned her selected weapon. She had many, and had been tutored in the use of sniper rifles, revolvers and automatics, but as she planned to get in close to Shemyaza, the equipment she had chosen for this task was a semiautomatic fitted with a suppressor. It was designed to be fired at close range, ideally with its muzzle actually touching the skin of her victim, so that any detonation not muffled by the suppressor would be absorbed by the soft tissue of the target.

The windows of the hotel room were shut, but the air conditioning effectively cooled the air. She laid out the pieces of her weapon on the bed. Plastic: designed to be hidden in luggage and escape airport detection. It did not need cleaning, but this was a ritual she performed before every task.

The news reports on TV were full of the troubles in the Middle East. Fundamentalists were running riot in Egypt. Only a fool or a potential suicide would want to visit the place as a tourist nowadays. Western holiday-makers were fair game, and subsequently non-existent, so the terrorists had turned their attention to the ancient monuments that attracted people from all over the world to their country. Several sites had been bombed, and there had been international outrage over the severe damage perpetrated on the Osirion at Abydos. Stones that had stood for millennia now lay in rubble. Even Melandra was disgusted by it. In thousands of years' time, the creeds that approved of such vandalism might be forgotten, but the brooding monuments of the past would have continued on, perhaps until the day when no humans were left upon the earth, and the desert sands would blow over the last of their bones. Melandra shuddered. The thought was too disquieting.

Shemyaza had been traced to a house in London. Melandra had received an encrypted e-mail message via her notebook computer, which had given her a script for the job to come. It appeared her target was booked into his hotel under the name Michael Jacobs. Melandra would pose as an employee of a company called Prussoe Estates, which she presumed was a Grigori outfit. She would arrive at the hotel under the pretence of delivering some documents to Jacobs, and intended to talk her way into his room. It sounded too easy, but she had prepared herself mentally for unexpected developments.

Melandra wondered from where Fox got his information. Surely the Grigori would be aware of any human infiltration, and the only other explanation was that a Grigori himself was leaking data to the Children. That seemed even more unlikely. Some things didn't quite add up for Melandra, and it made her uneasy. Still, she trusted her instincts and had faith in her Lord. A silver cross hung at her throat; her protection. She would prepare herself with prayer before she left her room.

Lighting a cigarette, Melandra went to the window, where she lifted aside the nets. Down on the street, traffic surged up and down. He was out there somewhere. Did he know about her? She shivered and dropped the net. Later that night, she would find him and kill him, or die in the attempt.

Melandra walked through the city streets in the early evening. She felt tranquil, almost euphoric. The light was benign, the air balmy. Music filled the sky from the bars and cafes whose doors were thrown open to the summer night. She had effected a disguise, which she called her 'secretary look.' Curly, mid-brown, shoulder-length wig with blond streaks; high street store fashion clothes; make-up copied from the pages of a glossy women's magazine. She wore unflattering, but apparently fashionable, spectacles and discreet gold jewelery.

It took her half an hour to walk to her destination. For a while, she stood opposite the old building, smoking a cigarette in the arched doorway to a dusty dress shop, conveniently situated near a bus stop, so it would look as if she had left work for the evening and was waiting for her bus home.

He must be in there. It did not look like a hotel; it did not look like anything particularly, except perhaps the offices of a registered charity, which set up camp wherever the generosity of patrons manifested itself.

Melandra threw her cigarette end into the gutter and crossed the road. No traffic about. A group of young people ambled past her, their voices high with excitement. They did not appear to notice her. Why should they? She looked like a thousand other young women on the streets of London.

She had her orders, her instructions, her methods, her bolt-hole ready. When the job was done she would disappear as quickly as a cat, and within a few hours be on her way back to the States.

She mounted the three shallow steps that led to the closed front door. There was a peep-hole in one of the panels. She would be looked at through it. She rang the bell.

All seemed silent and dead behind the door. She could not sense life. Was it empty? She pressed the bell again, and the intercom beneath it buzzed into life. "Yes?"

"Hello, this is Nancy Oakes. I have some documents for one of your guests." Each statement sounded like a question. She exaggerated her own accent.

There was silence for a moment. Then, "none of our guests are expecting visitors."

"Oh," Melandra answered. "Well, I believe my employers did call. I work for Prussoe Estates. I am expected." This was a crucial moment. If they checked with the man himself, he wouldn't know what they were talking about, but someone, somewhere, had called this establishment earlier to provide back-up to her story. She shouldn't have had trouble at this stage. "Will you check at the desk, please?"

After a moment, the door opened a little. Melandra pushed it and walked inside. There was a tall woman waiting for her, an incredibly tall woman. Was this one of *them*? Her heart wanted to increase its pace, but she wouldn't allow it. She mustn't think about the implications; it was too awesome.

"Hi!" She smiled widely and held up a document wallet. "Hope there wasn't a problem." She held out her hand for a friendly greeting, but the tall woman only looked at it in disgust. She extended a hand of her own, but not to shake Melandra's.

"Perhaps I'd better take those, Ms Oakes. Who is it they're for?"

"Michael Jacobs. I'm sorry, but my instructions are to hand them directly to Mr Jacobs."

The tall woman assessed her. "Well, I'm afraid you're too late. Mr Jacobs checked out a short while ago."

"What?" She knew she'd let her voice and expression change too much.

The tall woman's eyes narrowed. "Perhaps you'd better call your employers, Ms Oakes."

Melandra chewed her lip, hoping to reassert her disguise. "Oh dear, this is kind of inconvenient." She laughed. "Trouble is, I'm late for the appointment. It's my fault I've missed him. Do you know where Mr Jacobs has gone?"

"No." The woman walked to the door and opened it again. "I'm afraid you must go now."

"Hey, I've been travelling all day! I have to find Mr Jacobs. There must be someone here who knows where he is."

The woman laughed coldly. "My dear, this is a private guest house. We do not pry into the affairs of our visitors. Mr Jacobs has left, and so must you. I'm sure your employers will understand."

Melandra sighed and tapped her foot for a moment, then reached into her large shoulder-bag. The woman's eyes widened at the sight of the gun. "Shut the door," said Melandra.

Hesitating for only a moment, the woman did so. "Explain yourself!" Her voice was deadly calm.

"I have to find Mr Jacobs," Melandra persisted. "Now, you know and I know that if we should have a little accident, if this gun should accidentally go off, no-one here will call the police. You'll just die. Is Jacobs worth that? I'm quite prepared to kill you, lady, so just tell me: where is he?"

The woman seemed to grow in stature. "How dare you threaten me, you little..."

Melandra shot her in the leg before she could finish. The sound of it was louder than she'd liked, but then she hadn't been that close to the target.

The woman slid, still graceful, to the floor, stared aghast at the blood pouring from the wound.

"I can shoot you quite a few times before you die," Melandra said. "Where is he?"

The woman looked up at her with an unreadable expression. "Whatever you're planning, you're wasting your time. He's at Heathrow, on his way out of the country by now, no doubt."

"Where?"

"How should I know?"

Melandra fired again, taking the woman in the arm, nearly severing it. "I think you do."

"Istanbul." The woman leaned back against the door, blinking at the ceiling, her blood pooling around her. "That's all I know."

"Well, thanks." Melandra walked to the door, opened it, pushing the woman aside. She paused for a moment. "Sorry about this, but I don't want you making any phone calls." She put her weapon against the woman's head and shot her, more quietly than before, then put her gun back into her bag and went out onto the street, closing the door behind her. "Bad security. They should have more sense."

Quickly, she walked down the street, then turned into a side road, making for the bustle of the main streets and the anonymity of the nearest tube station. First, she ducked into an alley and removed the wig and glasses, which she threw into a pile of cardboard boxes. She let down her hair and went back onto the street. Istanbul. She would follow him there.

Chapter Six
The King of Babylon's Daughter

Babylon

The princess dreamed her father's dream of war and victory. She hung somewhere up in the sky, looking down, and saw him ride a high-stepping grey stallion, amid a forest of fluttering banners that bore the seal of their royal house. His Magian generals rode behind him, dressed in robes of scarlet and gold. Her father looked so handsome; his coiled, oiled hair black against his uniform and his moustache shining like combed silk.

The sun shone down and made the stench of war more horrible. The princess knew that angels had fought here, for the battle-field was a tangle of broken wings and blood. The bodies of the defeated had rained down from heaven to die.

The king's stallion stepped daintily on its polished hooves towards a rocky outcrop that rose up from the battlefield, which was otherwise quite flat. Here, on a shawl of wet redness that was spread out over the stone, a tall figure leaned against an erect spear, gazing down at the carnage. The princess was in no doubt that this was a prince of angels. He was a giant, tall and lean. His long, pale face was clean-shaven and he was clad in bloodied leather; his white-gold hair wound up on his head, decorated with what appeared to be human bones. Cruel and dangerous he seemed, yet so beautiful.

The princess watched this angel warrior turn lambent blue eyes upon her father, silently watching him draw closer. Presently, fixing the king with an expression of disdain, he spoke, in a low voice that rang out like a clarion over the field. "Where is my brother, ruler of men?"

The princess looked on as her father drew his mount to a halt beneath the rock, looked up. "Who is your brother, lord?"

"He wears your chains, lies deep beneath Etemenanki, suffers in silence."

The princess saw into the mind of her father, understood then its workings; cunning and twisting. She knew that the king remembered the angel lord he had taken prisoner from a tomb, but he was not afraid. The prisoner was currency. "Penemue," he said.

The giant straightened up, flexed his fingers upon the spear. "Deliver him unto me."

The princess saw sly patterns curl through the mind of her father. She saw the words he discarded, heard those he selected. "Lord Penemue has many enemies," he said. "He is under my protection. By what name are you known, lord?"

The angel sneered then, and the princess knew he could see into the mind of the king as well as she could. "I am his sovereign lord. I am Shemyaza. And if you do not release Penemue, then I shall come for him."

The king bowed upon his horse. "But you are welcome always in my palace, lord. Return with me to the jewel of Babylon, and I will command a great feast be set for you. There, you may dine with your brother, in my house."

The angel nodded. "I shall come to your house," he said and various meanings twisted through his words.

The princess woke up then, roused from her dream by the echo of a clamour in the house. All was silent now.

She opened her eyes on the tawny darkness, blinked at the swaying canopies above her bed, where reedy chimes of metal swung like singing stars. Then, she heard feet running on the marble floors beyond the great double doors of her bedroom, as if they approached swiftly from a great distance, and she sensed a pulsing excitement in the air, like the memory of a shout in an empty room. They were not mortal feet.

She was not afraid. Like her mother, she was a prize and knew no fear in the house of her father.

Quietly, she slipped from between her linen sheets and cast aside the draperies that swathed her couch. Beyond, the room was vast and seemed empty; the bed a great splendid island in its midst, where she might lie enchanted awaiting kisses. A robe of dark silk lay in a puddle of fabric beside the bed. Without haste, the princess lifted it and pulled it around her shoulders, before venturing on her naked feet across the black and gold polished floor. Her feet left marks, like the feet of an angel. It was the heat of sleep seeping out from her.

The princess was a part of her father's dream of Ancient Babylon. She had been raised to believe in it, and knew no other life. She was Sarpanita, daughter of the Lord of the Four Quarters of the World and she lived in the house that was called the Marvel of the Land; the Shining Residence; the Dwelling of Majesty.

Outside the bedroom, she found her mother Amytis, also belting her robe and surrounded by a bevy of hand-maidens— Egyptians, all adorned in the manner of antiquity.

"What is it, Mama?" Sarpanita inquired politely. She was wary of her father, for she had seen him kill, but for her mother she reserved a quiet terror, blended with awe and a sliver of love. Although Amytis had never raised a hand against her, and rarely spoke sharply, the girl appreciated that, given the opportunity, Amytis was capable of being far more deadly than her husband.

The queen yawned, gave her belt a final yank. Her feet were slippered in pearled velvet, sewn with gold wire. "A commotion," she said. "Perhaps we have been invaded, though I think not. News, then, or a message." She shrugged and extended a honey-coloured arm like a shining serpent, out from her robe. "Come, my child. We must see for ourselves."

Sarpanita was pulled into the embrace of her mother, felt the heat of her body through the cool silk, the ripple of her muscles. The hand-maidens were left behind at the door to Amytis' apartments. Their eyes were wide; fingers fluttered before their mouths.

Before her marriage, Amytis had been a guerrilla fighter and was in fact a captive of war, which suited her husband's designs admirably. Now, she was less fiery, but smouldered on, slinking and sliding around the palace, a dangerous cat-serpent wearing a gold collar, kept docile by fresh meat.

Long ago, in the bed of their passion, Amytis had coaxed
her husband's dream from him. She knew how he regarded
himself and was wise enough to realise that collusion in the
dream helped consolidate her position at the king's side. Amytis
was not her original name.

"Mama," Sarpanita said. "Where is Tiy?" The old woman
would normally be found in Amytis' quarters at night.

"I think she is with your father," Amytis replied, "but we
shall see."

Tiy was a fearsome seeress, whom Amytis had brought
with her from home, ostensibly as a hand-maid. Sarpanita was
not sure whether she was related to this terrifying crone, because the relationship between Amytis and the seeress was
odd and nebulous. The girl knew they practised strange, old
rites in private together. Sometimes Amytis seemed in awe of
Tiy, while at other times the old woman behaved like a servant. Despite the fact that Nimnezzar clearly despised the
seeress, it seemed he was objective enough to appreciate her
strong psychic abilities. Much to the disgust of the Magian
priests who flocked around him, Tiy had become one of his
close advisors. The fact that Tiy was at this moment with the
king must mean that something momentous had occurred.

Mother and daughter walked through the high-ceilinged
corridors that were tiled in blue and decorated with designs of
lions and trumpet flowers and the images of tall columns gar-
landed with leaves. Brass lamps depended from the ceiling,
looking like censers. Electric light gleamed from them dimly
like burning oil. "I dreamed of an angel king," said Sarpanita.
"And names came to me: Shemyaza, Penemue."

"Ah yes," replied the queen. She squeezed her daughter's
shoulder. "You are a seeress like old Tiy, sweet child. The
names are pertinent."

Amytis actually believed her daughter to be rather more than
just a seeress. When the child had been conceived, Nimnezzar
had come to his wife's bed as Shemyaza and she had received
him as Ishtahar. This ritual union had been fruitful—surely an
omen—as before then she had never conceived with any man.
Sarpanita was therefore an angel princess, not quite human, for
her parents had risen above their mortal spirits to create her.

Sarpanita, unaware of this aspect of her creation, only recognised the tone that she must not question her mother further.

The king's private apartments were some distance from those of the royal women, and they had to cross an open balcony to reach them. The courtyard below was filled with flowers, all breathing sweetness into the night. It was a special garden the king had designed for the queen, and all its blooms came alive at night. Amytis liked to walk there, slowly, in moonlight. She kept her peacocks there; all tame and named and collared, and there was a trefoil pool, where opal-white carp dozed beneath a mat of lilies.

"Why did we hear them running?" asked the princess, because all was tranquil in the garden. "It had nothing to do with us."

"There was no-one running," answered the queen, "but you heard it nonetheless. An echo through the grilles, that came from your father's quarters, perhaps, or a premonition."

"But you heard it too," whispered the princess.

Amytis laughed. "It is my business to do so."

They came now to the gates of the king's apartments, where guards stood to attention. The gates were bronze, decorated with the images of striding, winged gods. The guards were ceremonial; they did not carry guns, but curved swords. When they saw Amytis and her daughter, they opened the gates for them. Amytis smiled at them vaguely and led her daughter past them.

Beyond, a dark, columned hall-way unfurled before them, grander than the corridors of the women's quarters. Noise could be heard here; the whisper of voices talking quickly and a sense of imminence in the air. Servants flitted across the passage-way ahead of them like ghosts. It was clear that the king had been roused, and that his staff hurried to attend to his wants.

Statues stood motionless in niches; tall feather-cloaked men of black basalt, taken from the ancient city discovered by the king's archaeologists. Sarpanita glanced uneasily at their long, stern faces and slanting ophidian eyes.

Amytis paused before one of the statues, gestured at it. "He is one of the Arallu," she told her daughter, pulling her close against her side. "A frightening thing. A long time ago, the legends say that Great God Anu made a garden, which he called Kharsag. His messengers and warriors, the Shining Ones, attended him there, but some of them went bad and stole out of the garden in the night. They went down to the lower plains to seduce the daughters of men. A great war was caused by this. The children that the rebel Shining Ones conceived on their women were monstrous, and hunted down by Anu's fierce warriors. Those that survived were forced into hiding. Some of their descendants became a demon race called the Arallu. They lived in the city your Papa's diggers found. They lived underground to hide from the wrath of Anu."

Sarpanita shuddered. She knew vaguely of these things, but her mind had always shied away from them. "They are just stories," she said, in a small, precise voice.

Amytis nodded. "Indeed they are, and yet remember you can make a story of playing with your kitten in the light and shade of your inner room. History *is* stories, some of it embellished to make it more colourful, some of it remembered only in half-light, fragmented." She squeezed Sarpanita's shoulder. "My dear, Penemue was a rebel Shining One. For his sins, he was buried beneath hard, heavy rocks in a tomb of black glass. He did not die. The Arallu kept him hidden."

"Why didn't they set him free?"

Amytis shrugged. "We may never know. I think it must be because they were afraid of his power. But your father is not afraid, little Nita. He opened the tomb, he took away the rocks."

Sarpanita swallowed convulsively. She did not want to think about what her mother was telling her, in case she remembered something that was buried deep within her mind, older even than her body, or her soul. "He's alive?" She felt as if dark, flapping pinions beat the air around her, invisible. For the first time, she knew fear in her father's house.

Amytis laughed softly. "He is not *dead*, my daughter."

"I dreamed of angels…"

"The Shining Ones are remembered as angels in many faiths. It is just a name. The old stories were carried far across the world, and were changed along the way."

"Mother, I feel strange. It is as my dream described. An angel prince imprisoned in our city."

"That is your Penemue," said the queen languidly, pointing at the statue before them, "or rather his image." She smiled down at her daughter. "I think it is time you learned certain things. Your father protects you, because he looks upon you as a child, though of course you are not. I will take you to him now and we shall discover what the fuss is about."

At the doorway to the king's private salon, they found his Magian vizier, Jazirah, in the act of closing the doors behind him. He was exceptionally tall, like so many of Nimnezzar's closest staff, but his height was unusual in an Indian. His face, which was contemplative as he emerged from the salon, changed when it saw the queen and her daughter. It became closed. He straightened up.

"I am here to see my husband," said Amytis, stepping up to him.

Jazirah smiled, made a languid, open-palmed gesture with both hands, bowed a little. "Madam, he is not within."

"What has happened, Jazirah?" asked the queen. She was irritated by his oily politeness, for she knew he had no liking for her. To Jazirah, she was a common gypsy, risen above her station.

Jazirah pulled a quizzical face. "Happened, my lady?"

Amytis composed herself for argument, already bored by it, but Sarpanita touched her arm. "What was that cry, mama?"

Amytis turned. "Cry, my daughter?" She had heard nothing.

Jazirah stroked his chin, his short, neatly-clipped beard, and kept silent.

Sarpanita glanced along the corridor that led away from her father's rooms. "From there," she said. "I heard a cry. It was terrible." She raised her arm to point, and its tawny flesh was pimpled as if from cold or fear.

"Etemenanki," said the queen, realising something. She eyed the vizier, who shrugged. "Is my husband at the temple?" she asked.

"He may well be," said Jazirah.

"A strange hour to be worshipping," said Amytis and began to walk in the direction Sarpanita had pointed. Jazirah loped to catch up with her.

"Perhaps not a good time to intrude," he suggested.

Queen Amytis ignored him. "Come, Nita," she said, and her daughter came to her side.

In the days when the kings of Babylon had ruled all the known world, a tower had been built, a great ziggurat that was remembered in legend as an edifice designed to reach up into heaven. The Tower of Babel. In the old tongue, it had been named Etemenanki, and had been a fire temple, sacred in earliest times to the Shining Ones, the men and women of an advanced race revered as gods, and later to the god Marduk. Its name meant 'the Temple Foundation of Heaven and Earth'. The original Grigori, known as Watchers, had visited a shrine at the top of the temple, where they had lain with the comeliest daughters of the city in the ceremony of sacred marriage. From these unions had come the line of kings, who always bore Grigori blood. Later, once the Grigori had melted away into hiding, men had assumed the roles of gods and continued to re-enact the ritual. The ziggurat had been destroyed and rebuilt many times. This was its latest incarnation, constructed far from the site of the original.

Etemenanki dominated the city, rising over it incredibly. Smoke from the eternal fires and their offerings purled from its summit, visible only on the clearest of days. Amytis knew what her husband the king had incarcerated within the labyrinthine chambers beneath the temple. Tiy had told her about the strange being Nimnezzar had brought back with him from the *tell*. The king had refused to talk about it when Amytis had questioned him, and had forbade her strictly to enter the chambers beneath Etemenanki until he gave word otherwise. It was for her own safety, he said. She knew Nimnezzar was wary of allowing his wife to view the captive. He was either afraid of it or of its possible effect on her, or perhaps vice versa. Amytis was patient. She did not push the issue, nor had need to. For the time being, she could glean all the information she needed from Tiy.

Amytis guessed, or perhaps instinctively knew, that something had occurred in the dark passages of Etemenanki. Tiy had divulged that since his arrival, some weeks previously, the strange captive had not spoken, nor eaten anything but an occasional small fruit. Water, he drank copiously, but it seemed the long incarceration beneath the earth had damaged his immortal mind. He seemed, so Tiy reported, hardly aware of his surroundings. The king had many scholars in his court, some of whom were familiar with several of the ancient tongues. All these had been tried on the visitor without success. No ancient word, of any known dialect, attracted his attention. Now, Sarpanita had heard a cry from the temple, and Amytis wondered whether her husband had resorted to torture to coax a reaction from the dead-alive angel.

A private walkway, used by the royal family, led from the palace to a back door of the temple. On the way there, Jazirah clearly realised that the queen would not be stopped and became more communicative. "The king was roused from his bed only a few minutes before you arrived, my lady. The temple priests came for him."

"So what has happened?"

The vizier shrugged. "I was just on my way to find out."

"Then we shall find out together," said the queen. She knew her husband well enough to be sure that, in the midst of a crisis, he would forget about how he had refused her admission to the rooms beneath the temple.

The lower levels of Etemenanki comprised a series of linked shrines. Above ground, on the rising tiers, the flame was worshipped, and djinn conjured from the sacred smokes, but sometimes the priests of Babylon needed to invoke the elementals of earth and this was done deep underground. Here, the king had imprisoned his find, perhaps so that he was as far as possible from the flames, from which he might draw power and escape. Penemue was an unknown quantity. He had apparently survived for millennia, and no-one knew the extent of his power, only that he could not be remotely human.

The queen and her companions passed through several empty shrines, and then came to the door of a room where a peering cluster of people was gathered, dressed in the scarlet and orange robes of Magian priests. Amytis parted them with a wave of her hand and, with Jazirah keeping pace, stepped to the threshold.

Sarpanita hung back. She could not speak, for her head was still full of the terrible cry that she could not hear with her ears. Within the shrine, something suffered and twisted in pain. She did not want to see it. She was afraid.

Her mother's body stiffened, and Sarpanita knew she beheld something almost indescribable. Then, she turned. "Come, Nita. Come here at once."

Sarpanita froze. She heard her father speak her name in surprise, then from within the room, Tiy's voice, "It is time, now."

Something else within the room became aware of her. She could feel it. And it drew her towards it inexorably. Her feet moved numbly and the doorway came closer. She had no choice.

He sat upon a great stone chair within a cage of iron. His hair hung over his chest, a strange red in colour, like slender metal wires. They had dressed him in plain linen trousers and tunic, yet still his body seemed inhuman—too big for the room. One of his hands, which hung over the arms of the chair, could have crushed her head like a seed. His face was alien yet beautiful; the face of one of the statues. He was looking directly at her with eyes that were unnaturally blue. *Penemue. I dreamed of your name.*

Slowly, Sarpanita approached the cage and the angel watched her like a large animal would watch a small creature coming towards it. She could not turn her head, but heard her mother's voice, speaking to her father.

"See, my love. See! He recognises her for what she is!"

The voice seemed to break a spell and Sarpanita looked at her parents. Her father had his arm around his wife's shoulder, but it seemed as if he was restraining her rather than showing affection. Tiy stood to the side; a dark, wizened creature. Her milky blind eyes were like polished pearls. The three figures seemed to be a long distance away; small and unreachable.

The princess put her hands upon the bars of the cage and the angel let his head drop to one side. He tried to smile, although his face was haggard and tired. She saw then that they had chained him by the ankles to the floor.

The king came up to her and put his hands upon her shoulders. "My daughter, do you know who this is?"

She nodded, whispered, "Yes. It is Shemyaza's brother. I dreamed of it." She felt her father's fingers convulse upon her shoulders.

"He has lived for a very long time."

"I know. You found him under the earth." She wanted to say, "but he does not belong with us," and warn her father that to keep Penemue in chains might be dangerous, for then his fierce brother would come looking for him. But, as she also knew her father was not afraid of anything, there seemed no point in saying this.

Amytis came to her husband's side. "When did he...wake up?"

The king flicked a quick, sardonic glance at Tiy to indicate he disapproved of Amytis knowing about the captive and that he understood exactly where her knowledge came from, then relented and spoke. "Not long ago. He was sitting there peacefully as usual, then jumped in his seat and let out a great scream."

"Sarpanita heard it," said the queen.

The king patted his daughter's arm. "I am not surprised."

"What are you going to do now?"

"Give him to the linguists again. What else can be done?" The king eyed his daughter. "Speak to him, Nita."

Sarpanita did not want to. If she was to speak to this being, she should do it alone, not in front of others. She shook her head.

The king made a sound of annoyance. "You must. Can't you see that he is aware of you."

"I don't want to, papa. I'm afraid."

"Nita, this great angel is to be your..."

"Hush!" interrupted Tiy, who had so far remained uncharacteristically quiet. "It should be carefully explained to the girl in private. Women's talk."

"Nonsense," snapped the king. "In the ancient days, the daughters of the settlements were not given careful explanations as to what must happen to them. We must continue the tradition. We conceived this child for this very moment, and who knows, our sacred act might even have influenced the Shining Ones to allow me to find Penemue. She belongs to him already, and on her, he will conceive the sons of a great race."

"Yes," hissed Tiy. "That is true. But she is only a child, great king. And you are a man. The knowledge of this intimate subject should not come from you."

Nimnezzar laughed. "You'll get your chance, old woman. My daughter is yours to instruct, as we have discussed."

Sarpanita listened to their conversation without feeling. They wanted to give her to this creature, who would tear her body with his great size, perhaps kill and devour her. Angels were terrible creatures; she had always known that. She wished her father had not found Penemue, yet over the past couple of weeks, her body had thrummed to strange rhythms. She had been waiting for something, her blood had been waiting for it, and here it was.

"Speak to your husband," said the king.

And Sarpanita felt her blood turn to dust. The angel shuddered before her, flexed his shoulders; his nostrils quivered, scenting her. It made her think of bulls and stallions. He moved his body upon the chair, trying to stand, and but for the princess, everyone in the room took a step back from the iron cage.

The angel uttered a groan and collapsed back into his seat. Then he gripped the stone arms of the chair and threw back his head, screamed out a single, deafening word that shook the foundations of the ziggurat: "Shemyaza!"

Chapter Seven
The Summoning

Essex, England

The tall man rinsed his long, pale hands at a small, porcelain sink, having already removed the rustling plastic gloves. On his examination couch, his patient sat rearranging her clothing in the afternoon light that came in diffusely through the blinds at the windows.

"Well, it's all going splendidly," said the man, a gynaecologist. "Only a few more weeks." He remembered to smile as he turned 'round.

The woman smiled back, her face radiant. Later, that might change when the realities of parenting stubbed out the pink fantasy. The consultant thought suddenly that he too might have had children once, but now his life was an arid desert, and the past seemed inappropriate, somehow messy. He felt disassociated from it and pushed the unwelcome, intrusive idea from his mind. It was absurd. He lived alone, had never married.

The woman, his patient, chattered on as she put on her coat. He uttered platitudes in return. She really was in superb health and as far as modern medical technology could predict, so was her budding child. There was little to say to her.

At the door, she pressed a slim hand into one of his, which was still slightly damp. "Thank you for everything. You're always so reassuring, Mr Murchison. Forgive me for saying this—I hope it doesn't sound too personal—but I think you must have been born to look after the needs of the female body."

He smiled again, unembarrassed, but unwilling to comment. "Thanks. You take care of yourself." Gently, he propelled her out of his office.

Once the door had closed behind her, he went to sit behind his desk, which was virtually empty. She had been the last patient of the day, yet he felt as if there was something else he had to do before he could leave the hospital. All day, he'd been plagued by strange urges to keep looking in his diary. Had he forgotten an appointment? Perhaps it had not been written down. He buzzed his secretary. "Pamela, is there anything that needs my attention before I go home?"

A slight pause. "No, Mr Murchison. Would you like me to bring you a cup of tea?"

"Thanks, but I think I'll just be off."

He stood up and took off his white coat. What was it that nagged at his mind? What morsel of information had he mislaid? Before he left for the day, he was driven to roll up the window blinds. Sunlight splashed into his consulting room, an August invasion. When he turned away from the window, the room seemed too bright, everything held in a caul of radiance that weirdly immobilised it. Pieces of furniture had taken on a sinister stillness, as if they might move of their own accord once he'd left the room. He shivered in the warm air. Perhaps a summer chill was presaged.

When he opened the door to leave, his name on the doorplate seemed the name of a stranger. Cameron Murchison. He felt it did not belong to him. He was not usually prone to such fancies.

He drove in his car through the city heat to the suburb where his lonely house was situated. Along the sides of the roads, the tamed gardens were parched, and melting hose-pipes lay useless upon sticky drive-ways; their use was temporarily banned. His long, elderly car rolled quietly up the short avenue where he lived, to the tall narrow house at the end, hidden behind a screen of yews trained into a hedge.

He had a housekeeper, Mrs Melrose, who came in every morning to attend to the slight disorder his presence in the house created. The only times he saw this woman was on the weekends, when she cooked his breakfast also, and sat opposite him at the wide kitchen table to talk about the newspapers, which came through the door in a roll.

This evening, Murchison would have welcomed the company of the housekeeper. He felt odd. Driving home, he thought he had seen a star high up in the bleached, daytime sky. It must have been the sun reflecting off a plane.

The house was utterly silent. Not even the tick of a clock broke through it. As he went into the spacious, airy kitchen, the refrigerator began to hum, which made him jump. Mrs Melrose had left him a note on the table. He picked it up and stared at it, but was unable to decipher the words, as if they'd been written in a language he did not know.

An evening meal of select cured meats and crisp pale salad had been left for him in the fridge. He found it by accident looking for the milk; presumably this was what the housekeeper's note had been about. She didn't leave him a meal habitually, only when she had something she wished to use up; then she'd bring it with her from home.

Murchison sat in the silent kitchen and ate the meal. It seemed delicate, the food of a rarefied being, its subtle flavours exploding on his tongue. It needed wine to complement it; a light, sand-dry vintage. He drank some fresh orange juice instead.

Something was happening to him. Would madness feel like this? His life was mostly without textures; its greatest highs being the enjoyment of good food and wine. He never went out socially, and listened to music only at home on his hi-fi system, which had cost thousands of pounds. Films did not interest him, particularly, and he liked only books on archaeology. He had an arrangement with a local antique dealer who made polite phone calls on the occasions when merchandise came into his hands that he thought Murchison might appreciate. He owned many artefacts dug up from far sands that were arranged in a glass-fronted cabinet in his study. Sometimes, he would stare at them for hours, searching for a memory that never came back to him.

His life comprised small, precise pleasures. Most people liked him, for he was quiet and gentle, but he did not yearn for their company. His ironic smile, springing auburn hair and attenuated good looks pleased women, yet he seemed not to notice the messages in their eyes. Several of his patients had fallen in love with him over the years, but it had escaped his attention. He liked and respected women, enjoyed his work, and knew he had a healing touch that often smoothed the path of difficult pregnancy. Despite this, he never wanted lovers, and felt, for the most part, asexual. Perhaps that was what his patients liked in him. Yet sometimes, a woman might come to him who gave off an invisible aura that felt to him like a fierce, open wound. These women he knew he could not help, and usually they did not take to him and even distrusted his opinions. It did not necessarily mean they would have trouble with their pregnancies. He did not know what it might mean.

As the sun sank, Murchison went into his music room and slid a Mozart CD into the hi-fi. The music did not please him; in fact, he felt quite irritated by it. Silencing the equipment, he pulled a book from one of his tall book-cases. It fell open in his hands and the long face of the pharaoh Akhenaten, captured in stone, stared back at him. A strange coldness filled his belly; it seemed as if his heart had slowed. What significance was there in this? He had seen the picture a hundred times before, yet now he felt that if he only gave himself up to the sensation squirming in his body, he would be transported back in time and the statue would be rough stone beneath his fingers. It might even speak. A thick, pungent aroma as of church incense tantalised his nose. He heard the distant ringing of bells. It was all coming up to him, out of the book.

Murchison slammed the pages shut and pushed the book hastily back onto the shelf. There was no temple scent in the house, no haunting chime.

He went to the drinks trolley and poured himself a large Scotch. Normally, he drank only in moderation as all his liquors were obscenely expensive and wanted only to be enjoyed in small sips. Murchison drained the glass, blinking water from his eyes conjured by the fiery trail in his throat. Then he poured another. He was shaking. He felt ill.

Upstairs, things were no better. He felt watched in his bedroom and closed and opened the curtains several times, unsure of whether he felt safer with the world let in or shut out.

He knew there were dreams waiting for him, and could even feel their shadowy presences rustling in the corners of the room, among his clothes in the wardrobe, beneath the bed. He was afraid, yet also resigned. Something was going to be shown to him, something which had been approaching him all day, from a great distance. He could feel it drawing nearer. It might be terrible.

But how could he sleep? His mind raced, juggling a myriad random thoughts. He closed his eyes and listened to the drumming in his breast. It was tribal, a summoning.

In his dream, he owned a great house that spread out around him like a great, sleeping monster. It was full of secrets and darkness, and unexpected splashes of colour. This was his real life. He sat in a study far larger than the one to which he was accustomed, though in many respects they were similar; antique curios littered every surface and he knew that books on ancient lands were crammed onto the floor to ceiling shelves that lined the room. This house was filled with his family, who spanned many generations. He had a gracious aloof wife, who ruled the domain. He had sons and daughters; aristocratic creatures who obeyed his word and the will of their mother. Below the house, was a vast labyrinth of work-rooms. He knew that in this place, he performed medical procedures; it was a link with the life that he knew. But who was he at the moment?

In the dream, he rose from his desk and turned round, gazed up into a massive stained glass window depicting a giant peacock. Was he awake now?

A voice spoke to him. "Go back to the ancient domain. It is time."

When he turned round, the room was empty. Really empty. The furnishings had vanished, leaving only an echoing shell.

Cameron Murchison woke up abruptly, a short gasp expelled from his lungs. He stared into the blue darkness, blinking. The dream had been so vivid. He had felt more comfortable in it than he did in waking life. In the dream, he had a full history and each detail was available to his memory. He felt that if he could only go back there, he'd learn a lot about Cameron Murchison.

I am always waiting for something, he thought, kept on hold: but for what? What is it that I have forgotten?

Memories of his past were hazy. Only dimly could he recall the training he had undertaken at university, and the faces of his parents, long dead, were simply blurs. He did not know if this was the same for other people, because he had never discussed it with anybody. His life, for the past twenty-five years or so, had been filled only with work. He had lived here in this house all that time, but could not remember moving into it, or where he had lived before.

For the first time in twenty-five years, Cameron Murchison considered the possibility that something had happened to him in the past, something which his mind had blotted out completely. A strange feeling of anger filled his heart. Someone should be blamed for this, but who?

He lay awake until morning light filled the room, then got up. Something was very wrong. He had never felt this way before, as if the foundations of his life were moving beneath his feet, about to open up and reveal a startling abyss of buried truth. He was afraid and nervous, but also weirdly excited.

When he looked in the mirror in the bathroom, it seemed to him as if another face was hiding beneath his own: not different in feature, but in expression. It was the face he should have. Lines scored his face, but he no longer felt they belonged there. They had been imposed on him. He straightened up, a toothbrush in his hand.

They have aged me, he thought, and through that have sentenced me to an early death. He didn't know why he should think that. The thought was unreasonable, crazed.

Mrs Melrose arrived at half past nine, letting herself in the front door and calling, "Hello-ee!"

Murchison was waiting for her in the kitchen, unfamiliar in his posture, pacing around the table, tapping it with his fingers. The housekeeper paused in the doorway, surprise on her face.

"Is something wrong, Mr Murchison?" An understatement. Something was clearly wrong.

He paused in his table circuit. "Tell me, Mrs Melrose, how much do you remember of your childhood?"

She raised her eyebrows. "Excuse me?"

"Can you remember details; times, dates, faces? This is a serious question. Please answer me."

She folded her arms, thought about it. "Well, some things, yes. Why, Mr Murchison?"

"Would you consider it strange if a person had barely any recollection of their formative years?"

She laughed uneasily. "You're the doctor. Surely you're more qualified to answer that!"

He turned away from her to gaze out of the window. He could not open up to this woman; their relationship was not that kind. She would think him mad, and he was sure any hysterical confidences from him would be unwelcome. He should not have spoken at all, but Mrs Melrose was the nearest he had to a friend.

"It's clear," she said.

"What is?" He still did not face her.

"You must go back to the ancient domain. It is time."

"I beg your pardon?" He turned round quickly. Her face was blank.

"I didn't say anything."

"You did...you said..."

She frowned, shook her head. "Look, are you sure you're all right, Mr Murchison? You don't seem yourself today."

He pressed fingers against his brow. "No, perhaps it's a touch of summer flu."

"Then go back to bed," Mrs Melrose said, coming forward. This was safe territory.

"Well...I..."

"Go on. I'll bring you a tray." She put her hands on his arm and pushed him towards the door. "My, you feel hot! I'll get you some aspirin, too."

He could not rest. He did not want to get back into his bed. Sleep? Impossible. Mrs Melrose appraised him as he meekly took the aspirins she had brought for him. He did not like the intensity of her stare.

"Mr Murchison…" A pause. "Have you any family I could call, perhaps?"

He laughed bleakly, handed back to her a glass of water. "I look that bad, then?"

She looked uncomfortable. 'Well…It's more than just a chill, isn't it?"

He frowned up at her. There was something in her tone— a covered nervousness. "What do you mean exactly?"

She went to his bedside table, put down the glass and tidied the already-neat pile of medical journals that constituted his rare bed-time reading. "It's just that I couldn't help noticing…"

"What?" Was she afraid of him?

"Your study. As I walked past. The strange mess it's in."

"I don't know what you mean." He stood up. "What mess?"

Mrs Melrose cowered away, her hand reaching behind her for the door handle. "I know it's none of my business…."

Murchison jumped up from the bed and strode towards the door, his house-keeper flinching away. He heard her voice calling after him as he ran down the stairs. His feet seemed hardly to touch the carpet. It was like flying.

In the doorway to the study, he came to a staggering halt. Someone had been in there. Desecration. Vandalism.

All the furniture had been pushed to the sides of the room. The cases that held his precious artefacts gaped wide, as if they'd been flung open from within. The shelves were bare. Everything stolen. No.

Murchison's panicked eyes swivelled downwards. There, on the carpet, in the middle of the room, the ancient relics were arranged in a perfect circle: small, stone heads, fragments of pottery, funerary figures.

Their owner stood trembling in the doorway. Mrs Melrose crept up behind him, perhaps intent on sneaking to the front door.

"I didn't do this," Murchison said. "No matter what you think."

His voice, now, was calm. Mrs Melrose stopped behind him. "Then who did? Surely, you'd have heard intruders?"

Murchison scraped his hands through his hair. "Yes, I would have thought so, but I slept deeply...What kind of joke is this?"

Mrs Melrose was clearly moved by the ragged edge to his voice. She put her hands on his arms. "Perhaps we'd better call the police," she said.

He nodded, gulped. "Yes..."

"I'll see to it. You go back to your room and lie down."

Wearily, Murchison obeyed. As he went slowly back up the stairs, he was wondering what kind of housebreaker moved furniture around and arranged artefacts on the floor. In his heart, he suspected no-one had entered his house in the night. Whatever had done that in the study somehow lived here already.

He lay on his bed, fanned by the air that came in at the open window. Outside, the sound of children playing braided with the cacophony of traffic, of distant crowds. He smelled warming tarmac, cut lawns, the scent of the rose that grew against the wall of his house. His eyelids drooped involuntarily. The sounds outside tumbled around themselves, resolving into a skirl of eastern music, the jabber of foreign voices, the creak of carts and the braying of mules. There was an aroma like that of a great slow-moving river—stagnant yet fecund—frilled with the smells of human waste, sweat, cooking meat and rare perfumes.

Lead me, he thought.

Before the police arrived with questions that could not be answered, he had already packed a bag to leave.

Chapter Eight
And Saw That They Were Fair...

Istanbul, Turkey

Shemyaza had no fear of pursuit: Melandra was sure of this. He had used the name Michael Jacobs on the flight over to Istanbul, flying business class with two companions. She had been unable to elicit any information from the airline herself, but a quick call to Nathaniel Fox's office had been sufficient to set wheels in motion elsewhere. After securing a last minute cancelled seat on the next available flight to Istanbul, she'd sat in an airport bar awaiting a return call. She'd not had to wait long.

Fox told her that the Children of Lamech had operatives in Turkey, who'd already been mobilised, and once her target had landed in Istanbul, would follow him discreetly to his accommodation. Melandra questioned whether her services would actually be needed now. Her words were greeted with a brief but eloquent silence, then Fox spoke, "My child, you have your duty as others have theirs."

"We have to presume he'll be alerted at some point," Melandra said. "My operation at his previous address will have been discovered by now."

"That is inevitable."

Melandra detected a faint note of censure in his voice, but what else could she have done at the Grigori hotel? "I'll be taking off soon," she said stiffly. "Shall I call you when I reach Istanbul?"

"Call me only when you have something to report," Fox replied, and broke the connection.

Summer in England had been stifling, but the heat that enveloped Melandra's body when she stepped off the plane in Istanbul seemed almost unnatural. She'd been brought up in the wet, cool north of America, and disliked hotter climates. As instructed by Fox, she took an expensive taxi ride into the city some kilometres away, and booked into the appointed hotel in the Sultanahmet, the old district of the city. Here, she awaited contact from one of Fox's operatives. She sensed tension in the air all around her that did not simply originate from her own stress levels concerning the job she was here to do. A vibrating sense of danger and repressed fury seemed to seep through the walls of the hotel from the air outside. Political tensions were high, of course, but it was more than that. She could not dispel the impression that something was forming invisibly around her—an event of some kind. For a few brief moments she felt as if her whole purpose was preordained, but not just by the Children of Lamech. She had a part to play, involuntarily, and had already embarked upon it.

Dismissing the sensation as paranoia, she calmed herself by assembling her weapon, which had been concealed, dismantled, in various items of luggage. Her cases had hidden compartments, but not *suspiciously* hidden. Their presence might seem convenient, rather than sinister; a way to keep certain parts of her luggage separate from her clothes. In the event of surveillance equipment discovering them, the compartments were filled with innocent-looking devices such as a hair-dryer, a travel iron, jumbo canisters of deodorant, hairspray, air freshener. The light-weight components of the gun itself were concealed within these items.

A sniper rifle might have been useful here, but in the event her semi-automatic proved unsuitable, she would have to improvise. First, she wanted to pinpoint her target and observe him. She felt that, in London, the job would have had to be swift and anonymous, but out here she sensed she had more time to be elegant and thorough. What was Shemyaza doing here? Fox hadn't discussed that with her.

Melandra looked out of the window: stark lines of modern buildings, but within and below and beside them, the ancient sub-city, the perfume-breathed seductress who held all the secrets of history. Car horns might blare and the stink of traffic eclipse the incense aroma of the forgotten past, but still to a sensitive ear, the land rang to the plaintive call of archaic instruments, and the swish of women's hair in darkness. This land was not of Melandra's Lord, Jesus Christ. She shivered as she thought this, attempting to dismiss it from her mind. The whole world was Christ's. But still, a heavy, brooding female power seemed to sway and murmur at the edge of her perception, its curling hands undulating through smoky air, calling out to her, demanding recognition. She turned away from the window. The people here mostly worshipped Allah. What female deities could possibly hold sway in this place?

She did not make personal contact with the operatives who were effectively working for her. A letter arrived, written by hand, and seemed to have originated from an old friend of hers, given the tone. The letter chatted informally about a mutual acquaintance and how Melandra could look him up while in the city.

By now, he'll know, she thought. His people will have told him about what happened at the hotel. Is he waiting for me?

The letter didn't give any indication of a problem, but she felt her nerves tighten within her body, almost as if his evil mind had suddenly become aware of her thoughts and had homed in on them. In America and England, she had simply thought of Shemyaza in terms of a target, but out here, so close to the sacred centre of the world, he seemed to have become large and terrible in her imagination. For some reason, the Children of Lamech had been unable to take a decent photograph of the man, and all she'd been shown were blurry representations that told her nothing. Therefore, her own mind provided the details. She knew he was blond, yet couldn't help imposing Satanic features onto him; dark, leering face, greasy black hair, cruel, hard eyes. The Devil.

In the morning, she took breakfast in her room, eschewing the traditional Turkish meal of bread and jam, and ordering a selection of fresh fruit. She could almost taste the fermenting sugar in the ripe flesh. By the time she went out into the city, she felt slightly heady, dressed in a modest long-sleeved cotton dress and dark glasses, her hair pinned up on her head. She carried a large shoulder bag, of the type used by many Western women; the contents, however, differed radically from what you'd normally expect to find in a woman's bag. The city hummed and rustled with secret life. Again, beneath the blare of car horns and human shouts, she detected the eerie wail of a female voice raised in song; a song of invocation or adoration. This seemed peculiar, because she knew it was not the time of day when the voices of temple callers would normally ring out over the city. Also, she thought it was usually men who sang the calls. The woman's voice seemed to be all around her, and did not originate from any particular area.

Melandra had a finely honed sense of direction and had little trouble in locating the hotel where her target was staying. For a while she sat outside a café, under the awning, drinking strong Turkish coffee and dreamily watching the stuccoed doorway to the hotel. The heat pulsed around her. She noticed how the bodies of the Turkish women swayed in their concealing robes as if they danced within their purdah. *You cannot suppress the female celebration of life.* The thought came unbidden. She visualised an image of dark, shady hallways, where fans turned slowly on the ceiling, parting the thick smoke of hashish; dark eyes behind a lattice, the low chuckle of feminine laughter, the swish of light cotton against polished floors. Such a strange summoning. Melandra smiled to herself. The demons of the east might attempt to seduce her, but she was made of fibres too tough to yield.

It seemed the day was unwinding around her, in a slow, measured pace. She drank more coffee, smoked cigarettes under the shade of the awning, and watched the hotel entrance. People came and went. The double doors were open, and she could see part of the darkened hall-way beyond. She felt no fear, even though he might be watching her from an upstairs window, aware of her purpose.

A slight, warm breeze lifted her hair like exploring fingers. She shook her head to dispel the impression, her attention caught by a sudden commotion nearby.

A number of scrawny dogs had run out from a shadowy side alley and were fighting in the dusty street, rolling over and over, their jaws slavering, their howls high-pitched. Melandra experienced a deep revulsion as she stared at them. Passers-by ignored the hysterical creatures, even when more dogs, perhaps excited by the noise, started to whine and bark excitedly in shuttered courtyards. The whole street was suffused with the clamour. Almost as if the animals had been enacting some bizarre invocation, a wind started up, spiralling the dust into eddies and swirls. Again, Melandra heard a woman's voice ululate loudly over the din; a proud, eastern song. Then the doors to the hotel slammed shut.

Melandra cricked her neck turning to see. At the same moment, the dogs broke apart and ran off in different directions. The sobbing echoes of the woman's song streamed away down the twisting alleys and the last particles of dust fell back to the street.

The doors to the hotel opened once more, slowly and seemingly without the agency of a human hand. As they hit the white walls, their handles rattled. A figure stepped out from the shadows and stood at the top of the shallow flight of steps that led to the street. He was tall, clad in traditional Arab dress of white cloth, his head and most of his face concealed from view. At his appearance, the environment around him seemed to slow to utter stillness, and become bleached of colour.

It's him, Melandra thought.

He did not look at her, or make any other sign that he was aware of her presence. After surveying the scene around him for a few short moments, he stepped down onto the street and walked right past where she sat beneath the awning.

Sound and colour and movement returned, and Melandra came back to her senses. He was walking away from her, out into the labyrinth of the city. She got to her feet, knocking the table and spilling the dregs of her coffee onto the cloth.

There was no doubt in her mind that the man who'd emerged from the hotel was her target. She could see his tall shape moving slowly but purposefully ahead of her through the bustle of the streets, and checked her pace to keep a short distance behind him. His height made him easy to keep in sight above the heads of other people.

He walked into the bazaar and here paused. Melandra thought he had sensed her presence behind him, but maybe he was only examining merchandise on one of the stalls. Melandra was surrounded by the aromas of spice and coffee, hot pistachios and sweet corn. Sunlight off brass dazzled her eyes. The stall-holders all seemed to be grinning at her with long teeth, as if in some private joke about her. She stopped as if to examine an array of floating coloured scarves, keeping her target in the periphery of her vision. He did not look 'round.

When he moved on, Melandra followed. He turned up a side alley, where the tall, white buildings seemed to meet overhead. Awnings flapped above them, and brightly-coloured carpets hung from balconies. Sunlight was scant in this area. Shops and stalls still lined the narrow street, but Melandra sensed a subtle difference in the air. The people sitting cross-legged behind their merchandise looked at her blandly; their dark eyes the only visible features showing, faces swathed in striped cloth. There were fewer people browsing among the stalls.

Ahead of her, she saw a low wall before a courtyard, where a group of tall women sat upright, with legs apart, their strong feet firm against the ground. In front of them, a wanton array of sumptuous fabrics was cast. They did not look like typical Turkish women. Their faces and arms were bare, and covered in curling black tattoos. Heavy gold jewellery studded with hunks of lapis lazuli and turquoise adorned their ears, throats and nostrils. Their languorous movements and heavy yet sinuous bodies exuded an almost visible aura of sensuality. Melandra was suffused with disgust at the sight of them. They might have stepped from one of the stories about the Fallen Ones; lustful wantons who had seduced the sons of God. The women turned their heads to stare at her as she approached. Whores, Melandra thought. They are whores waiting for custom. She tossed back her head and forced herself to hold the long-lidded gaze of the women, filling her expression with contempt. Momentarily, all thoughts of her target were forgotten. Something about the whores' confident stance made her feel uncomfortable. They radiated an essentially female power, as if they sucked it up through their feet from the earth itself to shine from their eyes and hang like an aura around their voluptuous bodies. She had read legends of the sacred prostitutes of ancient times. They would have been like this.

Closer now. The women seemed to be waiting for her. They would speak. One ran her fingers through her long, tangled hair, another fanned herself with a broad leaf. Melandra felt as if their sly gaze willed her to draw close to them. They whispered together softly, and each time one of them bent her head to murmur in the ears of another, Melandra heard the chime of tiny bells. When the breeze lifted the hair of the women, the air vibrated as if a rattle-snake had shaken its tail nearby.

One of them raised a hand and beckoned. Her hair was henna red and fell over her shoulders and breasts in a lascivi-ous cloud. Almost hypnotised, and unable to pass by, Melandra halted before the group. Even seated, they seemed to tower over her. They stared at her in the manner that cats stare; inscrutable. It made her feel like a child again.

I have always been a child, she thought. Never a woman. The secret territories these harlots know are unknown to me.

Her mind felt hazy, overwhelmed by the chime of bells that jingled at the women's wrists and ankles, and the per-fumes exuded by their bodies: jasmine, sandalwood and clean sweat.

Swaying where she stood, removed from reality, Melandra was held in the snare of dark eyes. The women disgusted her no longer. She was envious of their pride and beauty. A des-perate longing uncoiled within her, rising up from the empty pit that had lain within her all her life, poised to strike its venom into her heart. These women had power she had never had. She wanted to understand it, possess it.

The woman who had beckoned to her stared unblinkingly into Melandra's eyes for what seemed like an eternity. Melandra found herself taking tiny steps, nearer and nearer. Her head was pounding, and pin-pricks of light sparkled be-fore her eyes. She thought she must collapse, but then the woman reached out and touched her face. At once she felt strengthened; intoxicated perhaps, but nowhere near losing consciousness. Long, ring-encrusted fingers caressed her cheek, then curled behind her neck and pulled her closer. Melandra felt the moist heat of the woman's sweet, spicy breath upon her lips. Her whole body tingled as if it was being stroked by loving hands. Melandra closed her eyes. Her lips met those of the nameless woman and for a time-less, endless moment, they kissed like lovers.

Melandra's heart seemed to have stilled within her. She had no thoughts, no opinions, and had become a ringing nerve of pure sensation. Then the heat and perfume, the pressure of lips, drew away, and Melandra opened her eyes. The woman now stared down the street. The breeze blew the banner of her hair in the same direction. Melandra followed her gaze. A tall, white-clad figure stood motionless, some feet away, his back towards her. It was her target; the demon Shemyaza. Melandra began to walk towards him. She glanced back at the women behind her, but they ignored her now, staring only at the man in white. Shemyaza began to walk away, and Melandra followed him. She did not think about what had just happened.

Soon, the stalls became more widely spaced, until eventu-ally, Melandra found herself walking along a narrow alley, tall buildings to either side, but no sign of human life. Sunlight came down in patches and her target moved through these golden pools, briefly blazing before swimming into shadow. She thought that he must be aware of her by now, but still he did not turn or change his pace. An ephemeral blade of panic touched its point against her heart: was she following him into danger? Perhaps he was totally aware of her pursuit and planned to lure her into some hidden spot, where his followers would jump her before she could defend herself. The feeling did not persist. Melandra became convinced the man ahead was unaware of her. His gait and posture were relaxed, as if he was taking a stroll to mull over some private thoughts.

She realised she was tired, and had perhaps been walking too long in the sun. It seemed as if she was moving in slow motion. When she looked up, a carpet hanging overhead seemed to flap at an unnaturally sluggish pace. She heard a delicate tinkling chime that seemed to keep time with her steps, as if she wore invisible bells around her ankles. Simultaneously, an oceanic rushing sound invaded her ears. It was quiet at first, hardly even a sound at all, but gradually built in intensity, as if she had two giant shells pressed against her ears. Then, a distinct salty smell, like the sea, washed over her, perhaps conjured by the ghosts of breakers in her ears. She thought that the man ahead of her nearly turned his head, although he did not look 'round. Her hand was damp upon the clasp of her bag. She thought about removing her weapon, for there were no people about. She could shoot him now quite easily.

He turned into another side street. Melandra walked into shadow. For a moment, it seemed there were stars in the afternoon sky above her. She should do it now; end the mission. She reached inside her bag to take out the gun, and her fingers curled around its hard handle. The sun must have penetrated the strengthened cloth, for the weapon felt absurdly warm and alive to her touch. She ran her fingers over it, trying to establish its familiar form in her mind. Something wasn't right. Her exploring hand was running over what seemed to be a long, hard fleshy shape, its surface covered in a loose, soft skin. It was full of living heat; she could feel blood coursing through its length. Where the muzzle of the weapon should be, she found a bulbous but delicate knob of flesh. Melandra realised what it was she was touching, and yet a surreal sense of indifference washed over her. A tiny voice within her cried out in disgust at the phallus in her grip. *It should be a gun, this is not possible.* But the voice was drowned out by the rushing in her ears, and the state of non-reality that enveloped her. Melandra withdrew her hand from the bag and let it dangle at her side. She kept on walking.

Her target's pace was almost hypnotic. She felt driven to keep following him. A strong aroma of ozone and corn drowned out the smell of the sea. For a brief instant, she had the impression she was walking through a field of swaying wheat that was starred with blood-red poppies. The horizon seemed to rush out on all sides. She felt dizzy, blinked, and the narrow alley-way swam back into focus. The haunting sound of a woman's voice came again, so close. Could it be her own voice singing? The images of the whores' faces floated across her mind. The sensation of the kiss lingered on her lips.

Somewhere ahead, a door slammed and there was a sound of running feet, a short ripple of laughter sharply silenced.

Shemyaza paused ahead of her. He still did not look 'round. Melandra put out one hand to lean against the nearest wall for support. She felt breathless, and her heart was beating painfully in her chest. She could hear its soft yet urgent boom.

She watched as Shemyaza began to unwind the cloth from around his head. A wave of snow-gold hair tumbled down over the aching white of his robe. He shook his head, then continued walking down the alley. She could do nothing but follow. Now, her sandaled feet seem to follow the secret dance steps of the eastern women she had seen on the streets. Around her, the rushing sound had become the gossiping rustle of thick corn, overlaid by the chimes from her braceleted feet. She made music as she walked. Now she felt powerful like the whores, she felt alive.

Then, a flash of blinding whiteness dazzled her eyes. Something blocked her way. All the strange sensations ceased abruptly. She heard a dog bark somewhere and the wail of a peevish child.

She looked up to find the tall figure of Shemyaza before her. He had the most beautiful face she had ever seen; the face of a pharaoh or a god. His eyes, the deepest blue, stared unflinchingly into hers. His musky smell was overpowering; she could taste it, taste his spirit.

"Who are you?" Shemyaza asked her reasonably.

"I am yours," she said. And the world transformed itself around her.

They lay down together in the corn. He held her gently, kissed her closed eyelids. "You are an angel," she said, and knew it to be true.

He lifted her dress and put his long hand flat against her naked belly. "And you are a woman of the earth."

Melandra was a virgin. As she lay in Shemyaza's embrace she thought about how she'd never considered how it would be when the time came for her to lose this maiden state. Against her instincts, nurtured by the beliefs of those who'd raised her, she realised that she was blessed, and being given an experience few women would enjoy. The pain was just a small spark that kindled a greater flame of pleasure within her. She gave herself up to the drunken delight of his body upon her. No thought of guns or killing, only simple, natural experience. She became pure feeling, devoid of intellect. The delicate petals of poppies drifted down upon her face. She was enfolded in feathers, in great wings.

He breathed a single word in her ear. "Ishtahar."

Melandra woke up feeling cold. Before she even opened her eyes, she was aware of the rough sacking beneath her. Her dress was drawn up over her hips and her underwear was gone. She sat up abruptly, and saw that it was dark. Faint lights burned in some of the high windows of the buildings around her. She was alone.

Melandra jumped up, skidding on the sacks, and pulled down her dress. Her face was flaming. What had happened to her? How could she have allowed it to happen?

In numb despair, she ran back the way she'd come, expecting threatening figures to jump out at her at any moment. She couldn't believe that she'd allowed Shemyaza to seduce her. Yet wasn't that his original evil? She had given up the most precious gift to him, her enemy, and he had taken it cruelly and left her abandoned in a potentially hostile environment. His vile hand-maidens had initiated her violation even before he looked upon her face.

Melandra reached the end of the alley, already trying to decide before she turned the corner which direction she could take. And yet, amazingly, when she stepped out into the next street, she found she was back where she started. There was the café where she'd sat earlier, and there was the hotel where Shemyaza was staying.

Melandra ducked back in to the alley to catch her breath and try to calm her mind. "Bastard!" she hissed and punched the wall with a closed fist. He had mocked her, shown her his power and she, believing herself immune, had fallen beneath his unholy spell. She cringed inside to think what Nathaniel Fox would say if he knew of this. She had failed in her duty, soiled herself in God's eyes. Shemyaza must know what he'd done to her. It was abominable.

"Right," she said aloud, spreading her hands on the air before her. "Get a grip on yourself. It's not over yet."

She peered round the wall at the hotel. Its doors stood open, and a few people were talking just inside the entrance. Melandra felt her skittering heart turn to steel. She would kill him now. She did not care if she was caught. He had defiled her, in body and mind; rendered her worthless.

Calmly, she walked towards the hotel. People moved aside to let her enter the lobby. She brushed her hair back behind her ears and marched purposefully up to the reception desk. A thin Turkish youth stood behind it. He smiled at her in open friendliness.

"Good evening," Melandra began. "I'm looking for a friend of mine who I believe is staying here. Mr Jacobs. Michael Jacobs."

The youth frowned, shook his head, with a moué of apologetic denial.

Melandra sighed. "I know he's staying here. Perhaps he's using his…professional name." She leaned on the desk and smiled widely, with what she hoped was charm. "Look, I'll describe him. He's very tall, with long blond hair. Handsome, I suppose. Travelling with two companions?"

The youth thought for a moment, then grinned and nodded. "Yes, yes, Mr Shenley. He's gone now, I'm afraid."

"Gone?" Melandra's heart stilled for a moment. Then she collected herself. "He's checked out then. When?"

The youth nodded. "This morning, Miss. Very early."

Melandra stared at the youth. "That's impossible," she said. "I saw him coming out of the hotel this afternoon. Would you check for me please?"

The youth shrugged. "He left, Miss. He and his companions hired a truck and drove out of the city this morning. I helped them load their bags. You must have been mistaken about seeing him. I'm sorry."

Melandra couldn't prevent herself from drooping over the desk. Her mind felt as if it had just been put into a liquidiser. "Don't think about this yet," she told herself. "Stay calm. Get information."

She raised her head. "Have you any idea where Mr Shenley was heading?"

Again, the youth shrugged. "He didn't say exactly. But they took supplies, even blankets. Looked like a long journey."

Melandra tapped the counter with one hand. She sighed. "Thank you."

"Miss?" The youth looked expectant.

Melandra found him some coins in the bottom of her bag and threw them over the desk. "You've been most helpful."

Outside, she stood in the street, tears running uncontrollably down her face. Devil, demon. What had seduced her? Possibly not even flesh and blood. She must find him now and finish her task. It was her destiny. It was war.

Back in her hotel, she drank an entire bottle of wine and, her nerves calmed, called Nathaniel Fox. It was early morning in New York. It surprised her how easily she kept the panic and horror from her voice as she reported that Shemyaza and his companions had fled.

"Was he aware of your presence?" Fox demanded.

Melandra ignored the faint note of criticism. "No. Unless he's psychic, of course."

Fox laughed dryly. "We have to assume he has some inkling of your presence." He paused. "You said he drove out of the city. We can only presume his destination is the east. Given his affluence, it's strange he hasn't flown out of the city. Are you sure he left in a truck?"

"As sure as I can be," Melandra answered. "Perhaps you should put some of your spies on to it."

Fox's voice was clipped. "He'll be making for the whore of cities, Babylon. You will be contacted with further instructions." The line went silent.

Melandra stared angrily at the phone for a moment, then replaced the handset.

Chapter Nine
Freedom Fighters

Turkey

The road they travelled was wide, the landscape desolate, almost lunar, and the truck thundered along at a fast pace. Their guide and driver was a cheerful and garrulous young Turk named Hasim, whom Salamiel had engaged after making discreet enquiries in the city. Hasim was clearly sympathetic to the Yarasadi, although he identified himself as Turkish. Daniel, unsure of the young man's heritage, understood about a quarter of what Hasim said, as he spoke in a continuous babble that seemed to be half Turkish, half English. Hasim knew about the prophet Gadreel and accepted Salamiel's story that they were a team of journalists researching the story for a Western magazine. Before leaving England, Shemyaza had bought an expensive camera, which Daniel now carried in its shop-new case.

The previous day, they'd met Hasim in a local bar in Istanbul, where Shem had made delicate enquiries about the best way to reach the Yarasadi prophet. It was clear that the subject was sensitive and that the Turkish authorities would discourage any Westerners from approaching the Kurdish rebels: that had been the way of things for many years in Turkey. Hasim told them they would need documents from the rebels to guarantee them safe passage through the mountains where terrorist units held sway, but being caught by the Turks with such papers would mean instant imprisonment and gruelling interrogation. Hasim suggested that they should drive to the city of Diyarbakir, where there was a large Kurdish population, including a number of Yarasadi. Here, a guide could be found to take Shem and his companions into the mountains. They would need someone who knew the safest routes, and who could direct them to the places they'd most likely run into Gadreel. Hasim warned them that the journey would be hazardous, especially once they reached the mountains, where what semblance of law and order remained in the lowlands had broken down altogether.

"Terrible things have happened," he said. "Whole villages massacred. The Yarasadi have few friends because their acquaintance means trouble. I've heard that even other Kurdish factions view them with wariness."

"This Gadreel character must have stirred up what was already an explosive situation," Salamiel remarked.

Hasim nodded. "Yes. Neither the Turks nor the Babylonians look kindly on the way Gadreel has fired up this faction of the Kurds. The Turks, they say the Yarasadi are devil-worshippers and secret followers of the new king of Babylon. But from what we hear, Nimnezzar wants to rid the world of Yarasadi as well. Some say he is afraid of them."

Salamiel peered at the others over the top of a newspaper. "Seems things are getting pretty hairy all around the Middle East at present. Another hotel has been bombed in Cairo. Wouldn't want to be out there at the moment."

Hasim rolled his eyes. "You have seen nothing yet, my friend."

It would take several days to reach their destination.

Shemyaza had been subdued all day, since they'd left Istanbul. He sat beside the driver in the front of the truck, while Salamiel and Daniel sprawled out behind on blankets. There was no air conditioning in the vehicle and only the breeze from the open windows provided any relief from the heat. A tinny, meandering strain of Turkish music spluttered from Hasim's cheap cassette player. Salamiel smoked a chain of vile-smelling cigarettes and flicked through the English papers they had brought with them from the hotel. Salamiel seemed happy to follow Shemyaza's lead. He didn't question anything and was apparently enjoying the trip, as relaxed as if they were simply on holiday. At one point during the morning, Daniel asked Salamiel quietly if he thought Shem was all right.

Salamiel glanced up at the back of Shem's head, and pulled a wry face. "He's fine. Leave him be, Daniel. He doesn't need you to analyse him all the time. He's just full of thoughts."

What thoughts, though? Daniel wondered what was going through Shemyaza's mind. They hadn't contacted Enniel before leaving England, and when Daniel had suggested it, Shemyaza had almost snapped at him. "Enniel is not involved in this. None of them are. It's my business."

Daniel had been tempted to call Lily, but realised the consequences could be awkward. She would be concerned for his safety, and would therefore tell Enniel anything Daniel said to her. Perhaps Shemyaza was right. The Parzupheim should not be involved in this, nor any other sly Grigori cabal.

Daniel found it difficult to talk to Shem now. They behaved like awkward strangers with one another. Daniel could not help but be slightly offended that Shem had booked a twin room for Salamiel and himself in Istanbul, while installing Daniel in a single room next door. Once, they had been close, making plans in the dark of a shared bed, dreaming the future. Daniel wondered whether he himself was responsible for this estrangement. When he and Shem had met in London, he knew he'd been cold and defensive. As a result of that, Shem appeared to have shut Daniel out of his personal life, and Daniel's pride wouldn't let him broach the subject himself. He realised there was no point in brooding about it now. Other, more important matters must occupy all their thoughts at present.

Daniel was uneasy about the journey. He was unsure whether Shem could maintain their safety or not, and knew that he would have to keep all his senses alert for signs of threat, on both a physical and psychic level. They were travelling into one of the most politically-sensitive areas of the world to look for someone who might well be nothing more than a terrorist. It hadn't occurred to Shem that Gadreel might not welcome him with open arms.

Unable to elicit conversation from Salamiel or Shem and unwilling to listen to the prattle of the driver, Daniel dozed as they travelled. He picked up one or two vague psychic suggestions of threat, which seemed to involve a woman, but the information was too nebulous to interpret.

That evening, they stopped for the night at a small town. Here, ancient and modern Turkey again nestled uncomfortably side by side. This land had seen many empires rise and fall. Ottoman ruins lay everywhere, declining forlornly alongside the brash newness of petrol stations and glass-fronted shops.

Hasim arranged accommodation, while Daniel and the others waited at the truck. Daniel took out the camera and ran off a few shots of the landscape. He felt they should be keeping a record of their journey. Salamiel disappeared in search of more cigarettes, and Daniel used the moment of privacy to mention to Shem the psychic impressions he'd received.

Shem offered an unexpected response. "Yes, that will be the American woman."

"What American woman?" Daniel asked. "What have you been keeping from me?"

Shem shook his head in irritation. "It's nothing. I found her outside the hotel in Istanbul. She wanted to kill me."

"Shem! I can't believe you haven't mentioned this before! When did this happen?"

"This afternoon."

Daniel stared at him, wondering whether this was a joke.

Shem sighed deeply. "I'm changing, Daniel. I was drawn back to the city in spirit, and led the woman into the ancient heart. She is a follower of mine. And yet an assassin."

Daniel tried to keep his voice even. "Where is she now?"

"She won't follow us—immediately. Daniel, you mustn't worry. She's not a threat. There are other things…"

"What?"

"This afternoon, something else intruded into my visions. I realised it's something I've been dreaming of for some nights. Disturbing. It involves another Watcher. I couldn't identify him, but he was in terrible pain—incarcerated, or being tortured. Would you see what you can pick up about that?"

Daniel nodded. "I'll try. Information's not coming through too well. Seems you're picking up more than I am."

Shem waved this remark away. "Just get on with it, Daniel. I don't want your excuses."

They are not excuses, Daniel thought. As time progressed, he was seriously beginning to wonder whether his talent was deserting him.

The following day, their journey towards the east began in earnest. It would have been easier to make the trip by plane, but Shem wanted to experience the country firsthand. He seemed to have no sense of urgency. Daniel was entranced by the landscape; here Shem's heritage seemed very close. Despite the concessions to modernity, the land still retained the grandeur of its past, and a lot of its magic. A rolling vista of stone-strewn grassland stretched away to either side of the road. Occasionally, rocky outcrops rose up like heat-blasted, alien castles. Here, hidden within the scenery, lay the remains of the Hittite and Phrygian empires. Long before those races surged with conquering zeal across the Middle East, the Grigori had walked here. The remains of their civilisation had vanished. So many ruins; so many conflicting lives. Daniel extended his senses into the countryside and picked up fleeting images, but none that seemed particularly pertinent to their situation. Perhaps there was just too much information for him to interpret, and the important symbols were lost in a confusing maelstrom of ancient memories. Or perhaps the fault lay within himself.

Shemyaza sat in the front of the truck, his eyes closed. He was very conscious of Daniel behind him, this strange new Daniel who was as cold and distant as a star. He was concerned about Daniel's claims of losing his psychic ability. Could it be possible? Daniel could not know how much Shem relied on him, while doubting his own powers. Shem couldn't help feeling that Daniel's insistence on having changed was his small act of rebellion for having been abandoned after what happened in Cornwall. And all that had come before it. Daniel had had five years to mull over those things. Shem could sense his bitterness. Now, all he wanted to do was turn to his vizier and say "Help me, I am afraid," but he could not speak. The episode with the American woman had shaken him as much as he sensed it had shaken her. It had been unexpected, a total, disorientating yanking-back to act out an archetypal role.

He'd had as little volition in it as she, as if they'd been the puppets of higher powers.

Shem opened his eyes, his head resting on his hand, his elbow on the rim of the open window. He gazed down at the blurred passing road, and it seemed an oily black streak was keeping pace with them. Shem blinked. He saw it was a black serpent, a cobra with folded hood that wriggled with unnatural speed beside the truck. As he stared at it, the serpent raised its head. "Shemyaza, I am the symbol of your doom. You journey towards your ultimate sacrifice. Have you no will of your own? Turn back. Turn back. Your father laughs down at you from Heaven."

Shem uttered a sound of surprise, which prompted Salamiel to call, "What is it?" from the back of the truck. Shem could not tell him. There was no serpent on the road, no sly hissing voice in his head, only his own doubts and fears. He closed his eyed again, resting his head against the back of the seat. He saw Ishtahar before him, as he'd known her so long ago. She walked past him in the oaty gloom of a room shuttered of sunlight, fanning herself with a palm frond. "Shemyaza, get rid of the boy. He watches us. You have no need of him now. You have me."

Had she ever said that to him? He couldn't remember. He had lost her and now he had lost Daniel. Perhaps it was preordained that he should fulfil the final agonies of his destiny alone.

Their next major stop was Sivas—at first sight a grim and forbidding town. The stark concrete buildings of the outskirts gave way to more historical sites in the centre, but apart from stocking up on supplies and a night in comfortable hotel beds, the group had no desire to linger. Daniel tried, and failed, to acquire some information about the Watcher whom Shem had glimpsed in dreams. Shem did not mention the subject that evening, and again seemed wrapped up in his own thoughts.

From Sivas they travelled to Elazig, entering the Tigris and Euphrates Basin. Daniel felt his skin tingle to the echo of a thousand memories. If he closed his eyes, he fancied he could hear the thunder of hooves as warriors poured across the landscape. Ragged banners waved and fell; blood was spilled in an eternal libation to lost gods. In contrast, and like so many of the towns they had passed through, Elazig seemed relentlessly modern and scoured of its ancient heart, but once its environs were left behind, it was clear that the truck was venturing into areas of Turkey unfrequented by casual tourists. Nearer Diyarbakir, the land became more rocky and barren, providing a scant living for smallholders and herders. The harsh terrain shimmered and baked beneath the summer sun.

The further east they travelled, the more the Turkish authorities became inquisitive about their presence. At every junction, armoured cars and troops could be seen, and there was a tangible atmosphere of tension in every small town they passed through. The truck was stopped continually, and dark faces, lean with suspicion, were forever peering into their belongings.

Diyarbakir was a city of contradictions. It was contained within a wall of black basalt, built in Byzantine times; one of the oldest cities on earth, with a violent and dramatic history. Hasim provided a tour lecture, gabbling the names of lost empires: Urartian, Assyrian and Persian. Alexander the Great had once conquered this city, when it had been known as Amida. It was now hard to credit that such exotic people had ever once thrived there. Over the years, the city had spilled out of the walls, and its outskirts consisted of the now familiar modern, concrete buildings. Tower blocks soared in the pulsing heat. The city walls were punctuated by four main gates, as well as several smaller ones. Its remaining length was dotted with defensive towers. Hasim explained that a large Turkish military installation lay to the south, while to the north a NATO airbase provided a constant back-drop din of screaming jets and throbbing helicopter blades.

The atmosphere in the city was chaotic; fume-gushing traffic hurtled around them in disorganised, honking streams. Nearer the centre, the modern buildings concealed edifices of ancient times, although there was evidence of extreme poverty and squalor along the narrow streets that coiled away from the main thoroughfares. The heat was almost unbearable and, to Daniel, the heavy, tense ambience of the place was equally oppressive. Here, Kurdish refugees had flocked for over a decade, driven from their homelands by war and persecution. They regarded Diyarbakir as their capital city, but the might of powerful nations around them denied them autonomy. Hasim installed his charges in one of the better hotels and went off scouting for a guide.

Daniel sat in his room drinking heavily sweetened tea. A fan turned lazily in the air above him, complemented by a raging air conditioning unit that provided physical relief in equal measure to aural discomfort. They had reached the first of their destinations, but Daniel was anxious about what might come after. After all he'd seen and heard, it seemed the Yarasadi would be too concerned with their political troubles to accept Shemyaza as a representative of all they worshipped. Would they be seen as madmen or, worse, people who mocked the conflict of the Kurds? They had become distanced from the object of their journey, caught up in the grinding cruelty of the real world, where nations were oppressed and irreplaceable ancient sites violated and destroyed. The faint psychic impressions Daniel received only served to emphasise these things. The eternal conflict of angels seemed rarefied and unimportant in comparison.

In the next room, Shem lay on his bed while Salamiel went out sight-seeing. He longed to bang on the wall to summon Daniel, needing help to banish the whispering, deceitful voices in his head. *Only your death can bring back the knowledge of the past. Your soul must be snuffed out like an exploding sun. Run away from it, Shemyaza. Disappear into the world. Become Peverel Othman again. It is what you really want. You're not a saviour, you never wanted to be. Others have shaped you in the image of their desires.*

In the past, when he'd been assailed by doubts, Daniel had been there to reassure him. Why couldn't he simply go into Daniel's room now and tell him the truth of how he felt? It seemed impossible. He must find Gadreel instead.

In the morning, Hasim took them to a tea-garden; an oasis of calm in a shaded courtyard, separated from the noise and smoke of the street outside by thick walls. Here groups of young Kurds in Western-style clothes sat chatting together. Some sat alone, engaged quietly in studies, drinking Coke or small glasses of sweet tea. Daniel was struck by the way that the sexes mingled here without stricture; Kurdish women were not generally secluded or veiled.

Hasim led them to a table beneath the branches of a spreading tree, and here introduced them to a young Yarasadi named Yazid, who was sitting waiting for them. Daniel was surprised by Yazid's appearance, for he was quite pale of skin with thick, dusty blonde hair and dark blue eyes. His lively manner and fine features combined to make him very attractive. After the introductions were made, and everyone was seated with a drink before them, Yazid explained that he was eager for Westerners to witness the atrocities against his people first-hand and was therefore more than happy to take them into the mountains. He told them proudly that he was a peshmerga—a warrior committed to the struggle against oppression.

Shemyaza questioned him carefully about Gadreel. "Your prophet has made astonishing claims—that you are descended from the angels. I thought the angels were spiritual beings."

Yazid nodded earnestly. "We were led to believe that, yes. The memory of our history has been hidden from us, but Gadreel made us remember. It is important that the whole world understands what is happening here. In the past, the Ancient Ones were wiped out and now we, their descendants, suffer the same fate. It must not happen. You will tell of our troubles, so people will know."

Yazid owned an ancient Transit van—even more rickety than Hasim's vehicle—into which they piled their belongings. After bidding farewell to Hasim, who seemed as grieved to see them leave as if they were life-long friends, they began their journey further east. Yazid said they should go to the town of Van, on the shores of Lake Van, a vast inland sea surrounded by mountains. Here, he would be able to make provisions for them to make contact with Gadreel's immediate followers, who were the only people who could feasibly arrange a meeting with the prophet.

The roads were now almost impassable, so full of potholes that the travellers felt as if their insides were bruised by the constant jolting. The landscape became even more bleak. Yazid drove through the sites of military attack—

Kurdish villages and towns reduced to rubble. Daniel felt as if he were travelling through the scenes of a post-Holocaust movie. The world had been scoured of greenery and those who survived had to scavenge in order to live. He forced himself to look upon the horrifying scenes: people squatting in the ruins of their homes that had been bulldozed flat; children riddled with disease from impure water; casualties of the fighting hobbling around with missing limbs and ruined faces. The people they saw sometimes had blond or red hair with green or blue eyes: true Kurdish stock with the physical traits of their long-forgotten ancestors still visible upon their bodies. Despite their adversity, the people were cheerful and welcoming. Daniel felt humbled by their spirit, then felt guilty, for his feelings seemed absurdly patronising. Shem seemed particularly disturbed by the torment he witnessed, perhaps because it evoked memories of what had happened to his half-human children many millennia before. Only Salamiel seemed unmoved by all they saw.

They had come here seeking the past, and maybe they had found it. But not in the way they'd imagined.

The countryside around them changed, becoming more mountainous; rugged and sparsely populated. The journey now became slower, owing to the increasing deterioration of the roads and more frequent check-points. On nearly every occasion, the travellers were grilled by suspicious guards as to why they were in the area. Now, their story had to be changed. They were a group of post-graduates from an English university, travelling to Old Van to visit the ancient tombs there. Yazid seemed unperturbed by these interrogations; Salamiel barely held his contempt in check, while Shem acted indifferently. Daniel, sometimes, felt sickened by the atmospheres he picked up. He could sense that violence was never far from the soldiers' thoughts.

Finally, they reached Van, approaching it in late afternoon. The town was like so many others they had passed through; modern and grid-like, held in the splendid cup of the mountains. Both Daniel and Salamiel voiced their disappointment about the towns they'd visited. They had expected softly decaying cities of minarets and domes; not miles of concrete

and glass. Yazid explained that Van's appearance was mainly
due to a serious earthquake which had devastated the town in
the 1950s and had destroyed what remained of the ancient
buildings there. Old Van, the original town, had been demolished by war in the early twentieth century, although ghostly
remains of it still existed, arrayed around the Rock of Van, a
huge natural formation that rose up beside the lake. The new
town did boast an airport, and Yazid told them that there would
be more amenities for travellers.

As they drove in, the great Rock of Van was visible from
the road, rising up from the sprawling remains of the old town.
Shem began to speak quite openly about how this site had
once been the location of an ancient Grigori stronghold, during the time of the wars after the Flood. "I have read the
ancient manuscripts that describe it. Rituals were held on the
shores of the lake, in the early morning and evening when the
water shone like gold. The towers of the ancient city rose up
around the Rock, and there was a palace built upon it, crawling over the stone like moss."

Yazid eyed him speculatively as he spoke, but did not comment. Daniel was sure the young Kurd was privately surprised
and intrigued by what he heard. Shem made no attempt to
hide the fact that he was directly connected with the ancient
race. Daniel wondered whether Shem was dropping these clues
into the conversation deliberately, in the hope that Yazid would
report them back to Gadreel's followers.

In Van, the group booked into a comfortable hotel, where
Yazid told them he would take them into the mountains the
following morning. Yazid disappeared before dinner, presumably to contact the people they had come to meet.

In the morning, their journey resumed, taking them higher
into the mountains, heading south towards Babylonia. Here,
the landscape seemed so vast, it was as if they were exploring
a new world. Rolling grassy slopes reached up to distant peaks
that were capped with glowing snow. After a day or so of slow
travelling along less-frequented and therefore nearly impassable routes, they passed the invisible boundary between the
countries. There was a check-point, but Yazid bribed the
Babylonian guards effortlessly with the money and cigarettes

that Shem gave to him for that purpose. The guards seemed bored and swallowed without question the story that Shem and the others were archaeologists, intent on exploring the ancient tombs and wall-painted caves that were hidden amid the rolling landscape.

They drove slowly now, under cover of darkness, resting during the day. Often, when the gradient of the treacherous road permitted it, Yazid turned off the truck's engine and they rolled and bumped along in silence. Yazid never used the headlights, seemingly navigating by instinct alone. Overhead, the sinister throb of helicopters trailed them like powerful predators. Salamiel made jokes that at any moment they might drive into a Babylonian patrol that would be more officious than the Turkish border guards. Daniel suspected that in some ways Salamiel relished the idea of conflict. Yazid, however, seemed to know the mountains tracks so well, they managed to avoid any horrifying confrontations. Perhaps it was down to luck rather than strategy.

Now, they travelled through more abandoned villages, where the buildings looked as if they'd been clawed by frenzied monsters. Yazid wept openly as he described the atrocities that had been committed against innocent people. Entire communities had been gassed or shot; he also spoke vaguely of other, less tangible attacks.

"The weapons are evil and cruel," he said, "but those from the fire are worse."

"Those from the fire?" Daniel said.

"Djinn!" Yazid replied, in a defensive tone as if his passengers would not believe him.

"Djinn are used in attacks?" Salamiel said from the back of the truck. He glanced at Shem who was sitting beside Yazid up front, his arm along the back of the seat.

"I have heard of that," Shem said. "More precisely, the rumour is that Nimnezzar's Magians invoke djinn into the Babylonian soldiers. I'm not convinced of this. It could just be an exaggerated story."

"You have not seen it," Yazid said.

"Is he one of ours, Shem?" Salamiel said. "This new king?"

Shem shrugged. "I don't know. We'll have to find out."

Early one evening, Yazid announced they were only a few kilometres away from the village where they would meet with Gadreel. This news heightened everyone's spirits.

Daniel felt now as if the weight of history, the history of Shem's people, was pressing like a crowd of ghosts upon his mind. The setting sun brought out the hectic colours of the mountains; copper lichened with verdigris; rocks of poison-green malachite, and blood-streaked porphyry. The air was almost narcotic with the scents of greenery and summer flowers crushed by the delicate hooves of goats. The sheer rocks, veined with their ophidian colours, reminded Daniel of the serpentine cliffs at the Lizard peninsula in Cornwall, where Shemyaza had reclaimed his divine kingship. Perhaps the last thing the exiled Grigori had seen when they'd left these lands were the splendid colours of the mountains. The serpentine cliffs would have been their first sight of England too, when they made landfall at the Lizard. Was that part of what had drawn the giant race to those shores?

The village was half-ruined and many people appeared to be living in tents among the rubble. Smoke rose from cooking fires into the evening air, along with the cries of playing children. Women and men were dressed alike in army fatigues; the garb of modern warriors.

Armed peshmergas halted the truck and spoke to Yazid in Kurmanji, the local Kurdish dialect. Yazid answered their questions, constantly pointing at his passengers as if to illustrate a point. Eventually, they were allowed to pass on.

Yazid parked up and left his companions in the truck, while he went to speak with a group of men who'd watched their arrival with interest. Presently, he returned and led the group into one of the ruined buildings where men and women were clustered around a fire. They were all clearly peshmergas, dressed in military clothing and surrounded by weapons. The walls of the room were pocked with bullet-holes, and the windows were broken, with rough sacking taped over them. A broken child's toy lay in the corner of the room. Daniel had to shut his mind down in order to prevent any stray memory of whatever tragedy had taken

place there intruding into his consciousness. Lowering his
guard even for moment meant he was swamped with a sensation of terror; screams of pain reverberating through his brain.
When Shem and the others entered the room, its occupants all began to speak at once, gesticulating wildly. Yazid
answered back, with equally expressive gestures. Eventually,
he turned to Shem. "I have explained your situation and these
people are happy to let you stay here."

Shem frowned. "Are they Yarasadi?"

"They are friends of the Yarasadi," Yazid replied enig-
matically.

"When will we meet with Gadreel?"

"Soon, soon. You must wait here."

One of the group, an attractive woman in her thirties,
bade Shem and his companions be seated. She told them in
clear English that her name was Fatime and offered them the
hospitality of her hearth. This last comment was accompanied by a wry grin to indicate she was aware she didn't have
much hospitality to give. Her skin was as pale as Yazid's,
although her hair was a dark reddish-brown, complemented
by green eyes. She told them that as well as being a freedom-
fighter for her people, she was a doctor, who over ten years
ago had trained in France. She was in charge of this small
settlement, caring for the injured refugees and soldiers who
sought sanctuary there. Shemyaza told her they had brought
supplies with them from Istanbul, so Yazid went back to the
truck and unloaded what remained of the luxuries they'd
purchased. While the assembled company passed round raki
and beer, and distributed packets of cigarettes, Fatime initiated conversation with her guests. She admitted she was
sceptical that Gadreel would meet with them.

"Few have met him," she said. "He is the mountain goat,
the eagle, resting rarely. Some say he is not human at all."

Shem raised his eyebrows. "Really? Why?"

She shrugged. "He never shows his face. Perhaps it is
hideous."

"Or the face of an angel," Salamiel suggested.

Fatime narrowed her eyes at him. "Some might say you
have the face of an angel."

He grinned, shrugged.

"You are not Yarasadi," Shem said. "Are there any here?"

Fatime shook her head. "No, they are in the mountains, further south. You have to remember that Yarasadism is not like the other beliefs of our people. For thousands of years there have been the Alevi, the Yezidi and the Yaresan, but Yarasadism is new. Gadreel tells us it is very old, and perhaps it is, or perhaps it is just a new banner from which to draw strength. People of all faiths are drawn to it. They say they have woken up from the sleep of centuries."

"But not you?" Shem asked.

Fatime pulled an expressive face. "By birth, I am Alevi, but my beliefs now are political rather than religious. If Yarasadism can help my people to win their eternal fight, I have no argument with it."

The next morning, after an uncomfortable night spent on a concrete floor wrapped in blankets, Shem and his companions discovered that Yazid had disappeared during the night, along with his truck. Salamiel and Daniel were suspicious of this, but Shem thought that Yazid must have gone to seek his people and tell them about the strange Westerners who were asking for their prophet.

Over a sparse breakfast of bread and goat-cheese, washed down by sweet tea, Shem asked Fatime how long they should expect to wait for Gadreel's people.

She smiled. "I have no idea. You will just have to be patient."

Daniel watched Shem covertly. He sensed the mounting anxiety within him, and a sense of confusion. They should speak—he knew they should—but how could he break down the invisible wall that had come to separate them?

On the evening of their second day at the village, Daniel wandered off alone into the nearby crags, although he was tailed by several children and a three-legged dog. He emerged from a narrow pathway between high rocks to a natural look-out that hung high above a mountain valley of tough grass. Mountains rolled away into the distance. It was a dreaming landscape, seemingly oblivious of the human conflict taking place within it. Daniel put his hands against the ancient rocks, trying to project his mind back to when Shem's people had made their mark in this land, but he could not extend his senses beyond the mundane. He knew that in some way he was deliberately 'shutting down.' Perhaps he had been too affected by reality recently. He realised how different he was to the gauche youth whom Shemyaza had taken away from Little Moor. Never then could he have imagined being where he was now. For the first time in months, he thought of his sister, Verity, and had an urge to contact her. Was their father still alive? Homesickness swamped him. He yearned for the mellow glow of an English summer evening and the smallness of life in his old home. Kurdistan was stark and terrible and unremittingly honest in revealing humanity's failings. These mountains were washed in blood, and had been for millennia. The ambitions Shem had had in England seemed irrelevant here. What significance could the mythical conflict of angels have to people who daily had to fight for their lives? Daniel shuddered in the breeze that came down from the mountains. He felt like an impostor here.

A small hand tugged at his t-shirt. "Danee-ell, Danee-ell." He looked down and saw a grubby-faced girl smiling up at him; gaps in her teeth which he hoped were the result of growing rather than some obscene injury. She was dressed in a tattered, colourless dress, which was too big for her, and a brightly-embroidered purple jacket. Daniel recognised her as one of the children who had followed him from the village; he could see her companions, giggling and shy, hiding among the rocks behind him.

He ruffled the girl's hair. "Hi."

She held out a bunch of wilting, tiny flowers to him and chattered to him in Kurmanji. Despite the language barrier, he could tell she sensed his sadness and sought to cheer him. Tears came to his eyes and he pressed the fingers of one hand against them.

After five days, there was no sign of Gadreel or any of his immediate followers. Shem and Salamiel questioned Fatime every day until she became impatient with their demands. She did not know where the Yarasadi were. Perhaps they were too far away to receive the messages, or else engaged in combat. Daniel could sense she was really quite exasperated by Shem's constant questions. Daily, she had to deal with the influx of refugees that trailed in from routed villages in the mountains. Her scant medical staff were over-worked, with too few supplies. Sometimes, gunfire could be heard echoing from peak to peak.

One day, her natural courtesy deserted her. "What is so important about one man?" she snapped. "If you are here to report on our troubles, look around you. This is what should be taken back to the West!" All around her, the injured lay on make-shift beds among the ruins, or sat before meagre fires, staring into the smoke with blank eyes.

"We *will* take it back!" Shem answered. "We shall do more than that."

Fatime shook her head and walked away from him. Watching, Daniel could tell she thought Shem cared nothing for her troubles.

Daniel offered to help wherever he could, although he found it difficult to deal with the human pain of mutilated orphans and grieving women disfigured by appalling chemical burns. It was not the physical injuries that affected him, but the strong psychic effluvia of defeated despair and overwhelming grief.

On one occasion, he assisted Fatime to clean up the wounds of a young boy who had been brought in with a group of peshmergas. They had found him in the ruins of a smoking village. The boy's legs were hideously mangled, although Fatime told Daniel that she would use a poultice of local herbs on the injuries, which might prevent the need to amputate the limbs. Daniel doubted that the boy would ever walk again.

As they knelt together, mixing the poultice, Fatime said to Daniel, "Your friends have some business with Gadreel they are not speaking of."

And Daniel had to answer, "Yes, they have."

"They know him already."

Daniel looked into her eyes. "They know of him, Fatime. It is an old business. Very old."

"They are different from you."

He nodded. "Yes. They are like Gadreel, or rather they hope Gadreel is like them."

"What are they?"

Daniel was silent for a while. "Long ago, their people came from these mountains."

Fatime stared at him for a few moments, then changed the subject. "Here, open that jar for me. I need a handful of the leaves." Daniel realised she did not really want to know the truth, perhaps because she already suspected it.

Another week passed by, then another. Daniel and Salamiel occupied themselves by helping Fatime around the settlement. Salamiel spoke to Fatime often about the struggles of her people. Daniel detected a sub-text. Did Salamiel feel that Shem's task was to become involved in the conflict? Daniel couldn't dispel the impression this was so. He finished off the last of the films they had brought with them, tempering heart-rending shots of human misery with compositions of ragamuffin children grinning against the soaring landscape. The gap-toothed girl, Adina, who had once offered him flowers for his hurts, had become his shadow, having developed a strong crush on him. He knew that when the time came for them to leave, he would find it very hard to leave her behind in this place.

Each morning, Shem wandered off alone into the mountains, returning at sunset. He barely spoke to his companions. Salamiel confided to Daniel that he thought Shem was a maelstrom of doubts. "We are wasting time here. Why is he stalling?"

Daniel answered carefully, aware that Salamiel was liable to turn on him very quickly. "But we can't really do anything until we've made contact with the Yarasadi. We have to wait here."

"Nonsense!" Salamiel said. "He could show them his power instead of hiding it. Gadreel and the Yarasadi would no doubt appear with miraculous speed if Shem would only take control of the situation." He paused, then said. "Speak to him, Daniel. Only Anu knows what's going on in his head."

Daniel shrugged. "I can't, Sal. He won't let me."

"Then what are you here for?"

As the days passed, Salamiel's comments became more waspish. This did not help to restore Daniel's confidence in his unreliable psychic sight.

Daniel knew that Shem was becoming increasingly impatient about Gadreel's failure to appear, which was reflected in the terse manner in which he interrogated Fatime. Salamiel was convinced that Yazid had simply dumped them and had perhaps had not even contacted the Yarasadi. "Perhaps we should be looking upon ourselves as hostages now," he said.

Shem could not even articulate his feelings to himself. He was continually drawn to the mountains, almost as if, should he sit in solitude long enough, something would be revealed to him. He watched Daniel develop friendships with the Kurds, and recognised the barbs of jealousy in his heart. When the child Adina put her arms around Daniel and nestled against him, Shem yearned to be in her place. Daniel was his strength, his psychic eye. But it had been plucked out. In the past, this area had been where Shem's Nephilim sons had fought the might of the High Lord Anu. If he sat down and closed his eyes, he could almost hear the echoes of war still reverberating among the soaring crags. In mountains like these, where he'd taken Ishtahar in the last days of their life together, he had made his final stronghold. If he stared at any sheer cliff, he could almost see the fortress; a stark outline of cyclopean blocks; flat towers crowned with spreading spikes that were the rafters of the rooftops. Ishtahar had betrayed him there, by fleeing to Kharsag, where she'd revealed the whereabouts of Shemyaza's stronghold to Anu. She had condemned him to a horrifying death, and yet some part of him still loved her. He knew her actions had been the result of seeing the monster of hate and anger that he'd become. He could not blame her for her treachery. These mountains were full of her fragrance, her presence. He remembered that in lulls between the fighting, when his mood had swayed back to something like his former self, he and Ishtahar had strolled together among the valleys, gathered flowers and made love in the lush grass. The memories were too painful.

One day, Salamiel trailed Shem from the village and came upon him in his silent meditations. Saying nothing, Salamiel sat down beside him on the rock, staring out over a narrow gorge, where far below water spumed and crashed. Eventually, Salamiel broke the silence. "Shem, we can always go back."

Shem glanced at him, his expression unreadable. "I can't. I wish I could."

"Tell me what you're thinking."

Shem shook his head. "Nothing. Just remembering."

Salamiel was silent for a moment, then said, "I've been thinking about what we should do. It's obviously a waste of time hanging around here. I think we should take some action."

Shem raised his eyebrows. "Oh? Such as what?"

"Perhaps we could go to Babylon." He was clearly fighting to keep his voice calm, but an almost fanatical light had come into his eyes. "Shem, it is time for you to use your power. You are the divine king of angels. Isn't your job to change the world? You must rise up as the warrior, not the peace-maker. That has been tried and failed. We should go to Babylon and claim its armies for your own."

Shem laughed incredulously. "No, Sal. That doesn't feel right to me. I just have to find Gadreel. I have to find my brethren."

Salamiel snorted in contempt. "How long must we wait? What is going to happen?"

"I don't know. Daniel will discover this for me."

"Daniel!" Salamiel's voice was full of scorn. "Shem, why do you keep him by you? He's told us hardly anything of use recently, and let's face it, he doesn't even warm your bed for you any more. I think you're more than capable of taking on Daniel's role yourself. You are Shemyaza, more powerful than anyone."

Shem narrowed his eyes and his voice became harder. "How little you know me, Salamiel. I don't ever want to hear you speak of Daniel like that again."

"Someone has to point out the obvious to you," Salamiel answered, but the fire had gone from his eyes. "I'm sorry. I only have your interests at heart."

Shem shook his head once more, and stood up. "I have to speak to that woman again. Let's go back."

Shem had left Fatime alone for a few days, but when he returned to the village, he marched straight up to her and announced, "We can't stay here for ever. We need your help. I'd like you to send another message to Gadreel for us."

"I have sent messages," Fatime replied curtly, "and have received no answer. He might not come. You must face this."

"Send another message," Shem said. "I will pay for it."

Fatime shrugged. "Waste your money, then. I will do as you ask."

That night, after a brief private discussion, Salamiel and Daniel demanded that Shemyaza sit down with them to discuss what they should do next. The supplies they had brought with them had run out and they were now a burden on Fatime's limited resources. Shem was all for heading off into the mountains with the help of one of Fatime's people. He felt sure they could pay someone to guide them. Salamiel pointed out that they had no money left, and suggested they return to Van, in the hope of making contact with a Yarasadi there. Also, there were banks in Van where they could withdraw further funds.

"We are wasting our time here," Salamiel said.

Daniel felt Salamiel was right. "We've got to face it: Gadreel doesn't want to know about us."

Shem shook his head. "You're wrong. We can't give up. We are meant to be here. Gadreel will come."

Fatime had strolled over to where they sat, clearly interested in the outcome of their conversation. It didn't take long to work out she'd been eavesdropping for some time. "Your companions are sensible, Shemyaza. You should return to Van. Afterwards, if you still want to go down to the plains of Babylon, one of my people could guide you further south to the foothills, but first you will need supplies and transport. Your safety cannot be guaranteed."

"Two more days," Shemyaza said. "Then we shall see." He looked up at Fatime. "We shall repay you in full measure for your hospitality."

Fatime made a dismissive gesture. "No. There is no need."

When she walked away, Daniel went after her. He touched
her arm to get her attention. "I know how much you are helping us," he said. "Why?"

"Helping you?" Fatime looked puzzled. "I have done
little. You, Daniel, have done more these last weeks to
help me."

Daniel shook his head. "No. You could have used us as
hostages, Fatime. I'm not blind to the fact you are willing to
let us walk out of here back to Van. You wouldn't let us walk
out alone either, would you. Why?"

She smiled. "Instinct. Maybe. You could never be hostages." She glanced back at Shemyaza and Salamiel. "Your
friends, they frighten me, Daniel. But they belong here." With
that, she held up a hand to silence any more questions and
walked quickly away.

The two days passed, and as Daniel expected, there was
still no sign of the Yarasadi. Fatime offered to lend them a
jeep and a guide to return to Van, although she told them there
had been some trouble on the road out of the mountains and
some of it might be impassable.   .

"We have no choice," Salamiel said.

Daniel could tell that Shemyaza felt disheartened by
Gadreel's failure to appear. He had no doubt imagined some
dramatic reunion where everything would fall into place. To
Daniel, Gadreel's decision to keep a distance indicated that he
could not be a reawakened Watcher as Shem had thought. He
was probably nothing other than a Kurdish peshmerga, who
had simply adopted a name he considered to be powerful.

At dusk, they loaded their possessions into the covered
jeep. Most of the people seemed sorry to see them go.
Fatime embraced Daniel and wished him luck. Adina clung
to his legs, weeping, until Fatime prised her away and led
her to a group of women nearby. Daniel knew he could not
take her with them; they had no idea what would happen to
them or where they'd end up. He made a firm decision
that, once he returned home, he would try to help her people,
in whatever way he could. *If* he returned home. With this
thought, his mind became utterly still. For the first time,
he considered leaving Shem behind. His role as vizier

seemed to have disappeared. He had lost the keenness of his psychic sight. Shem needed a new vizier. Perhaps he would find one in these mountains, some native of his ancient homeland. Daniel rested his forehead against the canvas of the jeep, pretending to be engrossed in fixing it to the vehicle's frame. It's finished, he thought. I've played my part.

"Daniel?" Shem's hand curled around his shoulder. "What's wrong?"

Daniel paused for a moment, wondering whether he dared to speak his mind. Then the words were being spoken, almost independently of his will. "Shem, I think I'll be going home."

Shem was silent as he considered this statement, then he laughed softly. "That's good news. I know you feared we'd all get killed up here."

"No. I mean soon. Now. I don't want this anymore."

Shem sighed impatiently. "We'll return to Van, and see what happens. Something *will* happen. I'm sure of it."

Daniel pulled away angrily. "Will you listen to me for once? I'm going back to England. I could get a flight out of Van to Istanbul. It's over, Shem. I don't belong with you any more."

People around them had stopped what they were doing to listen to the argument. Fatime sucked pensively on a cigarette nearby, her eyes narrow and watchful.

"You can't go back," Shem said quietly. "There's nothing there for you. Your place is with me."

"No. I've changed. I'm no use to you now. I'm not the Taliesin I was to you in Cornwall. Give me one last thing. Give me the money to get home."

Shem's hands shot out and grabbed Daniel's wrists. He pulled Daniel towards him, making him wince in pain as the bones in his wrists ground together. "You are not trying, Daniel! You're forsaking your duty!" He shook Daniel like a rat in the jaws of a dog.

Salamiel sauntered over to them. "Let him go, Shem. He may be right. We're all exhausted. Let's talk about this back in Van."

Shem uttered an angry cry and threw Daniel against the side of the jeep. But for this movement, the entire camp around them had become still. Children watched with wide eyes.

Salamiel thrust himself between them and tried to break
Shem's grip on Daniel's arms. Daniel struck out with his feet
and caught Shem on the shin, which prompted him to transfer
his grip to Daniel's throat.

Salamiel punched at Shem's face, yelling, "You'll kill him,
for Anu's sake! Shem, let go!"

Daniel flailed and hit out with his arms, striking Shem
around the head. He retched and gasped in Shem's hold. So,
Shemyaza would kill him now. Was this the end of it? He
became overwhelmed with a numbing lethargy, and could no
longer feel the pain of suffocation. Sound became faint in his
ears, replaced by a rushing like the sea. His vision blurred.
Then, Shemyaza had let him go, almost as if something else
had attracted his attention.

Daniel slumped to his knees, wheezing and coughing, his
hands against his throat. Salamiel and Shemyaza were like
giants before him; inhuman and terrible, their hair coiling like
snakes around their heads and shoulders in the evening breeze.

"Daniel." Salamiel squatted down before him, took his
face in his hands. "Are you all right?"

Daniel swallowed painfully and croaked, "Yes." He was
surprised by this unexpected show of concern, but let
Salamiel help him to his feet. Daniel could not look at
Shem. Wiping his eyes to clear his vision, he saw ghosts
everywhere; dark shapes that had melted out of the dusk.
They seemed be floating down from the rocky crags around
them; dark cloth swirling round them like wings. One of
them came towards the jeep, and Daniel saw it was not a
ghost at all, but a man dressed in a dark robe with a red
scarf wrapped around his head. They had come then, at
last: Yarasadi. Daniel knew it had been decided for him: he
would not be going home just yet.

Shem had already caught sight of the robed figures. He
had straightened up and now stepped forward to address
the one who seemed to be the leader of the group. Fatime,
however, intervened, moving quickly to place herself between Shem and the stranger. She spoke to the leader in
rapid Kurmanji and then turned to Shem. "These people
are Yarasadi. It is unclear whether they are here because of

the messages, for they claim to know nothing of them, but they do wish to speak with you."

"Is Gadreel with them?"

Fatime shook her head. "No. But that is not unexpected. Nobody meets Gadreel."

Shem clawed his fingers through his hair impatiently. "Where is Yazid? Did he reach them?"

Fatime again spoke to the Yarasadi in their own tongue. "They will not answer clearly. They say there is someone they must take you to."

Shem nodded. "That must be Gadreel. Tell them we will go with them gladly."

Fatime studied Shem for a moment. "You have to understand, these people are an elite group. I do not know their activities and cannot vouch for your safety if you go with them."

"I understand, but we must still go."

Daniel knew Shem well enough not to expect an apology for his attack. To Shem, there seemed to be no difference between an act of cruelty or of love. The atmosphere in the jeep as they set off from Fatime's village was tense and silent. Salamiel seemed embarrassed or guilty about the episode and would not speak to Daniel, although he did offer a reassuring pat upon the shoulder as they climbed into the back of the jeep. Shem said he would drive, although one of the Yarasadi— a woman—climbed into the front seat beside him, presumably to act as guide. They could see little of their new companion, as she was disguised by her costume and the light now was dim. If she could speak English, she clearly did not intend to do so, and directed Shem by gestures and sharp remarks in Kurmanji. She kept her gun upright between her robe-swathed knees; a fearless female who had no anxiety about travelling with three male strangers. The other Yarasadi disappeared back into the shadows of the rocks.

They drove through the night, along mountain roads that looked—and felt—as if they had not been travelled by wheeled vehicles for centuries. Progress was slow and on several occasions the company had to alight from the jeep to manhandle it out of a deep rut in the road.

Daniel knew that he could no longer avoid speaking to Shem about their relationship. Shem's unexpected violence hid more than mere annoyance that Daniel wanted to leave him. At one time, their alliance had been intense and passionate, but it had been spoiled by Shem's long recuperation from his ordeal in Cornwall. Daniel wondered whether his withering psychic ability was something to do with the fact that he and Shem had become estranged. If he was to remain part of the Grigori's destiny, then he must face the resentments that had built up within him, and break down the barriers of hostility. How and when he had yet to work out.

Chapter Ten
The Daughter of Israel

Cornwall, England

Lily Winter was worried about her daughter, Helen. The child had had a mild fever for three days now, and the attentions of the young Grigori physician whom Enniel had sent to the cottage seemed to have done nothing to alleviate Helen's condition. Tonight, it was worse.

Helen's body was hot and dry, her breath sour as she tossed and whimpered on her bed. Lily bathed her daughter's forehead with the fragrant herbal concoction that the physician, Master Malagriel, had left for her. Five minutes earlier, Lily had again called Malagriel, who had assured her that the child was in no danger. Lily wondered how the physician had come to that conclusion. To her, Helen's condition looked very serious.

Again, Lily couldn't help wondering whether Helen had been affected by the strange insect she had found on the cliffs on the day of the eclipse. The creature had been dead when Helen found it, and resembled no beetle that Lily had seen before. She had showed it to Malagriel, afraid that the stiff lifeless form had somehow stung Helen. The physician had looked at the insect with interest. "It seems to be a scarab—and a very large one at that."

"But what was it doing on the cliffs?" Lily demanded.

Malagriel had shrugged. "Well, it could have come from High Crag. Enniel has the place stuffed full of old relics, as you probably know." He grinned. "Not least, some of his relatives."

Lily had been in no mood for jokes. "Are you sure it couldn't have hurt Helen?"

"Yes. Scarabs aren't poisonous."

In the early stages of her illness, Helen had insisted on keeping the creature in a jar beside her bed. She liked to turn the glass vessel in her hands, staring at the oil-bright colours of the insect's carapace. Now, the jar stood ignored on the table, next to the Winnie the Pooh lamp, amid a jumble of Helen's toy ponies. Lily's heart contracted within her. The little array of youthful belongings seemed pathetic standing so mundanely above the suffering child. Lily dreaded that Helen would never be able to play with them again.

Thunder growled in the distance; another storm. They had been occurring every evening recently; violent electrical tempests that brought no rain. The air was humid, yet Lily shivered. She stood up and went to the window, looked out. Another jagged spear of light cracked down to spike the earth. It was almost as if something were moving again beneath the Cornish soil, another monstrous serpent brought to life. Lily's mind was cast back to the terrifying time when she had first come to Cornwall. She felt unnerved, in need of company. Her brother, Owen, was out, but she could call Emma Manden.

Downstairs, Lily discovered that the phones were down again. Another peal of thunder came, followed by what felt like a minor earthquake. Lily cringed. Ornaments on the shelves rattled, pictures tilted, and the overhead lamp fitting swayed. "No," Lily said aloud. She could sense something creeping towards her home, shrouded in thunder, carried by it.

The lights suddenly went out and Lily jumped, repressing a cry that rose in her throat. She could not stay here. She would have to pick Helen up and carry her from the house. They would have to go to High Crag. Enniel would know what was happening. He would protect them.

Running to the stairs, Lily was horrified to see a spectral shape staring down at her from the first floor, limned in blue-white lightning radiance that came in through the landing windows. Her first instinct was to slam herself backwards against the wall, trying to make herself invisible. Helen was up there, though. Her vulnerable daughter. What could she do? There was no way Lily would abandon her.

Then the voice came. "Mummy! Mummy!" The ghostly shape came scampering down the stairs, and Lily realised it wasn't a ghost at all.

Lily scooped the child up into her arms and realised at once that Helen felt cooler. The fever had broken. Relieved, Lily pressed her face against Helen's cheek. "Helen, what are you doing out of bed? Are you scared?"

"No, I'm not scared, but I've got something to tell you."

"What?" Lily carried Helen towards the kitchen. As she pushed open the door, the lights came on again. Normality restored.

Helen wriggled in her arms. "Met-met wants to go home. He wants me to take him."

"Who's Met-met?"

"My animal. The one I found."

"The scarab beetle?"

Helen nodded.

"Where does he want you to take him, sweetheart?"

"To Khem. It's a long way."

Lily knew that Khem was one of the ancient names of Egypt, but how could Helen have known it? "Well, perhaps one day we can go on a holiday there and then we'll take him home."

Helen shook her head emphatically. "No. Soon."

Lily deposited Helen on a chair and went to the fridge to fetch milk. "We can't. It's not a safe place at the moment. People are fighting all the time."

"Mummy, we must go. Met-met jumped onto my face and folded the thing that made me sick up into a ball. He threw it away. Then he told me."

Lily paused, the milk carton poised over Helen's cup. A mother would normally dismiss such nonsense as make-believe, but Helen was no ordinary child. She was Grigori. "Why does Met-met want to go home so badly, Helen?"

"He wants to show something to me."

"What?"

Helen shrugged and took the milk drink from her mother. "I don't know. We mustn't be scared of the fighting, though. Mummy, will you ask Enniel to sort it out for us?" Already

Helen was wise enough to know where money and favours came from in their home.

Lily sat down at the table and folded her arms upon it, staring at her daughter. In many ways, with her perfect face and shadowed, sometimes commanding, gaze, she resembled a girl of Ancient Egypt.

The phone rang. Lily got up to answer it, but by the time she reached the hallway and lifted the receiver, all she heard was a crackle, a long-distance hissing. "Hello, hello?" No answer. She replaced the receiver thoughtfully, her mind suddenly full of Daniel. Did he need her? Was he thinking of her? Lily stared at the phone before going back into the kitchen. She could not dispel the suspicion that Helen's announcement was somehow connected with Daniel's disappearance. The phone call seemed like an eerie omen. Enniel knew that Shem had taken his companions to the Middle East, but there had been no news from them for weeks.

I can't just go out there, Lily thought. I can't.

But she knew that in morning, she would go to High Crag and speak to Enniel.

Chapter Eleven
The Keeper of the Key

Babylonia

Rocks cast long blue shadows over the twisting road. It was late afternoon, and they had been travelling for a day and a half. Shem dozed beside Daniel on the floor of the jeep. Daniel stared at his sleeping face, fighting an urge to reach out and touch it. Not yet. The time wasn't right.

Salamiel was driving. He had persisted in chatting to the Yarasadi woman and had gleaned the information that her name was Sabry. She spoke enough English for Salamiel to make himself understood, and had grudgingly responded to his friendly overtures. Daniel had watched him flirting, amused.

The truck careered to a stop in front of a group of armed men, who appeared to have materialised from crevices in the rock. Like the first Yarasadi they had met, these men were not dressed in modern military garb, but long, dark robes embroidered elaborately in gold and crimson. Their heads were swathed in scarlet cloth, which revealed only their eyes. "We are near the camp," Sabry said. "Very near."

The peshmergas approached the jeep and Sabry spoke to them in Kurmanji. After a wary inspection of the passengers, the Yarasadi waved them onwards.

"Is Gadreel here?" Daniel asked.

Sabry glanced round at him, frowned and shook her head.

The road suddenly turned sharply to the left and downwards. A hidden valley was revealed. Shem woke up and, as Daniel watched, wound a long white scarf around his head to conceal most of his features. Their eyes met. Daniel saw challenge in the gaze and returned it, obtaining a smug satisfaction when Shem finally averted his eyes.

Daniel leaned forward over Sabry's seat to get a better view. The valley floor was lush and fertile, surrounded by forbidding cliffs of green-veined rock, full of gaping caves, which appeared to have been utilised as dwellings. A forest of oak hugged the far side of the valley, while before them, bizarre natural monoliths reared up from the valley floor, dwarfed by the looming cliffs. These formations looked very much like the 'fairy chimneys' of Cappadocia, but here the terrain was remarkably different. Cappadocia was almost a desert.

"It's unreal," Daniel murmured.

"Bad in winter," Sabry said. "Cut off by snow for months."

As well as the permanent rock dwellings, the settlement comprised many temporary buildings of hides and canvas, which were all roughly circular. People wearing the distinctive dark clothing and scarlet head-gear could be seen moving among them. Goats were grazing among parked trucks, and horses were corralled nearby.

Salamiel crunched the gears and the jeep descended into the valley. People paused in their activities to watch its advance. Daniel could sense their wariness and suspicion. Everyone carried guns. It was difficult to determine who was male and who was female.

At Sabry's command, Salamiel brought the jeep to a halt between two tall chimneys of stone which stood before a wide sway-backed tent of goat hides. A tall figure stood at the entrance canopy, hands on hips. Golden fringes adorned his scarlet head-scarf. His proud stance declared his leadership. A group of other figures surrounded him, with guns slung over their shoulders.

"Qimir," Sabry said. "Tribe leader. The sheikh."

Daniel could sense a certain 'otherness' about the people before them. He felt almost reluctant to leave the safety of the jeep. How would they react to Shem? Would he reveal his true nature to these people, who had worshipped the angels for millennia?

"Wait here," Sabry told them and climbed out of the jeep. Daniel watched as she approached the tribe leader and spoke to him. Qimir stood motionless, listening to the rapid outpouring; his eyes, which were the only visible features of his face, fixed on the wind-shield of the jeep.

"He doesn't look very welcoming," Daniel said.

Shem smiled. "You see what you want to see." Without further words, and ignoring a protest from Daniel, he got out of the back door of the jeep and approached the tribe leader.

Salamiel uttered a small, worried sound.

"We can't let him deal with this alone," Daniel said.

Salamiel nodded. "You're right. Anu knows what he'll say!"

Together they got out of the jeep. Daniel saw Qimir's eyes widen almost imperceptibly as Shem drew close to him. What did the man see? Daniel wondered. Shem, even with his head and face covered, exuded a magnificence that went beyond appearances. Judging from the sudden stiffening of the sheikh's body, Daniel felt it was almost as if the tribe leader's worst fears or wildest hopes had been confirmed.

Shem halted beside Sabry and bowed his head. "Greetings to you, sir."

The sheikh nodded shortly, but otherwise made no move or sound.

Shem straightened up. "My friends and I are here because we would like to meet Gadreel."

"I have explained your purpose," Sabry said.

Qimir's eyes travelled slowly over Shem and his companions. "You are not journalists," he announced. "Just what are you?" He spoke English perfectly, and his voice was not heavily accented, almost as if he'd been brought up in the West. It was a soft, low voice, precise and careful.

"No, we are not journalists," Shem admitted. "but I assure you we have the interests of your people at heart. It is very important that I meet Gadreel."

"We shall talk," said Qimir. He turned and gestured towards the tent.

"Thank you." Shem turned to his companions. "Well, this is it. Shall we go in?"

Daniel and Salamiel exchanged a glance. Gadreel was not here. Did that mean they would have to endure another fruitless period of waiting?

Inside, Qimir's dwelling was adorned with flowers of white, purple and yellow that exuded a fresh perfume. Blooms splayed out of brass bowls and were hung in garlands on the canopied walls. The light from outside was dim, augmented by a couple of oil lamps flickering on the floor. Qimir bade his guests be seated on brocade cushions. As they sat down, the tribe leader summoned a young man from the shadows of the tent and spoke to him in a whisper. Then, Qimir unwrapped the red cloth from around his head to reveal a clean-shaven, tawny-skinned face of long, delicate features. "You have had a hard journey?" he enquired.

Shem smiled. "Tiring. But the mountains are beautiful and do much to restore the spirit." He also unwound his head-cloth and shook out his hair.

Daniel watched Qimir's reaction carefully; he suspected that the tribe leader knew already that Shem was no ordinary man.

A young boy emerged from beneath a curtain, carrying a large dish of dried fruit and nuts, accompanied by a girl who bore a tray containing a tall, narrow tea-pot and a number of glasses.

"Refreshment," Qimir said. "It eases conversation."

Shem inclined his head. "We thank you."

The company waited in silence as the tea and food were distributed. Unlike most other people they'd met since they'd entered Turkey, Qimir seemed taciturn and aloof. The silence was uncomfortable, yet Qimir himself displayed no sign of unease. He sat thoughtfully, his head resting in one long-fingered hand.

Taking a sip of tea, Shem said, "These are my companions, Daniel and Salamiel."

Qimir afforded them an appraising glance.

"And I am Shemyaza."

Qimir smiled thinly. "Yes? That is not the name of an Englishman."

"No," Shem answered, "my name is, as Gadreel's, from an ancient source."

"Shemyaza," Qimir said, "is a name known to me. It is a another form of Malak Tawus, also called Azazil, the Peacock Angel and the first avatar of the Divine Spirit. Do you understand what that means to us?"

"Yes," Shem answered simply. "I understand. I have lived with the knowledge of the meaning of my name for a long time."

Their eyes locked, and after a while Qimir looked away and helped himself to a handful of the nuts. "So what is your business with Gadreel, other than a comparison of names?"

"I cannot discuss it at this juncture. It is of a personal nature."

"You are known to Gadreel?"

Shem paused, then said simply. "Yes. I am known."

Salamiel shifted uncomfortably upon his cushion. Qimir indicated him languidly. "Your companion does not think so."

"Not at all," Salamiel said smoothly. "Shemyaza is certainly known to Gadreel, but perhaps not acquainted."

"That is a strange distinction," Qimir said, biting into an almond. "Gadreel is not here of course. You did realise that."

Shem shrugged. "I do not expect to find him easily, but I believe you can get word to him. We have travelled a long way and have waited a long time to meet him. Now, we are with his people. The next step must be a meeting with Gadreel himself. We would be most grateful if you could arrange this."

Qimir threw back his head and laughed, which seemed an inappropriate response. "I can *ask* for a meeting," he said. "If your request is granted, you can expect a surprise." He sobered slightly. "Tell me, what can I reveal that would entice our prophet into your presence?"

"Tell him that his brother, Shemyaza, wishes to speak with him."

Now it was Daniel's turn to squirm. As yet, they had no proof that Gadreel was Grigori, never mind the individual Shem believed him to be. If Gadreel showed up, it could be embarrassing, if not dangerous.

Qimir laughed again. "Brother to Gadreel, heh? I take it you have not met your *brother*?"

Shem shook his head. "No...well, not in this life."

Qimir nodded. Shem's answer seemed to have satisfied him. "I shall see to it that your message reaches the right ears. But you may have a wait. Until then, the hospitality of my household is open to you."

"It is more than we hoped for," Shem answered.

Presently, Qimir summoned one of his staff, a young woman named Shirin, and directed her to arrange accommodation for their guests. Shirin's head was uncovered, although she was dressed, as the men, in long, dark, embroidery-encrusted robes. Her abundant hair, which was henna red, hung unbound down her back. Into it was woven small mountain flowers. Her wrists were braceleted with curling tattoos. She led Shem and his companions to a small tent that smelled strongly of goat. Lifting aside an entrance flap, she revealed a dark interior where thick, hairy hides were laid out on the floor. Daniel suspected the hides might be alive with vermin. Nor was there much room for three grown males to stretch out. Still, it was more private than the quarters given to them by Fatime.

Daniel and Salamiel went back to the jeep to fetch their belongings, watched by curious Yarasadi. "Qimir knows more than he's letting on," Daniel said.

Salamiel nodded. "I thought that too. Yazid, of course, might have delivered a report."

Daniel sighed. "God, I hope we don't have another month of waiting to endure. I get the feeling this Gadreel character is playing with us."

"Perhaps he needs to be sure of us," Salamiel said. "If we are who we say we are, then we will wait. Gadreel would know this."

"I hope you're right."

That night, Daniel dreamed coherently for the first time since he'd left England. The wind cut through the valley with an eerie cry, and its noise intruded into Daniel's restless sleep, creating a maelstrom of sound that was like the advance of a great army or the summoning of a sorcerous storm.

He stood upon wind-swept rocks above a black sea that heaved beneath a boiling sky. It seemed as if he'd entered the dream half-way through, as if a part of him had been existing within it for some time. Echoes of words recently spoken resounded in his mind, but he could not remember them.

A shimmering blue sphere hung above the sea, illuminating the angry cresting waves. Daniel peered at it, feeling that he'd invoked it, although the memory of doing so had vanished. It would be Ishtahar, his goddess, bringing more puzzles to him, and obscure answers to his questions. He saw her again as a child, hovering with drooping feet above the water, encased in her own bubble of light.

"Ishtahar!" he cried and as if in response, a wave crashed against the rock beneath him, soaking him with spray that smelled strongly of brine and rot. Ishtahar looked odd to him; at once familiar and a stranger.

"Don't you know me, Daniel?" she asked, and the voice was that of a mature woman. The child smiled and spun before him in the air. "You have chosen to stay on this path, now follow it...The time of your rite of passage is at hand."

Then a blinding flash crashed across the sky, like thunder. The rock shivered beneath his feet; he heard the crack of stone. When his vision cleared, he found himself standing within a plain chamber that was conical like a bee-hive. The air was noticeably drier, almost sterile, and a low hum vibrated all around him. The walls exuded a perfect white glow that seemed to occlude his surroundings rather than illuminate them.

Daniel turned round in a circle, and looked down at his glowing limbs that were absorbing the light. He could hear strange whispers speaking in an unknown tongue, and distant echoes as of metal and stone ringing together.

Presently, a darkness formed in the light before him and out of it came a shape; an immensely tall male figure robed in white. He looked like a man, but Daniel sensed he was not. His towering body seemed full of light, as if he was made of it. Long, eburneous hair fell over his chest, and his face was like a caricature of Grigori features; attenuated beyond what seemed possible, with slanting eyes of a piercing blue. His skin was so pale, Daniel could see mauve veins pulsing with life beneath it, yet despite an undeniable grotesqueness of appearance, the figure was in his own way beautiful. In his outstretched hands, he held a conical crystalline object that he seemed to be offering to Daniel.

Daniel stepped forward and held out his hands, but the stranger would not relinquish the object he held. He loomed over Daniel, perhaps seven feet or more in height. His mask-like face held no compassion, nor any other emotion Daniel could recognise as Grigori, whose personalities were often more complex than human. He sensed a total amorality, a mind that viewed the world in a manner entirely alien to anything he had encountered before, in waking life or in vision. He was afraid of the creature, yet transfixed.

The tall being seemed to be aware of Daniel's feelings for the faintest suggestion of smile stretched his lips and he nodded almost imperceptibly. His features began to quiver with minuscule movements; his eyes blinked like a cat's. Daniel sensed that this was a language of expression, beyond words. He could not understand it, although it seemed to him that a stream of communication was flowing across and over him. There was no impatience. The stranger appeared to think that Daniel could understand every nuance of expression.

Daniel stood there for what seemed like half an hour, until the figure appeared to give up his attempt at communication. He shook his head and retreated into the white glow. Daniel felt he had left something important unsaid, failed to pick up a vital clue. The light grew dim around him. He hung in a void, wanting only to wake up.

It was the hour just before dawn. Daniel, feeling restless, crept out of the tent and stretched his limbs in the clear air. Goats moved like ghosts between the dwellings and the sentinel pillars of stone, chewing at the short grass. From far away, some distant peak, came the eerie lament of a woman's voice; no song, but a succession of wordless vowels. The hiss of the wind was its percussion, and also its strings, as it whistled through the trees and howled through the rocky passes. Daniel felt the hairs upon his arms rise. There was magic here.

He walked away from the cluster of dwellings towards the far side of the valley, where the caves were. Smoke from dampened fires curled lazily in the predawn light, and the scent of flowers was very strong. Sleepy guards made no move as Daniel passed among them, almost as if he was invisible.

His footsteps echoed loudly in the caves as he passed them. He was drawn to a fissure in the cliff-face, which proved to be the start of a steep, upward path, little more than a gully. Daniel paused, and once again caught a ghost of the lilting refrain, as if someone was singing alone high above.

The path led to a narrow valley which sloped upwards away from him, oppressed on either side by steep rocks veined with startling green malachite. The grassy floor was starred with white flowers, which exuded a heavy, fresh perfume. Daniel stepped onto the grass, and as he did so, caught sight of two pale figures flickering ahead of him. They appeared to be flashing in and out of reality, gambolling like children on their way up the valley, although they were too tall to be children.

Every hair on Daniel's body felt electrified. He smelled ozone, and his head began to ache. The figures became clearer in his sight; two males, completely naked, their skins unnaturally white. He could not make out their facial features, and their hair was a waving blur of indistinct colour around their heads and shoulders. They seemed to be involved in a game of some kind; their arms waved as if in the movements of a dance, and they were laughing. Facing each other, they moved sideways up the valley, gesturing at one another. Daniel knew immediately, without understanding how, that they were brothers.

One is incomplete, he thought. Unmade somehow...

As he watched them, the reason for this became apparent. The figure on the left looked perfect, graceful of limb with flawless skin, while his brother's movements were more jerky. Daniel also realised that the second brother's flesh was scored with long lesions along the flank, almost as if his body were seamed and splitting apart. The image was at once revolting and compelling. Daniel could not work out what it must mean.

Then someone called his name, and the image shattered, sparks of light and colour flying out to either side to be absorbed by the watchful cliffs.

Daniel turned and saw Shem strolling towards him. He uttered a low sound of annoyance. "Thanks!"

Shem frowned. "For what?"

Daniel sighed, shook his head. "I saw something, and your voice dispelled the vision, that's all." He related what he'd seen.

Shem nodded thoughtfully. "Could have been a memory of people who once lived here—Watcher descendants. The nomads of the mountains are referred to as 'pale tall trees,' did you know that?"

"No. But I don't think the vision was simply that."

Shem put a hand on Daniel's arm. "This country: you can feel the magic, can't you?" He inhaled slowly. "Smell it."

It was almost touching how at ease Shem felt in these surroundings. Daniel glanced around him. He'd always thought of Eden as being an oasis in a desert, but of course that was not so. It had existed somewhere in the mountains. How much did the Yarasadi know of their heritage? Was it all demons and angels to them, or did they realise that the Grigori still walked among them?

Shem put his hands upon Daniel's shoulders and looked directly into his eyes. "Well, it has to be said by one of us, so it might as well be me. Can we rescue what we once had?"

Daniel forced himself to hold Shem's gaze. He felt cornered, unable to organise his thoughts. "I don't know." He shook his head. "No. We can only move on."

"Together or alone?"

Daniel could feel himself responding to Shem's presence. He wanted to curl his arms around Shem's body, hold him close, but something still prevented him. Instead, he rested his hands upon Shem's arms. "I was only a child when you showed to me the secrets of your history and gave me extended life. I was in awe of you, Shem, dazzled by your beauty. You have to remember I had only recently discovered my own sexuality. You were a god to me then."

Shem smiled sadly. "Are you telling me that your feelings for me have gone?"

Daniel shook his head, frowning. "I don't know what I feel. After you retreated into yourself, I could not think of becoming close to anyone else. I've been alone for five years. That's a long time to live without love. It's changed me. I think I 'shut down' more than just my psychic abilities."

Shem brushed the fingers of one hand down Daniel's face. "Perhaps the two are connected."

Daniel pulled away, nodded. "Could be. I have to work it out."

Shem folded his arms. "Come back to me, Daniel. I will wait, but I want you back." He paused. "Is this anything to do with the fight we had at Fatime's village?"

Daniel stared at him. "No. I can't say that helped, but…"
He waited for an apology, but none was forthcoming. Resigned to the fact, he sighed. "Anyway, what happened there
is irrelevant. I know we have to talk, Shem, and it will be
soon, but I don't feel ready yet." He looked around himself.
"Maybe here, I can think more clearly." He smiled. "No doubt
I'll have plenty of time. How long do you think Gadreel will
make us wait?"

Shem accepted the change of subject without comment.
"Who knows? But he will come, Daniel. I am convinced of
it." He slung an arm around Daniel's shoulders. "Come on,
let's forget our differences for a while and just walk. This
country should be enjoyed through the senses."

That evening Qimir decreed that a feast should be set for his
guests. Gone now was the reticence of when they'd first arrived at the camp. The settlement was decked with garlands
of flowers, and the atmosphere was light and joyous, as if the
tribe were happy to forget their problems for the slightest cause
and give in to the urge to celebrate. Fires burned among the
dwellings, sending cascades of sparks into the night sky and
filling the air with the scent of wood-smoke. Musicians practised around the tents, playing stringed instruments named
tamburas, an oboe-like object called a zurna and drums they
called duhuls. Everybody's feet seemed to itch to dance; robes
swung more widely as people walked around the settlement
and eyes sparked with a desire for childish wickedness. Daniel
was caught up in the atmosphere of it, and felt his heart soar
like a bird over the mountains. Deep, throbbing echoes seemed
to boom from crag to crag, and he had a vague sense as of vast
wings flapping ponderously overhead. Something was due to
happen; he could sense it.

As dusk fell, and fires were lit around the tents to roast
spitted sheep, Daniel walked once more to the path that led to
the cliff dwellings. At the edge of the valley, he turned and
gazed back down over the settlement. It seemed to him that
he'd slipped back in time, that at any moment tall, robed shapes,
wearing cloaks of feathers would melt out of the trees, and
the people would fall down before them in adoration. Duhuls

beat a tattoo upon the night and above, the stars were pierc-
ingly bright. It was like the eve of a great battle; a certain
repressed hysteria in the air. Gadreel is coming, he thought,
but perhaps it was more than that.

On impulse, he began to ascend the narrow path that led
towards the caves. Something was drawing him there. Small
stones crunched beneath his feet, rolling down into the valley.
He noticed that one of the caves was illuminated by a red,
flickering glow. As he drew closer to the entrance, he saw a
straight-backed, seated figure silhouetted against the glow
within. Daniel had thought all the Yarasadi were present at
the feast below. Even in the dim light, Daniel sensed this
person was watching him intently, calling out to him with a
firm inner voice.

The sounds and sights of the night seemed more alive, as
if his senses had become more acute. It reminded him of the
time in High Crag, when Shem had bestowed longevity upon
him. At first, he'd been unable to bear the intensity of his
senses. Even inanimate objects had seemed threatening. Now,
Daniel did not feel threatened by his heightened perception,
but intoxicated.

By the time he'd reached the small fire at the cave mouth,
Daniel was panting, but not because of the climb. He could
now see that the seated figure was male, but before he arrived at the rocky entrance, the man stood up and retreated
swiftly into the cave. Daniel was compelled to follow. Music and laughter in the valley called him back, but the summons was weak.

The interior of the cave was lit by the warm glow of several oil lamps that rested on the floor and in niches in the rock.
The walls were covered in strange designs that looked very
old: figures seated in a cross-legged position, wearing tall, conical hats. There was no sign of the man who had been seated
outside, and but for the sputtering of oil, no sound. Daniel
called, "Hello!", and it seemed as if his voice conjured the
chuckle of trickling water that appeared to originate from the
back of the cave. Daniel noticed a narrow opening in the
stone there, partly hidden by a hanging rug. Cautiously, he
went towards it.

A mature male voice called from the chamber beyond. "Well, are you going to come through, or do I have to wait all night?"

Daniel hesitated for a moment, then squeezed through the crack in the wall and emerged into another chamber, small than the one he'd left behind. It was almost empty but for a pool of water that flowed out of a narrow fissure in the rock. The pool was about six feet wide, its surface glittering with the starfire reflections from an old brass oil lamp that hung on the wall. A couple of thread-bare, gold-embroidered cushions were scattered along the nearside of the pool, suggesting people came here to contemplate, or else scry, by the waters. The air was damp and fresh against the skin.

A man stood before Daniel, hands on hips, smiling in welcome. "Ah, here you are at last!" He appeared older than the other Yarasadi Daniel had met and was dressed in a white robe cinched with a crimson sash. His hair was short, his feet bare. "Come forward. Let me have a look at you."

Daniel ventured further into the cave. "Are you a priest?" he asked.

The old man sat down on one of the cushions by the pool, and gestured with his hands. "In many ways. I am Mani, the last of my kind."

"Why have you called to me?"

Mani's weathered face rippled with splashes of golden light that were reflected from the water. "We share similar gifts, young one. We have business together. Please, sit with me a while. We must talk."

Daniel sat down opposite the old man, on the brocade cushions. "What gifts do we share?"

"That of the sight," Mani said. He gestured widely. "I would like to tell you about myself."

Daniel shrugged, displayed the palms of his hands. "Then please do."

Mani settled himself on the cushions. "I am not of this tribe. My family were Magians, who lived in the city that now is Babylon. I was the last of my father's line and have no children of my own. When King Nimnezzar came to power,

he summoned me to his court and told me I must join the
ranks of his elite company of Magi. I would not join the pre-
tender and had to flee for my life. I already had enemies at
court who envied my powers. The Yarasadi gave me sanctuary, so here I am. Mani the Magian, at your service." He
bowed his head and spread his arms wide.

Daniel bowed his head in return. "I'm Daniel Cranton,
from England."

Mani nodded. "Yes. Daniel of the Lion."

Daniel smiled. "That's not the first time I've heard that."

Mani raised his brows. "Your soul has a long affinity with
the lion. An ancestress of yours once worked in the house of
Sekhmet, She of the Eye of Fire."

"The Egyptian lioness goddess?" Daniel shook his head.
"How can you know that?"

Mani grinned and made a languid gesture with his hands.
"I know much about you, Daniel. I've been waiting a long
time for you and your companions to arrive." He nodded to
himself for a moment, then said, "Tell me what you thought
of your vision of the holy twins."

Daniel could not conceal his surprise. "You know of that
too? Is it a common phenomenon around here?"

"Not at all. But I knew that you would see it."

"Why did I? Can you tell me what it meant?"

Mani rested his hands on his crossed knees. "Let me tell
you a little of what your coming here means. The prophet
Gadreel has spoken to Qimir, and has told him of the Grigori.
The Yarasadi have been made aware of their ancestry. I have
known of the Grigori's existence since I was a young man. I
was curious, and in those days a scholar hungry for knowledge. I learned much of the secret history of the Fallen Ones,
the *Daevic* race, for I was not afraid to delve into areas that
were fraught with danger. Often, I ran for my life, clutching
nothing but a fragment of papyrus containing a single sen-
tence that was only another tiny piece in the puzzle I was
trying to solve. I learned things that even Gadreel did not
know. Now, I instruct Qimir, for he too wants to share this
knowledge."

"So you knew that Shemyaza would come here?"

Mani shrugged expressively. "Not exactly. Gadreel would ask me questions constantly, for I too wear the mantle of the vizier. Gadreel was, like your master, driven to do certain things. But what was the great purpose of it? I searched the hidden world for answers, but all I learned was that the fallen Watchers must once again form a brotherhood. How would that happen? Gadreel had met no others, and I could find no trace of them through my spirit guides. When the news came to us that your master, Shemyaza, was seeking Gadreel, we all knew that the time had come for us to learn the answer to our questions. Shemyaza has returned to his home land to put right the wrongs of ancient times, to reverse history."

Daniel kept his face expressionless. "Go on..."

"When we received the news, Gadreel was suspicious. It seemed almost too convenient that Shemyaza would come seeking his own kind in this forsaken and ravaged country. Gadreel had always believed the Watchers would have to find their king for themselves. It was possible that Nimnezzar might have sent an impostor to infiltrate the Yarasadi. We had to have proof that Shemyaza is who he claims to be. Yesterday, he unveiled himself in the dwelling of Qimir and the light of the angels filled our little settlement. I watched, here from my cave, with the sight of my inner eye. I noted quickly that you were different from your two companions. They are Grigori, but you are not, yet you have an important part to play in Shemyaza's destiny. The vision of the twins was sent to tell you that something lies hidden within you. Your seams, too, are ready to split."

Daniel frowned. "What does that mean exactly?"

Mani gestured with one hand. "I cannot tell you the answer. You must learn it for yourself. But I can guide you. Shemyaza does not yet have awareness of the true nature of his destiny, does he?"

Daniel shrugged. "Shem is opaque at the best of times, but I know that he still feels confused. The role of divine kingship has been thrust upon him and I think part of him resents it."

"As his vizier, he considers it your job to answer the questions in his heart."

Daniel nodded, with a sad smile. "That's true. I keep failing him."

Mani leaned forward and spoke more urgently. "Daniel of the Lion, can't you feel what is happening? A new epoch is dawning, bringing with it a higher spirituality for the races of the world. Your visions lead you to a specific goal. Surely you have begun to work out their message?"

Daniel shrugged, perplexed. "All I know is that Shem felt driven to come here and find Gadreel. Back in England, I received information in trance about some kind of hall of records, where the lost knowledge of the Grigori's ancestors is stored. I've also been told about a key to this place, a key in the sky. Shem feels the answer to whatever his destiny is lies in Old Eden, but as yet, I've been unable to discover exactly what it is he must do here."

Mani nodded as Daniel spoke. "You are on the right path. Gadreel too has had visions similar to yours. Perhaps it would help if you examined Kurdish beliefs, for they relate to Shemyaza's task. Time, or history, for the spiritual Kurd is divided into a number of epochs. When the last epoch has run its course, humankind will walk the sacred bridge into heaven. In each epoch, there are seven avatars of the divine creator incarnated upon the earth. We are now at the last epoch. What comes after will be as different to anything this world has experienced before as a little crawling caterpillar is different to a butterfly. The lost knowledge of the Grigori belongs to the world, but until now it has not been ready for it. Shemyaza and his companions are the seven avatars for this epoch. You, Daniel, are one of these avatars. You represent the Khidir, the Kurdish Green Man of the earth. He is a spirit of nature, of love, beauty and emotion. It is the task of the seven to fulfil the world's destiny, so it may pass to its next stage of evolution."

"But Shem does not have six companions," Daniel said.

"They will come to him," Mani said, and smiled. "He is here to gather his brethren around him in order to rebuild his kingdom. Your task is to show him the vision of what that kingdom will be."

Daniel gestured helplessly with wide arms. "I feel my sight is deserting me. How can I show him anything?"

Mani laughed. "You saw the holy twins in the valley. Think, Daniel. What else have you seen since you have been here among these people?"

Daniel glanced at him sharply. "Well, I had a dream. There was a strange being in it, who seemed like a Grigori, but was not."

"Describe this dream to me."

Daniel told everything that he could remember. "The being seemed older than time. The more I think about it the stronger I feel that he was Grigori, or at least connected with them, but unlike the Grigori, he had no human elements within him. I don't think he was of this earth."

Mani nodded. "What you have described is one of the Elder Gods. They came to this world straight from the source of all creation and initiated the beginnings of life. The Elders came before the Grigori, long before. They are no more, but the Anannage and then the Grigori were their legacy to the world."

"But what was the Elder trying to show me?"

Mani considered, then made an abrupt gesture. "He was offering you the key to the Chambers of Light."

"The Chambers of Light? The hall of records?"

"Yes, it where the knowledge of the Elder Gods is stored and hidden. Once you have the key, you will discover more about them. For now, you must concentrate on the significance of the seven, and of forming this brotherhood."

"You said that I was one of them," Daniel said. 'But I can't see how. I'm not Grigori like the others."

Mani grinned. "In your vision, the Elder was offering back to you all that you have lost."

Daniel raised his eyebrows. "My sight?"

Mani smiled. "No, far more than that, Daniel of the Lion. You will see." He gestured around him. "There is a purpose to your coming here, more than just to talk with me. This cave is a shrine to Khidir. Through this shrine, and Khidir's help, a person may enter the hidden worlds. What is to happen to you cannot take place in this world. You must leave it for a time."

Daniel couldn't repress a shudder. "That sounds like death."

Mani shrugged. "Perhaps it is. There are many forms of death and not all are final. Are you afraid?"

Daniel uttered a nervous laugh. "Only a fool would not be."

"True. Yet will you trust me?"

Daniel rested his chin in his hands. "I was drawn here and my instincts tell me you mean me no harm. Yes, I will trust you. I've been in darkness. Whatever light you can offer me, I must take."

Mani smiled. "Good. Now listen to me. To summon the Khidir, preparations have to be made for forty days and forty nights. I have made these preparations in readiness for this night. Come, we must gaze into the sacred pool."

They sat together beside the dark water that shone with points of light. It was like staring at a reflection of the night sky, but no sky that had ever looked down upon the earth. Its constellations were unknown to Daniel. Mani pulled out a small, blackened pottery bowl from a pocket in his robes, along with other implements for the ritual to come. He began to chant in a soft sing-song voice, and crumbled what looked like dried leaves into the bowl. To these, he added a few drops of an oily liquid from a small, stoppered bottle.

Mani's voice was soporific; the more Daniel listened, the more his eyes felt heavy. He needed sleep so badly. From outside came the distant rhythms and wails of the Yarasadi music; now it was plaintive and eerie, like an invocation.

Mani set light to the crumbled leaves and a thick, stinging smoke arose from the bowl. "Breathe deep, Daniel," he said.

Daniel leaned over the bowl and inhaled. His eyes began to water copiously as the thick, bitter smoke filled his nose, searing up inside his head. Whatever Mani burned within the bowl was extremely potent. After only a few moments, Daniel felt so dizzy he had to lie down beside the pool. Fighting nausea, he rested his head right on the edge of the rock, so that his hair trailed in the water.

"Be still," Mani murmured and reached out to sprinkle a powdery substance over Daniel's body. "The sleep that Khidir brings is a blessing. He will touch you with dreams." He leaned

forward and slowly stirred the glinting water with one hand, so
that a ring of ripples lapped towards Daniel's face.

Daniel could barely keep his eyes open. All he could see
of the pool was a shifting surface of sparkling stars.

Mani's voice seemed to come from very far away. "Sleep,
now. Sleep and dream."

The voice died away, absorbed by the music of the water.
Daniel was alone. His eyes were barely open now and, as he
blinked, it seemed the light in the cave became dimmer. The
stars upon the water went out, one by one. In the dark, he felt
his body stir, independently of his mind. He could not move
his arms, which seemed paralysed by his side, and his legs
were pressed firmly together in muscular spasm. His body
flopped and wriggled like a landed fish. He edged gradually
towards the pool, until he slid into it without causing a single
ripple and the water closed over his head.

Daniel swam, undulating his body. A fast current pulled
him along. Water was sucked into his lungs; he breathed it. A
low, humming sound filled his head. He swam for an eternity,
yet it seemed like a single instant. There was no light. Then,
it seemed as if the darkness was dissipating and a dim radiance appeared in the distance, ahead of him. Daniel swam
towards it. He could not feel his body; perhaps he was nothing more than a spark of consciousness. The light loomed
larger and brighter in his sight and he no longer had to swim;
the current dragged him onwards. He spiralled in the water,
turning over and over, dragged towards the underwater sun.
At its centre, a shadowed core pulsed in time to his heart-beat;
a solid shape within the light. As he drew closer, he could see
that it was an immense serpent, resting with raised head upon
its coils, surrounded by a greenish aura of light. Daniel thought
at first that it was a stone idol, but then he saw the creature
move, sway its gargantuan head from side to side. It seemed
unimaginably ancient, a prototype of all the serpent gods. It
radiated power, and Daniel could sense that not all of it was
benign. This was ancient wisdom, but it also had the capacity
for ultimate evil, or ultimate amorality. Daniel resisted being
drawn towards it, terrified his personality would be eclipsed
by it, swallowed whole. He tried to move his limbs, to fight

the strong current, but any movement on his part only seemed to increase the speed of his forward flight. He was afraid he would be dashed against the serpent's immense body and destroyed.

The current carried him relentlessly upwards now, towards the serpent's head. Daniel was filled with an instinctive fear so profound, it struck at the most primitive core of his mind. He felt like the first human who had ever beheld the ineffable countenance of a god. The eyes of the serpent spat sparks of viridian radiance. As Daniel grew closer, it uttered a roaring hiss and opened its mouth; a lightless maw so vast it could have swallowed five men in one gulp.

Unable to scream or save himself, Daniel was sucked into the serpent's jaws.

He was aware of falling downwards, incredibly fast, within what seemed to be a waterfall. Scalding hot and freezing cold liquid splashed around him, but did not arrest his flight. There was no light at all. He could have been tumbling through the void of the universe. Daniel closed his eyes, praying for the vision to end. It was too real, too terrifying. He dreaded the moment of impact.

Then, without warning, he was simply floating. For some moments, he lay perfectly still, eyes closed, hardly daring to breathe. He could hear the lap of water and sensed fresh air upon his face. When he opened his eyes, he found that he was floating, belly down, in a cool, refreshing pool. His vision seemed abnormal, as if he saw the world through eyes that were not his own. His body too felt unfamiliar; constricted yet fluid. He could not feel his arms and legs and could only move by wriggling his shoulders and spine; an action that produced swift movement and propelled him forwards across the surface of the water. He realised he was a water snake, no longer human at all.

Daniel swam to the nearest bank and slithered up it onto a flat lawn of short grass. He raised his upper body and surveyed the scene around him, tasting its scent with his flickering tongue. A waterfall plashed down into the pool, which lay at the base of a cliff, surrounded by a lush garden. Large, exotic flowers of every hue exuded a heavy, sensual perfume.

Wide-leafed ferns collared the trunks of immense primordial trees, whose bushy crowns rustled and swayed high above. The garden was filled with a dazzling, unearthly light, but his serpent eyes were not blinded by it.

One tree in particular drew Daniel's attention. It was hung with garlands of wild flowers and coloured ribbons. Daniel felt compelled to approach it. As he did so, a tall figure emerged from the foliage beside the tree. The figure shone with a blazing white light and stood gazing down at Daniel with eyes that emitted a piercing blue radiance. Daniel recognised him at once. It was Shemyaza, his hair cascading down over his breast. He wore a white robe that was slashed at the sides to the waist, revealing braids of ribs and muscle, and his feet were adorned in sandals of intricately-worked golden leather. "Daniel," he said. "Come home. Return to the source."

Daniel reared up before Shemyaza, yearning for the touch of his hand. But as he gazed up into his master's face, Shemyaza began to change. Behind him, as if somehow joined to his spine, an enormous tail of peacock feathers fanned out to frame his body. His face elongated and his body became thinner and taller. The tail feathers became a spectrum of light around him. For a few moments, he resembled a radiant feathered serpent, poised as if to strike, then he had transformed into the Elder who had appeared to Daniel in his dream the night before.

As before, the Elder did not speak, but the muscles of his mobile face flickered with expressions that conveyed communication. "It is time, my son, for you to shed your skin."

The Elder bent down and lifted Daniel in his hands. Daniel hung there, letting his ophidian body grow limp. He was not afraid now, but drowsy. His skin itched all over and he yearned to be rid of it. He gave his entire being, with trust, to the care of the Elder. The pain, when it came, seemed like the ultimate betrayal.

With one sharp fingernail, the Elder clawed into Daniel's serpent hide. Daniel felt himself split. His skin was not ready to shed at all. He was being torn apart. Helplessly, he wriggled in the Elder's grasp, his tail lashing the air. He uttered agonised hisses, yearning to scream, to make some human sound. This was the death that Mani had hinted at, and it was terrible. The Elder was skinning him, pulling his bleeding carcass from the black skin. It was pulled over his eyes and his sensitive tongue tasted the scent of blood and raw flesh. He would die now, flayed. The caress of the air was an agony against his exposed flesh.

Daniel found that even a serpent can weep tears.

Then he was falling.

He hit the grass with a thud that knocked the air from his lungs. He realised at once that he was once more in his own body. Rolling onto his back, he looked up and saw the Elder standing over him, an empty snake-skin dangling from his bloodied hands. Daniel ran his hands over his chest, and realised with relief that he still possessed a skin. He tingled all over, as if someone had rubbed him down with gravel. Already the stink of blood was being erased by the perfume of flowers.

The Elder dropped the skin onto the grass without even looking at it, and knelt on one knee beside Daniel, his alien face hanging like a mask before Daniel's eyes. He slid one giant hand behind Daniel's neck and raised him from the grass. Daniel wanted to turn away from the inhuman countenance, but was too weak to move. The Elder pulled him against his body and kissed him on the mouth. He did not speak, but his expressive face seemed to say, "You are whole, my son. Go forth from this place and meet with your brethren."

Daniel closed his eyes and rested against the Elder's chest, enfolded in his arms. He remembered then what it was like to be held. He had missed it so badly.

Then someone was calling his name, from a long way away. Daniel resisted this summons. He wanted to drowse where he was, but the voice kept on calling, growing louder and louder. It was intrusive; a harsh, human sound.

The light of the garden faded until Daniel was enveloped in blackness. He could not hold on to the vision. A hand was shaking him. "Daniel! Wake!"

He woke with a start, wholly alert, and sat up abruptly, uttering a cry of shock. Mani squatted beside him, his face full of concern and perhaps fear. Daniel realised he was back in the shrine of Khidir. The vision was over.

Seemingly satisfied that Daniel had completed the spiritual journey unharmed, Mani nodded and grinned at him. "I thought you would never wake. How do you feel now?" He held out what looked like a bowl of milk, although when Daniel tasted it, he realised it was spiced with liquor and cinnamon.

"Fine," Daniel answered. "I think." He smiled and handed the bowl back to Mani. "Whatever was in that smoke has some kick to it!"

"Not just the smoke, Daniel," Mani said, and looked around him, "but this place."

Daniel started to get to his feet and found he was lying on something that rustled beneath him. It was only then that he realised he was naked. Some vision! He wondered if Mani had taken away his clothes while he'd slept. "What is this?" Daniel asked, reaching down to touch the papery, slightly oily, material around him.

"Your skin," Mani replied.

Daniel uttered a horrified sound and jumped away from the spot. He felt sick.

"Isn't that what happened to you?" Mani asked in an even voice. "You shed your skin?"

Daniel shook his head in disbelief. "Yes, but...that was a vision."

Mani folded his arms and fixed Daniel with a steady eye. "Not just that. Look at yourself. Raise your hands."

Daniel did so and saw that his skin was shining with a weird light, similar to the way in which the Elder had seemed to shine. "What's happened to me?" He glanced at Mani. "It was more than a vision, wasn't it."

Mani nodded. "You have begun a change, a leap forward in your evolution. It will take a while to complete, but it is begun."

"What change?"

"You are Grigori once again, Daniel, as you were in the beginning, so long ago."

Daniel got to his feet and held out his arms before him. The light glowed through his skin. "This is impossible."

"Not at all," Mani said. "The Elders have granted you this gift. You have a place in the destiny of the world, and you need your Grigori form to fulfil it." He put his hands on his knees. "At one time, a sacred flame burned in this place, and its influence still prevails. You have walked through its memory and it has changed you."

"This is incredible' Daniel said, to himself more than to Mani. "A vision can't cause physical effects." He turned his hands before him in the air. His skin seemed almost translucent. He could see the delicate tracery of veins pulsing beneath it.

"You must not worry," Mani said. "From my visions, I have learned that this effect will not last. Go back to your people now. Your master awaits you. He has waited a long time."

Daniel stood up. "I can't go naked."

Mani laughed. "True! Although my adopted people have few taboos about such things. Still, I have a robe for you. Take it." He presented Daniel with a bundle of white cloth. "I will spare you the unpleasantness of sifting your old clothes from the sloughing."

Daniel pulled the robe over his head. His skin felt wet as if he'd actually bathed in the pool. He knew he would never know what Mani had done to him while he'd been unconscious or whether he had been physically responsible for what had happened to his body. Before he left the cave, he turned to Mani. "Thank you for all you have done for me. I'd like to ask you one thing."

Mani spread his hands before him. "Then ask."

"Where are the Chambers of Light? How do we find the key?"

Mani laughed. "You think I can tell you these things? I am flattered! I am sorry, Daniel, but that knowledge cannot be gained so easily. Also, it is Gadreel's place to lead you all to the next stage of your journey. I have played my part, small though it was."

Daniel reached out and clasped Mani's hands. "It was not small to me. Again, thank you."

Mani waved him away. "Go now, go! The feast awaits below and the music calls for your feet!"

Daniel walked down from the cave. He felt serene and tall, as if he could float above the ground. In this way, his ancestors had come down to the world of men and their bewitching women. He could almost feel a cloak of vulture feathers hanging heavily from his shoulders; the wings of an angel. He could smell the antique must of it, and felt the ghosts of scratchy pinions against his flesh.

He paused before entering the settlement, gazing upon the sparking central fire and the people who danced wildly around it. Their music had conjured him and he had answered their summons. His eyes searched the gathering, until he caught sight of Shem, who stood near the back of the circle of dancers, watching them with a contemplative expression on his face.

I am equal to you now, Daniel thought, *in some ways.*

He was absorbed into the spiralling complexity of the dance. The music became more frantic, the dancing more riotous. Skirts and scarves spun out, metallic threads catching the fire-light. It was almost as if the Yarasadi had been expecting Daniel to come, dressed in his angel robe, or else perhaps they thought he was someone else, a vision of one of their avatars invoked by the dance.

As he danced, Daniel was acutely aware of Shem's motionless presence nearby. Was he aware of what had happened to his vizier? For a brief moment, Daniel met Shemyaza's eyes. Shem nodded slightly, a secret smile upon his face. Then, the chain of dancers broke up and scattered into a whirling saltation of individual human motes, hiding Shem from Daniel's view. Daniel spread out his arms, and in the centre of the gathering, danced the dance of the vulture kings, led by the wail of the tambura, the charm of the zurna. Though most of the dancers around him could barely speak a word of English, Daniel felt a strong communion with them, beyond words. He was kin to them now, aware that within each of them, the secret of their heritage lay like a protected seed in winter darkness, awaiting the light and warmth of spring. They had waited so long.

He danced perhaps for hours, as the stars arced overhead, and the fire-smoke rose up in writhing coils. He did not tire.

Dimly, he was aware of people moving around him; talking, eating. Then he was dancing alone and the tribe were sitting around him in a circle. Women lolled against their men, fanning themselves with plucked leafy twigs. Their eyes were dark, yet bright with starlight. Eventually, Daniel fell into a swoon. There was silence now, but for the crackling of the dying fire. Between the eastern mountains, the first pale rays of dawn cast an ephemeral road of light down from heaven. Daniel lay on his back, breathing deeply. He saw Shemyaza standing over him, his hair catching the pale morning light. "Daniel, can you stand?"

Daniel barely had the energy to speak. He shook his head slowly from side to side.

Shem knelt down and lifted him in his arms. Daniel's head hung backwards; he saw faces upside-down that watched him as Shem carried him to their temporary home. Then, the entrance flaps to the tent were closed behind them and Shem laid him down on the musky furs. There was little light. Whatever had made Daniel's flesh shine had faded away. His feet and calves were aching severely.

"How did it happen?" Shem asked, then shook his head. "No, that is your business." He took Daniel's hands in his own. "This is the greatest gift to me. You know how I have mourned the fact you were born as a human in this life."

"Shem," Daniel murmured. "How do you know that I am Grigori now?"

Shem knelt beside him, his face almost invisible in the gloom. "I saw you walk down into the valley, Daniel, and your face was shining. Maybe only I saw it, but for a moment, I seemed to be looking at myself—not as I am now, but when I first went down to the lowlands and took Ishtahar as my lover. It shocked me, but it seemed so right."

"There is a sacred cave," Daniel said. "It happened there."

Shem stroked his hair. "I believed that you were shutting me out of your life, but perhaps I am as guilty as you of preferring isolation. Our path is hard, Daniel. We should not choose to walk it alone. You are my light."

Daniel held out his arms and pulled Shem into his embrace. Shem's voice was muffled against his neck. "When I saw you there, with a shining countenance, it seemed to me as if something shattered within my mind." He pulled away from Daniel's arms and looked into his eyes. "I understand my purpose now, and I understand what love really is."

They lay down together in the furs, and Salamiel, for the next few hours, elected to keep his distance from the tent.

Chapter Twelve
The Prophet's Tale

Later in the morning, Daniel woke up alone. He sensed excitement outside and rose from the goat-skins. His feet shrieked in pain, and he had to limp outside, although the rest of his body throbbed to a more languorous tide. Shem and he had been united in love once more. Shem had spoken of his doubts in the furry warmth of their bed and Daniel had been able to soothe him. "We will find the answers. Gadreel will come." He had also told Shem what Mani had revealed to him about the Elders and the Chambers of Light.

"The Elders were Anu's ancestors," Shem said thoughtfully. "I think we are beginning to touch upon knowledge that was forbidden even to the Anannage."

Now, as he walked between the towering stone chimneys, Daniel felt taller. The camp was a flurry of activity; people were shouting to one another; quick, eager voices. Daniel saw Shem and Salamiel standing with Qimir at the centre of the camp. They appeared to be waiting for something, or someone. Daniel hobbled over to them. Shem smiled warmly at him as he approached, but Daniel could sense his tension.

Salamiel uttered a cry of surprise when he saw Daniel. "I hate to say this, but whatever you two were doing last night has done wonders for your appearance! You look remarkably healthy, Daniel, and rather smug about it too."

Shem put his arm around Daniel's shoulders. "Flattering though it would be to think I'm responsible for the change, there's more to it than that."

"I'll tell you later," Daniel said. He did not want to discuss his experiences in Mani's cave in front of Qimir. "Do I take it the Yarasadi are expecting visitors?"

Shem nodded. "Qimir summoned me a short while ago. I didn't want to wake you. I thought you needed the sleep, but looking at you now, perhaps not."

"Is Gadreel coming now?"

"I haven't been told that in so many words, but I suspect that's who's on their way."

Daniel asked no further questions but, like everyone else, fixed his eyes on the steep pass down from the mountains. He expected a convoy of trucks, armoured vehicles of some kind.

They heard it first; a thunderous sound amplified by the towering cliffs. Then it was the dust thrown up from the rough road. Finally, a band of horseman came galloping crazily into the valley; the riders clad in black and red, the horses adorned with multi-coloured tassels and ribbons. At the sight of them, the whole camp uttered a joyous roar of welcome and surged into a knot of bodies. The horsemen urged their beasts right into the centre of the welcoming throng. Horses reared and screamed, exciting the animals corralled among the tents, who began cantering up and down, snorting and whickering. Dogs barked and goats ran in panic in all directions.

One horse leapt free of the crowd and its rider directed it to where Qimir stood. The animal stopped just in front of them, prancing and rearing. Its rider was clothed in the traditional costume, face covered.

Qimir bowed. "Gadreel, you are welcome."

For a few moments, the rider made no sound or sign of welcome, then jumped down from the horse, allowing it to skitter away. Its dragging reins were grabbed by one of the children, who had gathered expectantly to perform this duty for the Yarasadi peshmergas. Gadreel was tall, and the commanding stance spoke strongly to Daniel of Grigori blood.

"Gadreel," Qimir began in a careful voice. "This is Shemyaza, your *brother*." He made a sweeping gesture with his hands which included Shem in their orbit.

Shem inclined his head. "I have been waiting for this moment," he said.

The figure in front of them did not move, but stood with hands on hips, head thrown back. Only the eyes were visible, and even from a few yards away, Daniel could see their intense blue.

Shem seemed rather non-plused that Gadreel had not responded to his greeting. "Perhaps we could talk somewhere," he began.

The figure raised a single, admonitory hand as if to silence him.

"Gadreel," said Qimir. "You must not keep your brother in suspense like this. He has waited long to meet you...man to man." Here, Qimir uttered a delighted laugh.

Gadreel shifted from foot to foot, and then, with slow, deliberate movements, began to unwind the concealing face-scarf. Yards and yards of it, there seemed. Daniel could not help but be held in suspense, wondering what would be revealed.

Finally, Gadreel threw the scarf onto the floor and stared defiantly ahead.

"Great Anu!" Shem exclaimed.

Gadreel laughed coldly. "Yes, my brother. Great Anu."

"Shemyaza," Qimir said, still laughing. "There is no brother for you to meet, but I am delighted to introduce you to your sister."

Gadreel shook out her thick red hair. She was a stunningly beautiful woman, which perhaps indicated one of the reasons why she chose to hide her gender. For a moment, she still stood arrogantly before them, then took a few steps forward. "Do you not remember me, Shem?"

He nodded. "Yes. How could I not? I simply did not expect to find you female."

Gadreel laughed again. "I do hope you are not disappointed!"

He shook his head. "How could I be? But why the disguise?"

"It is easier for me if people believe me to be male. You have to remember we are in a part of the world where prejudice and injustice against women is high. Only the Kurds of the ancient beliefs think otherwise." She looked Shem up and down. "Well, you are as fine as I remember you, and Salamiel, you have hardly changed at all." Then she glanced at Daniel. "But who is this? I feel I should know you."

"It is Daniel," Shem said, "my vizier."

Gadreel narrowed her eyes and smiled. "Of course. You are different, Daniel, but then this is a changed world to the one where we once walked as friends."

Daniel had an inkling then that there was perhaps a history between Gadreel and himself, perhaps at a time in the distant past, when the young vizier had felt wounded by Shem's obsession with the human woman, Ishtahar. How would Gadreel react if she knew that until the previous night Daniel had been as human as Ishtahar? He did not have clear memories of the past as Shem and his companions did. He felt it best not to say anything, in case he betrayed himself, and merely inclined his head and smiled.

Gadreel walked past him, touching his shoulder briefly as she did so. She gestured at Qimir. "Is there no welcome feast? I have a hunger like the sky, and a thirst of the desert."

Qimir embraced her warmly. "We shall retire to my dwelling, where you may refresh yourself and speak with your brethren."

The rest of Gadreel's followers had dismounted and were now being dragged off by their families and lovers to separate homesteads. Shem exchanged a glance with Daniel and Salamiel, then the three of them followed Gadreel to Qimir's dwelling.

Qimir left Gadreel alone with his visitors for a while, perhaps sensing Shemyaza wanted to speak in private, although Daniel was sure that listening ears were concealed within the labyrinthine chambers of the tent.

Gadreel sat down on the floor cushions in a careless, less than demure sprawl. She scratched at her hair and stretched her limbs with a groan; a woman who oozed power and confidence. She seemed insouciant about meeting Shem, but Daniel sensed she was not quite as relaxed as she appeared. "I feel we should make small talk," she said, "catch up on old times, but the truth is I have much to tell you. When I have spoken, we can take wine together, but first I must tell you my story. I have waited long for this moment."

Shemyaza nodded. "I understand. But first I must ask you one thing. Do Qimir's people know what you are?"

Gadreel smiled, resting back on her elbows, her long legs crossed at the ankles. "Oh yes. The Yarasadi are quite aware of the Grigori. I, and Qimir's vizier, Mani, have made sure of it! When we first received news that you were looking for me, Qimir would not believe you were the original Shemyaza, but Mani and I both thought you would be of my blood. I cannot believe you came looking for me. I always knew we would be reunited one day, but I thought I would have to search long and hard to find you, perhaps even wake you from a tomb."

Shem shifted uncomfortably on his cushions. "I am glad that was not necessary! Where do the Grigori live around here? Is there a settlement?"

Gadreel shook her head. "No, not locally. As far as I know, our people have avoided settling in this area since the great wars after the Deluge. I was born in Egypt, into the Re-akim, the Grigori clan that lives in Cairo. My name then was Sofiriel. A few years ago, I underwent a strange...*change*. I had dreams, which seemed like memories, of the time of The Fall." She grimaced. "I remembered another life, being male. In my dreams, people called me Gadreel. Also, my life became haunted by portents and omens. It was as if the universe were trying to tell me something, but I did not know what it was. I told no-one, neither family nor friends, about what was troubling me, for in some way, the experiences made me feel unwholesome. But gradually, I accepted the knowledge that in some way, I *was* Gadreel, reborn into this time."

"So what urged you to take on the role of a prophet?" Shem asked. "To essentially create the Yarasadi?"

Gadreel wrinkled her perfect, straight nose. "It is hard to explain. I knew I had a purpose, and once I assumed the name Gadreel, my dreams changed. I saw visions of the Elders, when they lived upon this earth, in Egypt. I knew that other brethren of mine would also be born into this time, and the approaching epoch was important. The Elders implied to me that the time was approaching when the Chambers of Light could be opened again, and all that was lost through our Fall could be regained."

"Mani mentioned those to me," Daniel said. "Some kind of hall of records. I also had a vision about the Elders. One of them attempted to hand me a key." He related the vision to Gadreel, who listened intently.

When Daniel had finished his story, Gadreel smiled wistfully. "Perhaps, in whatever region of space or time the Elders exist, they think this world has suffered enough, or that humanity and Grigori alike are now ready to receive their knowledge." She shrugged. "Anyway, one day I left my home and let my instincts guide me. I had many strange adventures, but eventually found my way to the homeland, Eden in the mountains. Perhaps I was searching instinctively for Kharsag. I met a group of Yezidi, and while in their camp, had another dream of the Elders. I wasn't conscious of receiving information in the dream, but when I awoke, I just knew that the tribes-people were Grigori hybrid descendants. They had been scattered, perhaps during the Deluge, and the knowledge of their ancestry expunged from their minds. The Kurds have been persecuted throughout the centuries, perhaps because of their heritage. They are the results of the experiments in Eden, Shem, *successful* results."

Shem frowned. "I find that hard to believe. We were sorely punished for interbreeding with humanity."

Gadreel nodded. "We were. That is the injustice of it. What we did was illegal under Anu's law, but his own loyal Watchers were involved in clandestine breeding experiments with select individuals from the tribes of the lower plains. It was all done under controlled conditions, and I think that few people, other than the higher echelons, knew about it."

Shem smiled bitterly. "Perhaps we should have guessed. Our race is famed for its cabals within cabals. It is typical that we were made scapegoats for a crime that Anu was committing himself."

Gadreel smiled ruefully. "Obviously, over the epochs, the original Kurds have interbred with other races, which has diluted the blood, but certain individuals in the tribes carry the genes of these ancient ancestors. I knew it was important to re-establish these people as a nation, and the best way to do that seemed through religion. The indigenous belief systems have never faltered from the worship of the angels, and because, deep inside, these people *know* what they are, it wasn't that difficult to reawaken the awareness and knowledge within them."

Salamiel was staring at her, as if entranced. "And what is your aim now? To send your reawakened armies out into the world and fight a holy war?"

Gadreel shook her head. "No, that would be doomed to failure as all other attempts have failed. My task is simply to make sure that all the Yarasadi are aware of what they are, and that they have a special place in the future of the world." She raised a closed fist before her face. "They must take their ordained place amongst humanity. They are the leaders, the guides. For too long, they have suffered persecution, and have sought aid from other governments, but that is not the way for them. We must gain access to the Chambers, for I believe that once they are open, all the senseless bloodshed will cease. The eyes of the world will be opened to the truth."

"A miracle," said Salamiel, dryly.

"Yes," Gadreel agreed. "Something of that type." She fixed Shem with steady eyes. "There are four of us now. We must find the others."

"How many?" Salamiel asked.

"Our company should number seven," Gadreel answered. "Of this I am sure. It is the sacred number of the Yarasadi, and also of the Watchers. Once we have formed this cabal, we shall be able to gain entrance to the Chambers."

"But first we need to know where they are," Daniel pointed out.

"Don't you know?" Gadreel asked Shem.

He shook his head. "No. I haven't thought about it yet, but I imagine they must be somewhere near or in Kharsag."

"We need to find the key first," Daniel said.

Gadreel frowned. "I had hoped you would already be in possession of such an artefact."

Shem tapped his lips thoughtfully with steepled fingertips. "Perhaps this is where your knowledge of this area will help, Gadreel. Daniel has received information that the key will be found in a Cave of Treasures."

Gadreel thought about this for a moment. "There is a place known as the Cave of Treasures in these mountains. I have heard of it, although never visited it. It is a secret and holy shrine, to where adepts of the Yezidi have made pilgrimages for centuries. Qimir should be able to offer more guidance." She paused, then said, "Perhaps the entrance to the Chambers will also be found at the cave."

"That's possible," Shem agreed. "But what do we do first? Wait for or find our remaining three cabal members, or go looking for the cave?" He turned to Daniel. "Can you work on finding these other Grigori?"

Daniel nodded. He felt more confident about his abilities now. "I'll try." He shrugged. "It seems likely that your brothers—and perhaps sisters—are already looking for you."

"We shall speak with Qimir and search for the cave," Gadreel said. "Why waste time? Once the others find us, we should be ready for them."

Chapter Thirteen
Advice of the Seeress

Babylon

The king of Babylon stood before the great cedar wood table in the sunny cavern he called a study. He was sifting through a pile of photographs, laid out before him. Tiy, the seeress, sat nearby, upright on a chair, her fingers gripping its arms. Nimnezzar had never seen her relax; she always seemed to be straining forward against life.

Every day, the king's daughter, Sarpanita, had been led into the presence of Penemue. The Watcher lord would not speak to her, but stared at her without blinking, as if she was an exotic animal, tamed and purring before him. He seemed content to gaze upon the princess. In turn, Sarpanita always sat before him with eyes modestly downcast, a faint blush upon her face. Nimnezzar suspected the two were somehow communicating, but when he asked his daughter if this was so, she only shook her head.

"He gazes upon her for long hours at a time," the king had confided to his wife in the privacy of her bed-chamber. "What is going through his head? What has Tiy said to you?"

The queen had stroked his chest, resting her head upon her hand. Her shining hair had spilled down upon him like the coils of a lamia. "Sarpanita has said nothing to us. Perhaps she likes to sit there with his eyes upon her. For now, it seems that nothing else of his will touch her." She had laughed.

The king, annoyed that she made light of such a matter, had begun to wonder whether a conspiracy of women was involved in this scheme of silence.

He had summoned Tiy to his study, intent on prising the truth from her, but what seemed feasible as an idea now seemed unlikely in Tiy's presence. Not for the first time, Nimnezzar thought about how Tiy told him only so much as she wanted him to know. Jazirah, his vizier, disapproved of the apparent power that Tiy wielded at court, and often hinted that the king should not be so lenient with either the seeress or the queen. Nimnezzar sometimes hated and distrusted Tiy, but deep within, he respected her age and her female strength. When she deigned to help him unreservedly, her assistance was worth more than the might of all his Magians. Amytis too, for all her slippery guile, he admired. He knew that her loyalty to him was unassailable, despite its selfish motives. Jazirah would not understand or agree with these sentiments, therefore the king kept silent about them. Jazirah had worked for Nimnezzar for many years, yet was still unaware of the regular private meetings the king had with Tiy, and how he sometimes acted upon her advice even when it contradicted the vizier's suggestions.

"Tell me how my daughter progresses," Nimnezzar said casually, arranging a set of photographs in front of him. They were all images of the buried city.

The old woman remained rigid, her white eyes blinking. "She is shown to the angel lord at dawn and dusk."

"This I know. Have they yet communicated?"

Tiy shook her head. "He cannot speak."

Nimnezzar sighed. Even though he was not looking at the old woman, he sensed a smugness in her words. He was impatient with the manner in which women seemed to enjoy keeping secrets from men. He turned to look at her, but her head was directed away from him, as if her sightless eyes watched things he could not see in the corners of the room. "I was not referring to speech," he said, "but a more subtle contact. I think you are aware of what I mean. Tell me now; what transpires between my daughter and the angel?"

Tiy turned her head towards him, and he glanced away from her. The sight of those milk-pearl eyes always made him uneasy, as if, lacking the power to see the physical world, they could spy all too well into the human heart. "My Lord, I speak to the girl morn and night. Whatever occurs between her and the angel lord, she cannot speak of it clearly. This is not wayward behaviour on her part, but simply a human inability to articulate matters beyond her understanding. Sarpanita is a sensitive child, and neither I, nor anyone else, will profit from bullying her to give more information."

"Do they commune through thought?"

Tiy got to her feet and glided across the room in the unerring and nimble manner that always made Nimnezzar shudder. "More than that, I feel. Their language is that of dreams and memories. Sometimes, when I question her, she murmurs the name "Shemyaza". I believe Penemue fills her mind with images of his brother."

Nimnezzar forced himself not to take a step away from the old woman, even though the musty incense smell of her voluminous robes filled his nostrils. "This Shemyaza," said the king, tapping the photographs thoughtfully with his fingers. "In a way, he is Sarpanita's spiritual father." He did not expand further, confident that Amytis would have provided her aged mentor with every detail of her relationship with her husband.

Tiy nodded. "Yes. It can be seen that way."

Nimnezzar knew Tiy was waiting for him to say something; the words that would act as a key to the lock upon her tongue. He had played this game in the past. "I am building Shemyaza's city for him," he murmured, more to himself than to the woman. "Should I call him to me?"

"In ages past, the Watchers offered their divine seed to enrich the blood of the royal lines," Tiy said, nodding. "Penemue, in his prime, would have been a great and powerful being. I have no doubt that should he once again unite with his brother-king, his faculties would be restored. And if Shemyaza has manifested in the world..." She shook her head. "Great king, you need him. It is unthinkable that the empire of Babylonia could once again thrive without him!"

Nimnezzar forced himself to stare into her face. He could detect no guile in her expression, and yet..."There is something we have not yet considered. My Magian priests have reminded me recently that in the form of the Peacock Angel, Shemyaza is worshipped as a god by the wretched Yarasads! Is it possible their adepts are as aware of

Shemyaza's manifestation as we are? If so, with whom will he ally: those who have worshipped him for millennia or Babylon, who seeks to recreate the sacred empire of the past?"

Again, Tiy nodded. "Babylon has stamped upon the worshippers of the Peacock Angel. This could be a dilemma indeed!" She grinned, displaying unnervingly strong teeth. "However, all is not lost. Whatever Shemyaza's feelings on the matter, I am sure that Babylon can bring him to her breast."

"Speak," said the king.

Tiy sighed patiently. "Since I came to your court, I have pondered long upon how best you may realise your ambitions. I made many journeys into the realm of spirit seeking knowledge. I learned that until Shemyaza has reclaimed the wisdom of his ancient ancestors, he will be virtually powerless in this world. Now is the time to secure him, before his strength waxes."

Nimnezzar looked sceptical. "He is the king of the fallen ones. Surely, his power will be great?"

Tiy raised a finger. "Think of Penemue and his condition. Shemyaza too has yet to regain his full powers. You need him, Great King, because he has the power to rule the world. You need that from him. Therefore, Shemyaza must be brought to Babylon very soon, before he attains his strength."

"Where is he?" Nimnezzar asked. He had no doubt by now that Tiy knew the answer.

"I believe Shemyaza is searching for an ancient artefact of his people—an artefact that you too could use. You will find him in the old land."

Nimnezzar uttered an angry snort. "With the Yarasadi!" He punched the table-top with his fists.

"Yes, he will go to them. Their prophet will have drawn him. Remember the name: Gadreel too was one of the fallen ones."

Nimnezzar now paced around the table. "If Shemyaza is with the Yarasadi, it will be difficult to find or capture him. The Yarasadi are lords of their terrain. I'm unsure my men can best them in their own territory. There are too many secret places in the mountains where they can hide. I have no desire to waste my troops."

Tiy followed him and laid a hand upon his arm. "My sight can guide you into the secret places. All you will need is a force of warrior-priests, a small one."

The king glanced at her askance. Led by a blind woman into hostile territories: was this the action of a hero or a fool? "You know exactly where?"

Tiy smiled. "Oh, great king, do not doubt what my eyes can see! In dreams, I have beheld a Cave of Treasures, where the artefact Shemyaza seeks has lain for millennia. Your Magians could never discover it, but Shemyaza will. All that is required of you is faith and trust. Remember, it is the way of human men to scorn the power of women, but do you not claim the blood of angels runs in your veins? Honour and revere the power of the female, Nimnezzar, if you would re-claim your heritage and become a god-king!"

Sarpanita sat before the cage, deep below Etemenanki, ab-sorbing the dream-images that Penemue sent to her. Incense smouldered, filling the air with smoke that smelled sweet, but which burned her throat. Sarpanita stared at her hands, which were folded in her lap. She could not look at the angel while he sent her the pictures, for his face was a distraction and her mind became filled with it.

Over the days, she had learned much about the history of the Arallu. Penemue had not been able to witness the con-struction of their underground city firsthand, for by the time the first excavations were made, he'd been incarcerated be-neath rocks in his life-tomb, but as he'd lain there, suffering beneath the weight of the stones, his mind had flown out of his body, and had witnessed much of what had happened. He'd seen the dour Arallu lords stalk the bare corridors, heard the screams of captive women, and had smelled the bloody in-cense the Arallu used in their rites. He had sensed their fear of Anu and his faithful Watchers. He had heard the stories of those who had been discovered by these loyal forces and how they had been murdered, their new cities destroyed so thor-oughly that not even a memory of them would remain.

The Arallu had found Penemue by accident, as their hu-man workers burrowed deep into the earth. His sarcophagus had been uncovered, in the place where Anu's engineers had buried it. No-one was supposed to discover it, but they had.

At first, the discovery had caused argument. Some had wanted to open the sarcophagus, while others, thinking that Penemue, if he survived, would take control of their city, had advised against it. Quickly, they had learned that their priests could communicate with the captive, and that he could be questioned like an oracle. They had been puzzled that he made no demands for release.

Even now Penemue was distressed that he had been disturbed.

Had he been asleep all these centuries? Sarpanita wondered.

No, not asleep. Dead more than alive, but eventually the heaviness of the rocks and the eternal darkness lost their power to hurt his mind and body. He had felt weightless, insubstantial. His body had become merely a numb vessel to which his mind could return and rest, whenever astral travel became too tiring.

On the rare occasions when Penemue pined for activities of the flesh, he had found that he could inhabit a living body. Sometimes, under ritual conditions, the Arallu would provide an unwilling host for him, seized from their human work-force. Otherwise, Penemue would steal a body, slipping into its owner's mind without them even realising it. Through these vehicles of flesh, he could experience the pleasures of food and wine, of lovers' bodies, even experience the act of killing. He could ride into battle without ever fearing death or injury, for his mind could quit the host body whenever he willed it so. Sometimes, gripped by a strange anger, he had driven his unwitting hosts to suicide. Or else, to experience the farthest reaches of emotion, he had killed the loved ones of the human vessel he inhabited.

Sarpanita could not judge the Watcher for these acts. His mind, she knew, worked in a way very different to her own. It was not that he did not perceive a difference between good and evil, but that he didn't see what she termed 'evil' as bad, or thought what she knew as 'good' was somehow worthy and desirable. Acts had consequences, as did thoughts. The tapestry woven from the different strands of consequence was valid, and if some of the threads required for its construction caused pain to others, it was simply a necessary part of the whole.

He asked her a question in the form of a feeling that invaded her heart, "Why have they woken me?"

"Because you were there," she answered in her mind. "And you are what my father desires to be. He wants to rule like a god over his angels."

She sensed the Watcher's amusement. "He wants me to be like the Arallu were in the past and breed a line of little kings for him, with you."

"Yes," she answered and he observed the distress in her heart without sending any reciprocal thought or feeling. She felt as if he'd touched her feelings somehow, held them and looked at them, and then put them down again, for they did not hold his interest for long.

"It is a circle," Penemue told her. "I was incarcerated for tasting and honouring a human woman, and now I am exhumed for the same purpose." His humour was bleak. Perhaps he would not be able to perform in the way Nimnezzar wanted.

"Now I am here in the air, it is difficult for my mind to roam," Penemue said. "I once saw a dim spark that was a tiny flame. All that was left of my brother and master, Shemyaza. I do not believe that he is dead."

"He will come here looking for you," Sarpanita said, to please him. "I dreamed of it."

"Shemyaza was love, but it was terrible," said the angel.

And Sarpanita shuddered to think what kind of monster made the amoral Penemue think that way. "How can love be terrible, lord?" she asked.

The angel's sigh was a dark breeze through her mind. "Shemyaza loved a human maid, a young woman like you. Their union was that of spirit and the earth. But it was forbidden, and they were discovered. Shemyaza lost his heaven for it. At first, he was a willing sacrifice and became the scapegoat, cast out into the desert, to atone for the sins of his brethren who had also taken human lovers. I was one of them. I saw his fall and turned away to eat the festival meat. In the

desert, Shemyaza learned bitterness and hatred. He felt we
had betrayed and abandoned him, that his sacrifice meant nothing. Eventually, he raised an army of half-breed Nephilim,
terrible warriors, and filled with their father's rage they ravaged the sacred ground of Eden. Many died, and our Father
released the Deluge to cleanse the earth. Shemyaza was captured, his earthly body burned alive, while his soul was cast
into the constellation to Orion, where it was sentenced to hang
for eternity. Perhaps eternity is over, for now Shemyaza is free
in the world."

Sarpanita listened to this story with rising dread. She was
becoming part of this terrifying history. It was leaking into reality.

In the afternoon, while the palace shimmered like a mirage,
aching and white in the sun, a foreign woman came to the
court of the king.

A soft-footed courtier approached Nimnezzar in his cool,
cavernous study, and here whispered of a fair-skinned Western woman, who had travelled long, perilous roads in a truck,
with only an idiot Turkish boy for protection. The woman
wished to see him.

Nimnezzar raised his eyes from his work, and wondered
for a moment what manner of female, Western or otherwise,
could burrow her way through the morass of officials, protocol and obstructions that were set like a maze around his inner
sanctum. He frowned. "Why are you bothering me with this?
Who is this woman and what is her business?" He looked
around for his vizier, Jazirah; the shadow who normally eclipsed
all intruding lights from his presence. He felt strangely vulnerable being accosted in this way, no matter how fearful the
servant might be.

The official bowed low. "Great King, she claims she is
looking for a Watcher lord and that she has information you
will find useful. She insists on speaking to you."

Nimnezzar had wooed the lands of the west; perhaps this
woman knew she would not be dismissed out of hand. "Who
does she represent?"

The official shrugged. "She has indicated she represents
no-one but herself, great king."

"Indicated?"

"She will speak to no-one but you, great king. She is fearless and tenacious."

For a moment, Nimnezzar felt annoyed by the woman's audacity. Perhaps he should order a group of his personal guard to molest and humiliate her for this effrontery. She claimed no connection to a government or official agency. He was mindful of causing diplomatic upset, but at the same time resented the way this unknown female felt she had the right to march up to his palace and demand audience. However, it was possible she really did have information.

"Find Jazirah and ask him to question the woman," Nimnezzar said, and dismissed the official from his attention, carefully lifting a sheaf of papers before his nose. His minion backed, bowing, from his presence.

Melandra Maynard felt as if she had invaded the court of hell. Here she was, through wits and impudence alone, sitting in an ante-chamber to the court of one of the devil's followers. She could not believe she had achieved her objective. Her hands were steady on her shoulder bag, which perched upon her knees. The guards had divested it of its secret—the weapon—but did not appear to find it unusual that a woman would carry a gun of its type. She had surrendered it without argument. This was a cross-roads.

In Istanbul, she had discovered it was possible to hire guides to take her anywhere in the dangerous east. People there lived with the troubles; they knew how to negotiate them. So, accompanied by a Turkish guide, she had made her way to Babylon. The journey had not been uneventful, and sometimes they had had to buy their way out of trouble, first with the Turks and then the Babylonians, but by degrees, they had made progress. Now, Melandra was in Babylon, in the palace of the king. She was quietly surprised that she had achieved her objective. It seemed to her now that the journey had been almost too easy.

Of course, Americans were welcome in Babylon. Since the country was no longer Islamic, the West had lost no time in befriending the Babylonian government. In time-honoured tradition, the West chose to overlook the atrocities committed in Babylon's name, in order to profit from the commerce of oil and arms. To them, Nimnezzar seemed tractable and co-operative in comparison with other Middle Eastern rulers. Babylonians on the street might glance askance at a Westerner, but officials couldn't be more helpful.

Melandra had been stricken by the signs of prosperity she'd encountered in the country: copies of ancient monuments littered the stark countryside; new towns reared their columns and minarets towards the sky. Conflict in the north did not sully the tranquillity of life further south. It might not exist. In Babylon itself, the streets were wide and clean. The ugly old buildings of late twentieth century architecture were being replaced everywhere by elegant constructions of marble, granite and basalt. Traffic was restricted in the city centre, but there was an efficient, modern public transport system that looked like something out of an SF movie. Even the people were part of this expressionism; their clothes were neither Western-style nor traditional Eastern, but a newly-conceived meld of both, fashioned from soft, elegant fabrics. Babylon was like a fantasy artist's impression of an exotic alien culture that had developed sophisticated futuristic technology. The ancient and the ultramodern blended together to create an aesthetically-stunning whole. Only Melandra knew that this was the work of the devil. Its beauty was furled around a maggoted heart.

Melandra found that the word Grigori acted like a cantrip— it opened doors and minds. Her guide, staunch at her side for the promise of American dollars, had led her to the right offices, speaking the words that allowed her access to the next platform of the game. The magic charm of the Grigori had broken every barrier until it had led her unharmed into the lair of the monster himself. At the last gateway, her guide had been taken from her. She wondered whether Shemyaza was already here in the city.

Melandra sat for over an hour, thirsty and hungry in the cool, dark room. The journey from the walls to the heart of the palace complex had taken over a day, and she had neither eaten nor rested during this time. Now, she felt light-headed and reality seemed a plastic, unreliable thing.

Fighting dizziness, she eyed with longing the pool in the garden visible beyond the windows. Soon, she might find she had wandered out there involuntarily and was scooping aside the lilies to drink the water like an animal, lapping with dry tongue. Melandra did not want this to happen. She must remain in control and aloof. The first thing she would do the next time she saw someone—anyone—would be to ask for a drink. They would grant her that, surely, in this court of Pandemonium whose demons aped civility and manners?

When the tall man came to her, she jumped in alarm, for she had not heard him approach. He was handsome and sinister, clad in embroidered silk robes, like a prince from the Arabian Nights. He looked at her with cold eyes, his lips smiling slyly, then bowed his head. "Madam, I am Jazirah, vizier to the great king, Nimnezzar. What is your business here?"

Melandra put her bag onto the floor, feeling too ordinarily female with it clutched to her lap. She clasped her hands loosely on her thighs. "My name is Melandra Maynard. I am American. I believe, sir, that your great king and I have certain interests in common."

Jazirah laughed soundlessly, throwing back his head so that his jaw dropped open. Then he shut his mouth with a soft snap; a reptile capturing insects. "My dear lady, I am quite sure that many people would like to have interests in common with our great king, but that alone does not have them clamouring at our door demanding an audience. Your sheer impertinence and determination has aroused our curiosity. I hope the reason for your being here is a good one."

"Shemyaza," said Melandra. "I met with him in Istanbul. Is he here yet?"

Jazirah did not flinch, although Melandra felt sure an invisible shudder had passed through his body. For the fleetest of moments, his pupils might have widened a fraction. "Who is this Shemyaza?"

The question had given her power. It was not a good question, and revealed more than Jazirah intended: his uncertainty, perhaps even fear. "He is one of the Grigori, from whom your king claims descent. I am surprised you have not heard the name before." She risked a small, if polite, smile. "*Is* he here?"

Jazirah shook his head and smiled indulgently. "No."

"He is on his way here. I know this."

Jazirah raised his brows, but made no comment to her revelation. "What business have you with such a...person?"

"I represent a body of men in the West who are eager to meet Shemyaza. He is a difficult person to locate and once he has arrived here, might prove difficult to negotiate with. Babylon and my organisation can be of help to one another."

"We do not need your help," Jazirah said. "Whatever plans our great king has, he is quite capable of realising them by himself."

"Of this I am sure," Melandra said carefully. "However, no-one upon this earth but your people and mine are aware of the fallen race—the Grigori, who walk among us. This is a shared secret. My people have watched the Grigori, in every land, for a long time. King Nimnezzar might be interested in our intelligence."

Jazirah stroked his chin, his eyes never leaving the gaze of Melandra. She could tell she had surprised him, and thought that perhaps the Babylonians, for all their worship of the fallen ones, were not aware just how great was their influence or how far their numbers extended.

"What exactly do you want from us?" Jazirah asked her.

Melandra lowered her eyes. "Something happened to me in Istanbul," she said. "Shemyaza touched my soul. I am drawn to follow him, and where else will he want to be, but here with his people. I come here as Shemyaza's hand-maiden, and as the servant of his king on earth."

Jazirah regarded her with scepticism. "And what of your masters? Are they all this Shemyaza's followers?"

Melandra nodded. "Yes."

"And they send you to us; a woman alone in a dangerous country. It is strange. Why has there been no official communication concerning this matter?"

"I am chosen," Melandra answered simply.

Jazirah exhaled through his nose. "We shall see," he said.

At least it seemed she was to be given some hospitality. Jazirah summoned servants, who escorted Melandra to a salon nearby—a woman's room of drapes and tinkling chimes.

Here sweet cakes were brought to her, as well as a selection of nuts, a salad and fruit tea for refreshment. These foods were like nectar to her eager mouth, their flavours delicate and somehow antique. But for the telephone extension on a nearby filigreed table and the electric lights, she could believe she had somehow been transported back to ancient Babylon.

A young girl, dressed in flowing green veils, stood silently beside the door. Melandra felt drawn to communicate with her in some way, if only by a smile, but her instincts warned she should not. It was important that the Babylonians realised her words were for the king and his courtiers alone.

A thought intruded stealthily into her mind. But what if they should find me out? She dismissed it firmly. It was vital that she ban from her heart all thoughts of death and bitterness. She must act her role.

After she had eaten, Melandra lay down on the cushions that smelled of incense, and dozed for a while. She was exhausted. Warm breezes came in through the swaying diaphanous drapes at the window and fanned her softly. She was awoken later by a contained commotion at the door.

Rising, she saw an old woman come into the room. Her eyes were milky-white; blind. She wore layers of diaphanous robes of different shades of grey. Around her neck: a golden necklace fashioned like a serpent biting its tail. Her carriage was erect, her step firm. Perhaps she was the mother of the king.

The old woman put her head on one side as if in appraisal. Melandra found this unnerving. She could not help feeling that the woman could see inside her perfectly well. The woman inhaled, seeming to draw in the scent of Melandra. She nodded and smiled, extending gnarled yet elegant hands. "Welcome, my child."

Melandra was unnerved by this familiar address. She composed herself on the cushions, straight-backed. "When shall I see the king?"

The old woman glided towards her, the blind eyes staring out above Melandra's head. "That I cannot say. I would like you to tell me what you can about the one they call Shemyaza. You know him, don't you?"

Melandra shook her head. "I can speak only to the king."

The old woman sighed. "Ah, my child, there are some things you most certainly must not tell the king, but you can unburden yourself to me. I am Tiy, the king's seeress."

Melandra went cold inside. A witch! Perhaps this hag already knew Melandra's purpose. "There is nothing to tell," she said, "that I cannot tell the king."

Tiy smiled. "Not even that you surrendered your maidenhood to the fallen one?"

Despite herself, Melandra felt her face redden. She turned away from the old woman, even though she could not possibly witness the blush. "How do you know that?"

"I can smell it on you—his spirit, his fire." Tiy sat down. "You can speak to me, Melandra Maynard, for I understand your purpose. You are here to kill Shemyaza."

Melandra uttered a surprised cry. "No!"

Tiy raised a hand, shrugged. "It is of no consequence to me. I would hear your story. Tell it to me."

Melandra was aware of a strong sense of support and empathy emanating from the old woman, but wasn't this simply the sorcery of a witch? She must surely resist it. "I can't."

Tiy reached out and touched Melandra's hand. "But you can, my child. You can. You think me a witch, yet learn one universal truth. We women, all of us are witches. Every one. No matter what we call ourselves."

Melandra rubbed her forehead with one hand. "I don't know…"

Tiy pushed her back into the cushions with one firm hand. Melandra could not fight it, and felt as if it took an eternity for her body to hit the embroidered silk. Perhaps she fell a thousand times. A headache was beginning behind her eyes. She could smell burning. "So long ago…" she began in a small, slurred voice. "It started before I was born…"

Tiy sat beside her, idly caressing Melandra's hair as she talked. Her heart beat strong within her. She too could smell the fire.

Chapter Fourteen
The Cave of Treasures

The Mountains of Babylonia

Qimir knew of the Cave of Treasures, although he had not visited it in person. "Its location is known to the adepts of my people, and some have travelled there to connect with the spirit of our ancestors. But the journey is long and arduous."

"How far?" Shem asked.

Qimir shrugged. "Days, at least. You must head southeast. Most of the journey is impassable for trucks, so you will have to travel on horseback."

It was decided that they would take an escort of half a dozen Yarasadi, for the route was sometimes hazardous, and rival Kurdish factions prowled the shadowed passes, as well as agents of Babylon. Qimir summoned an old woman of the tribe, Tahira, to his dwelling, explaining to his guests that she had visited the cave fifteen years previously and would make an excellent guide.

Tahira was tall and unbent by age, although her advanced years showed in the weathering of her face. Long, grey hair, that looked as strong as steel wire, coiled down over her shoulders. She wore heavy jewellery of malachite-inlaid silver at her throat and wrists, and around her spare shoulders hung a large, fringed shawl of red and yellow silk. She listened without expression as Qimir explained what he required of her. Once he'd finished speaking she spent several minutes arguing with him in Kurmanji. It was clear she did not welcome the suggestion of acting as Shemyaza's guide.

Gadreel translated her words quietly for the others. "She says she's too old to risk such a journey. And she's demanding to know why we want to go there. She says there's nothing left there but bones."

While Gadreel was whispering, Tahira turned to her and uttered a question in accurate English. "Why are you making this journey? Do you seek guidance from heaven and will visit the Cave to find it?"

Gadreel shook her head. "Not exactly. We are looking for an artefact."

"No artefacts there!" Tahira snapped, waving her hands. "Many bones, old memories, but no artefacts. Barren place, home of the vulture spirits."

Gadreel smiled patiently. "Perhaps the artefact we're looking for doesn't look like much. It could be a stone or even one of the bones. We don't know yet what it is. It *is* very important, Tahira. The future of our people might depend on us finding this thing."

Tahira considered for a moment, then shrugged. "I did not want to be called upon this late in life, but if the journey must be made again, then so be it. But finding artefacts—that is up to you."

"Thank you," Gadreel said, in obvious relief. "We could not do this without your help."

Tahira asked Qimir if she might take her grandson, Jalal, with her, for she claimed the boy had a sensible head on his shoulders and she'd feel safer with him there. "And you know, Qimir," she added, in English for the benefit of the visitors, "what you must do before they leave."

Qimir regarded her thoughtfully for a moment, then nodded. He rose from his cushions and went over to what looked like a pile of rugs in the corner of the room. These he threw aside to reveal an old wooden chest, covered in intricate carvings. "Come here," he said to Shem.

Shem joined him and watched as Qimir reverently lifted the lid with both hands. Inside, lay an article wrapped in layers of multi-coloured silk and bound with seven ribbons of the different colours of the rainbow. Qimir reached in and lifted out the bundle. Shem heard something clank inside it; metal. Qimir gestured for Shem to hold out his arms and laid the bundle into them. Then, he unwrapped the coverings to reveal a collection of ancient, blackened short swords.

Shem looked down at them steadily, although his instinct was to wince away from the blaze of power they emitted. He could sense their great age, and also that they had been used in ritual for centuries, if not millennia. He realised he was looking at treasured artefacts of Qimir's clan.

"These swords have been passed down my family since our blood-line began," Qimir said. "They have great power. In the distant past, they may have tasted blood, but now we use them in our most important rites."

"They *have* tasted blood," Shem said, almost absently.

Qimir nodded. "Before you begin your journey, we will join in a ritual to ask for the protection of the highest god. You must be confirmed as divine avatars of the last epoch."

Shem nodded. "Whatever you think best."

The ritual would take place at daybreak, when the first rays of the rising sun slanted over the mountains and touched the valley. In the dim pre-dawn, Shirin and two of her sisters came to Shem and his companions in Qimir's dwelling. Here, they offered robes of bright colours; gold for Shem; green for Daniel; red for Salamiel and violet for Gadreel. The robes were embroidered with gold wire and when Daniel held the cloth to his nose, he could smell a faint aroma of flowers.

After they'd dressed themselves in the robes, the Yarasadi women wove fresh blooms into their hair and circled their necks, wrists and ankles with bracelets of flowers. Then they were led out into the central area of the camp. Qimir and his personal guard were already waiting, adorned in multi-coloured robes and similarly decorated with flowers. The air was filled with their heady scent, and the green smell of cut stems.

Qimir bade the avatars stand in a circle around him; his personal guard forming a wider ring around them. Then, quietly, every other member of the tribe gathered beyond them.

The crowd waited in silence until the blue-grey twilight turned rose and the sun lifted between two mountains, sending a golden-pink road of dawn light down into the valley. Along such a road, the angels might once have walked to enter the ancient settlements of humanity.

Qimir bowed three times to the rising sun and gestured for
Shemyaza and his three companions to follow his movements.
Then Qimir began to chant in quick, lilting tones, his voice
rising and falling rapidly, his tongue flicking around complex
sounds. Beyond the circle, in lower voices, his guard echoed
responses, pausing to bow at regular intervals.

Qimir fell silent and made a gesture with his hands. A
young girl entered the circle, carrying the sacred swords. They
seemed to weigh heavily in her thin arms. Qimir lifted the first
of the swords, kissed it and held its blade up to the light. Now,
he spoke in English, presumably for the benefit of the avatars.
"Let all present bear witness upon these oaths I swear today.
You with eyes aloft, behold the splendour of *haq*, the universal spirit, shining forth through my will."

Everyone's eyes focused upon the sword Qimir held high.
He turned round slowly. "I, Qimir, create *baba ba* and open
the gate through which all holy avatars may pass from *dun ba
dun*, from oblivion to oblivion." He bowed and then plunged
the sword into the earth at his feet. This ritual was repeated
with five more of the swords, which he positioned in a tight
circle. Projecting his voice across the valley, he held the final
sword above his head for several minutes.

Standing at the edge of the circle, between Salamiel and
Gadreel and opposite Shem, Daniel felt the hairs rise on his
arms. Qimir was attracting the attention of powerful forces,
who now hovered invisibly around them, observing the proceedings. Power was gathering, swirling above them; a maelstrom of memories, emotion and purpose.

For a moment, Qimir fell silent and lowered his head.
A bird cawed from the cliff-face; the only sound. The sunlight burned a furrow of light across the grass. Then, with
a great cry, Qimir drew himself to his full height and thrust
the final sword into the earth, spearing the centre of the
circle of blades. Sparks flew up as hard metal bit into the
ground, grinding against stone. Qimir fell to his knees, collapsing upon the pommel of the seventh sword. Daniel
saw the energy from Qimir's own body, the strength of his
beliefs, cascading into the vibrating metal. Radiant lines
of power emanated from the central sword to each of its

companions; they rang like tuning forks, filled with Qimir's light and energy.

The circle of guards began to chant rapidly and made complicated gestures with their hands, augmenting their leader's ritual actions. The tribe swayed beyond them, all hands extended with fingers splayed, towards the swords.

Daniel gazed at Shem. His eyes were wide, his head thrown back, as if he could see something coiling up from the ground that was readying itself to strike him. Daniel sensed it as another layer of responsibility preparing to enshroud Shemyaza. *Part of him is fighting this,* Daniel thought.

Qimir rose slowly from the ground and, after a few moments' silent contemplation, drew in a deep breath and straightened his spine. He turned to Shem and strode up to him, placing his hands upon Shem's shoulders. Daniel saw Shem wince, very slightly. Qimir chanted a repetitive phrase, which Daniel could tell meant he was calling down the power of Malak Tawus into Shemyaza's body. It was ironic really, for wasn't Shem, in his original incarnation, the prototype of the Peacock Angel? After a few moments, Qimir fell silent and hugged Shem, then kissed him on both cheeks. Shem bowed his head, as if in respect, and Qimir nodded approvingly.

The tribe leader returned to the centre of the circle and repeated the whole process with Gadreel, before moving on to Salamiel. When Daniel's turn came, Qimir paused. Daniel wondered whether it was because he had only recently risen to the state of Grigori, but when Qimir met his eyes, he realised this was not so. Qimir seemed moved almost to tears. When he came to place his hands upon Daniel's shoulders, he spoke in English before beginning the formal chant. "Son of the mountains, who recognised you," he murmured. "Your soul is old, Daniel, yet irrepressibly young. Stay by your master, for he needs you."

Daniel bowed his head, unable to speak. His throat felt constricted and he closed his eyes. Then Qimir's voice rang out and over him, like a stream of crystal clear liquid. He felt *something* move through his flesh, his bones, and realised that Qimir was actually giving something to all of them, part of his soul and the soul of his family. Before Qimir moved away,

Daniel whispered, "I will treasure the gift." Qimir met his eyes and smiled. Then, with a brisk turn, he positioned himself at the centre of the circle once more.

Raising his arms, Qimir uttered the final lines of the ritual and once it was concluded, the whole tribe raised their voices in a great cheer. The air became thick with petals that were thrown from baskets carried by the children. The tense, solemn atmosphere broke up, and someone began to play a merry tune on the zurna.

The party set off later in the morning, amid a din of cheering and shouting. As they prepared their animals to leave, Qimir pulled the seven sacred swords from the ground and presented them to Gadreel. "Take these divine weapons with you," he said. "Do not use them to take life, but to preserve it. Use them only in a time of dire need, for away from their home, my heart, their power diminishes and you will have no means to restore it."

Gadreel nodded and carefully stowed the swords, safely wrapped in several yards of cloth, onto her pack horse. "I will return them to you," she said, and Qimir nodded once, clearly trusting her word.

Leaving the camp in style, Gadreel led the way by urging her horse into a gallop. Everyone followed; the horses kicked up clods of earth, the tassels on their bridles swinging wildly. Cooking utensils clanked and clanged on the pack animals. The whole tribe uttered a haunting ululation as Gadreel's company careered off towards the mountain path.

Before long, the riders left the wider path-ways and headed off up narrower trails, where the cliffs seemed to lean towards one another, until they virtually met overhead. Birds arced over the high rocks, uttering occasional mournful cries. There was no sound of gun-fire, but what seemed like an eternal silence beyond the natural noise of wild-life. Daniel felt that he and his companions could be the only creatures on earth.

The journey proceeded, unmarred by any dramatic events, and after a few days, once the saddle soreness had abated, Daniel was able to enjoy the untamed surroundings. Here, in

the wilderness of the world, among the very crags where the
Nephilim had fought and the Anannage had worked their ar-
cane technologies, it was easy to believe he had somehow
moved backwards in time. At any moment, a Watcher whose
shoulders were adorned with the wings of a vulture might appear around a corner. Daniel experienced no sense of danger.
He felt held by the mountains, protected.

At night, he held Shemyaza in his arms. Shem would not
speak of his worries, but perhaps sensed that Daniel was aware
of them. There was little Daniel could say. Behind every
conversation, every shadowed glance, every stone on the road,
every bird overhead, lurked a hidden threat: that the climax of
Shem's task would be his own sacrifice.

Daniel said, "You must not look for omens, Shem." He
himself fought not to think of them.

Gadreel seemed to think the greatest danger lay not in the
approach of human adversaries, but in the djinn. She felt that
if Nimnezzar's Magians had sent elemental spirits out into the
mountains, they would probably be attracted to the light of
Shemyaza's soul. Every night, Gadreel and Tahira muttered
incantations around the camp and placed bowls of water and
flowers at strategic points, which Gadreel said would ward off
any djinn that might sniff them out.

One day, late in the afternoon, as the horses plodded along the
trail, Salamiel drew his mount up alongside Shem's. "You've
hardly uttered a word since we left Qimir," Salamiel said.
"What's going on in your head?"

Shem, who had been lost in his own torturing thoughts,
detected a sharpness in Salamiel's voice. He shrugged. "I'm
just thinking about what I'll do once the key is found."

"*If* we find it," Salamiel said. "What exactly are we doing,
Shem? Will our journey end with the opening of the Chambers? You must know."

Shem smiled. He could not speak of his doubts to Salamiel.
"I don't know any more than you do."

Salamiel shook his head. "I don't believe it. Tell me everything, Shem, or must we follow you as blindly as we did
before, when we were cast out of Kharsag?"

Shem glanced at him sharply. "You did not follow me blindly, Salamiel. You came with me because you believed what we were doing was right. Isn't that why you're with me now?"

Salamiel did not answer immediately. Shem detected a tightness to his companion's expression, and also a faint corona of angry crimson fire around his body. "We have never really talked about the past," Salamiel said. "Perhaps it is time to. I, and your other supporters, despised Anu's hollow sanctimony. We were filled with a fire to rebel against all that Kharsag stood for. You made us see the truth, Shem, the lie of it. You were our glorious leader. We would have followed you anywhere."

Shemyaza glanced across at him, but did not speak.

"Don't you understand?" Salamiel snapped. "We have the chance to redress our failings now. We should go further than we did before. Our people rule this world behind a veil, believing themselves to be superior to the human race, but in truth they are dissolute, power-hungry and selfish. It is the same as it was in the days of Kharsag, when you recognised that, Shem, and yearned to change it. We are wiser now and less impulsive. We should destroy the dominion of the Grigori, squash the tyrant of Babylon and any others who wield oppression in this world. Think, Shem, this is our destiny. We must raise an army."

Shemyaza laughed quietly. "We already have an army. There will be seven of us."

Salamiel uttered a harsh caw of irritation. "Seven? Shem, wake up! I followed you ten thousand years ago because I believed in your strength and in our power to change the world. You fought so hard, and suffered the worst of agonies because of it. But you had fire! You had courage! Remember your Nephilim sons and how you led them in battle."

Shem did not respond, but gazed silently ahead. His head was filled with images of war and darkness. He closed his eyes briefly. His sons had been monsters, trained by him and inspired by him. They had been bred in bitterness and had wanted to destroy the world rather than change it. "That was not the way," he said softly. "I was wrong."

Salamiel shook his head. "No, you were right, and you had the support of your brethren. We knew you had doubts, even then. Perhaps I should not reveal this, but the brotherhood made me swear an oath. You had led us so far, we could not return to our old, comfortable lives, but towards the end, we saw signs of weakness and indecision within you. Therefore, it was decided that should you renege on your promises to us, and seek peace with Kharsag, I would be the one to kill you."

Shem frowned. "You were the closest to me, but for Ishtahar and Daniel. Would you have done it?"

Salamiel sighed. "I would have had to, Shem, no matter what I felt for you. We would have carried on without you." He paused. "We were parted for millennia, but in Cornwall, fate brought us together again. I have stayed with you since, even though I might have had to wait another ten millennia for you to regain your strength. I was prepared to do it, because I believe in you." He raised a closed fist before his face. "Our revolution failed in Kharsag, Shem, but we can succeed now."

Shem pulled a wry face. "Salamiel, you seem to have charged off down a side road. We are not travelling together at this point."

"You're not listening to me, are you!" Salamiel hissed. "I had hoped we'd returned to Eden to turn back history, to win the war we lost. We have an army, Shem: the Yarasadi, who are desperate to regain their kingdom. You have ever been their spiritual king. Inspire them now! Find the power within you and wield it! We've become immersed in these meaningless rituals of swords and avatars and keys. I don't understand it, Shem, and I don't like it."

Shem could see that Salamiel was close to becoming emotional, a rare condition for him. "You are too impatient," he said. "Reflect upon what you are saying."

This answer only seemed to inflame Salamiel's temper more. "What has happened to you?" he cried, incurring curious glances from their travelling companions. "And what has happened to Daniel? You don't really believe he has become Grigori again, do you? It's preposterous!"

Shem smiled. "Not preposterous, Salamiel. It happened, because it was destined to happen. It is a sign, a star that we must follow."

Salamiel expelled a derisory snort. "It's all too rarefied. We should be warriors, not ascetics mumbling over rituals and searching for omens!"

Shemyaza laughed. "Your rage gives me strength, as it always did. Haven't you ever wondered *why* our plan to bring lasting change failed in the past?"

"Well, we were thwarted," Salamiel said, mulishly. "By the treachery of Ishtahar and by the superior force of Anu's militia. We didn't have enough time to educate humanity, we..."

"No," Shem interrupted. "It was because we did not act with love."

"Love!" Salamiel rolled his eyes in exasperation. "How could we? Our position demanded courage and fire."

Shem sighed and leaned forward in his saddle, resting his forearms on its pommel. "I have had time to think in these mountains. It has helped me to analyse the past. I have learned to appreciate that to understand what love is, you have to understand what it is not. It is the not the fire that lovers feel, it is not desire or lust or need, those ultimately selfish cravings. Love is not a feeling, but an action. We should not feel it, but *do* it; an act of unconditional giving. Daniel has shown me this."

Salamiel looked at him sourly. "I don't see what this has to do with our failure in Kharsag or what we have to do now."

"Ah, but you're wrong," Shem said. "Daniel's experience in Mani's cave made me realise something. When we rebelled against Anu's law, we wanted to civilise the human race and give them our knowledge. But that act of giving was not unconditional. There were things we wanted in return: women, submission, reverence, power. Humanity were barely more than children then, and children learn by example. They learned from us and became what they are now. If the world is a hell on earth today, it is the result of our past selfishness. I know you don't think we need Daniel, and that I am capable of doing what he does myself, but he represents our aim and what the results of success should be. A flowering."

Salamiel sniffed derisively. "I still don't see what this has to do with finding keys, and dancing around sacred swords!"

Shem shook his head and sighed. "We are approaching our return to the source, the Chambers of Light and the knowledge of the Elders that Anu kept hidden from us. In Kharsag, we thought we were so advanced, but we lacked awareness of what we were. We looked upon humanity as children, but we were barely their seniors. They were not ready for the knowledge we gave them, and we were not ready to accept the consequences of our actions. We made changes happen, but they were too quick. Qimir's swords and the key we seek are some of the tools through which we will channel the bringer of real, lasting change."

Salamiel frowned. "Which is?"

"I told you. Love. It is what I must give and *be*."

Salamiel uttered a scornful sound. "Why don't I just nail you to a cross? It seems like you think you must you be a sacrifice again. *Are* you going to die?"

Shem shrugged. It unnerved him how accurately Salamiel had just described his own fears. "I don't know. Probably. If that's what it takes. Sometimes love is cruel. Sometimes it goes beyond death."

"I can't believe I'm hearing this. I know you, Shem. You won't accept sacrifice that meekly. You fought your destiny in Cornwall. Have you really changed that much?"

Shem forced himself to laugh. "No, I haven't. I'm merely telling you what I've thought about these past few weeks. It doesn't mean I've wholly accepted it."

"Gadreel and the Yarasadi don't want love, Shem. They want action."

"No, they want change. The Yarasadi believe that we, as divine avatars of Malak Tawus, herald the advent of the last epoch of the old order. The world will not end after this, but change. Humanity and the Grigori must move on. This is the last chance, for both our races."

Salamiel frowned. "And how will *we* change?"

"Humanity's destiny is to become more like us; Daniel is the symbol of this. Our destiny is to regain our lost heritage, to become the Anannage once more, but this time we will interact freely with humanity. There will be no lies and no secrets. We will not guard our knowledge jealously, but share it."

"A dream, Shem." Salamiel sighed deeply. "Riding along here, I find it hard to believe. I have lived too long and suffered too much. So have you. Ultimately, you will rise up with fire. You'll not be able to let yourself die for this destiny."

"I may not have a choice."

"Oh, you will. It would not be that easy. You wait and see."

One night, they camped in what Tahira called the Valley of Stones. It was a bleak, desolate place, where incessant winds wailed between the dark cliffs on either side. Tahira told them it was a place of ghosts, but that sometimes an open mind might receive a message from the dead there.

No messages were forthcoming, however, and in the morning, the company resumed their journey. They found the cave entrance in the late afternoon. The horses stepped around a corner in the path and there it was; a cliff face that seemed to lean backwards into the landscape, lighter in colour than the surrounding rocks. The cave entrance gaped blackly upon it, like a giant stain. It seemed, from a distance, to have no depth. A narrow, treacherous-looking path led up to a small rock platform before the cave. Two other paths appeared to lead from either side of the ledge, disappearing into dry and prickly shrubs that hung precariously from the mountain-side. The area had a strange atmosphere that made Daniel's flesh prickle. Weird echoes bounced from rock to rock, but were weirdly muffled. Wide-winged birds circled above that looked suspiciously like vultures, even though they were reputed to be extinct in this area.

Leaving their horses with Jalal and the other Yarasadi at the bottom of the path, Tahira led the avatars upwards. She climbed nimbly, like a ragged goat, her brightly-coloured shawl and long grey hair flapping in the wind.

At the cave's entrance, there were signs that others had been there before them; small bunches of wild flowers had been left as offerings and were scattered, wilting, over the hard, dry rocks.

Tahira had not been exaggerating her description of the place. From the moment Shem and the others stepped up to the entrance, they could see that the entire interior was filled with bones, piles upon piles of them. A warm wind seemed to emanate from the depths of the cave; it smelled of singed hair. The scene within looked like that of a hidden massacre: bleached bones, broken bones and bones arranged in decorative heaps. They glowed like phosphorous in the afternoon light coming in through the cave mouth. Farther back, ghostly white lattices gleamed in the dark.

A few yards in from the entrance, someone had cleared a small circular space. An uneven stone floor, polished by generations of human feet, showed through a scattering of grey ashes. Tahira turned around in a circle, nodding her head. "I remember it," she said, and then pointed a rigid finger at the cleared space. "This is where we must pray."

Shem glanced at Daniel and raised his eyebrows. They were not here to pray, although no-one enlightened the old woman.

Daniel examined some of the bones. "They look like bird skeletons," he said, "there are still feathers..." He sifted through a clacking pile. "Some are recent, too. Meat still on them." He looked around himself, shaking his head. "This place must have been used for..."

"Millennia," Salamiel said, stepping forward and lifting a bone. Almost absent-mindedly, he slipped it into his hair, behind his left ear.

Shem came over to them. "Birds and goats and serpents. In this place, the people—perhaps *my* people—once wore the wings of the vultures and flew in trance." He reached out and touched one of the white, delicate bones, but withdrew his hand before lifting it free of the pile.

Daniel turned in a circle to inspect their surroundings. "So where do we begin to look for the key? Is it under the bones, or even *one* of the bones?" He shivered. The atmosphere in the cave was not wholly benign, and he sensed curious presences feeling out for him.

"I think you should try and make contact with whatever spirit entities guard this place," Shem said.

"I had a feeling you might suggest that." Daniel put his hands on his hips and gazed up at the roof of the cave, which was blackened with ancient soot. He sighed. "Right, let's see what can be done, but I want you, Gadreel and Salamiel to share this meditation."

Gadreel asked Tahira to wait outside, and once she had left, the four of them arranged themselves in a circle, sitting cross-legged on the ground. In the silence, they heard the hollow, wooden sound of dislodged bones shifting their positions. A dry carrion scent filled the air. It was not easy to close the eyes and surrender sight to begin the meditation.

Because Daniel wanted to concentrate on whatever entities were present in the cave, Salamiel led the group through the preliminaries of the meditation. He asked them to visualise a cone of white, protective light growing up around them. Once this was done, he invited any spirit forms that might be present to make themselves known.

For a while, nothing happened as everyone extended their senses out into their environment. In his mind's eye, Daniel could still see the interior of the cave; the darkness, the jumbled heaps of bones. As he concentrated on this image, he became aware that a fire was burning in the middle of their circle. He could hear it crackling now and smelled the pungent smoke—wood mixed with broken bone. A tall, hunched shape was lurking in the shadows behind Shem's back. It looked like a shadow itself, but even as Daniel concentrated upon it, its shape became more solid. Mentally, Daniel called out to this image, and without hesitation, it came forth into the light of the flames.

Daniel forced himself not to wince away. The figure before him was monstrous, in both height and appearance. He wore a skirt of bloodied feathers around his hips, while a cloak of vulture wings hung over his shoulders. The flesh was still raw and red where the wings had been hacked from the bodies of birds. Smooth white knobs of bone jutted out from the shoulders of the cloak. The guardian's face was fierce, his eyes shadowed and predatory. His hands were curling and uncurling like claws that yearned to tear and rend. His mouth was set in a gargoyle sneer.

Daniel almost gagged from the carrion stench that enveloped this entity. It took some effort for him to ask it to name itself. The name came immediately, aggressively: *Rabisu.* Daniel sensed that this was an ancient spirit-form, perhaps placed millennia before by the Nephilim warrior-priests who had used the cave. The guardian was most likely a thought-form that embodied, in a limited way, the personality of one of the priests. Its duty would be to remain there over the centuries, guarding the sacred site.

"Do you see it?" Daniel asked the others.

"I sense something," Gadreel said.

"Shem?" Daniel said.

He heard Shem shift restlessly on the floor. "It's the guardian. Tell him who we are and what our purpose is."

Daniel addressed the guardian aloud. "Rabisu, we are Shemyaza, Gadreel, Salamiel and Daniel. We are searching for the key to the Chambers of Light. Is it here?"

Daniel saw Rabisu pull himself up to his full height, which was at least seven feet. His eyes sparked blue in a face that was otherwise unrecognisable, owing to the quantity of ash and pigment that was smeared across it, augmented with dirt and grease. A voice boomed painfully in Daniel's head. "To whom does my key belong?"

"To whom does my key belong," Daniel repeated. "Did you all hear that? You must answer."

There was silence for a while, then Gadreel said simply, "To us, its inheritors."

Daniel saw the guardian draw back his lips into a snarl. He made a sudden movement, as if about to pounce. "No," Daniel said bleakly. "That's not the answer."

"To Anu," Salamiel said, "the first Lord. It is his key."

Again the guardian snarled and stamped his feet, sending a spray of bone-dust up into the smoke of the fire. "No," Daniel said. "Think! Rabisu is impatient with your answers."

"What do you think, Daniel?" Salamiel said. "You're the vizier. You answer the question."

Daniel shook his head. "I don't know." His mind was whirling; it was impossible to organise his thoughts. What *was* the answer? He felt the air move around him as Rabisu struck out with hooked fingers towards his face. Daniel uttered a gasping cry. He could feel the guardian's power building up, his impatience and scorn. They should not have considered summoning him until they were more sure of what they wanted from him or indeed from themselves.

"The key belongs to the Yarasadi!" Gadreel said. "This is their secret place of worship."

Rabisu growled and his long, black fingernails raked Daniel's brow. Daniel heard Salamiel and Gadreel utter soft cries of surprise, and knew that the spiritual guardian had left a physical mark. He could feel a trail of blood begin to seep down his face.

"Shem!" Daniel yelled. "You answer him! Speak! Do it now or everything will be lost! Say it, Shem! Say what I know you can say!"

Shem stood up and Daniel opened his eyes. The two realities were overlaid upon each other; the cold cave in afternoon light; the fire and the guardian. Daniel blinked blood from his eyes. Shem seemed contained and almost dazed, as if his mind was elsewhere. "The key," he said, "belongs to me. Shaitan. It belongs to me."

Abruptly, the guardian uttered a wild scream, which everybody heard, then jumped up into the air and vanished. The company all opened their eyes and looked around themselves in astonishment for a few moments, then Salamiel said. "I can't see any key. Where is it?"

Gadreel glanced at the ground and sighed, "No key."

Daniel shook his head. His brow was stinging now; he felt dizzy. "We failed," he said. "I don't know if we'll get another chance to speak with the guardian. It won't trust us, and probably won't even make another appearance."

Gadreel slapped the ash-strewn stone floor with the flat of her palms. "Damn! We should have been more prepared!"

"But how were we to know what the guardian would ask?" Salamiel said.

"I should have known," Daniel answered in a dull voice. "Site guardians often set riddles, ask questions. Gadreel is right. We were too impetuous."

Shem was staring out of the entrance to the cave. Daniel looked up at him and sighed. Shem was an unpredictable creature; he could not be relied on. "What do you want to do now?" Daniel asked him.

Shem did not answer, but walked out of the cave. His three companions swapped a few incredulous glances, then followed him.

Shem stood upon the narrow ledge gazing up at the sky. Tahira and the other Yarasadi, standing below with the horses, were looking up at him. For a moment, Daniel wondered whether Shem was possessed by Rabisu, for he was acting strangely. He laid a hand upon Shem's arm. "What is it? Are you all right?"

Again, Shem said nothing, but slowly raised an arm to point up at the sky.

Daniel shaded his eyes with one hand, and squinted to where Shem was pointing. He saw a pin-prick of light against the clouds.

Gadreel came up beside him. "What's that light?"

Daniel shrugged. "I'm not sure…"

Suddenly the light began to zoom towards them, becoming larger and brighter, until it hung above their heads as a hovering sphere of radiance about two feet in diameter. The Yarasadi below began to cry out in Kurmanji and gestured at the apparition in surprise and fear. The sphere emitted a high-pitched hum. It swerved to the left a few feet, then to the right, before shooting off to the left, towards the cliff face further along the path. Here, it collided with the rock and exploded with a deafening blast. Everybody on the cave ledge cowered down, while the Yarasadi below uttered panicked cries and covered their heads. Stones showered downwards, and a cloud of rock dust billowed out from the cliff face.

After a few moments, when everything seemed quiet, the group straightened up, brushing dust from their clothes and faces.

"Incredible!" Salamiel said. "Our own UFO."

Shem glanced at him inscrutably, then said, "Daniel, come with me." He began clambering along the tortuous path that hugged the face of the soaring rocks. Daniel followed him. Dust clouds still hung in the air and there was a smell of ozone. Daniel didn't know what it was they'd seen and questioned the wisdom of going to investigate the explosion. "Shem, shouldn't we wait a while?"

Shem glanced back at him. "It's quite safe." Shattered rocks shifted beneath his feet. He stumbled, yet kept on moving. Daniel could not let him go alone.

Presently, Daniel saw light reflecting off something that lay in a pile of rubble that had demolished a stand of shrubs. Shem said, "There!" and increased his pace, clawing his way through the debris. He bent down and sifted through the stones. "Daniel, come here!"

Cautiously, Daniel approached. Shem squatted with his arms resting on his thighs. He gestured at his feet. "Look. There."

Daniel looked over Shem's shoulder. In the rubble, he saw a shining shape that lay partially buried. "What is it?"

Shem gestured for him to come forward. "Take a look. Pick it up."

Daniel paused for a moment then knelt down. He saw a perfect crystalline cone about the size of his fist. Strangely, he could not tell whether it was green or red. The colours seemed to shift within it. Carefully, he picked up the cone and dusted it with his sleeve. "What kind of stone is this?" he asked Shem.

Shem shrugged. "It must be alexandrite. In daylight it appears to be one colour, in artificial light another."

"So what kind of light are we in at the moment, then?" Daniel held the stone up before his face, turning it this way and that. Still, the colours merged and flowed.

"It must be an effect of the earth-light that carried it," Shem said.

"It's incredible," Daniel said softly. "*This* is what I saw in my dream vision of the Elder. He was holding it out to me. And in Cornwall, at the eclipse. I saw it in the dark sun…"

Shem reached out and touched Daniel's hair. "It's the key," he said.

Daniel handed it to him. "And it's yours…apparently. Apported straight to your feet."

Shem nodded distractedly and put the crystal cone into his jacket pocket. He looked around himself. "It's very close."

"What is?" Daniel stood up.

"Kharsag, the garden," Shem answered shortly. "This is Eden, Daniel."

Daniel observed the barren terrain, the harsh cliffs of splintered rock, the wheeling carrion birds high above. If this was indeed the ancient land of Eden, then not even a memory of its former splendour remained.

Chapter Fifteen
Finding Kharsag

Eden

The group elected to spend the night in the Valley of Stones, and here they erected their tents. Jalal built a fire and together with his grand-mother set about preparing a meal. The other Yarasadi sat around smoking and laughing, but their laughter sounded forced. Everyone felt tense.

Shem sat down on the ground and asked Daniel to massage his shoulders. "Invoking ancient entities is bad for the bones!" he said.

Daniel could not share Shem's light-heartedness. As he dug his fingers into Shem's muscles he said, "I should have guessed the Elder was offering me the key. Mani virtually said so. What would have happened if I'd had the sense to take it in my vision? Would the key have manifested at Qimir's camp?"

"We'll never know," Shem said, reaching up to squeeze one of Daniel's hands. "But we've found it now, and the next stage must begin."

Salamiel sauntered up, his expression tight. "It's at times like that that our beloved Shemyaza shows his true colours," he said.

"His true power," Daniel amended.

"You knew exactly what to say to the guardian, didn't you," Salamiel said. "Why did you wait until Daniel got attacked before you said anything?"

"He didn't know!" Daniel said, before Shem could answer. "The Elders were working through him, then. He spoke with their voice."

Salamiel snorted contemptuously. "Oh, *of course.*" He laughed to lessen the sting of his sarcasm. "Why did you refer to yourself as Shaitan, Shem? What's the significance of that?"

Shem shrugged. "Rabisu would not have recognised the name Shemyaza. Shaitan is a local form of my name. It seemed obvious to use it. As for knowing what to say, it wasn't the Elders speaking through me. Something much more prosaic." He turned and glanced over his shoulder at Daniel. "Remember when I entered the underworld in Cornwall? I was asked a similar question and by some miracle—or perhaps divine coincidence—got the answer right."

Daniel frowned. "I don't follow."

"I said that I and the serpent of the underworld were one. It's all the same thing, really. God, king, serpent, light, chamber, keeper and key. All one. They key had to be mine. I'm learning the script. It's not that original."

Salamiel laughed again. "You are unbelievable at times."

"Many people have thought so," Shem answered dryly, "but despite unbelief, I still exist."

While they waited for their meal, Gadreel and Salamiel wanted to examine the key. Shem handed Gadreel the crystal. She turned it in her fingers, watching the colours, refracted by firelight spinning over her hands. "It holds all the light of the world," she said, "and it feels so unbelievably cold. Where did it come from, and how?"

"It's what we call an apport," Daniel said. "An artefact that simply manifests out of thin air. The arrival of this one was more spectacular than I've ever seen, though. The key itself was never at the cave. We simply had to perform the right actions there, say the right words for it to be summoned."

"Then *where* was it before?" Gadreel asked. "It must have been somewhere. If we knew the answer to that, I feel we would be approaching the answer to everything."

"Yes," Daniel agreed. "Unfortunately, nobody really knows the science behind the appearance of apports."

Gadreel pulled a wry face. "Perhaps it will disappear just as easily."

Daniel shrugged. "It's possible, but it has been summoned for a purpose. We have to suppose it will remain with Shem until that purpose is realised."

"Presumably, there's a niche somewhere," Salamiel said, "that the crystal fits into. The gate to the Chambers of Light? All we have to do now is find out where they are."

"Are they here?" Gadreel asked Shem.

He shrugged. "I'll go and investigate in a while, after we've eaten."

"Shall I come with you?" Daniel said.

Shem shook his head. "No, I want to do this alone."

"But it might not be safe," Daniel argued. "Who knows what's wandering around these mountains. All it would take is for you to go into trance and anything could jump you— spiritual or human. Let me test the waters, Shem. You were never averse to that before."

Shem shrugged nonchalantly. "Whatever..."

After they had eaten, the group sat around their horses in a circle, and passed 'round a flagon of rough wine. Conversation was easy, to the point where Daniel almost forgot why they were there. He listened to the musical language of the Yarasadi, watching Tahira and Gadreel placing brass bowls of water around them in a wide ring, in which floated crushed flower petals. This was their protection against whatever stalked the night. Once the ritual was complete, Tahira sat down among the men and began to regale the company with colourful tales of her youth, most of which sounded like fantasy, but perhaps were not. Daniel lay on his side, his head supported by one hand, staring at the fire, while Tahira's lilting voice washed over him. The fire held them in a capsule of radiance. Beyond it was utter blackness, and the sigh of the wind against loose stones. The horses munched their fodder, snorting and blowing into the food, striking the ground with their hooves. Daniel almost fell asleep; his mind wandered, until in a hypnogogic state, he became aware of slow-moving, stooping forms hovering beyond the sanctuary of firelight. Drowsily, he acknowledged that these ancient mountains would be full of spiritual entities, who would be drawn by the fire and the brighter lights of living beings.

Then Gadreel snapped, "What was that?" She sat upright, her nostrils flexing like a cat's.

Daniel felt as if a cold wave had crashed over him. Reality came surging back and the sound of the flames suddenly crackled wildly in his ears. The horses had become nervous, flinging up their heads and whinnying to one another. Daniel sensed that there was something more solid than spirit forms beyond the fire, but they were not entirely human either.

Tahira sucked in her breath through her teeth, and hissed, "Djinn!"

Gadreel stood up and peered into the darkness.

"You placed the usual protections," Salamiel said, standing up slowly. "We should be safe...surely." The wind played with his hair so that it appeared uncannily like shifting flames. He could have been a djinn himself.

"I hope so," Gadreel murmured, "but this is strong, very strong."

Daniel said, "Where's Shem? I can't see him."

Everyone looked around. "Gone!" Salamiel said. "The fool!"

"He's slipped the leash, Daniel," Gadreel said. "He has gone looking for Kharsag."

Daniel groaned. "I can't believe he's done this!" He called out. "Shem! Where are you?"

"Sssh!" Gadreel hissed, grabbing hold of Daniel's arm. "Be quiet. Don't alert whatever is out there."

"I think it's already alert," Salamiel said softly.

"Just be quiet!" Gadreel said, raking her hair back from her face. Her eyes looked wild in the fire-light. Tahira stood gaunt beside her, muttering at the darkness, her shawl pulled tight against her lean body.

"Jalal," Gadreel whispered. "Calm the horses. If they take flight, we will be stranded in this place."

Jalal and the other Yarasadi guards obeyed her word, although Daniel suspected that if the animals panicked, there would be little anyone could do to restrain them.

For a few moments, everyone held their breath and listened, but the only sound was the crackle of the fire and the susurration of the wind. Even the horses had gone quiet, their postures rigid and alert.

Daniel's flesh crawled. Whatever stalked them had come looking for Shemyaza; he was sure of it. Perhaps it was fortunate the hunter had found only the fire. Now, he could hear a soft, crunching sound as of light feet pacing over the stones of the valley floor. It sounded as if it wasn't far from where they were all sitting, but he could see nothing. "Can you hear that?" he asked Gadreel.

She narrowed her eyes, concentrating, holding her hair back from her ears with both hands. "Yes."

"Children of the fire," Tahira hissed, "the evil ones."

Her words seemed to act as an invocation. Some yards away from the group, half a dozen new fires popped into life, glowing at ground level, before leaping towards the sky. Purple-blue flames danced in the dirt. "Ai," breathed Tahira. "They come. They smell us."

The horses began to shuffle again, although it seemed they were too petrified to try and escape. Gradually, tall, motionless shapes could be seen forming within the spectral flames. They illumined the small brass bowls of water and petals, and then the water began to bubble and steam, the flowers curl up into crisps.

"Yai!" Gadreel yelled. "Tahira! The swords! Quickly!"

She and the old woman ran to Gadreel's baggage, which had been taken off her horse for the night. Frantically, they tore at the wrappings and the swords spilled out in a clatter onto the stony ground. Gadreel took the largest blade and began to run around the camp in a circle, dragging the sword's point in the dirt to create a shallow channel. Tahira scuttled along behind her with the six other swords, which she plunged at intervals into the ground. Each time she struck the earth, silver sparks shot out from the blades.

Gasping and breathless, Gadreel and Tahira ran back to the others who had now all gathered in a huddle in the middle of the circle, the shivering horses in their midst.

"Will it be enough protection?" Salamiel asked.

"I don't know," Gadreel snapped back. "Pray!"

The Yarasadi had all begun to mutter a chant, their bodies stooped into postures of alertness, ready to defend themselves if necessary.

Tall figures stepped forth from the blue flames. Daniel
watched them examine the swords from a distance, as if con-
sidering whether the defences could be breached. The figures
were robed in black, faces and heads covered but for the eyes,
which glinted wetly. Then one of the creatures elected to test
the power of the swords. It loped towards the nearest one,
somehow transforming into a thick, twisting skein of red-shot
black smoke before it touched the blade. Upon contact, the
sword emitted a sound like a gigantic tuning fork and vibrated
in the ground. The creature was hurled backwards. Daniel
saw it regain a more humanoid shape. Its robes had fallen
from its head, and what he saw resembled a man who had
been hideously burned. The flesh was black and smoking,
only the piercing amber eyes uncharred.

For what seemed like an eternity, the djinn assaulted the
protective swords, but on each occasion were repelled by their
power. Those within the circle sat close together, holding hands
and uttering the same charm of protection. Daniel was sure
he had never experienced such terror. The djinn were so persistent; they never tired. And he could feel their passionless
determination. They were hunters, but he had a suspicion
they were seeking live captives. Being captured alive by the
djinn might be worse than death at their hands. Daniel hoped
that Shem was safe. It was impossible for him to try and concentrate on picking up Shem's presence psychically. Perhaps
he was meant to leave them. Perhaps, if Shem was here, the
djinn would be stronger somehow. Daniel knew that Shem's
power had two sides to it; the dark side was the lord of djinn.

Long before dawn, the group's firewood supply ran out,
and they had to watch in dread as the flames sank lower, until
only a crawling smoulder was left in their midst. The tall purple-
blue flames outside the circle gave off no heat and gradually a
numbing chill paralysed flesh and bone. Daniel could no longer
feel his fingers or toes. Would they die of cold before their
attackers gave up?

When the first pale rays of dawn came to the stony valley,
the djinn transformed themselves into smoky vapours and
purled upwards into the sky. For nearly half an hour afterwards, everyone was too frightened to move and sat shivering

in the circle. Nobody spoke. The horses were covered in a cold foam of sweat, their eyes rolling in their sockets.

Eventually, Gadreel got up and went to the edge of the circle where she stood, hands on hips, staring out beyond the swords. After a few moments, she turned to the others. "It's safe now. Some of you go and find some more fire wood. It's too cold. We need warmth. Jalal, get someone to help you rub down the horses. We must walk them, warm them up.'

While a couple of the Yarasadi ventured warily out of the circle, Tahira went to gather up the swords.

"Are they spent?" Gadreel asked.

Tahira shrugged and held out the largest sword to her, which she took in her hand, hefting it like a familiar, well-loved weapon. Gadreel turned it this way and that, staring at the blade.

"Well?" Salamiel asked. "Will they be of use to us again?"

Gadreel pulled a puzzled face. "I'm not sure. It's almost as if their power has retreated into them in some way. They don't feel empty, but neither do they feel...alive."

"So what do we do now?" Salamiel asked. "Look for Shem or wait here for him? Do you suppose he was attacked by djinn himself?"

"I don't know," Gadreel answered. "What do you think, Daniel?"

Daniel screwed up his face in vexation. "I don't think he was, but it's difficult to tell. I don't sense he's in danger, but neither can I trace him. The light of him has become invisible to me."

"Well, that's convenient!" Salamiel said. "We need to get out of here quickly, and Shem's disappeared!"

"Perhaps I should go and look for him," Daniel said.

"No," Gadreel snapped. "We mustn't split up."

"Then we'll all go!"

Gadreel shook her head. "No. We'll wait for him here. He knows where we are."

Salamiel sighed. "Well I, for one, am starving. Perhaps we should eat, then discuss what to do. Hopefully, Shem will have turned up again before we have to make any decisions."

Shemyaza knew he had to go into the mountains alone. He was not afraid of pursuit or attack. He was so close now. The terrain had changed dramatically, but he felt sure in his heart that over the next ridge, round the next corner, he would find evidence of his lost home. He trudged an uphill path towards the sky, towards the vulture-girdled peaks. He felt confident that once he reached the site of the valley of Kharsag, which he knew lay so close, the answers concerning the Chambers of Light would be given to him. He could not bring Daniel with him on this journey.

Close, so very close. He could not believe there wouldn't be some sign left of the garden, some impression left in the rocks of all that had taken place there, if only the channels cut by waterfalls.

In the distance, it seemed a faint voice called out to him. He could not pay it heed. The dawn was beginning to bloom around him, and already the land was held in that surreal still-ness that heralds the transition between night and day. The light was still grey on the mountain path. Shem did not recognise the terrain, but felt that it was familiar.

Father, the prodigal has returned.

In his mind, he saw again the fertile terraces of Kharsag, and screened by cedars, the great Mountain House of Anu. He saw the orchards, their trees heavy with fruit, and the serene, robed Anannage working among them, attended by their human labourers. He saw the tall, domed glass houses of obsidian, the coruscating waterfalls and the forests of cedar that hugged the mountainsides around the valley. So beauti-ful. He could almost drink in the memory of tranquillity as if it was borne on the air like the perfume of a woman walk-ing some yards ahead of him.

It could not be the same now, he knew, for the Anannage were millennia gone, but he hoped to find the ruins, ghostly outlines of habitation in the valley of the vanished settlement.

He felt swamped by an inconsolable homesickness. *I want it all back!* And yet, the last time he had been here, his people had burned his body and imprisoned his soul. Should he not also think of that?

Echoes of his own torment rang from crag to crag, thin as a baby's scream. A dancing figure, cloaked in ragged feathers, seemed to shimmer just ahead of him, leading him on, a vague shadow flickering rapidly on the edge of his perception. If he blinked to clear his sight it became more indistinct.

He took the key crystal out of his pocket and held it up before his eyes. "What am I doing here?" he asked it, as if the stone would speak back to him. "Lead me to Kharsag."

No voice came from the stone, but a cold whisper echoed in Shem's mind. The crystal became warm in his hands, and a pinprick of light glowed at its heart. "Heaven has gone, Shemyaza."

"I must see where it once lay."

The crystal glowed red as if a heart beat deep within it. "Your father, Anu, brought me to this place. He was the keeper of the key, as you are now. Through my power he created Kharsag in this land of Eden. I was taken from my place by the first keeper and carried to safety when the Chambers were sealed."

"Was Anu the first keeper of the key?" Shem asked.

"There have been many keepers, many fathers. The cycles of time repeat themselves."

"Are the Chambers of Light here in Eden?"

"No. Kharsag was but a replica of the Chambers in stone, leaf and life-giving water."

"Then where are the original Chambers? I must take you back there, open them..." He rounded a corner, one hand against the cold rock, and there the path seemed to rise up and end. Shem's heart beat faster. Here it was; the lip of the valley. For a moment, he stood still, fighting a maelstrom of nausea, dizziness and excitement. He put the crystal back into his pocket and made himself walk forward, pushing through the air.

He could see that a wide pathway led around the perimeter of the valley, lined with sentinel stones that did not look naturally-formed. Just a few more steps and the site of his old home would be revealed.

He faltered on the path. What had they done?

The valley lay below him; it had once been a bowl of fertility. Now, spreading wide, the land was thorned with a chaotic mass of metallic structures that looked like the tortured skeletons of monsters, their flesh long stripped away by the acid blue flames that burned like neon in the pre-dawn twilight.

What had once been Paradise was now a desolate vista of gas fields. Miles and miles of them, the land abused and gouged to surrender the sacred flame. Heaven had been destroyed.

Shem squatted down in horror, his hands pressed against the dirt. What had he expected to find: a mirage of the past, ghosts enacting bygone rituals? Not this. Certainly not this. He took the crystal from his pocket once more to ask questions, seek answers, drowning in despair.

A series of metallic clicks sounded around him. Shem stiffened. The crystal lay cold and dead in his hand, mere stone. He recognised the sound behind him. *Too late…*Slowly, Shemyaza looked over his shoulder.

Around the perimeter of the valley, the rising sun, which was just lifting through a valley in the peaks, reflected off a host of guns. Still forms surrounded him, their weapons all pointed right at him.

Shem felt confused. What was this? It did not form part of what he'd expected to find in this place.

A tall figure stepped forward from the shadow of a rock. It was robed in black, the head covered but for the eyes. Shem sensed the presence of corrupt power. He saw no point in rising or speaking; if this person wanted to communicate with him, they would have to initiate the contact.

For what seemed like minutes, the figure appraised him. Then spoke. "What is your name?"

Shem knew that these people had been looking for him. They'd known where to find him. "You know who I am," he said, sneering, "but who, might I ask, are you?" He expected a blow, but the man before him made no aggressive move.

"I represent King Nimnezzar of Babylon."

"Good!" Shem stood up, and the soldiers around him moved their weapons nervously. He raised his arms. "There is no need for this. I have long wanted to meet the man who claims to be of sacred blood." He put his hands on his hips and fixed the tall robed figure with steady eyes. "Is your king responsible for the depredations we see in this sacred place?" He indicated the valley behind him.

"These are the gas fields of the king," answered the man.

"I am curious as to why a man who claims to be the descendent of angels should rape their holy ground."

The robed figure narrowed his eyes, but would not respond to the accusation. "You are to come with us," he said. "Shemyaza."

"I know that," Shem answered.

The robed man reached out and with a deft hand, plucked the crystal from Shem's hold. "This I will look after for you."

"Take it," Shem said. "If Nimnezzar is what he claims to be, he should be the first to fathom its secrets."

There was no time to think of Daniel and the others. What had happened above the ruins of Kharsag had been preordained. Shem could tell that some of the Babylonians were Magians, and that they were not afraid of him; quite the opposite. As they escorted him down the mountain path towards a waiting army truck, Shem considered that King Nimnezzar might see him as a threat and want to dispose of him or incarcerate him. How must he behave in Babylon—as a king or a captive? Shem wasn't sure. Destiny unfurled his path before him; he could only follow it, whether in faith or not. If the Chambers of Light had once existed in Eden, they were no more. He could only hope the end of his task lay in Babylon.

Chapter Sixteen
Alliance of Angels

The woman sat in the hallway drinking a glass of milk. It seemed a quaintly childish thing to do, yet the woman was far from a child. Waiting to check in, behind a line of impatient guests, Cameron Murchison watched the woman drink. She sat beside a table on which a display of dried flowers stood. It was the kind of table found around hotels; people sat at them for brief moments as they waited for elevators or fellow guests. Murchison saw the woman's throat moving as she tilted back her head. It seemed, for a brief moment, as if a faint, purple light danced around her head.

He was tired. The plane had been full to capacity and he'd had the misfortune to be seated near to a woman carrying a baby that whined peevishly and continually. Once they landed, the heat of Egypt sapped his strength; his mind felt muzzy. The increase in political troubles meant that visitors from overseas had to be escorted by police to their hotels. Security was high upon the streets, the atmosphere fervid. The visitors' coach drove steadily through streets blanketed with thick smoke, in which the smell of burning flesh simmered faintly. An occasional gun-shot coughed in the distance. Down side-streets, people could be seen running in chaotic crowds, for no apparent reason. Some erupted from an alley-way and collided with the coach, banging their hands upon its sides, leaving dents. Women held screaming children up to windows. "Take my baby. Save my baby." Murchison could only turn away from these appalling things, helpless.

More than once he had thought 'What am I doing here?' and for just a few seconds panic welled within him, and he wanted to catch the next flight home. Then the inner need, the *sureness* he'd felt, which had compelled him to travel here despite the dangers, would reassert itself and he knew that soon the purpose of his flight would be revealed to him. It was like being a pilgrim to a holy land, and he had no doubt that, in some way, the ancient soil and sand of Egypt was holy to him. He was looking for the face of the pharaoh Akenaten in the crowd; the face that had drawn him here, long and faintly smiling.

The milk-drinking woman, he supposed, was similar in appearance to an ancient Egyptian. She was seated, yet still appeared to be very tall. Her dark auburn hair was cut square onto her shoulders. She wore no make-up, yet her features were strong, the lips full, brows heavy. It was impossible to guess her age; she could be anything from twenty to forty, exuding an aura of both youth and maturity. Her hand around the glass was like a man's hand, sure and tanned. She was not beautiful, but extraordinary. If he'd had a sister, she might well have looked like this woman.

Was that the secret? A lost heritage? A forgotten family? It seemed he had left any remaining grip on reality back in England.

Murchison smiled to himself. He had come to the front of the line now, and the formalities of mundane life must be attended to. When he had to sign his signature, the shape of his name felt unfamiliar to his hand. But what did he want to write instead? His thoughts were obscured; a troubled, cloudy sky. Outside, a siren wailed.

On the plane, he'd drifted in a hypnogogic state, dreaming of boiling clouds tumbling across the heavens, of tornadoes, and hurricanes. He'd had to swim through torrential rain, blind, looked up into the deadly crest of a tidal wave. Storms, changes. Perhaps it could be interpreted as cleansing.

Murchison expected the woman he'd seen to have disappeared by the time he'd finished with the hotel receptionists, but he found that she was still sitting in the same place. He'd have to walk past her to reach the elevators.

She'd finished her milk, and the glass now stood on the table by her elbow. She was staring straight ahead at the wall, as if deep in thought, as if trying to remember something. When Murchison drew abreast of her, she looked directly at him. A

smile hovered on her mouth, uncertain. Her brows drew together. She'd seemed to recognise him, but now clearly thought
she was mistaken.

Murchison paused. He could walk past now. It was in his
nature to do that, for generally he disliked potentially embarrassing situations. But still, he paused. His mouth opened of
its own volition and uttered a greeting. For a moment he
thought, *we are meant to meet here*, then dismissed the idea. From
the expression on the woman's face it seemed she was equally
confused.

"Forgive how this sounds," Murchison said, "but I get the
feeling I know you. I'm Cameron Murchison." He held out
his hand.

The woman stared at it for a moment, then took it. Her
palm was cold and wet, presumably from her drinking glass,
but her grip was firm. "I must admit you look familiar, yet I
don't know your name. Are you in pharmaceuticals?" Her
accent was English, yet Murchison would have sworn she was
of a more exotic blood.

Murchison grinned. It was surprisingly easy to conduct
this conversation. He knew that soon they would be drinking
together in the bar. "No, not exactly. I'm in the medical profession; gynaecology."

"Perhaps we've met at a conference, then." She smiled
more easily. "Lydia March."

"Here for business?"

Again her heavy brows drew together, and her eyes became reflective as if, for just a moment, she was confused,
unsure. "Well…I…just fancied a holiday, and Egypt has always fascinated me."

"Me too," Murchison said. "It was rather a last moment
decision flying out here."

"Yes, I know what you mean." She shrugged. "Well…"

"Look, I could do with a drink. How about you?"

She stared at him, so he babbled on. "I could just drop my
luggage off in my room and meet you in the bar. What do you
think?"

She nodded. "Yes, OK. I must admit I feel slightly at a
loose end right now."

On the way up in the elevator, Murchison's face grew hot. Would Lydia March think he was simply trying to chat her up? He was never so forward. Perhaps she would now discreetly go to her room, or venture outside into the turbulence of the city, unnerved by an importunate male. Was his purpose in being here simply to find a new, more impulsive side to himself? He would be the first to admit that might be an improvement.

The bar was dark yet airy, huge brass fan blades turning on the ceiling. The air conditioning made it almost cold, like a tomb. Copies of mummy cases, layered with gold paint, were positioned around the walls.

At first, Murchison thought his assumption had been correct and Lydia March had disappeared, then he saw her sitting at a table in the shadowy corner, beneath a canopy of palm fronds that rose from a gigantic urn. She smiled up at him, and in response to his enquiry, requested a glass of white wine.

At the bar, he wondered whether he should tell her the way he was feeling, that he was sure they were somehow destined to meet. No, it sounded too melodramatic, the worst of chat-up lines.

When he returned to the table, she took the wine from him and sipped it, then placed the glass carefully in front of her. "You know, she said, "this is most peculiar, and you'll no doubt think I'm mad, but I can't help feeling we were somehow…well.. *supposed* to meet here." She grinned cautiously. "Is that too bizarre?"

He wriggled in his seat opposite her. "No, not at all. I was thinking the same thing, actually, although I didn't think I'd have the guts to say it."

Lydia March leaned forward. "Tell me, why are you here in Cairo? Why are you really here?"

Murchison sighed. "It sounds insane. A day or so ago, I had an extraordinary day, and simply had a compulsion to come to Egypt. It was almost—and this sounds the most insane thing of all—as if I was summoned or drawn here."

Lydia March smiled—he saw relief in the expression—and nodded. "Yes! That's it! God, I thought I was going crazy! I had a dream, and in it, a lion came to me. It lay at my feet, and as I watched, transformed into a sphinx."

Murchison recounted his experiences at home, and the pull that the face of the pharaoh Akenaten had had over him. "I had no choice but to come. I could not ignore what was happening."

Lydia nodded. "Yes. After I had my dream, I felt as if I woke up being somebody else. Does that make sense?"

"Entirely."

Her eyes were alight with excitement now. "What's happening, Cameron? Are we part of something? Are there others like us?"

Murchison had not thought of that. "I don't know. Perhaps we'll find out. We've found each other."

Lydia touched her throat with her strong left hand. "I don't know whether to be afraid or ecstatic. This is so *strange*. I can't believe it!"

Murchison was thinking, *things like this don't happen in real life*, but it was happening now. He had to believe it.

They spent the afternoon together, weaving their stories, discussing their implications. Lydia was a rep. for a pharmaceutical company. She was single, not attracted by the prospect of marriage or children and, like Murchison, had only a dim recollection of her formative years. It was tempting to believe they were, in fact, related, and that somehow their memories had been mysteriously wiped clean. But perhaps this was too fanciful. Their conversation was like a dance, full of wild tarantellas, when their most speculative ideas would burst forth, only to be followed by slow, stately steps, when they considered they were acting like children, making things up, stepping too far into the domain of fantasy.

"But can anything be *too* fantastical?" Lydia mused, twirling her fourth glass of wine in her hands. "We don't know the truth, we only know it exists. Our reality, our truth, might be *anything*."

"I keep wondering whether I'll wake up shortly," Murchison said, "but the truth is, I've never felt more *real* than sitting here with you, talking about this absurd...idea."

By the time they decided to go out for dinner, both were feeling light-headed. Lydia took Murchison's arm as they immersed themselves in the furnace of the night. The stenches and perfumes of the city washed over them in suffocating fug; its cacophony howled in their ears. Along with a very visible military presence, hundreds of westerners filled the city streets, risking the dangers because they'd been drawn to Egypt for the approach of the new millennium. New Year's Eve was still a couple of months away, but already the atmosphere was building up towards it. A gigantic party had been planned to take place on the Giza plateau, with superstar bands, laser displays and various circus side-shows. Murchison found the whole thing a little distasteful, as if the New Age party plans threatened to cheapen an event that should be special and holy. He didn't know why he felt this so strongly, but voiced his thoughts to Lydia. She nodded. "Yes. I feel the same way. Are these feelings connected to why we're here?"

"You mean we might have been drawn here for the new millennium as well?"

Again, she nodded, then laughed. "Perhaps the New Agers are right and something amazing will happen. Perhaps we are part of it."

Murchison joined in her laughter. "Who knows? Maybe all these people booked themselves on last minute flights too!" In truth, he felt that Lydia and he were quite apart from other travellers.

Beyond the city, the pyramids loomed on the horizon like alien craft against the sky, weirdly sentient and watchful. Lydia shuddered. "I keep wanting to look up at the sky, as if something's hovering over me. I feel very strange."

Murchison patted her hand where it was hooked through his elbow. "Don't worry. If anything's going to happen to us, I'm sure it won't be bad."

Lydia glanced at him quickly. "I hadn't thought of it in terms of good and bad before. It just *was*. But you're right. I don't have a feeling of doom, just impendence."

They ate in a small restaurant, and talked about their work, their small lives. To both of them, it seemed increasingly as if some part of themselves had been shut away or even broken off. Lydia's careful questioning brought it home to Murchison just how unusual his lack of history was.

"Who *were* we?" Lydia asked, "and what have we to do with Egypt?"

Murchison took her hand. "It is a mysterious, ancient land. Who knows its secrets?"

"I want to be part of them," Lydia said, then grinned ruefully. "I think."

They wandered back to the hotel, and it seemed entirely natural for them to spend the night together. Both confessed to virginity, but the fact of it was inconsequential. They were meant to be together. As they undressed, without inhibition, in Murchison's room, Lydia mentioned the fact they might be brother and sister, but strangely, this only excited them. They imagined an affinity with the incestuous alliances of the ancient Egyptian kings and queens.

Lydia lay in the blue glow of night, her body pale and supple, beneath a single sheet which she held up to her breasts.

Murchison looked at her. He felt desire, but it wasn't urgent, more a simple need for oneness with this new companion. Once they embraced, they tumbled easily into lovemaking, almost as if they'd been lovers before, or at least were practised at the art.

For one moment, as he moved upon her, he looked down into her eyes. They were deep and tranquil, almost like smooth, dark beads of glass. What thoughts flowed behind them? He could not tell, although he did not feel embarrassed gazing upon her.

"Listen," she said, and he paused, conscious of being held, hard, within her body. He could feel her heartbeat pulsing closely against him.

"Listen to what?"

She flinched as if a sudden, sharp sound had squealed into her ears. She shook her head, smiled. "Nothing. Really. I thought I heard..." She brushed her damp hair back from her brow, curled her arms around his back. "We are moving back through time."

He heard it then. A faint skirl of music, a summoning, like a hypnotist's trigger to reawaken the memory of a hidden command. The harder he concentrated on the music, the more it blended in with the faint sounds of the city beyond the windows, filtered by double glazing. He could not hear the music now. Perhaps it had never existed.

Murchison felt sure that when they climaxed, they would both remember something, but his orgasm was like an ebbing of the memory tide, fragments of recollections sizzling away back into the deep. Lydia uttered a gentle sigh, her eyes closed. It seemed no revelations had come to her either.

Lydia lay beside him, curled along his side. "We were so close," she said. Both were too tired to make love again.

Lydia slept restlessly, and kept Murchison awake for several hours. She frowned in her sleep, murmuring phrases he could not properly hear. Her dreams seemed troubled. He held her in his arms, compelled to stare at her face.

In the morning, when Murchison awoke, he opened his eyes to see Lydia standing naked by the gauzy drapes at the window. She was staring through them at the hazy dawn.

"What is it?" Murchison asked, fearing she was distressed.

She turned to look at him with dark eyes. "I know who we are," she said, "who I am."

"How? A dream?" He had to swallow. He felt afraid now, afraid of what she would say.

"I am Pharmaros," she said. "That is my name. I know you, have always known you."

Murchison stared at her. Her words disturbed him; he didn't want to hear them. Yet wasn't this what they'd both wanted?

Then Lydia was gripping the drapes with both hands and he was out of the bed in an instant to catch her as she fell. She lay against his bare chest, shuddering. "They took it all away from us...all of it. I hate them!"

"Who?"

"Remember!" Her voice was a snarl. "You can. It's there! Just *think*! This morning, it all seems so clear, as if the last twenty years of my life never even existed. We've woken up now, truly woken. It can't just be me. Think!"

Murchison's mind was like a TV screen, and some madman was constantly changing the channels. He caught glimpses of images, memories, but they refused to remain static. He could not interpret them. "It's no good…I can't…"

Lydia, or Pharmaros as she'd claimed to be, pulled away from him and got to her feet. "I was not always a woman," she said, looking down at him.

Crouched before her, gazing up at her full, statuesque body, Murchison found, strangely, that was not difficult to believe. She was voluptuously feminine, but there was a masculine steel about her. He remembered his first sight of her hands.

She put her strong, agile fingers against her body, below her breasts, and stroked down her stomach in one graceful movement. "I have become the thing I desired, that initiated my fall…" Her eyes became glazed. "In the age of Eden, in its prime. I am he who taught the children of men the resolving of enchantments, and for that I was cursed. Look at me now, my brother. Remember with me the moments of our wretched, glorious history!"

For a brief moment, Murchison felt as if he'd been engulfed in flame. He saw a woman's face, blond hair, arms reaching out for him in terror from an inferno of blue fire. He put one hand over his mouth, froze, stooping, gazing at the floor. Then he said in a quiet, wondering voice, "Helen, my god." The moment of his fall was far closer to the present moment than millennia before. Twenty years previously, he had sought to enact forbidden rituals with a daughter of man—Helen Winter. He had been seized by the Parzupheim from his family domain in the village of Little Moor, and a new personality had been grafted onto him. Something, or someone, had now released him from the prison of forgetfulness. The memories had come back to him entire, as if he'd never lost them. He knew now what the face of Akenaten meant to him: it resembled the long-faced countenance of an ancient Watcher.

Pharmaros held out her hands and lifted him from the floor. They stood facing one another, of a similar height, eye to eye. "Who are you?" she asked.

"Kashday," he replied. "Kashday Murkaster."

They embraced for a moment, the room stilled around them. Then Pharmaros lifted the drapes. "It's been so long," she said, "this punishment."

Chapter Seventeen
The Jewelled Serpent

Daniel and the others waited two days in the Valley of Stones. By the end of this time, the Yarasadi were getting impatient and wanted to return home. Gadreel said she felt they should still wait, but Daniel could tell she was no longer as sure about this as she had been.

"Oh, for Anu's sake, let's go back to Qimir's camp," Salamiel said. "It's obvious Shem isn't coming back here. What good is it doing hanging around? Our supplies are running low. Remember we have to feed ourselves on the journey back."

"We can't just leave him!" Daniel said. He'd already made some short forays into the surrounding mountains, but had been unable to pick up any sign of Shem, physical or psychic. He'd also meditated for hours, trying to contact Ishtahar, hoping she could give him information, but she either wouldn't or couldn't co-operate. Daniel had never felt so alone. He couldn't dispel the feeling that Shem was now far away, but still felt it would be a betrayal if they returned to Qimir without definite proof that Shem had gone elsewhere. There was still a chance he might be meditating somewhere up in the mountains.

Gadreel ran her fingers through her hair. "One more night," she said. "That's all. This afternoon, we'll have another thorough search and if nothing's found, or Shem hasn't turned up by tomorrow morning, we'll leave."

Daniel uttered a suppressed cry of outrage and turned away from her.

"Salamiel is right," Gadreel said softly. "We can't wait here for ever, Daniel."

"Then what *do* we do?" he snapped. "Without Shem we have no purpose, no idea what to do. We are the limbs; he is the brain. Do we return to Qimir and forget all about the key and the Chambers, and the other avatars who must be waiting for us somewhere?"

Gadreel sighed. "I understand your anxieties, but I still think we should go back, not least because of what Salamiel has pointed out about our supplies. At Qimir's we could apply ourselves to working psychically to trace Shem. We could work intensively on what to do next."

"We have no key," Daniel said. "No master and no key. No knowledge."

"We have no choice!" Gadreel said sharply. "We can't stay here until we starve. And don't think of waiting here alone. I'll tie you up and drag you away kicking and screaming before I'll allow that!"

That night, Daniel lay in his blanket, listening to the comforting sounds of horses around him, and the snores and breathing of his companions. *This is my last chance*, he thought. *Ishtahar, come to me. Advise me as you always have.*

His mind was totally blank. There was no buzz of psychic contact, just deadness, and the soft cacophony of mundane thoughts. "Damn it!" Daniel said softly and sat up abruptly. Why was his ability so unreliable? He remembered how, when he'd first worked with Shem, he'd had psychic information tumbling out of his mind whenever it was needed. Now, it was such hard work, for so little reward. Maybe he was too old, too closed off. But he was Grigori now, no longer human. Perhaps that meant whatever blocks he was experiencing were self-created.

Daniel felt an urge to walk around and got to his feet. Creeping away from his companions, he ventured beyond the circle that Gadreel had drawn with the sword, and which they still kept intact, punctuated by the bowls of flowers and water.

"Come to me," Daniel murmured. "I'm waiting. Come."

He sat down on the cold stones. The circle, with its smouldering fire, seemed miles away. Wind fretted his hair, reached into his clothes with icy claws. He shivered. "Ishtahar! Come to me!"

There was no sign of the blue glow which presaged Ishtahar's presence, either in reality or in his mind. Daniel concentrated harder, bellowed her name with his inner voice, willed her to manifest.

After a few moments, he opened his eyes. He felt dizzy, sick with the effort. Nothing, still nothing. He pressed the heels of his hands against his eyes, uttered a groan of defeat. "Where are you, you bitch?" He knew that in insulting his goddess, he was castigating himself, and yet the suspicion lurked within him that now he was Grigori, Ishtahar would no longer have dealings with him. He had become the person with whom she'd once had to compete for Shemyaza's affections.

A rattle of stones alerted him and he dropped his hands from his eyes. For a moment, all he could see was sparkling stars of light, then his vision cleared. A serpent was undulating over the stones towards him. It was as thin as a whip and even in the meagre light of the distant fire, its scales glinted and glistered with a gold-shot blue radiance, as if it were made of lapis lazuli. Its eyes were sapphires, each reflecting a single, purple spark.

Daniel stared at the creature, hardly daring to believe it might have come in answer to his summons. "Ishtahar?" His voice was a whisper.

The serpent reared up and hung before him, its blue-black tongue flickering in and out of its lipless mouth. "Ah, Daniel, you chide me so sorely," it said.

Daniel's shoulders slumped in relief. "You came. Thank God!"

"Thank who?" lisped the serpent. "You should thank me, and me only."

Daniel detected a new tone to Ishtahar's remarks, a sharpness that had not been there before. "Then I thank you, Ishtahar. My sore words are inspired by desperate need."

The serpent undulated before him; a private dance. "Ssso, you are Grigori now, my Daniel. You have regained what the years have taken from you, while I still languish in my grief."

"We both deserve respite," Daniel said carefully. "Yours will come."

The serpent dipped and swayed before him. "Yet in even
in your elevated condition, you still need me—as I have ever
been needed by men!"

"You sound bitter," Daniel said. "You never were before."

The serpent emitted a sound like a sigh. "It is my curse to
be a goddess to others," it said, "yet who will be a god for me?
Must I wait for an eternity to live again?"

Daniel thought about this, and saw how he could, in some
ways, be seen as instrumental in this continuing torment. "You
are a goddess because you allow it. People petition you, and
you hear, you respond. Surely only you have the power to end
the curse?"

The serpent contemplated him silently for a moment.
"Daniel, I am a forgotten goddess. My shrines are ruins, visited only by lizards and birds. Only you call to me now and
hold me to the form I am."

"I do not wish to cause you suffering," Daniel said. "You
came to me as an advisor. It was you, not I, who initiated our
contact."

The serpent lunged forward, but Daniel did not flinch. "It
was love that drew me to you," the serpent lisped. "Love for a
man, your master. You do not need me now, yet you bind me
to the earth."

"I do need you," Daniel said softly. "And I will always be
grateful for what you have done for me. But I don't want to
bind you."

Purple sparks flared in the serpent's eyes. "You are releas-
ing me, Daniel, from our confederacy?"

"If you want me to, yes. If my word alone will provide
that release."

The serpent swayed a little. "Then I accept that release
with gratitude. You may ask me one last question."

Daniel considered for a while, knowing that the way he
worded this question was extremely important. Ultimately, he
opted for simplicity. "How can I regain my inner sight?"

The serpent did not hesitate. "You have never lost it. Your
dilemma is that you do not trust yourself, which is why you
stare into darkness. You have been so close to the answer,
walked the ground where it lay absorbed by the stones, yet did

not recognise it. You can hear the things that even Shemyaza did not hear. The answer the key gave to him."

"I *can't* hear it. I have tried—walked these mountain paths. They are silent."

The serpent expelled a short hiss. "Oh, Daniel, Daniel. Look within. Must I hold your hand at every turn? You are more now than I was in life. You have reclaimed your angel blood. Listen to its music."

Daniel closed his eyes and summoned a quiet within him. Have faith, he told himself. He listened to the beat of his own blood and it resolved into the sound of feet trudging a stony path. An image bloomed in his mind: Shem climbing and climbing. He could feel all that Shem felt as he walked towards the site of vanished Kharsag. He saw the devastation that Shem had seen and then, almost in slow motion, relived Shem's communication with the crystal. When the time of Shem's capture came, he was aware of the sound of the guns, but in his head, louder than any metallic threat were the words, "Go to the old kingdom. Carry me to the Chambers. In Khem." The words Shem did not hear.

Daniel opened his eyes with a gasp. "Egypt!"

"Yesss!" hissed the serpent. "Shem has gone to Babylon, but you, my Daniel, must lead your companions back to Egypt."

"*Back* to Egypt? We have not yet been there."

"It is the place of beginning, but not your beginning."

"But *where* in Egypt? What must we do there? Will Shem join us?"

"Remember, Daniel, you are of the Lion," answered the serpent. "Seek the lion of the desert who guards Orion." It began to retreat, back into the darkness.

"Wait!" Daniel said. "You must answer me, Ishtahar. It is not enough just to tell me we have to go to Egypt. I need more! Stay! I command you!"

The serpent uttered a long, soft hiss. "You released me, Daniel. You are on your own now." Presently, it disappeared into the shadows. Daniel uttered an anguished cry and jumped to his feet.

"Daniel!" Gadreel's voice.

He turned and saw her approaching him from the circle. It was nearly dawn. He could see that Gadreel's eyes looked sleepy. "What are you doing out here?" she asked, rubbing her face and yawning.

"Trying to get answers," he said.

"And did you succeed?"

He shrugged. "We have to go to Egypt."

"What? Why?"

"Ishtahar came to me. That's the only information I could get."

"But where in Egypt?"

"She told me to seek the lion of the desert who guards Orion. I can only hope that was a reference to the sphinx."

Gadreel reached out and squeezed Daniel's shoulder. "Good, good. This is what we need."

"But it's hardly enough."

"No, it's more than enough. Much more than we had before tonight. We know now what to do. I'll wake Salamiel and tell him. The others might as well go back to Qimir's camp."

"It's so far, Gadreel. We can't ride there."

"It's not that far to the nearest town, despite how desolate and lonely it feels up here. We'll get transport. You and Salamiel still have money, don't you?"

"Yes, but..."

"No buts. That's all we need. Our final destiny has been revealed to us. We have only to follow it."

Far away, in Cornwall, Helen Winter woke up in her narrow bed. Blinking from sleep, it seemed to her as if a shower of blue sparks were falling down onto her, disappearing as they touched the quilt that covered her body. She could not move at all, but sensed that the sparks were pouring out of her scarab beetle Met-Met's jar. At the same time, she was gripped by a strange sensation. It was similar, in some respects, to when she fell over and the air was knocked from her lungs, but this feeling was a reverse of being winded. Something was gusting into her with the same sudden impact. Helen was not afraid. She was used to seeing and feeling strange things.

Released from her paralysis, she gulped for breath and sat up in the bed. Should she call for her mother? Not yet. The sparks and the peculiar sensations had gone now. She hopped out of bed and went to the window, where the curtains hung open.

Outside, the garden had disappeared. The cottage was surrounded by the sea, and now rose up from its own small island. Helen saw a shining figure walking towards her across the dark waves. It was a golden-haired man, dressed in a white robe. He seemed to be walking fast, but he came no closer to the island. His arms were held out to her, yet he could not reach her.

"Do not worry," Helen said to him, touching the glass of her window with small fingers. "Your love has brought me back. I am coming to you."

She drew the curtains across the window and went back to bed.

Chapter Eighteen
Bound in Babylon

Melandra Maynard was beginning to get impatient. She had been kept waiting for a couple of weeks now, and had still not spoken with the king. The old woman, Tiy, kept Melandra close to her and questioned her often. She appeared to be intensely curious about Melandra's life and history. Melandra had been selective about the facts she released, but Tiy had a knack for extracting data. Almost without realising what she was doing, Melandra found herself describing her insular childhood. When she looked back into her memories, all that she could remember was winter—bare trees, cold weather—and never any summers. There *had* been summers while she'd been at the school, so where had the memories gone?

"You were a lonely child," Tiy pronounced, "and you are a lonely woman."

"No," said Melandra, frowning. *But I am,* she thought.

Tiy shook her head at the description of Melandra's secluded school and its dusty teachers. "Such creatures have never grown up to be women," she said. "They should not be entrusted with the mind of a child."

Melandra described her teenage years defensively, although Tiy offered no comment. At the end of it, she merely patted Melandra's arm and said, "All that fire and energy poured into a desire to kill. You have much fire, Melandra Maynard, and one day we shall all see its flames."

Melandra hesitated, then said, "You know why I'm here, Tiy. I am sworn to kill the Fallen One."

Tiy sighed. "Yes. We are friends talking across a fence."

Friends? Melandra hadn't thought of that, but realised that over the last couple of weeks she had spoken to Tiy more

than she'd spoken to anyone in her life. Here was the grand-
mother she had never known. It was most peculiar and certainly inappropriate. Tiy was little more than a devil-worship-
per. Why then did her words make more sense to Melandra
than anything her teachers had ever said to her? Tiy's opinions gave her new insight into her past. Tiy did not say so, but
Melandra could tell the old woman thought she had been treated
very badly. There had been no love in her life, no excitement,
no childish happiness. These revelations disturbed Melandra
greatly, although she strove to ignore the needlings of doubt
that now pricked her mind. Tiy's careful words attacked the
citadel of Melandra's schooling and conditioning, but as yet
the walls remained unbreached. Babylon might act as a narcotic upon the senses, lulling Melandra into a dreamy state of
unreality, but bitterness still burned hot within her. Tiy would
never understand the reason for it. Melandra knew she would
always feel that Shemyaza had shamed and polluted her to an
extent where her own survival now meant far less than the
destruction of the Fallen One. After what had happened to
her, she doubted she could ever return to the life she once
had. Here, in the wilderness of the world, she might hide her
dishonour, but among other Children of Lamech in the States,
she felt her defilement would be burned upon her brow like
the mark of Cain. She could never forget the violation in
Istanbul, no matter how dim—or changed—her memories of
home might become.

It was clear to her that Shemyaza was not yet in the city
himself, and she resolved to use the time before he arrived to
ingratiate herself with the Babylonians. In some way, she must
become part of their society, so that, to a degree, she would
become invisible. Perhaps it was no longer important for her
to speak to the king. She realised that at some point in the
future, Tiy might well try to obstruct her work. Melandra
shrank from dwelling upon the consequences of that. It was
not inconceivable that Tiy too might have to be killed. I should
not get too close to her, Melandra thought, but it was difficult
not to respond to the offered warmth and confederacy.

Under any other circumstances, Melandra might have enjoyed the exotic luxury of Babylon and treated her stay there

as an unusual holiday. She knew there was a queen and a
princess in the city, but never caught sight of them. Their
quarters lay behind cyclopean doors at the end of a wide
corridor roofed in green glass. Melandra was free to wander
around the areas of the palace where the servants, musicians
and companions of the queen were housed, but soon discovered that guards at the doorways leading to other regions of
the palace would not allow her to pass by. Effectively, she
was a prisoner.

In the women's quarters, she had her own room. It was of
modest size but opulently appointed with drapes and cushions
and a private bath-room. There was a phone she could pick
up to order food or drink, like room service in a hotel. Outside the long windows to her room was a cloister that surrounded a pleasant water garden, where the women would sit
under canopies in the late afternoon, brushing each other's
hair, or painting delicate patterns with henna upon their hands
and feet. The Babylonians were respectful to Melandra, if
distant, and although the women were fond of whispering together and giggling whenever she was present, they always
offered her sweetmeats or hashish or wine, all of which she
refused. She was not invited into their circle, but they smiled
at her, watched her, discussed her.

Melandra liked exploring the labyrinth of the women's quarters. It was decorated with ancient art—statues and wall paintings—which despite their heathen nature were fascinating to
study. One of the more mature women noticed her interest
and confided to Melandra a secret. Thus, she discovered that
the women had access to a maze-like system of corridors that
wove like a secret web through all the levels of the palace.
Her benefactress told her in halting English of a story associated with these secret ways. She said that when King
Nimnezzar's Magian priests had invoked the djinn to help build
Babylon, Queen Amytis and Tiy had trapped one of the elemental spirits, and ordered them to give the women of the
palace entry to all the places from which the men would bar
them. The woman said that even to this day, Nimnezzar and
his male staff were blind to these ways and were unaware the
women watched them in all they did. Melandra found the

story amusing, but gave it little credence. To her, Babylon must have been built by very human hands. Still, she was now able to explore the palace more fully and marvel at its eccentricities and indulgences.

The secret passages led to screened balconies high above ceremonial chambers, where presumably the women were free to watch in privacy, without fear of rude male interruption, whatever proceedings took place there. Whenever Melandra went exploring, the rooms below her were always empty.

Most impressive of the secret places was the gallery that ran along one entire side of the palace's throne room. Behind its filigreed screen lay a miniature hanging garden. Fountains made soft music in ivory pools and languid ferns hung down to the marble flag-stones. The gallery's presence must be entirely obvious to anyone in the room below who happened to look up, thus proving to Melandra that Nimnezzar himself must have commissioned the secluded balconies and walkways for his wife. Still, the legends were compelling, and she could understand why the pagan, superstitious women of Babylon would prefer to believe in them rather than plain fact.

Melandra had noticed that the palace itself had moods, which were affected by the lives of those who lived within it, or perhaps even vice versa. She soon realised she didn't have to hear any sounds of activity to know that something momentous was going on. She could simply *feel* it.

One morning, she awoke with an intense feeling of oppression that seemed to have fallen upon her like a fog some time during the night. After bathing, she wandered into one of the communal salons, where some of the women were sitting on cushions, whispering together. They ceased speaking when she entered the room, their gaze sliding furtively around her. Melandra smiled, uttered a bright greeting, and went to help herself to a breakfast of fruit, milk and nuts, putting the women's behaviour down to some petty intrigue or quarrel. Perhaps a storm was brewing, which was affecting everybody's mood.

Later, as the morning lengthened, the feeling of oppression lifted somewhat, but was replaced by a tension. Melandra eventually asked one of the girls what was going on, but she only shook her head, apparently unable to speak English. For once—perhaps no coincidence—Tiy was nowhere to be found. Melandra prowled the secret corridors, peeking through lattices, peering round drapes. There seemed to be fewer people around than usual, but those she did see hurried about their duties. She knew something was about to happen. The air was full of the scent of incense, which drifted in enormous clouds from across the city. Melandra climbed out onto the only roof to which she'd found access. It was wide and flat and presumably covered the servants' quarters, because over a dozen long washing-lines were stationed upon it, from which a colourful assortment of laundry hung. Melandra shielded her eyes to gaze out over the city. She could see the enormous ziggurat of the temple a mile or so away, its summit shrouded in dense smoke. Tiy had told her it was the Tower of Babel, and despite her despising of its purpose, Melandra could not help but be awed by its construction. It was like an enormous stepped pyramid, its slope punctuated by wider terraces at certain levels where the entrances to shrines were situated, or outdoor altars. Even from where she stood, the incense fumes were strong enough to make her eyes sting. She heard male voices raised in an eerie, wailing chant and a cacophony that sounded like the cry of goats. A couple of drops of moisture fell onto her bare arms from the sky, but there were no clouds.

Melandra sensed a presence behind her rather than felt it, and turned round quickly. A woman stood behind her, looking as if she'd stepped down from one of the wall paintings of ancient times. Her apparel, Melandra deduced, must be a copy of the original Babylonian costume; a long, closely fitting robe of shimmering green cloth, whose golden fringes rippled in the slight breeze. Her black hair was squarely cut in an almost Egyptian style; its braids tipped with brightly-coloured beads; it could have been a wig. Her arms and throat were adorned with heavy gold jewellery. The woman was perfectly still and regarded Melandra through hooded black eyes. Melandra stared back at her.

After a few moments of intense mutual scrutiny, the woman spoke. "You are the American," she drawled, speaking the words as if they were an insult.

Melandra made no response but turned back to studying the Tower. The woman came up beside her. She was shorter than Melandra but was surrounded by an air of confidence and power that gave an effective illusion of height.

"What is an American doing here?"

"Seeking Shemyaza," Melandra answered shortly. She had no wish to converse with this woman; her aura of voluptuous sexuality made Melandra feel uneasy.

"We both know there is more to it than that."

"I don't think that's any of your business," Melandra said. "I'm here as a guest of the king. If I have anything to say, I'll say it to him."

"And I am Nimnezzar's queen. I am Amytis."

Melandra's eyes widened in surprise. She was annoyed that this intelligence impressed her and fought an instinct to treat the woman with more respect. She must use this meeting with care, although she had no idea what honorific title was due to the queen, or even if it was expected in this barbarous country. "Why won't your husband see me?" she asked. "I have come a long way."

Amytis shrugged. "He is a busy man. Very busy."

Melandra paused, then forced a smile. "Is there anything you can do to help me obtain an audience?"

Amytis glanced up at her with disdain. "You must wait until he is ready. He is the Great King, American woman."

Melandra abandoned this train of conversation before she became impatient with it. "What has happened today? It's obvious that something's going on."

Amytis walked to the very edge of the roof, her sandalled toes hanging over its edge. "Why do you ask? I think you know as well as I do how a woman may learn things here."

"What do you mean?"

Amytis flashed her dark eyes at Melandra and smiled. "Well, as you creep around my corridors, I follow you. You do not know that I am there. I watch you. I see your mind working, planning. You think you are dangerous, American woman, but you are not. You know not in what you meddle."

"I know well enough."

Amytis laughed; a display of full-throated hilarity, hands on hips. "Tiy tells me of you," she said. "You intrigue us with your strange, misguided thoughts."

Melandra realised the futility of responding to this affront. It would be pointless to rant about how Shemyaza was the ultimate evil. These pagans were too ignorant ever to understand that. They were waiting for him to come to them; their dark god.

Melandra swayed upon the roof as if the intense blue sky was pressing down upon her. A terrible loneliness surged unbidden through her mind. She felt abandoned by God, by Jesus. They were not present in this nest of infidels, but shut out by unbelief. Melandra could not even remember the last time she had prayed. How effectively this whore of cities had drugged her mind. She had eaten of its lotus and lost the memory of her faith. These revelations came to her as if she'd just awoken from an intoxicated sleep. *What am I doing here?* she wondered. *How did I get here?* She was so far from home, so far even from what had happened in London. It was as if she had been led into a desert by a seductive mirage, only to come to her senses and find nothing there, with no way of getting back to the point from which she'd started. She shivered in the hot air. How would she kill Shemyaza here? Babylon was an alien world, and she no longer had a gun. Women here would use poison, snakes and scorpions to kill their enemies. They would use knives, perhaps, or a twisted skein of their own hair. She was not like the women of Babylon.

Amytis turned to face her. "I have decided to take notice of you," she said, and held out a slim, dark hand whose fingernails were lacquered in dark, shining green like insect carapaces. "Come, we shall go and see what my husband's people are so excited about."

Melandra looked at the hand for a moment, then saw her own hand within it, enfolded in fingers. Somehow, she had reached out and been taken.

Nimnezzar sat upon the peacock throne, his courtiers arrayed around him; the Magians a black presence in dark-blood robes in a line beneath a canopy. This was a court of men; no women were present to witness the judgement upon Shemyaza, seducer of all women.

The men of Babylon were dwarfed by the immensity of the throne room. Twenty-foot statues stood to attention along its walls, some of them pillaged from the ancient sites Nimnezzar's archaeologists had excavated. Some had been commissioned and represented Nimnezzar and his family.

The priests of Etemenanki had proudly informed Nimnezzar that the angel king had been located and secured, although they were rather sparing on details concerning the manner in which their elemental creatures had failed to capture Shemyaza's companions. They had muttered vague excuses as to why this had happened, but concluded that despite this small failing, their magic must be strong indeed, for had not Shemyaza come to their hands like a lamb? The ease with which they'd accomplished this task made Nimnezzar uneasy. It did not ring true to him.

The king had not yet told Tiy that Shemyaza had been located, never mind that he had been brought to the city. He knew that Tiy would want to be present at this meeting, and for now Nimnezzar wished to keep the old woman's meddling hands out of it. Superficially, she appeared to advise and support him, but some instinct warned him that Tiy had her own agenda.

The doors to the throne room were thrown wide and a phalanx of ceremonially-dressed militia marched into the room, led by Jazirah, who was dressed in deepest crimson, his large turban adorned with nodding peacock feathers. Nimnezzar swallowed involuntarily, anxious for a fleeting moment that he had no control at all over these events.

The soldiers came to a stand-still, surrounding a tall figure, whose head rose several inches above their own. Nimnezzar tensed. Was this the angel king? He looked like a man, less inhuman than the inscrutable Penemue. Nimnezzar wondered whether he'd been duped, or his Magians had captured the wrong person.

Jazirah stepped forward and performed an obeisance to the king. "My lord, I bring to you the captive, Shemyaza."

Nimnezzar raised a hand and gestured to Shemyaza to be led forward. His hands were manacled together before him. The supposed angel king was dressed in dusty khaki, a traveller. His long white-blond hair was tied loosely at his neck, tendrils of it hanging over his face. His skin was tanned to a pale shade of honey. He seemed bemused.

"So," Nimnezzar said in his most royal tone. "You are Shemyaza. I have been waiting to meet you."

Shemyaza smiled and inclined his head. He seemed perfectly at ease. "My sentiments are the same." He paused, then raised his hands. "Is this the way to treat a guest? There is no need for chains, I assure you."

Nimnezzar narrowed his eyes. "You have not yet attained the status of guest. You are my prisoner. Answer my questions with honesty and we shall see about the chains."

Shemyaza flared his nostrils, but did not appear particularly outraged.

"You do not look like a king," Nimnezzar remarked.

Shemyaza shrugged. "I have not claimed to be one. Others own that privilege."

"So, reluctantly, you assumed the role. Tell me, how have you survived these long millennia? Why now have you shown yourself in the world?"

Shemyaza raised his chin. "I had a destiny thrust upon me. I follow it, because I have no choice."

Nimnezzar was not pleased with the answer, which he felt was hardly an answer at all. "And what are your plans? Will you raise an army against humanity? Will you breed a race of warrior sons?"

Shemyaza opened his eyes wider, and for the first time Nimnezzar saw how blue they were and flinched slightly beneath the directness of the gaze. "My destiny is not that of the warrior."

"Where is your kingdom? Have you come to reclaim Eden?"

"I have no earthly kingdom. That is not my role."

Nimnezzar risked a smile. "You are a king without a kingdom or an army. Some might say that is not much of a king."

Shemyaza shrugged again and continued to smile, while the courtiers laughed at the king's joke.

Nimnezzar thought, he has charisma, but he is just a man. He seems deluded, a dreamer. "What were you doing in the mountains?"

"Visiting my old home."

"Just a visit? Why were you in the company of Yarasadi? Are they your people now?"

"The Yarasadi guided my friends and me through the mountains, that is all."

"I am wary of any who keep the company of Yarasadi. They are the enemies of Babylon."

"The Yarasadi have ever been somebody's enemies, yet all they yearn for is their own land, and to be able to live in it as they wish."

Nimnezzar raised sardonic brows. "A political statement, yet you claim no kingship over them."

Shemyaza lifted his manacled hands in what was designed to be a casual gesture. "I was merely stating the obvious. Whether I support that desire or not is irrelevant."

Nimnezzar leaned back in his chair, pointed an accusing finger. "You are lying to me. You lead the Yarasadi now."

Shemyaza frowned. "No, I lead no-one."

"What were you doing at the gas fields? Planning a terrorist attack?"

Shemyaza stared back at him. "Not at all. I was just looking."

"What were you looking for?"

Jazirah made a small sound to attract attention and, bowing, approached the king. "The captive had this in his possession when we found him." He held out the crystal cone.

Nimnezzar took it and turned it in his hands. "What is this?"

"A stone," Shemyaza said, "a curio."

"Did you find it in the mountains?"

"Yes. It is probably very ancient—a decorative stone that perhaps once adorned a statue or was inlaid into an altar."

"He was muttering into it," said Jazirah, "when we found him."

"It is a stone of power, then," said the king.

"If it is, I cannot fathom it," Shemyaza replied. "Why not enshrine it in your Tower of Babel. There it might remember its function."

Nimnezzar narrowed his eyes. "What do you know of my tower?"

"Only what I saw as your people drove me through the city. It is a good copy for an edifice built from guess-work."

"Not guesswork," Nimnezzar said. "The Magians learned from the sacred fires how it should be built. Djinn breathed life into its stones."

Shemyaza grinned. "Djinn are capricious creatures. You should use them with care."

Nimnezzar objected to the tone of this remark. "If you *are* Shemyaza, hear this. I am the appointed heir of Anu, the father of all gods. I command djinn, I command men. And now, I command angels. Shemyaza fell, he lost his power. His time is past. He should now submit to me, the rightful heir and give me what remains of his power."

Shemyaza laughed aloud at this. "Should he? By what right do you claim this kingship? Does Anu speak to you? If so, you are truly privileged, for he has neglected to speak to the thousands of his descendants who inhabit this earth."

The word thousands clearly took Nimnezzar by surprise. "Enough of this craziness. Tell me now of your plans. I am the true inheritor of the sacred blood-line. I will not tolerate rivals."

"I am no rival to *you*, Nimnezzar," Shemyaza said.

Nimnezzar was beginning to feel slightly numb. The interview seemed unreal. He had power over Shemyaza—he could feel it in his blood—yet how could this be so? If Shemyaza was who he claimed to be and who the Magians believed him to be, surely he would not submit to this treatment? Nimnezzar decided to test the situation. "I shall give you one more chance," he said. "Where are your armies? What is your first target? If you do not answer, I will have you beaten and cast into a pit."

Shemyaza laughed again. "Would you dare to do that to the king of angels?"

Nimnezzar did not hesitate, although his heart beat fast and painfully behind his ribs. "I see no angel king. I see a man. If you had power, true power, you would have evaded capture. You would blast us now with divine fire." Nimnezzar sneered. "No. If you have strength, it is in the weapons and hearts of others, many others. And I want to know who they are."

Shemyaza stood straight-backed before the king, his eyes gazing unwaveringly into Nimnezzar's own. "If you would be the true inheritor of the royal blood, you should learn that true strength comes not from brute, physical force, but from the heart and soul. You say you do not see a king in me, and you may be right, but all I see in you is a bullying child."

Nimnezzar snarled. "Enough! Perhaps in the pit you will realise the folly of your insults and learn to be more informative."

For a moment, Shemyaza seemed to become taller, and a light blazed from his eyes. Then he lowered his head, and his shoulders slumped. "So be it."

"Take him away!" Nimnezzar ordered the guards. "Teach him to respect the King of Babylon."

Chapter Nineteen
Secret History

Amytis, Tiy and Melandra had watched the proceedings from the gallery high above the throne room. Tiy had objected to the American being present, but Amytis was insistent. "She should not be here," Tiy had said in her own tongue, so that Melandra would not understand. "You know she has a mission. She might cause a disruption, which would be inconvenient to us."

"It is my wish to have her by me," Amytis had answered. "She won't do anything here. You have befriended this woman, Tiy, and have heard her stories. I too want to hear them, so she must also see me as a friend. We both know that Nimnezzar won't speak to her and soon he will send her away from the city."

"That woman holds more in her heart than she'll ever tell you!" Tiy had snapped, but relented. She was annoyed that Amytis had become involved in the matter of Melandra, for Tiy had been carefully nurturing a relationship with the American. The reason Nimnezzar had yet to grant her an audience was because Tiy had advised him against it, and had assured him he could let her deal with Melandra's interrogation. Nimnezzar was so obsessed by Shemyaza and Penemue, he saw Melandra as of minor importance. Tiy knew otherwise, but now, Amytis, with her brash, voluptuous presence, might spoil the delicate machinery of words and suggestions that she had constructed.

Tiy had sensed Melandra's tension when she had beheld Shemyaza. The old woman knew that Melandra had wanted to kill him there and then, but fortunately lacked the means. Melandra's hour would come, but perhaps not quite in the form she imagined. That morning, Tiy had experienced a revelation.

She was still reeling from its effects. Ever since Melandra's arrival in Babylon, Tiy had been visiting the temple of Etemenanki in order to scour the astral world for information about the woman and the men who held dominion over her. She knew the Magians felt extremely uncomfortable about her using the power of the temple, and would have liked to ban her from their sacred premises, but she ignored their complaints, confident that Nimnezzar would ultimately sanction her presence there. What Tiy had recently learned from trance was rather more than she'd expected, and was of severe importance to both Melandra and Shemyaza, but the moment was not yet right for Tiy to use this information.

"I must talk to the king," Tiy said, once Shemyaza had been led from the throne room. "It is time for me to meet Shemyaza."

"We should *all* like to meet this Shemyaza," Amytis said. "He did not *look* like a king, I must agree with my husband on that! Still, he was beautiful."

"I have seen his power!" Melandra blurted, causing Amytis to raise her eyebrows in surprise.

"Of course," Tiy said in a soothing voice, and reached out with her twiggy fingers to squeeze Melandra's arm. The muscles were tight beneath Tiy's touch. "Go now with Amytis and stay by her. I shall go and see how the land lies."

"Be quick," Amytis said. "I'm now quite impatient to learn what my husband plans to do next."

Tiy smiled and swept off up the passage-way. She had many tasks before her now, but her first was to convince Nimnezzar that Shemyaza was who they all thought he was. She could not see the angel king with her eyes, but his power had radiated into her mind like a burst of fire. Nimnezzar, the clod, could not perceive that with his muddy senses. He saw only a man. Tiy guessed that was what Shemyaza had wanted him to see. Still, she was surprised the angel had apparently allowed Nimnezzar's thugs to lead him off to a beating. His motives were yet more complex than she'd imagined. Up until the moment she'd 'seen' Shemyaza, Tiy had been prepared for infinite patience in this matter. Now, her energies and emotions were stirred. She had to act.

Nimnezzar, as Tiy had suspected, had been unsettled by his meeting with Shemyaza. When she entered his private office, she sensed the king was relieved to see her, but was striving not to reveal it. Fool! Didn't he know she had always been able to read his feelings? Now, he wanted advice, but he'd be condescending and aloof, attempting to disguise his need.

"I have spoken with the captive," Nimnezzar said in a haughty tone, "and am now unsure he is what you said he would be. He looks like a vagabond and talks like a man out of his depth. I think he is just a vain fool who has read the ancient stories and has cast himself in the role of Shemyaza. He's a misguided crusader who has duped the Yarasadi. A lunatic from the West."

"And you had him beaten," Tiy said.

Nimnezzar sniffed. "Yes. It was expedient for he was insolent. I have already received reports from Jazirah that he offered no defence as the guard beat him senseless. Is this the behaviour of a king?"

Tiy sighed quietly. She was not pleased to discover that Nimnezzar had actually carried out his threat, and had hoped Shemyaza would have offered some resistance. For whatever reason, he must be playing with Nimnezzar. "Do you doubt my counsel, Great King? Perhaps I am too old, and my 'sight' isn't what it was."

Nimnezzar uttered a sound of annoyance. "I would like your opinion."

"Then you must let me speak to him."

Nimnezzar paused, then said, "Very well. I shall send Jazirah with you."

"I would like to speak with Shemyaza alone." When Nimnezzar didn't respond, she said, "You must trust me. Haven't I helped you well in the past?"

"Very well. Speak to him, if he *can* speak."

Shemyaza had been confined in a dank hole, far below Etemenanki. The smell of the place offended Tiy's heightened senses as she was led by two of Nimnezzar's personal guard to the steps that disappeared down into the dark. She reached for the wall with her left hand and began her descent, dismissing the guards from her presence. They withdrew reluctantly and she heard a heavy door slam behind her. There was no source of light, but this did not matter to Tiy.

As she went slowly down the steps, Shemyaza's feelings drifted up to her like smoke. He was hurt and bitter, yet still she sensed no urge to fight in him. He felt defeated, confused. Tiy shook her head in bewilderment. He was a creature of contradictions, unsure himself of what and who he was. But there was no denying the flame of his soul, burning strong and true. Nimnezzar was more blind than she, for he had not noticed this flame.

At the bottom of the steps, Tiy stepped onto soiled straw. Others had been confined here, and perhaps still were, hanging dead in their chains. The smell of death hung in the air like unholy incense.

"Shemyaza," she said, and heard a rustle nearby.

She moved towards the sound, feeling in front of her with sensitive fingers. Presently, she felt cloth beneath her touch and the warmth of living flesh. Shemyaza appeared to be half lying in the straw. Almost greedily, her hands moved over his body, up to his face. She felt his fine bones, his high brow, but also the swelling there, the patina of dry, crusting blood. "You have been enjoying the hospitality of Babylon's king," she said.

Strong, agile hands gripped her own, lifted her questing fingers away from his face. "Who are you?"

"I am Tiy, a seeress. I came to the city with Nimnezzar's queen."

She heard him sigh. His breath rattled slightly in his chest. Perhaps they had damaged him there. "What do you want?"

Tiy squatted down before him. "To speak with you, to learn why you have allowed Nimnezzar to abuse you so."

"He cannot kill me. It is not yet time for me to die."

"How bravely you suffer your pain."

He paused, then said, "It is inconsequential."

Tiy became aware then that part of him gorged itself on pain because it justified the fear he was again to be a martyr. She spoke carefully. "I understand that Babylon is graced by your presence only because that is your wish. You want to be here. Why?"

She heard Shemyaza shift position slightly upon the straw, his soft grunt of discomfort. "I wanted to meet the man who claimed to be the heir to my people's kingdom."

Tiy's voice became insidious, an invisible serpent in the dark. "You could have come with fire. You could have come victorious. I know you have that power."

"Do you?" His voice was weary. "Your king sees only the weakness of a man."

"You cannot blame him. That is all you let him see."

Shemyaza was silent for a moment. "Then why do you think differently?"

"I am blind," she answered. "Therefore I see by other means."

Shemyaza again hesitated before speaking. "It is more than that. I feel that you..." His voice trailed into silence.

"Yes, I *know*," Tiy murmured. She reached out again to touch him. She could not help herself. Words came quickly that she had intended to preserve within her until later. "Shemyaza, I have waited long for the moment when I would meet you again."

"Meet me again?" Shemyaza echoed faintly. "When have we met before?"

She did not pause. "You were conceived in me, cut from my own body. I am your mother."

There was again silence for a moment, and Tiy knew she had managed to shock him. Then he laughed. "You can't be."

"But I am," she said patiently. "The body you wear is fifty years old. I bore it that long ago, when I was still lovely."

"You are human..."

"Yes. But your father was not."

Shemyaza took one of Tiy's withered hands in his own. "I was brought up by a Grigori clan—the Othmans. They told me my parents were dead. I heard nothing of a mother in the east."

Tiy squeezed his fingers. "They kept it from you. Now, I will tell you, because it is time for you to know. Whether this conflicts with their plans or not, I will still tell you."

"*Their* plans? Whose? The Babylonians?"

Tiy shook her head, although he could not see it. "Hush. Soon, you will know all, but listen...I bore you in the land of Persia."

Tiy explained that she had been born into a Gypsy clan, who were remnants of a Magian cult. They had worshipped one of Shemyaza's many forms—the Hanged One, Azazel— and believed they were descendants of the people who had given succour to the Scapegoat when his father had cast him out into the desert. Azazel had given sons and daughters to the women of Tiy's ancestors, so that their human blood had mingled with the essence of angels. The old histories had been handed down through the generations by word of mouth; it was a secret tradition. Tiy's clan had roamed across Persia, feared by some, scorned by others, but always held in a grudging respect.

When Tiy was twenty years old, a strange man had approached the camp of her people one evening at sunset. He was not a Gypsy, but neither was he like the people who lived in the cities and towns, or upon the farms. He was tall and, for those who were able to see the inner world, his countenance shone like the sun. Tiy, he singled out for attention, and that very night she took him to her bed. This Angel of Annunciation told her that she would bear a special son, who was of the gods.

"He was Grigori," Tiy said. "I sensed it, for even then, before my sight faded, I could see more with my inner eyes than others could."

"Your people knew of the Grigori, then," Shemyaza said.

She nodded. "Yes. We knew the children of angels walked the world, although it was your father who told me their name. When the time came for your birth, you were too big for me and the women of my family had to cut my belly to bring you forth. Your skin and eyes shone like the sun; there was a glamour about you. I named you Ra, after the Egyptian god of the sun."

Tiy sensed a stillness within Shemyaza's mind as he struggled to uncover some memory of his early years. "I cannot remember," he said.

Tiy ran her fingers over his hands. "It was so long ago," she said. "You stayed with me only for three years."

Tiy never forgot the words of her lost lover, that she had borne a son of the gods. Ra was living proof of this promise. In her heart, she had known she'd not be able to keep the boy with her. The days while her shining son played beside her were gifts from Azazel. She cherished them, knowing that eventually all she would have would be memories of those gilded hours. "You were a lovely child," Tiy said, "kind and strong and sensitive. It was so hard for me, because even then I knew your future held agony, fear and darkness. I tried to fill you with my love, that it might be a candle in the darkness to come."

One day, Tiy's fears were justified and three tall men came out of the desert to the camp of the Gypsies. They told Tiy they had come for her son, to take him back to his father's people.

"I could not fight them," Tiy said. "Your destiny had already been written. I knew I had been chosen to bear you, for I carried the royal blood of the Shining Ones. Their only gift to me, after they had taken you back, was that they gave my spirit entry into corners of their world, from where I could watch you grow into a man."

Shemyaza uttered a sound of anger and anguish. "But this means…" He could not say the words.

"Yes, my son. Do not doubt that the Grigori have always known who you were. Your reincarnation was planned from the first moment. What you have perceived as rogue fortune in your life has been crafted by the most secret cabals of your people. Many dark rituals have been conducted to drive you along your path."

She could sense confusion emanating from Shemyaza's body like a physical force. The news was so astounding to him, he could barely react, but there was also a secret, cynical part of him that wasn't surprised at all. "Tell me more," he said.

She squeezed his hands. "My son, the race of the Grigori is like a living thing in its own right, a complex creature. Secrets within secrets within secrets. There are those who guide you towards your destiny, but equally there are those who would stop you achieving it. Some Grigori do not want change to come."

"How do you know all this?" Shem held her hands so tightly, she felt her bones bend in her flesh.

"Because, with my inner sight, I have remained alert to the beacon of your presence in the world. The Grigori were merciful and granted me knowledge of your growth, but I also used that connection carefully and learned much about the Grigori themselves. When the time came that the ancient fragments of your soul were freed by the boy, Daniel, I felt it."

"Daniel," Shemyaza said, and groaned. "He is lost to me again."

"Have no fear," Tiy answered. "He and your other companions escaped Nimnezzar's clutches. They fared better than you, but then they had more spirit to fight."

Shemyaza sighed and released his tight grip on her hands. "I am relieved to hear that." He paused. "It is strange that my mother—if that is truly who you are—should be one of Nimnezzar's followers."

Tiy laughed. "His follower? No! I have acted as his advisor, but in many ways he has been my pawn."

"You knew that I would come here?"

"Of course. I knew that long ago, before Nimnezzar ever dreamed he would be king, which is why my protégé, Amytis, is now Nimnezzar's wife. I needed a pathway into the city, and I built one. But that is not important now. Shemyaza, the time of your destiny approaches. You know what you must do."

He laughed bleakly. "Do I? I have learned I am half human, and that makes sense to me. It explains why I could do nothing but fall beneath the fists and feet that beat and kicked me. Nimnezzar is right about me. I am hardly a king."

Tiy made an impatient sound. "Stop feeling sorry for yourself! You need to understand more about the past. You know so little. I have spent fifty years scouring the astral worlds for grains of truth and now I have a desert's worth of grains! The Elders of your race came out of Egypt, where they seeded the first great dynasties of kings. Their civilisation foundered—something happened to them which has been lost to memory—and their race fragmented. The great chambers where they stored their knowledge were closed down and hidden. Anu was a descendant of one of the Elders. He was an ambitious and industrious man. His forefathers had entrusted the keys to the Chambers of Light to their sons, and through the power of the key he kept, Anu created Kharsag in Eden. But that too went wrong. You know of that sorry history."

"Yes," Shemyaza said coldly. "I feel it is my task to open the Chambers once more, to redress the wrongs of the past."

"They were not wrongs," Tiy said, "The Elders did what was necessary at the time, but perhaps the world is ready now to know what was lost. It is indeed your task to open the Chambers. Let me tell you what I have learned about them, for you will need this knowledge."

Tiy explained that the Magians had advised Nimnezzar how to build Etemenanki, intending to use it as a focus for their considerable powers, but if anything, the Tower responded more to Tiy. The spirit of what it represented attuned to her, and gave her dreams of the past. She was a priestess of the Great Earth Mother, and the earth remembers everything that happens upon her body. Combining these two influences, Tiy had been able to learn about the Chambers and their history. She discovered that they had been built by the power of the Source of Creation, which had been channelled through a great alexandrite crystal, housed in a gigantic chamber in the centre of the complex. Twelve smaller chambers had been constructed around it in a circle and within these the Elders had placed miniature replicas of the great crystal. In these lesser chambers, twelve Elders would use the smaller crystals to enter deep trance and leave their bodies. A pattern of deeply-cut circles and lines on the chamber floors created a pathway for the astral bodies, enabling them to enter into the great central crystal. This gargantuan stone acted as a portal to the gateway of the stars of Orion. There, folding space and time itself, the astral bodies of the Elders were able to journey back to the Source of Creation at the centre of the universe, and there commune with it.

Shemyaza interrupted her narrative. "When I possessed the privilege of astral flight, I was always drawn to pass through Orion, but entry was always forbidden to me. Then, as part of my punishment, Anu decreed that my soul should be bound within those terrible stars, for what I thought would be eternity."

Tiy spoke softly. "Yes, my son. I have felt your pain."

"I strove to commune with the Source as the Elders once did. I wanted knowledge, I wanted the universe and I wanted the earth and her fires of ecstasy." He laughed ruefully. "I wanted it all."

"The Chambers of Light *were* the all," Tiy said. "They facilitated a union between spirit, earth and source. Through the crystal, the Elders could attain the answers to any question. They even learned of the great plan of the universe itself. The destiny of this planet was mapped out, recorded and initiated through those chambers."

Tiy then went on to talk about the Elders themselves. There had always only been twelve in existence at any one time. Before they had settled in Egypt, they had lived upon a great continent that came to be covered by ice and was therefore inhospitable to life. Tiy thought this was probably Antarctica. "But before that, my son, I know only that the seers of ancient times believed the Elders had come from between the stars."

"*Between* the stars?" Shem murmured. "What does that mean?"

"The earliest legends speak of how before the Elders came to earth, they were not creatures of flesh at all, but entities of a powerful, life-giving energy, similar in some respects to the power of your own aura or life-force, but increased a thousand times."

Tiy spoke of how her own tribe had referred to these most ancient forms as the Renowned Old Ones. She had since discovered that they had moved through the universe by resonating sonic vibrations that folded space and time. They had not possessed consciousness or emotion as humanity or Grigori knew it, which gave rise to another name by which they'd been known: the Unmoved Ones. They were perpetually functional like thinking machines, devoid of personality and instinct. Their actions and judgements had been undertaken with complete amorality, that same trait which, to a small degree, was still present in the Grigori. The Renowned Old Ones were not part of the great karmic cycle of incarnation and soul-evolution, but represented a kind of universal caretaking force. When they arrived upon earth, the energy of their life-giving presence affected the cycle of evolution that was already under way, and set into motion a more advanced form of life. The Elders came into being when the Renowned Old Ones initiated the creation of a higher life form, to comply with the universal plan. This accomplished, the Renowned Old Ones departed earth, leaving it in the care of their fleshly descendants.

"The Elders built the Chambers of Light in order to commune with their ancestors, the Renowned Old Ones, and the source of all creation from whence they had come."

"Why did they close the chambers?" Shem asked.

"That is known only to those who undertook the task," Tiy said. "They had their reasons, no doubt. All that is known is that the chambers were closed, the Elders disappeared, and the families of the twelve spread out into the world, each taking one of the smaller crystals with them. Anu was the son of one of the twelve. In Kharsag, he committed transgressions against the laws of his people. It is ironic that centuries later, he punished you for an indiscretion that, in some ways, leaned more towards the original plan of the Elders."

"How did he transgress?" Shem demanded sharply.

Tiy sensed she had touched a sore nerve. "Listen. Some of Elders' half-human families went far into the world, and settled in Australia, Tibet and South America. But Anu made the shortest journey into what is now Kurdistan. As he travelled, a sign came to him; a rainbow appeared over the mountains peaks. Anu looked upon the seven colours of the rainbow, and interpreted this as meaning there should now be a council of seven rather than twelve. In the mountains, he tried to recreate the Chambers, using the power of the crystal his father had given to him. This is probably the same key you found at the Cave of Treasures. Anu and his engineers harnessed the energy of a mighty blue flame that they found within the mountains, to act as a gateway to the stars of Orion."

"Yes," Shem said. "A temple was built around the flame, protected by a great tower. The gardens grew up around it."

Tiy nodded. "Thus Kharsag came into being: the High Place, the paradise in the clouds, remembered by the peoples of the world as heaven. Anu set himself up there as a god.

The Anannage were supposed to interbreed with humanity, to an extent where the Elders' influence became disseminated throughout the peoples of the world. You have to remember that, from the very beginning, the Anannage were hybrids, like you. But Anu, and others like him, became elitist and jealously guarded their knowledge. The Elders had withdrawn from the world, but the souls of their sons had not evolved enough to make wise judgements without the guidance of their fathers. They created isolated enclaves where they experimented with the power of the crystals and the sacred blue flames that burned within the earth. Anu thought he could atone for whatever mistakes had occurred within the Chambers of Light. He sought to reconnect with the divine source. But he was a rebel, Shemyaza, and it is my belief he identified those same traits within you, and could not tolerate them. He was fired by false piety and a lust to be all-powerful. He always wanted to know more than he was meant to know. What he saw in you made him afraid, for you were a dark mirror. That is why he made you the scapegoat for *his* mistakes, his fall, and the sins of his followers."

Shem was utterly silent as he digested this knowledge. Tiy gripped his arm. "You must see, my son, that this cycle has been replayed throughout history. Only you can end it."

Shemyaza had put his head into his hands. "He made me suffer! I can't believe the injustice of it!"

Tiy reached out to stroke his hair. "It is true. You must believe it, but don't let it become a burden. It is knowledge, and therefore freedom. You cannot reverse history here, nor in Eden. You must journey to Giza in Egypt and there, through the power of your father, Anu's, blood, reopen the gateway to the source and put wrong to right."

Shemyaza was silent for a moment, then took a deep breath. Tiy gave him time to compose himself, and did not interrupt his thoughts.

When Shemyaza finally spoke, his voice was brusque, without feeling. "The Chambers of Light are in Egypt. Perhaps I should have guessed that. But where exactly in Giza is their entrance?"

"I wish I could tell you," Tiy replied, "but their exact location is a secret that history has kept too well. I believe that you have the means to find them though. You have the crystal key."

"Nimnezzar now has the key."

Tiy made a dismissive sound. "Oh, you will get it back, have no fear, but first you must stop this senseless game. You are not a martyr, Shemyaza. You must cast off this hair mantle you insist on wearing. Babylon is your seat of power. You must claim it. Nimnezzar is a mote before you, a beetle in your fingers. He is puffed up with pride and arrogance because he believes he has captured two angels..."

"Two?"

"Yes. Penemue is here, waiting for you. Very soon, you will be reunited with your companions and together you will open up the Chambers that have lain so long in darkness. Later, I will tell you what I have learned of the rival Grigori factions and how they threaten you, but for now, you have enough to think about."

Shemyaza laughed sadly. "I feel your pride in me, and your faith, little mother. You forget that I am presently incarcerated in a hole. How do I begin?"

"That is simple. I will leave this place and tell Nimnezzar you have agreed to show him the secrets of the crystal. He trusts my word and will believe me when I say that you truly are the one we have been waiting for. Your only difficult task will be to convince him you accept him as the heir of Anu and are prepared to assist him. He is a suspicious man, which is partly why he is king. Once you are free of this place, you must follow your heart. Let the key speak to you."

Shemyaza touched her lined face and spoke softly. "Mother. The word feels strange upon my tongue. Can it be true?"

"It is. Listen to the words of your mother, Shemyaza. I have planned long for this moment."

After Tiy had given the news that Shemyaza was ready to speak to the king, Nimnezzar ordered that Shemyaza be brought to one of his gardens. Here, beneath the shade of an awning, Nimnezzar nibbled fruits, fanned by peacock feathers wafted by mute, castrated slaves. His body was robed in ceremonial dress, his oiled hair falling upon his shoulders. He felt truly the lord of his kingdom. Tiy stood behind him, her limbs loose. Somewhere, Amytis prowled behind a window, Melandra in her wake.

Shemyaza was brought into the garden by two guards. He was still dressed in his bloodied, dusty travelling clothes. Nimnezzar was satisfied by the sight of his wounds, glad to note his beauty had been marred. Yet the sun was captured by Shemyaza's bright, blood-streaked hair. It dazzled.

"Now you will speak," said Nimnezzar scornfully.

Shemyaza raised his head, and his eyes blazed blue from the bruises around them. "Yes, I will speak," he said. It was not the voice of a man who had been recently beaten.

"Do you command the Yarasadi peshmergas?"

"No," Shemyaza answered. "I spoke the truth when I said I had no kingdom and no army."

Nimnezzar shifted on his seat. "Then tell me what you are."

"You have my brother in bondage. Let me speak to him, free him of his chains, and I will tell you what you want to know."

Nimnezzar laughed coldly. "You are in no position to bargain. Do you desire another beating? Speak, or suffer!"

Shemyaza folded his arms. He smiled. "In the mountains, I was searching for an ancient artefact of great power. It was the stone your vizier took from me."

"I know this much," Nimnezzar said. "What is important is how you intend to use that artefact, and more importantly still, how *I* may use it."

"It will call down fire from heaven."

Nimnezzar frowned. "Explain!"

"If you like, it is the ultimate weapon."

For a moment, a thought passed swiftly through Nimnezzar's mind. He remembered the American woman whom Tiy had advised him not to see. Americans: ultimate weapon. The two seemed parallel. Was that the real reason the woman was here? "How is it used?"

"First, it must be empowered."

"How?"

Shemyaza shrugged, a grimace of pain passing over his face. "Take it to the top of your temple and have your priests call down the thunder-bolts. The stone must be held into the fire of a lightning fork."

Again, Nimnezzar laughed, but with less sureness. "This sounds a dangerous enterprise."

"Not to an adept," Shemyaza said. "Speak to your priests about it."

Nimnezzar narrowed his eyes. "Why should you speak the truth to me? I do not trust you."

Shemyaza took a step forward and, unexpectedly, the guards beside him took a step back, almost as if they'd been pushed. "You are right, Nimnezzar. The time for angels is past. This is the time of men. I cannot regain my kingdom, but through your dynasty the blood of my ancient line can flow once more in the veins of the world. Your seeress, Tiy, has told me that through your daughter and my brother, Penemue, you intend to initiate a new line of human-angel kings. For the reinstatement of this ancient practice of the sacred marriage, I am prepared to offer you my support. All I ask in return, is that once I have helped you secure the world, you will give me Eden. I yearn only to return to the soil of my ancient home, where I may live out the days this body has left to it."

Nimnezzar was astounded by this offer. He flicked a glance at Tiy wondering how the old woman had managed to cajole Shemyaza into co-operating. Visions marched across his inner eye. Glory. Victory. Empire. Lord of the World. He salivated. "Shemyaza, if you would swear fealty to me, bend now to my feet and kiss the earth between them."

Shemyaza approached, looming larger in the king's sight, until he cast a shadow over the swaying awning. Nimnezzar was forced to look up. Then Shemyaza knelt gracefully. As he kissed the dirt, his hair fell upon Nimnezzar's feet, through the straps of his sandals. Shemyaza raised his head. "Let me speak to my brother."

Nimnezzar's heart was beating fast. He felt aroused, and gestured quickly at the guards. "Take him to Penemue."

Tiy stepped forward. "I will accompany him—as a precaution."

Nimnezzar waved a hand. "Go!"

Sarpanita was sitting in the temple, before the prison of
Penemue. She had stared at him for over an hour and her
hand-maidens were becoming quite restless. To them, there
had been no communication between the captive and the princess. They were deaf to the silent conversation.

The moment Sarpanita had stepped between the great
bronze doors, Penemue had roared a statement into her brain.
"My brother is here!"

Sarpanita had had to stoop a little as if she was walking
against a strong wind. "He is here!" she screamed in her mind.
"Don't hurt me!"

The pressure lessened. "Have you seen him?"

Penemue's emotions were an indigo-red maelstrom in
Sarpanita's mind. She could barely think. "No, but my mother's
woman, Tiy, will have done so by now."

"You must see him yourself! I command it! You must
bring me tidings!"

Buffeted by his thoughts, Sarpanita sank wearily into the
lion-footed chair that was positioned before the cage. "I will
try...Penemue, is he really your brother? In blood?" In the
visions he had shown her there had been no hint of family ties
between them.

"Blood does not make a brother," Penemue answered.
"The Watchers were all brothers in spirit, but only Shemyaza
was the son of Anu's flesh."

He drifted off into his memories then, and Sarpanita's mind
was filled with dusty images, like ancient paintings hung too
long in the light. She fell into the dream of them, lived them;
saw Shemyaza as a young man, heard his laughter. He *was*
beautiful in the alien way of the Anannage, with his incredible
height and his long, serpent face. She knew that Penemue had
loved him as more than a brother. He showed her their lovemaking, and she could witness it without shyness. "The woman
killed him, killed his soul," Penemue thought mournfully and
Sarpanita knew he was speaking of Ishtahar. She found herself wondering what the world would have been like if
Shemyaza and the others had never disobeyed the laws of

Kharsag and taken human wives. She also wondered what business Shemyaza might have with her father. Had he been captured like Penemue or had he ridden into Babylon as a king? Like Melandra, Sarpanita had sensed Shemyaza's advent. Unlike Melandra, and because of the Magian Gypsy blood in her veins, she had also been able to detect the hot, confusing smoke of his emotions. Since she had been communing with Penemue, her ability to read people's feelings had been heightened. Strange how people so seldom said what they felt.

Penemue uttered a physical gasp and opened his eyes. The pageant of his memories were eclipsed from Sarpanita's mind in an instant. "What is it?" she asked him aloud.

At that moment, the doors to the chamber crashed open and several of her father's guard tramped inside. Sarpanita did not like them. Penemue had shown her how they had less honour than dogs. She stood up quickly. "What is the meaning of this intrusion?" she demanded with dignity, remembering to behave like a princess. Her women cowered about her.

Tiy came into the room and cleared a path for herself through the guards. Sarpanita saw how Tiy appreciated the change in her. *You are nearly a woman, and a wondrous woman at that!* "Your Highness," Tiy said, "There is an important visitor for Penemue."

Sarpanita touched a hand to her throat, as she'd seen her mother do. She knew at once who it was. "Then, come in." Behind her, she felt Penemue tense. *Still!* she cried in her mind. *We must be cautious.*

She wanted to be tall and aloof, her mother's daughter, the future mother of kings, but when Shemyaza came into the room, she sank to her knees—not through fear or weakness, but because she could see what he was. His power shone from him. He had been dressed in one of the gold-fringed robes common to the court of Babylon, only the fabric was white rather than of a primary colour. His hair hung freshly-washed over his chest, still half dry. She saw the marks of bruises on his face, and that he looked far more human than Penemue, yet more of a king than her father would ever be.

"Shemyaza," Penemue said aloud, then uttered a string of sentences in a tongue Sarpanita could not understand.

Shemyaza walked past Sarpanita and laid a hand upon her head as he did so. She felt the burn of his touch and was able to get to her feet. He still had not spoken. She watched his svelte back, the bright banner of his hair against it, as he put his hands upon the locks of the cage. For a moment, he bowed his head in concentration, although his fingers lay lightly against the metal. Then, the doors to the cage swung open. Sarpanita glanced at Tiy; she was smiling benignly almost in the manner of a woman who had just seen her son take his first steps.

Penemue spoke again, and this time, Sarpanita was able to see beyond the words and intuit their meaning. *Is it you? Is it really you? You look so different.*

Shemyaza gazed at him silently, then climbed up into the cage. He took Penemue in his arms, even though he was dwarfed by him. Words at last. "My brother."

Sarpanita saw that Penemue was weeping. He was telling Shemyaza of his torment since his release from the tomb, how he'd craved only solitude for eternity.

"It is now a time for life," Shemyaza said, and his language was the universal language of the heart. "Cast off your pain, Penemue." He ran his hands over Penemue's long face, pulled at his hair.

"You are born into the body of a human," Penemue said.

"Not exactly. This is the form we have become; Grigori. This body is of a long line of half-breeds. The differences between us and humanity are fewer now." Shemyaza turned and glanced down at Sarpanita, where she stood outside the cage. "And you are the daughter of Nimnezzar."

"Yes."

He nodded thoughtfully for a moment, as if deciding her fate, then smiled. "Your future husband is now free." He stepped down from the cage and gestured for his brother to follow him. Sarpanita could tell it was hard for Penemue to take those first steps. He had been imprisoned for so long. He stood at the door to the cage, his hands gripping its rim, looking out. With the potential for freedom scored upon his face, he appeared more alien than ever, but he was afraid.

Impulsively, Sarpanita walked forward and took hold of his hands. His height terrified her, and her slim fingers looked like the tiny paws of a monkey in his loose grip. "Come, my love," she said, and her voice shook only slightly.

Penemue stepped down from the cage and for a moment her arms had to take his weight. She thought they would break, but then his feet were upon the ground, and he was staring over her head around the room, as if he'd never seen it before.

"You must care for him, princess," said Shemyaza. "He has been away from the world a long time, and a cage is no place to reacquaint yourself with reality. We have work to do, but first give him the comfort of women. Teach him your language."

"We need no common language," Sarpanita said. She leaned against Penemue's side and his arm enfolded her like a wing. She could hear the boom of his heart, unnaturally loud and strong. Shemyaza joined their hands and uttered a blessing in the ancient tongue.

"I must leave you now," he said, "but only for a short time."

"Where are you going?" Sarpanita asked, for she guessed it was a question in Penemue's mind. Penemue still found it difficult to speak. "Tell us what is to happen."

"I am about to make it happen," Shemyaza answered. "Be patient."

"But my father," Sarpanita said, "my mother. What will become of them now that you are here?"

Shemyaza glanced at Tiy, who remained motionless. He stroked his chin for a moment, then spoke. "You will make a great and legendary queen."

"My father…" Sarpanita murmured, but Shemyaza was already stalking from the room. After a moment, Tiy followed. The guards looked uneasy but made no move to depart.

Sarpanita stood beside her angel lord in the slanting sunlight of the early evening. The palace seemed very still around her, not a sound. What must she think now? Her life was fracturing, changing. She looked up at Penemue who was gazing down at her, his face full of patience and interest.

"Come," she said, and led him to the long windows that opened out onto a balcony festooned with climbing vines.

"Look, you can see some of the city from here." It looked so small below them, like a child's model.

For all his height and long disuse of limbs, Penemue was as graceful on his feet as a deer. Out on the balcony, he blinked against the mellow light. The guards had followed them, but it did not matter.

"I do not know this world," Penemue said to her silently. He was looking at the domes, the minarets, the towers; so like his memory of the past, yet so different, interpreted as it was by modern minds.

"I do not know much of it either," Sarpanita said. "This palace has been my life since I was very young. I recall little before that. We must learn together."

"Do not be afraid," Penemue said, and touched her brow with his fingers.

"I am not afraid," she answered, and she wasn't.

From where they stood, they could see the Hanging Gardens spilling down from their terraces. They could see the roofs of other, lesser palaces, where the men whom Nimnezzar had made into nobles lived with their families. They could see the Museum of the Ancients and the basalt statues that adorned its roof. They could see the long, straight roads that cut through the city, fitting around market quarters, residential areas and parks. The walls of Babylon, some miles away, glinted with gold leaf. Nearer, they saw the temple, Etemenanki, dominating the sky. Smoke rose from its summit, high into the sky, thin and twisted like a tortured djinn.

Chapter Twenty
Fire From Heaven

The temple of Etemenanki smoked against the evening sky, as if a thousand offerings burned upon its altars. The royal party walked along the processional road that led to the temple steps. Magians led the way, holding lit torches and waving thuribles of incense. Behind them came their acolytes with shaven heads, scattering petals. Next came the king, dressed in his finest robes and attended by a group of male attendants. Behind him, Jazirah, with the key held in both hands. Shemyaza walked at Jazirah's heels, his head tilted back to take in the unimaginable sight of the temple. The party was followed by a formation of palace guards.

Shemyaza could feel Jazirah's fear as if it exuded from his spine like a skein of ill-smelling smoke. When the time came, the vizier would not be strong enough to control the power of the key. He was a cunning and forceful man, and therefore clever enough to know that Nimnezzar was demanding from him a performance beyond his capabilities. Shemyaza almost pitied him. Greed had brought Jazirah low. But for that vice he would not have heeded Nimnezzar's call and hurried to his court to glut himself on Babylonian luxuries. He would undoubtedly still be practising the ancient rites upon the altars of a hidden temple somewhere in India. There would be a price to pay for that desertion.

The party passed through the ceremonial gates of Etemenanki and walked across the smooth flag-stones of its outer court. Before them, a steep ramp soared upwards to the initial tier of the building. The Magians poured up the ramp in their scarlet robes, trailing perfume and fire. Shemyaza paused at the bottom and breathed deeply. Nimnezzar looked back. "Why do you linger?" he demanded.

"I am smelling the cedar wood that burns on the altar of the shrine up there," Shemyaza replied. "It reminds me of home."

Nimnezzar made an irritated sound, glancing keenly at Shem's face. He seemed unnerved by the fact that Shemyaza's bruises seemed to have faded greatly already. "If you attempt trickery, I will have you killed."

Shemyaza looked at him directly. "Your vizier holds the key, not I."

Jazirah's face indicated how little he enjoyed the privilege.

They began the ascent of the great ramp. Beyond the first tier, thousands of steps led up to higher levels. It would take at least an hour to climb to the top of the ziggurat.

Shemyaza overtook Jazirah to climb beside the king. "You have recreated the past so well," he remarked. "In your position, I would have installed an elevator, perhaps, or a moving stairway."

Nimnezzar clearly sensed sarcasm, but Shemyaza kept his face sublime. The king chose not to respond to the comment.

On the first terrace, they entered the temple, and here mute junior priests clad in sepia robes brought refreshment to them. The temple was gloomy, lit only by the light of candles. Tall columns disappeared into the darkness. The air had been hot, but now a cool breeze snaked into the building. Jazirah shivered. "I smell a storm," he said.

"Good." Shemyaza went out into the darkening sunlight. The sky was becoming occluded by clouds. He had not summoned them himself, but he felt that someone had. The clouds tumbled about the sky, already muttering with thunder. Tiy came to his side. "Let me take your arm for the next stage of the climb," she said.

Shemyaza hooked her fingers through his elbow. "Are these your clouds I see above me, mother Tiy?"

She laughed. "I cannot own the sky."

Shemyaza glanced down at her. He still wondered whether she had actually carried him in her body or was simply the victim of a delusion. Still, she had advised him well, imbued him with courage. She appeared to know about the Grigori. Whether she was mad or not, she had helped him in an hour of need.

The knowledge Tiy had given him concerning how the Grigori had manipulated his conception and covertly directed the path of his life was not a pleasing revelation. He hoped it was untrue, a paranoid theory, but some part of him was all too aware how likely it was. The Grigori were skilled in intrigue and conspiracy. It made him wonder whether Nimnezzar's rise to power had also been organised by some nefarious Grigori cabal. Nothing seemed impossible now. He could only follow his instincts.

By the time the royal party reached the seventh final tier, the evening had become black, although a weak and troubled sunlight still fought its way through the gloom. The light was altogether eerie. Shemyaza experienced a strong sense of déjà vu. This was the light that had haunted the earth in the days before Anu had released the Deluge to cleanse the land of the Nephilim warriors. Shemyaza could smell ozone in the air.

Etemenanki's summit was a wide, flat expanse of open air temple. It was adorned only by a large cubic altar of green stone. Here, a fire of cedar wood burned.

Nimnezzar approached Shemyaza, eyeing with disdain Tiy's fingers, which were still hooked through Shemyaza's elbow. Perhaps he wondered why his seeress seemed to have developed a friendship with the angel lord so quickly. "Shemyaza," Nimnezzar said, "you must now tell us how to use the stone."

Shemyaza took Tiy's fingers from his arm. "Your priest must hold it up to the sky and summon down the lightning."

Jazirah expelled a caustic laugh. "Do you think I am so stupid?" he snapped. "If I do that, I will be burned!"

Shemyaza raised his eyebrows. "But that is the way to empower the stone, the way it has *always* been empowered."

"And was the sacrifice of priests part of that empowerment?" Jazirah said.

Shemyaza shook his head. "If the right person holds the stone, there is no danger."

Jazirah uttered a contemptuous snort. "It is a trick, Great King. He plans to see me, your vizier, killed,."

"Silence!" Nimnezzar snapped. "Jazirah, do as Shemyaza tells you."

Jazirah stared at the king for a moment, then made an effort to smother his fury. He turned to Shemyaza with a thin smile. "Very well. You must tell me the correct incantations and gestures."

"There are none," Shemyaza replied.

"None? How else is the lightning summoned?"

"With your heart, Jazirah."

The vizier glared at Shemyaza for a few moments, then stalked to the altar at the centre of the platform. Here, he composed himself, and stood motionless with erect spine, focusing his energy. Shemyaza realised the man had some idea of what he was supposed to do. Jazirah held the key stone up to the sky in both hands. He closed his eyes.

Everyone was silent, and the only sounds were those of the wind scraping granules of sand across the granite flag-stones and the distant rumbling from the sky. Jazirah's lips moved, although he uttered no sound. His brow was unfurrowed as he projected his intention towards the clouds.

A fork of lightning splashed down, and hit the dirt some distance from the city. Jazirah did not flinch.

One of the other Magians approached the king and murmured softly, "We should move your servants and guards down to the next tier for a while." Some of the king's attendants were indeed looking anxious.

"No," Nimnezzar replied. "They stay where they are."

Veins stood out upon Jazirah's forehead now. He frowned with effort. A web of light spun briefly across the undersides of the clouds and then a mighty crash of thunder split the air. The younger attendants covered their heads and cried out. It sounded as if someone was shaking the sky, banging upon it, breaking it. Jazirah's head snapped backwards. He gasped. And then the chaos of the elements fell upon Babylon.

Lightning speared down as if cast by angry gods. It hit nowhere but the temple platform, creating a cage of light around the upper tier of Etemenanki. No-one was struck, but many of the guards and attendants cowered down upon the flag-stones. The Magian priests and their acolytes prudently removed themselves to the steps that led down to next tier, in defiance of the king's command. Nimnezzar's eyes were wide with fear as he watched the lightning spit down around him, but not a single fork struck the key stone.

"It is not working," Nimnezzar said, his voice shaking. "The bolts strike everywhere but where they are summoned."

Shemyaza folded his arms and shook his head. "It appears the stone is drawing the lightning, but is also repelling it. Unfortunately, it looks as if it will not absorb the power while Jazirah is involved."

Nimnezzar gestured. "Then *you* go. You take it." His face was unhealthily pale in the blue-white radiance of the lightning.

Shemyaza looked at him wryly, apparently at ease. "Are you sure? Do you trust me?"

Nimnezzar glanced around at the wild elements. "The lightning has been summoned, but it is out of control. Destruction must follow. Empower the stone!"

"Very well." Shemyaza unfolded his arms and walked to where Jazirah stood stiffly at the altar. For a moment, he had to wrestle with the vizier to prise the stone from his hands. Jazirah's fingers had locked upon it. "It holds me!" the vizier cried. "I can't let go."

Shemyaza slammed his bunched fists down onto Jazirah's wrists. The vizier cried out in pain, but his frozen fingers spasmed, so that Shemyaza was able to pluck the stone from his hands. "Go back to your master," he said. "You have done what you can."

Jazirah clenched and unclenched his numb fingers. He stared at Shemyaza as if trying to think of something to say. Then, with as much dignity as he could summon, he walked slowly to the side of the king.

Shemyaza dismissed all other occupants of the temple platform from his attention and tossed the crystal cone idly from hand to hand for a few moments, to get a feel of it. The lightning still stabbed down around him, and in some places the flag-stones had been scored and splintered by its assault. Shemyaza sensed that the spirit of the key was glad it was once again in his hands. He held it against his heart, and projected his mind outwards to control the wild elements. The growling in the sky gradually died down and the lightning merely flickered across the undersides of the clouds. It is waiting, Shemyaza thought.

He held up the stone in his right hand, the fingers of his left hand pointing down to earth. In his mind he called out, "Father, I am here! Ormuz, give to me the power of the foundation!"

For a moment all was still; even the wind died down. Then, with a monstrous cymbal crash of thunder, a brilliant blue trident of lightning snaked down from the clouds and struck the stone in Shemyaza's hands. He felt its powerful volts course into his body. His back arched, his body lifted onto the balls of his feet.

Nimnezzar cried out. "He is dead!"

The lightning twisted and coiled as if trying to wrench the stone from Shemyaza's grip. He could not have released it if he wanted to. The power of the skies poured into the key. Shemyaza waited until he had taken as much as he could bear, then projected his will to shut down the empowerment. At first, the elements resisted and he was afraid his body would be used as a conductor for the power until it was destroyed. His arm had gone beyond the sensation of burning. Now it was numb and cold. Energy poured through him, down into the stones of the temple. "Enough!" he cried in his mind, and visualised a dome of protective insulation around him. Then, it was over. The lightning disappeared instantaneously and the silence left in the wake of the thunder was absolute.

Shemyaza staggered forward against the altar, his right hand still held high. The stone glowed red in his hold. The Magians came back onto the summit, murmuring together. Those who had cowered down got to their feet.

Nimnezzar hurried forward. "I have never beheld…"

Shemyaza uttered a snarl that interrupted Nimnezzar's words. The king halted, uncertain.

"Come no closer," Shemyaza said in a cold, calm voice. He felt different now, as if a new personality had come to inhabit his body.

"The crystal…" Nimnezzar began. Suspicion, then fear, came into his eyes.

"Did no-one ever tell you not to trust a fallen angel?"
Shemyaza said. "They tell lies."

Nimnezzar's mouth dropped open. He raised a hand to
summon his guards, but before he could complete the gesture,
Shemyaza thrust the stone out before him.

"Too little, too late," he said. He knew he did not appear
beautiful now, but a sneering demon. He held the key stone
out before him and uttered a few words in the ancient tongue.
A brilliant gout of energy exploded out from the stone, a blinding radiance that created an immense cage of light around the
summit of Etemenanki. Everyone upon the temple platform
screamed and fell to their faces, clutching their eyes. Shemyaza
laughed at their agony, possessed by the power of the stone,
by the bitterness of his father's spirit.

After only a few seconds, the radiance faded and the madness left him. He felt an invading presence depart his mind
and dropped his arm to his side. The crystal weighed heavily
in his hand. He looked around himself. Jazirah lay prostrate
some distance away. His turban had fallen from his head and
his hands flexed in his hair. Servants hugged one another,
whimpering. Guards flailed their arms about, uttering curses,
while the Magians sat still, believing themselves to be victims of enchantment. Salamiel's words on the journey to the
Cave of Treasures whispered in his mind. "You will rise up
with fire…" Love seemed far from this place, but then, had
he not predicted himself that love could be cruel and stronger than death?

Nimnezzar sprawled on his back at Shemyaza's feet, his
fingers pressed against his face. Slowly, he lowered his
hands and blinked his streaming eyes. Realisation came a
moment later. "Blind! I am blind!" he screamed. "Guards,
seize him!"

Shemyaza laughed softly. "Fool to trust me, little king. I
have work to do. You stood in my way. Don't bother calling
for your guards—they are as blind as you are! You are a victim
of your own mindless greed. This land will radiate glory, but
you will never you look upon it."

Only Tiy stood erect beside the altar. She alone was unaffected by the gale of energy, for her eyes were already blind.

Shemyaza held out his hand to her. "Come, mother." She stepped unerringly over the fallen, writhing bodies and came to his side, dainty as a girl.

"Now, my son, you are ready for what I have to tell you next. Soon, you will be meeting someone. I must prepare you with information."

Together they descended Etemenanki and went towards the palace.

Melandra sat in the salon of Queen Amytis, chewing the skin around her finger-nails. Everything had got out of control. She shouldn't be here. It was dangerous. She'd gone too far. Nathaniel Fox seemed like the figment of a dream. She was alone. Her god turned his face from this whore of cities.

The oppression of the electric storm outside terrified and enervated her. Shemyaza was here, working his evil magic. She could feel it. But what could she do to stop it? It was all far bigger than Fox, or any of his confederates, had realised.

Amytis was chatting with her women, seemingly unaffected by the tension in the atmosphere. Then, a mighty explosion of thunder made the windows rattle and all the lights went out. The women uttered cries of surprise; some were frightened, others excited. Melandra got to her feet, her skin crawling. She saw Amytis sashay over to the window, lift aside one of the wafting drapes. It was very dark in the room now, and the light outside looked unnatural; greenish, as if they were underwater.

"What's happening?" Melandra went to the queen's side.

Amytis shrugged. "Something. No matter. Tiy is with the men. She will tell me everything later."

If there is a later, Melandra thought.

"There is a glow on the top of Etemenanki," Amytis said, pointing.

"We mustn't look at it," Melandra said and pulled the thin curtain fabric from Amytis' hold, arranging it hurriedly back over the window.

Amytis looked surprised and amused. "You are afraid, American. Why? The ways of men have no power over us."

Maybe I am afraid, because I am not a woman like you, Melandra thought. The ways of men *do* have power over me. She wanted to pray, but lacked the heart for it, aware in a dismal corner of her mind that it would provide no comfort. She had walked into Hell and must deal with its abominations alone.

"Yes, I am afraid," she said. "I know what Shemyaza is capable of."

"Tell me."

"He will kill us all!"

Amytis frowned. "He is the king of angels, the martyred one who gave his life that we might have knowledge."

"It was never our knowledge," Melandra said. "He stole it and we accepted stolen goods. We are as guilty as he is and our only hope of redemption is through God." Melandra reached for the queen's hands, which Amytis bemusedly let her hold. "Shemyaza is the great seducer. That is his dark power. We must fight it, see him for what he is. A demon! A prince of Hell!"

Amytis laughed uncertainly. "You are mad."

Melandra let go of her hands and shook her head. "No." She kept her voice calm. "People must be made to see Shemyaza as he really is. I came to the king to warn him."

Amytis stared at Melandra in amazement for a few moments, then sneered. "Tiy told me of your mission to kill," she said. "You will not do it. Your gods are false, so you do not have the power to destroy the king of angels." She turned away, and went to sit with her women, eyeing Melandra coldly.

Melandra dropped down onto a silk cushion. Her head was aching. It felt as if all the fibres of her body were being stretched.

After a while, some of the women, who had been sitting near to the windows, began to chatter and point. It was clear that they could see something outside. Amytis rose languidly to her feet and lifted the drape again, ignoring Melandra's protest.

"Tiy is coming," Amytis said. Quickly, she let the curtain drop back into place. Her eyes were shining in the gloom like black jewels. "Come, American, we will go into the garden and greet her."

Melandra could not control the terror that gripped her heart. It was almost as if she'd been given a fear-inducing drug. Something more than Tiy was approaching through the twilight. Something terrible. Melandra could sense its fatal footfalls. Once. Twice. Closer. It was slower than the beating of a heart, yet more empowered by blood. She didn't want to go into the garden with Amytis, but lacked the will to resist.

The queen of Babylon dragged Melandra through the window. Outside, the cries of peacocks echoed around the garden. Birds ran haphazardly in panic across the manicured lawns, dragging their tails through the marble pools. A flock of doves lifted and fell in alarm, like a curtain of pale light. Amytis cried out in delight and pointed towards the heavens. "Look, American! The gods are at work."

The heavy clouds that had once carried the storm were beginning to break up. Dense fragments rolled across the sky, amassing substance as they did so, forming themselves into gigantic balls, like wool or snow. A few had already become perfect gaseous spheres and were wheeling away in all directions. Melandra had seen nothing like it, nothing so unnatural. Then her eyes were drawn to more earthly matters.

Something was shining in the garden, something that had excited the peacocks and the doves. It was a column of light upon the path, and within the column, a shape.

Melandra sank down to her knees, aghast at what she saw. A man stood on the path, but not a demon. She could see clearly who it was: Jesus, dressed in white.

"My sweet lord," she murmured, and clasped her hands before her. Was this possible? Had he come to save her and cleanse this city of whores and idolaters? Jesus walked steadily towards her, holding out his hands. She saw the holy wounds there, dark against the pale palms. He looked exactly like he'd appeared in all the countless paintings and crucifixes that had supervised her childhood; a pale, thin man with tawny hair and neat beard. Rather than wearing the rather scanty costume of his execution, however, he was chastely robed from neck to ankle.

Jesus paused before her, and she reached up to take his hands. She pressed them to her lips, and felt the heat of living flesh against her own. "Forgive me, my lord," she said. "Save me."

"Rise," he murmured and his voice was the music of flutes and bells.

Melandra stood. He towered over her, taller than she'd ever imagined Christ to be. She looked at him more closely and realised his hair was golden, not brown at all. Neither did he have a beard, although his skin still appeared honey pale. His face shone with light. He touched her cheek with long fingers. "Well, my sister, will you kill me again?"

Her brow clouded. Kill him? Did he refer to the cross? Did he hate humanity for what they had done to him? "No, my lord. I will worship you."

He laughed at her, shook his head. "See me," he said, and brushed his fingers over her eyes.

She saw then, the long face, the piercing blue eyes, the remembered smile. She uttered a screech and pulled away from him. "Demon! Satan!" He had touched her again, touched her soul with his lies, made her see him as her ultimate god. He was evil incarnate. She must kill him now, but how?

"If you would fight evil," he said, "cast off the cruelties that were perpetrated upon you as a child."

"No!" She put her hands over her ears, backed away. Tiy and Amytis were vague presences in the garden; their forms were blurred. All that existed with any clarity was the demon before her.

A heavy decorative urn filled with flowers stood near to the path. Melandra rushed over to it and tried to lift it in her hands. She would smash him, smash his evil face. Behind her, she heard him laughing, his approach.

"Melandra, you will damage yourself. Calm down."

She turned on him, pointing a shaking finger. "The Lord shall strike you down!"

"The Lord?" Shemyaza laughed. "He left his heaven a long time ago. I have seen what is left of it, so I know. God does not care enough to strike me down. He, and all those like him, have abandoned their children—me, you, humanity and the Grigori."

"You're lying!"

He shook his head. "No. You have been lied to, but not by me."

"I don't believe you!" She could feel her resolve slipping away. Even now, he could seduce her. Her head blazed with pain and tremendous pressure. Blinking her eyes, she whispered beneath her breath, "Preserve me, my God, for in thee I do put my trust..."

"Melandra," Shemyaza murmured, "look at me." His voice was so gentle. For all her yearning and prayers, she could think only of the words of the Song of Solomon, "His eyes are as the eyes of doves by the rivers of waters...His lips like lilies, dropping sweet smelling myrrh..."

"No!" she screamed in her head and spoke aloud, "Be not thou far from me, O Lord; Oh my strength, haste thee to help me!"

"Look at me..."

She was sobbing now. "No. I must not. Oh God, deliver my soul from the sword!"

"Scriptures," Shemyaza said. "Ancient words. They are strange to your tongue now, Melandra. How long since you've uttered them? You lost your god here in the flower of Babylon. Why not speak the first lines of that pretty verse: "My God, why hast thou forsaken me?""

Melandra gripped the edge of the urn, blinking at the stars of the flowers. They sparkled in her sight, viewed through tears. Something black and terrible gleamed among the petals. She saw it. Metal. A gun; lying there, with a blue serpent sheen upon its muzzle. Her eyes followed the exact and precise lines of its body. "For thou hast heard me from the horns of the unicorn..." she whispered. It was not her gun, something smaller, but a weapon nonetheless. Why was it lying there, waiting for her, if not sent by God, or her beloved Christ?

Melandra reached out and took the weapon in her hands. It was warm, like the body of a basking snake. Pausing only for a moment, she grasped the gun in both hands, wheeled around and fired, crying, "In the name of God, die, you bastard!"

She saw the red explosion, smelled blood and cordite and the hideous reeks held within the human body. She had killed him, blown him apart. For a moment, she bowed her head, and a few sobs of relief shuddered through her. She had

returned to her god at the last moment, even though the per-
fumes of Babylon had clouded her mind. She had sinned,
but He had heard her. "Have mercy upon me, Oh God," she
said, "Wash me thoroughly from mine iniquity, and cleanse
me from my sin."

The smoke purled away slowly to either side. The gun-
shot still seemed to echo and echo from the palace walls.
Amytis and Tiy were mere smudges upon the evening, and the
floating veils of the other women, who had come out into the
garden, were less substantial than smoke. Melandra leaned
against the urn, breathing heavily, as if she'd been running.
She had done it: accomplished her mission. She felt light-
headed in her success.

Then the smoke cleared and he was walking towards her,
the white of his gold-fringed robe unmarked. She should have
known it would not that easy to kill a demon.

"You hold death in your hands," he said.

Melandra expelled a sobbing shriek and tried to fire again,
but the gun writhed in her hands. When she looked down she
saw an enormous, shining black scorpion wriggling around in
her hold, its sting lashing over her fingers. She threw it away
with a cry of disgust. Illusions! Lies! What could she do?
"Oh, God, I cry in the daytime, but thou hearest not; and in
the night season..."

Amytis' women were all staring at her with wide eyes, as if
they thought she was mad. *I am,* she thought. *I am mad.* She
put her hands over her face and tried to gather her thoughts.
In the chaotic darkness, she felt someone touch her shoulder
and knew the touch was his.

"No!" She tried to pull away, but he would not let her go.
She felt weak now, drained of energy and emotion, a child
looking out through the back window of long, black car, watching her life becoming smaller in its wake.

Shemyaza dragged her hands from her face. "You are important," he told her. "You did not follow me here, but were
drawn. You are not my executioner, but my protector."

Melandra shook her head wildly. "Don't say these things!
You are evil!" She began to recite a another psalm, "The Lord
is my light and my salvation; whom shall I fear?"

"Listen to me," Shemyaza said. "What you want and what I am are one and the same. I can be your sacrificed king."

"When the wicked, even mine enemies and my foes, came upon me to eat my flesh, they stumbled and fell..."

Shemyaza held her wrists tightly, his thumbs pressing against the delicate skin where blood ran blue beneath its fragile integument. "Those words will not help you, Melandra. Listen to me. I have walked in the desert as the scapegoat, I have fallen from grace to atone for the sins of others and myself; for humanity I have died a thousand deaths throughout history. The Roman Christian empire distorted my image into a symbol of fear, through which they wielded control over the masses of humanity."

"No! No!" Her voice rose in pitch, becoming feverish.

Shemyaza leaned forward and kissed her brow. "Walk with me now, Melandra. I am your Christ, the slaughtered son of god. I am Tammuz, Adonis, Icarus. I am the Iblis and the Peacock Angel. I am love and its dark brother. I am Lucifer, son of the light."

Melandra opened her eyes. "Hide not thy face far from me; put not thy servant away in anger..." She paused. The devil had such serenity about him. He looked upon her with the eyes of an angel who had never transgressed the laws of heaven. He was beautiful, and the beauty shone out of him rather than merely resting upon his body like a mantle. He was not like Jesus—he was not wholly good—she could see that, but what was good in him was pure and strong. The dark was the beast in him, the night and the abyss.

"You have been ordered to kill me," he said, "but what you would really kill is all that is sacred within you."

"How can I believe you? If you are telling the truth, then all that I have ever believed is a lie."

He grimaced, and for a moment she saw fury in him. "We have both been lied to." He shook his head, as if to clear it of this anger. "In Istanbul, I gave you the fruit, but you are yet to acquire the taste for it." He leaned down and kissed her lips lightly, then let go of her hands. "Come with me to Egypt, Melandra. I, and my brethren, have work to do there, and we will need someone to be our eyes, ever alert for danger."

Melandra laughed nervously. "You want to hire me? To be your bodyguard?" She raked a hand through her hair. "This is absurd! My task is to kill you. How could you ever trust me?"

Shemyaza smiled gently. "Perhaps that is one of the reasons I want you to be there."

"I don't know," Melandra said. "I need to think..." She looked up at him. "You don't know how much I hate you for what you did to me."

"It was done to both of us," he answered. "You are intact, Melandra. I never came to you in the flesh. My spirit was dragged to you."

She frowned. "That is not possible. You felt...so real. It *was* real."

"Do not be angry," he said. "I am not denying you your experience. I merely want you to see that it was arranged for both of us."

"Who arranged it?"

Tiy rustled forward. "There is something you must know, something I have only just told Shemyaza himself. Those men you work for, who are dedicated to ridding the world of the Grigori, they are ruled by a higher power."

"Yes, it is God!" Melandra snapped.

Tiy shook her head. "Oh no. Since your arrival here, I have visited the temple, Etemenanki, and breathed the smokes of dream to learn about you. I found obstacles, veils I could not rend, but today I broke through. What I learned is terrible indeed."

Melandra felt as if Tiy's emotions were floating off her like a vapour, infecting Melandra's own heart with disgust and shock. She felt breathless. "What did you learn? What?"

Tiy paused, perhaps for effect, then spoke. "The Children of Lamech murder Grigori in the name of God, but its leaders defer to men and women whom they have never met. They believe these people to be senators and judges, individuals whose identity must be kept secret, but the truth is more sinister than that. Today, the sacred fire showed me that a hidden Grigori faction, who calls itself the Brethren of the Black Sun, rules your organisation. This dark fraternity is opposed to Shemyaza fulfilling his destiny, because it will destroy their power. The victims of your organisation's assassins *are* Grigori, but individuals whose activities inconvenience the Brethren. They are one of many secret cabals within Grigori society, but they are perhaps the most dangerous."

"This cannot be true!" Melandra cried. "You lie. Why would Grigori want to murder Grigori? It's incredible."

"Girl!" Tiy said firmly. "I do not lie. Men murder men, don't they?"

"This news is as calamitous for me as for you," Shemyaza said.

Melandra shook her head. "But where is the evidence? I need more than just an old woman's dreams."

"In your heart," Tiy said, "you know I speak the truth. In your homeland, the Brethren of the Black Sun sent a demon to fill you with fear. You saw it at your leaders' headquarters, as you received the fatal instructions from them to kill Shemyaza."

Melandra stared at Tiy in mute shock.

Tiy nodded at her, as if she could see the younger woman's expression. "Oh yes, Melandra. Believe it. You and your colleagues have been, and are being, used by the very people you are sworn to eradicate."

Shemyaza took her hands in his own. "Nothing is as it seems, and that applies to both of us. I am not asking you to abandon your faith, for all faiths are one faith. I just want you to open your eyes and see that your directive to kill me is merely the hands and minds of dark Grigori at work, not God's. There was no gun among the flowers, just the symbol of your fears, but if you had truly believed in it, and your god had been with you, it would have destroyed me."

Melandra rubbed her aching brow with shaking fingers. "I can't believe you...I can't!"

Tiy came forward and laid her hands on Melandra's arms. "We will go into the palace and find an empty room. There, we will all talk together."

Melandra stared at the old woman's face. Her feelings were torn. Tiy's claims were preposterous, and yet Melandra did not wholly disbelieve them. Some part of her wanted to co-operate and was curious about what else Tiy had to say, while another was chained to the creed of the Children of Lamech. If she gave in to what her instincts told her was right, she might only be damning her own soul. She knew Shemyaza was adept at seducing women. Seduction takes many forms and not all of them involve the body.

Tiy shook her gently. "You know what is right, Melandra. But you are afraid."

"She must learn about the Chambers of Light," Shemyaza said.

"Yes, my son," Tiy answered.

Melandra threw back her head and searched the sky. *I need a sign. Please, God, give me a sign of what is right…*

Perhaps Shemyaza read her thoughts. The doves were still flying around the garden, filling it with the whirring music of their wings. He reached out and plucked one from the air without even looking at it. This, he held out to Melandra.

She stared at the bird, which now lay quietly in his hands. Then she took it from him and looked into his eyes. She had never held a bird before. It felt so fragile, its small heart beating rapidly against her fingers. Words rippled through her mind like a clear stream. *His countenance is as Lebanon, excellent as the cedars. His mouth is most sweet, yea, he is altogether lovely…*

"I'll listen to you," she said, slowly, "but I shall know if you lie. I shall know." She closed her eyes and pressed the soft feathers of the bird to her face. She hoped that what she said was true.

The streets of Babylon were filled with bewildered people. Public transport was stilled and the powerful energy that had struck the temple had caused a black-out in the city. People from every area walked silently towards the palace walls: men, women, children, young and old. Many had witnessed the storm and the fork of light that had struck the temple. Others had simply heard it. Everyone sensed in their hearts that something had happened to change their lives, but they needed confirmation and reassurance from their king. Surely he would address them now?

On the walls of the palace was a balcony, high up, where sometimes the king would speak to his people on public holidays. Now, as if by instinct the citizens flocked towards it. The crowd was strangely subdued; they spoke in whispers. Enormous torches were fixed to the walls on either side of the balcony. They were lit on ceremonial occasions, and were lit now. Sparks fled up into the darkness.

The people of Babylon saw their queen come out onto the balcony. The king was not with her. She held up her hands and they fell silent. "My beloved people, listen to my words, for they are the words of Shemyaza, King of Heaven."

Sarpanita waited in the shadows beyond the balcony. How would their people take the news that Nimnezzar and all his Magians were no longer in power? She had learned that Tiy and Shemyaza had confronted the generals of Nimnezzar's army and told them what had happened on the summit of Etemenanki. Shemyaza had told them that Sarpanita was their queen now. If they chose not to support her, they could leave the city. If they chose to fight for Nimnezzar, the power of the crystal key would smite them down. Sarpanita imagined how Shemyaza must have appeared to these cruel and violent men. The Shining One, with a divine wrath still burning invisibly around his body. They had had no choice. They had bowed to him.

But perhaps that had been the easy part. The generals, and after them, the courtiers and advisors, had ever been proficient at self-preservation. They would accept her as queen because it was in their best interests, but how would the populace of the city feel about this change? Would they accept a queen instead of a king? Then there was the greater picture: the country beyond the city, and beyond that, the world. Her father's fall had dramatic implications for many countries around them. Shemyaza had told Sarpanita that the city and the country were hers now, but she was so young to rule. At first, her mother and Tiy would be there to advise her, and she would have a husband to nourish her spirit. But she would need a government and ambassadors to speak for her abroad. She had so much learn and there would be so much to get used to. Childhood was over. Her husband was not even human.

When Shemyaza and Tiy had come to her in Penemue's room, only an hour before, she had protested when they told her she must be queen. "Make Penemue king," she said. "Make Mother queen." This last suggestion was made in fear. She was sure Amytis would not be pleased her daughter was to take the crown.

Shemyaza would not agree with her, neither would Penemue, who intimated to her that he did not want to be king. His only purpose was to love her and support her and provide her with children, who would be kings and queens in their own time. Tiy explained that Amytis could not rule in her husband's place and did not expect to. The people would not accept her, but Sarpanita had been a special child, ritually conceived. Now, she must assume her responsibility.

"You will not be alone in this," Tiy said. "I and Penemue have a journey to make with Shemyaza, but when we return, we will be here to sustain and counsel you. We shall gather those left of your father's court who will remain loyal to you. They will help you find the right men and women to form a government. But this is a time of change, Sarpanita, and you must learn to become strong very quickly. Do not forget this was always your destiny. You were born for it, and will be able to call upon resources you did not realise you had."

Hearing this, Sarpanita felt reassured, but there were other demons of doubt poised to strike. "What about my father and the others? What must happen to them?" She imagined potential enemies then; blind, bitter men plotting in the dark against her.

"The Magians will be returned to their own temples," Shemyaza said, "to suffer whatever penalty their superiors feel necessary. You must deal justly with the guards and the servants and make provisions for them."

Sarpanita glanced up at him. "You should not have hurt them."

Shemyaza gazed back at her steadily. "No, I should not, but the power your father had me conjure is beyond moral judgements. He bade me invoke it, and it possessed me."

"You knew what would happen. You could have refused…"

"Your father hurt himself," Tiy said, before Shemyaza could answer. "Shemyaza was just the catalyst. And Nimnezzar had had him beaten."

Shemyaza raised his brows at her. "What he did to me is of minor importance. The major issue is what Babylon represents and must become. This land is where civilisation began, and now it will take centre stage in the world once more." He turned back to the princess. "This is a time of sadness for you, but also one of celebration. Tonight, you shall be married. Be at peace, Sarpanita. Enjoy this time, for you have work ahead of you. Your children are destined to become world leaders, just and fair. This will be your gift to the future. Your first task will be to make peace with the Yarasadi and end the eternal war between your people and them. It will be an example to other nations."

The first task of many difficult tasks. Now, standing out of sight, behind the balcony curtains, Sarpanita felt sick with fear, yet also elated. She was sorry for her father, who had lost his sight and his kingdom, but knew in her heart that he had been proud and cruel. He should not have dared to challenge Shemyaza. If he had been less arrogant, and had not put Penemue in chains or treated Shemyaza so badly, he would have been out on the balcony now, but he had lost his chance.

Outside, her mother had fallen silent. Sarpanita could feel the presence of the crowd—her people—although they too made no sound. They were waiting. She saw Amytis turn round and beckon to her. "Come, Nita. Don't be afraid."

It took an eternity to walk the short distance out into the torch-light. Below, an ocean of eyes looked up at her, filled with the reflections of flames. They covered the great square before the palace, and the roof-tops of surrounding buildings. They filled the trees. She felt totally alone, naked before the expectations of the masses.

Then Amytis spoke. "All hail, Queen Sarpanita! All hail!"

And the crowd raised their arms and roared. Whatever Amytis had said, she had succeeded in touching the hearts of their people.

Sarpanita smiled back at them, mostly terrified. Her regency would not be easy, she knew. Below her, the people were filled with excitement and fervour, but in the morning, they would reflect upon what had happened. She would be breaking a long tradition of male rulers, and some would find that hard to take. But for now, she basked in their cheers and thought of Penemue who waited for her at the palace, and of tonight, when she would begin to learn the secrets of love.

Chapter Twenty-One
Millennium Fever

Cairo, Egypt

Pharmaros and Kashday had no doubt that they had shed their old lives for good. They had been living in the city for a couple of months now, running up an account at the Rameses Hilton, living off their diminishing credit. They spent their time making excursions out to ancient sites. On one occasion, they indulged themselves in a cruise up the Nile, although this had been a trip fraught with hazard. They had seen fighting taking place in the villages along the river banks. They had seen bodies polluting the sacred waters. Eventually, the boat had turned back to Cairo. It was no longer possible to pretend the country was in anything but a state of war. Rival Islamic factions fought bitterly. Westerners were killed every day, yet still they flocked to Egypt. The pull of the ancient land and the significance of the turning millennium was too strong.

"I can't bear it," Pharmaros said, as the boat moved swiftly back to the city. They stood on the deck in the dark, watching the water. "I don't want to be here. I'm afraid."

Kashday kissed her and tried to comfort her. "It won't be for long. It will soon be over. We have to stay; you know that."

"But where are the others?" Pharmaros asked. "There must be others like us." She glanced at Kashday with cautious eyes. "Shemyaza. Where is he? Is he alive, do you think?"

It was the first time either of them had spoken his name. Kashday had wondered in silence whether Shemyaza's long exile was now over. If so, they could expect something momentous to occur. Shemyaza, in the past, had ever been associated with disruption. Kashday put his arm around

Pharmaros. 'My love, that ancient business…It was never ended. We might have lived and died a thousand times, but what happened so long ago has never been resolved. It has been hanging over us."

Pharmaros leaned her head against his shoulder. "Not more suffering. It isn't fair. We are different people now. It might as well have not happened to us."

Kashday's eyes were distant as he gazed into the water. "We let Shemyaza take responsibility for all our actions. Our punishments were mild in comparison to his."

Pharmaros shuddered. "Then, if he lives again, he will hate us now."

"Hush now." Kashday squeezed her shoulder. "I said that nothing bad will happen to us, and I meant it. We must have faith."

"I remember him," Pharmaros murmured. "Do you? When they made us watch his execution?"

"Yes," Kashday answered grimly. "I remember." He did not want to talk about it; the memory was far from comfortable.

"He had become a monster," Pharmaros said. "His face was that of a lunatic. I denied him. I hated him. I blamed him."

"Yes. Yes." Kashday pulled her closer. He closed his eyes. Her words were painful, yet he sensed he must let her purge herself.

"We didn't know what we were doing. We were so young, and he was so forceful. He made me think it was right to teach humanity and to take a human wife. I was filled with the zeal of youth, of rebellion. I had no idea how terrible the consequences would be."

"None of us did," Kashday said. "Not even Shemyaza himself."

Pharmaros shook her head. "No. He knew what he was doing. He manipulated us." She pulled away from Kashday's arm. "Kash, I hope that what we have to do doesn't involve him. I hope he's still dead and stays dead. I don't want to go through any of that again."

"Nor I." Kashday pulled her close again. "We must strengthen each other."

Back in Cairo, they resumed their cautious existence, although the strain was beginning to show upon Pharmaros' face. Nearly every night, she dreamed of Shemyaza and woke up weeping. She became obsessed with the idea that he was about to walk back into their lives and bend their will to his.

Kashday was mercifully free of this fear. He had an open mind about what might happen to them, and if that included Shemyaza, then so be it. He did not fear Shemyaza and never had. Pharmaros had been different. In the past, Shemyaza had always intimidated her and this still haunted her. Secretly, Kashday hoped that Shemyaza *would* appear, although he kept this to himself. His dreams concerned the more recent past. In one of them he returned to his home in Little Moor, Long Eden, and there met a young woman in the garden. His daughter. Helen's daughter. She was very beautiful; a fey and wistful girl. In his waking hours he could not stop thinking of her, because he knew that somewhere in the world she was alive. The Parzupheim had stolen her from him, by stealing his life. He believed that the dream of her was, in some way, real. He was sure that, once, his daughter had gone looking for him at Long Eden and had found only a ghost.

As the days passed, Pharmaros incubated new fears. She became convinced that members of the Parzupheim were looking for them, perhaps to imprison them or worse. "Why did our memories return? Why were we driven to come here? We were supposed to stay ignorant and we didn't. They'll hunt us down now, won't they?"

Kashday had no answers, but he became infected by Pharmaros' rising sense of paranoia. They *were* in Egypt for a reason, and because they did not yet know what it was, they were prey to the wildest ideas. They lived like exiled criminals; eyes over newspapers, ever alert.

On the eve of Yule—a festival that seemed irrelevant in the hot land of Egypt—they went out for their habitual evening meal. They had not long returned from Sakkara and were still discussing the sights they had seen there. It seemed that while they'd been away even more people had flocked to Cairo in preparation for the coming millennium celebrations.

This perpetual influx had created a further surge in political tensions. In the newspaper that day, they had read of terrorist threats to bomb the sphinx. Would that ever happen?

Pharmaros stirred her coffee and said, "I know we've discussed this before, but we have to face facts. We can't stay here for ever. We'll soon run out of credit."

Kashday nodded. "I know, but something will happen by the end of the year."

"You're sure of that, aren't you."

He nodded.

"But *what* will happen? We've found no other Grigori. Time is running out."

Kashday sighed. "I know, but the worst that can happen is the New Year will pass us by and I will have been wrong. Then we can go home." He grinned boyishly. "To have to find new jobs, no doubt."

Pharmaros would not join in with his humour and frowned at the table, painting patterns in the spilled coffee with her finger-tips.

Kashday left her to her moody silence and stared through the window of the restaurant at the hectic crowds milling around in the street outside. He thought he heard the snap of gun-fire, a distant scream. "This place is madness."

"It will get worse by the new year."

He sighed through his nose. "Yes."

Taking a sip of coffee, Pharmaros peered at the passing crowds. "Everyone seems to be searching, searching. Everyone seems to be lost. It is Pandemonium. A true hell of lost souls."

Kashday nodded absently, wishing she wouldn't be so relentlessly gloomy. Perhaps she was right and they should return home. Perhaps the reason for their being here had simply been to meet each other. Then, he saw a face in the crowd and his right hand made an abrupt, involuntary jerk against the table-cloth.

"What is it?" Pharmaros asked.

He looked at her, winced inwardly at her obvious fear. It was so easily kindled. He shook his head. "I don't know. A face…" Then he was on his feet, throwing money onto the table cloth, far more than their meal was worth. It was the last of their cash. "Come on."

"Where?" She was already following him, out into the steamy heat of the night, the amorphous press of hot bodies. Kashday reached for her hand, dragged her behind him. Babbling crowds parted before them; their bodies felt insubstantial. Ahead, Kashday caught sight of a blaze of red hair, a head that stuck out above the seethe of the surrounding crowd. A shock-wave passed through his body. Grigori! But more than that; a sense of familiarity.

They emerged into a square, lined by awned shops, which even at this late hour were open for business. Kashday paused. He could see the red-haired man clearly now. He had stopped at one of the stalls and was talking to the merchant.

"He's Grigori," Pharmaros whispered. "I just know it. Shall we approach him?"

"I don't know. Perhaps we should watch him for a while."

The stranger seemed to hear their whispered conversation, for he froze and then turned towards them quickly. Pharmaros pressed herself against Kashday's side. "He's seen us!"

The stranger's expression was unreadable, but he was clearly waiting for them to make a move. Kashday drew in his breath. "Well, let's get this over with." He began to walk towards the stranger.

Pharmaros hissed, "No!" but still followed him, taking hold of his arm.

The red-haired Grigori had a flimsy, cheap necklace dangling from his fingers. The shop-keeper was attempting to grab his attention again, pawing his arm, gabbling in Egyptian. The Grigori stared at Kashday and Pharmaros and raised his eye-brows in enquiry. He appeared suave and haughty, although he was dressed casually in desert fatigues, his thick red hair spilling riotously over his shoulders. He would have stood out in any crowd.

"Do I know you?" he said.

"I think you might," Kashday answered. He could not keep a certain tightness from his voice. He might be wrong about this person, embarrassingly wrong. "My name is Kashday Murkaster and this is Pharmaros."

The stranger looked them up and down. He smiled. "Kashday Murkaster," he said and dropped the necklace he was holding into the aggrieved shop-keeper's hands. "I think I might know you, yes."

"Who are you?" Pharmaros asked.

"Salamiel," he answered. "Are you looking for me?"

"Yes," Kashday said. He laughed in relief. "We are."

Salamiel took them to a nearby bar and insisted on buying them drinks. He seemed at ease and strangely casual about having encountered them. It was almost as if he'd expected to, but perhaps that should not really come as a surprise. The whole scenario felt peculiar to Kashday. They *did* know this man, but he was a stranger. There was none of the acute stab of recognition he'd felt when he'd met Pharmaros, simply a vague sense of familiarity.

Pharmaros told Salamiel the story of how they'd come to be in Egypt. He listened patiently, swigging his beer. "Well, now you know why you were drawn here," he said, when she'd finished speaking.

Pharmaros frowned. "No we don't. We've only met you. Why are *you* here?"

Salamiel sighed. "Well, we were looking for you, although we didn't know it would be you, of course…"

"We?" said Pharmaros.

"Yes. I have Gadreel and Daniel with me."

"Gadreel, yes," Kashday said. "I remember him, but who is Daniel?"

Salamiel smiled. "The modern version of Gadreel is female." He gestured at Pharmaros. "Like you. Daniel, you might recall, is Shemyaza's vizier."

"Shemyaza!" Pharmaros murmured. Her face was set in a revealing expression.

"That's right. I'm afraid we have *mislaid* our esteemed leader. It's a long story."

"I want to hear it!" Pharmaros snapped.

Salamiel stretched languidly. "Of course you do. Look, I think it's only right that the others are here for this. We're staying in a hotel near here. Let me call them. OK?"

"Yes, of course," Kashday said.

They watched Salamiel slink over the pay-phone. "Well,"
Kashday said.

"He's like Shemyaza," Pharmaros said. "He always was.
The side-kick. The lackey. How can we trust him?"

Kashday, who had always had a soft spot for Salamiel, and
had once wished to be more like him, said, "Who did you want
to find?"

"Gadreel is all right," Pharmaros conceded. "But I would
have preferred finding Penemue to Salamiel. And this Daniel,
he was just Shemyaza's glorified concubine. Why is he involved?"

"These are Shemyaza's closest confederates," Kashday said.
"Yes. It's as I feared. He's come back to us."

Daniel and Gadreel were nothing like how Kashday or
Pharmaros remembered them. Gadreel had been a quiet, sensitive man, but was now a strong, opinionated woman. Daniel,
who had been hardly more than Shemyaza's shadow, a thin fey
youth, was now a pleasant and communicative individual.
Despite her earlier misgivings, Pharmaros was quickly won
over by Daniel's charm. It was he who oiled the social wheel,
effected the introductions and told the story of how he and
his companions had ended up in Cairo. He was clearly in emotional turmoil over Shemyaza's disappearance, but tried to make
light of it. "He'll show up, I'm sure. We just have to do what
we can to be ready for him."

"These chambers," Pharmaros said. "Do you know where
they are?"

Daniel shrugged. "Well, I've visited the sphinx three
times. I was pretty sure the entrance to the chambers must
be concealed nearby, but so far I've found nothing. I've pho-
tographed the monument from every angle. I had a theory
that the entrance would be between its paws, because then
the Elders could have emerged from the chambers to greet
the rising sun, due east. It's very strange. I could feel the
presence of the chambers all around me on the Giza plateau,
but I'm beginning to think the entrance is somewhere else
entirely."

"Away from Cairo?" Kashday asked.

Daniel shook his head. "No. I think it's in the city. I've been picking up images of a Coptic church. Perhaps, because there are now five of us, we should meditate together and see what information comes out of it."

"We need to work on discovering the dedication of the church," Gadreel said. "That will save us the time of investigating every one in the city."

Daniel scraped his hair back from his face and sighed. "Of course, we're limited in what we can do, because Shem isn't here. He holds the key and *is* the key."

"You said there should be seven of us," Pharmaros said. "If Shemyaza is the sixth, who's the seventh?"

"I don't know," Daniel said. "We can only trust they'll turn up over the next few days."

Kashday took Pharmaros' hand. "Well, now we know why we're here," he said. "Does it make you feel any better?"

Pharmaros nodded thoughtfully. "Yes. Opening the Chambers of Light is certainly something I can put my heart into." She smiled at Daniel. "I was afraid we'd have to repeat some terrible event from the past, be punished again."

"We *have* been punished," Gadreel said. "You've nothing to feel guilty about."

Pharmaros coloured slightly. "I don't," she said, without conviction.

They decided to conduct the meditation that night, at the hotel used by Daniel, Gadreel and Salamiel. There seemed no point in wasting time. On the short walk back, Salamiel fell into step beside Kashday and Pharmaros. "I know your daughter," he said.

Kashday glanced at him in surprise. "*My* daughter?"

"Yes. Her name is Lily. She is with a Grigori family now in Cornwall. I met her there. She used to ask me about you."

"Really? I have never met her."

"I know. She has a twin brother too. Owen. You should ask Daniel about him. They were very close friends."

Kashday paused for a moment, glanced at Pharmaros, then spoke. "What of their mother?"

"Dead, I'm afraid," Salamiel said. "But you have a grand-daughter. Lily named her for her mother. Helen. You can look forward to meeting them when all this is over."

"Yes. That would be…" Kashday shrugged helplessly. "I never thought I would."

"I believed I was the father of Lily's child for a while," Salamiel said casually, "but when she was born, it was clear I wasn't."

Kashday fell silent. Salamiel hadn't changed.

Chapter Twenty-Two
The Huntress

Helen sat beside her mother on the plane. They had managed to get seats by a window, and Helen could look out at the clouds. Lily sat beside her, reading a magazine. Helen knew her mother had gone to a lot of trouble to get them on this flight; not least a protracted verbal attack upon Enniel to wear down his objections. Helen had heard one of the restrained arguments, which had taken place in the kitchen of the cottage, following a phone call by Lily to summon Enniel to their home to discuss 'an urgent matter'.

"You cannot take a child into that part of the world at present," Enniel had said. "Especially not one of our children. Where's your sense, girl?"

Helen, listening beside the door, had gone taut with anticipation, expecting that her mother would not react well to being called 'girl'. For a moment, there had been silence. Then, Lily spoke, in a cool, collected voice. "Enniel, I am more than capable of looking after myself and my daughter. You should know that. I'm not asking for money, but a little assistance, just so the journey will be safer. You know the Grigori families in Egypt. Please contact them for me."

Helen had smiled to herself, proud of her mother.

Later, Enniel had spoken to Helen herself, asking why she wanted to go to Egypt so much. Helen had explained about the scarab, causing Enniel to frown.

"Can't you see that we are part of it?" Lily had said, unable to keep out of the discussion.

"Part of what?" Enniel had enquired icily.

"You know what. It began with the eclipse, when Daniel had that peculiar experience..."

Enniel had glanced at her sharply. "We do not know where Daniel is," he'd said. "Neither he nor Shemyaza have deigned to contact me."

"I think we *do* know," Lily had answered softly. "But you have been told to keep out of it."

Enniel had finally agreed to help them, although he suggested that someone else, perhaps Lily's brother Owen, should accompany them. Lily made it clear that she and her daughter wished to travel alone.

Helen was aware of the fact that, quite often, her mother instinctively deferred to her. Sometimes, it felt as if Lily was the younger of the two. But this wasn't the only reason Lily was so keen to support her daughter's desire to travel to Egypt. Although she was quite used to getting her own way with people, Helen knew that the man named Shemyaza had a lot to do with Lily's decision. Just the mention of his name made different colours shoot off from the aura of light around Lily's body. Helen did not know that only very few people saw these colours naturally, and that for most it involved a lot of self-discipline and practice. The name Shemyaza affected Helen too. It was a golden word and made her think of the sun. It made her tingle. There was blue in the word too, possibly in the last two syllables. Helen knew instinctively that she was connected with this mysterious person in some way, not least because of the vision she'd had of a golden man walking towards her across the water. Helen had not told her mother about this. The intense feelings that Shemyaza conjured in Lily made Helen uncomfortable. Helen wanted to meet Shemyaza and knew that, eventually, she would. She had once asked her uncle Owen about him because she knew Owen had met him. The word had affected Owen's aura too; it became muddy, shot with sparks of intense red. He would not speak to her. Owen was the only person Helen had any real trouble in controlling. She suspected, without knowing why, this too had something to do with the one they called Shemyaza. He affected everybody he met.

Helen fidgeted in her seat. They were nearly there. She knew that Enniel had superficially agreed to let them go their own way, but there were certain people on the plane she felt uneasy about.

She'd mentioned them to her mother, who'd merely pursed her mouth in annoyance and said, "Don't worry. If anyone's our unofficial bodyguard, we'll give them the slip when we land."

Helen could not suppress an involuntary shudder. Would operatives of Enniel's make her feel so troubled?

Daniel stared up at the Sphinx, shading his eyes against the blinding morning sunlight. The monument's enclosure was thick with tourists, but just by gazing on the mysterious, impassive countenance above him, Daniel could blot their buzzing presence from his mind. He remembered the time he had stood before Azumi, the rock sphinx of Cornwall, equally mystified yet desperate for answers. Why won't you relinquish your secrets, he thought. Will you only reveal them to Shem? He sighed heavily. Today was New Year's Eve. The new millennium was only hours away, and still Shem had not appeared. Daniel had no idea what he and his companions should do. He could only keep looking, keep guessing, until the last possible moment.

The Giza plateau was swarming with people, and there was a heavy military presence, supposedly to protect the road crews of the bands who were due to begin playing around mid-day. Mesh fencing had been hastily erected around the central stage area. A massive sound and lighting system had been installed, and a pyramid erected over the stage. Nearby, the original monuments seemed to look down in distaste. Daniel didn't blame them.

Where was the entrance to the Chambers? The meditation last night had been helpful in that they had all picked up imagery of a crypt beneath the church, but the dedication name of the church had eluded them, so they still had no way of locating it precisely.

Salamiel and the others had gone off on a field trip. They were investigating as many churches as possible, although it seemed likely that all Coptic churches in Cairo would have crypts and also priests who would object to strangers poking around them, in fear of Muslim persecution. Daniel closed his eyes and attempted to blot out all sounds around him. He had to get the information they needed.

As he tried to concentrate, he became aware of being watched and opened his eyes quickly. Quite a lot of people were milling around the monument, but his eyes were drawn immediately to a woman who stood smoking a cigarette, leaning against the eroded wall of the enclosure. She was dressed in jeans and a black shirt and wore shades, her dark hair pinned up loosely on her head. A large leather bag was slung over her shoulder. Why was she watching him? He got the impression it was more than a casual interest. Daniel stared back at her, although he could not see her eyes and could no longer be sure whether she was looking at him. She stubbed out her cigarette and walked away, quickly, pushing aggressively through a knot of sight-seers, who complained loudly. Daniel followed her, making people repeat their objections as he shouldered past them. He kept the woman in sight as they left the enclosure. She walked purposefully through the temple complex that lay before the Sphinx. Daniel was confused when she disappeared for a few moments as a crowd of sight-seers, freshly delivered from Cairo's centre, disembarked from a coach and milled around like mindless sheep in front of him. He clawed his way through them, and saw the woman ahead of him, about to board one of the buses that ferried people to and from the city. He ran after her and managed to climb on the bus just as the driver was about to shut the doors. Quickly, he sat down and scanned the passengers, finally catching sight of his quarry further up the bus. She appeared to be examining something in her lap.

Daniel clasped his hands together between his knees. What was he doing? He shouldn't have followed her. She was doubtlessly just a tourist who had no interest in him at all. Yet his instincts screamed otherwise.

Once they reached the city centre, the woman got off the bus, along with several other people, in a busy market area of the older part of the town. Daniel followed as discreetly as possible, lingering by the bus as the woman strode off across a stall-packed square, where reproductions of Ancient Egyptian art were laid out on tables to tempt the gullible tourists. Once the bus pulled off, Daniel could not see his quarry at all. Perplexed, he began to wander through the stalls, inspecting the crowd minutely. Stall-holders attempted to interest him in their wares with some persistence, but he ignored them. The woman had vanished very quickly.

Daniel had just given up the idea of being able to find her, when someone grabbed him and pulled him roughly into a narrow, empty side street, where the blank walls of what appeared to be residential buildings rose high to either side. His face was pushed roughly against the wall and he heard the unmistakable sound of a gun being cocked close to his ear. Something cold and hard was pressed against his hair. Daniel forced himself to relax. He sensed he mustn't struggle.

"Who the fuck are you?" a woman's low voice demanded.

"Daniel Cranton," he said. Would she kill him?

"Daniel…" With one final unnecessary shove, she released him. He turned round slowly. The woman was standing before him with folded arms. There was no sign of a weapon in her hands, but perhaps she had already secreted it in her shoulder bag. She smiled at him. "I thought I knew who you were, but I had to be sure. Sorry."

Daniel rubbed his head. "Who are you?" Could this be the seventh avatar they were looking for? She did not look like a Grigori, mainly because she wasn't tall enough. Her manners, however, had a certain rogue Grigori flavour to them.

"It doesn't matter who I am. I've been looking for you. You must come with me, now."

"I don't think so," Daniel answered, adding insouciantly, "I was always told to keep away from strangers."

She removed her shades and took a step towards him. Hands on hips, she tapped her foot impatiently. "Look, I asked nicely, so don't give me any trouble." Her eyes were hard. "Let's go."

"I think you'd better give me a good reason *why* first."

"Brave boy, aren't you!" She shrugged. "OK. A friend of yours sent me. You really want to meet him. So come on. We're wasting time."

Daniel's heart lurched. He knew then that he had to go with her. "All right. You go ahead. I'll follow."

"Right!" She stalked off up the street and Daniel went after her, maintaining a slight distance between them. They did not speak to one another. She led him through a maze of alleys to a cramped street of tall buildings with narrow door-ways approached by short flights of steps. The woman marched up to one of the doors and turned to Daniel. "Here we are. Come in."

Daniel followed her into the building. It was spacious in-side, yet bare, the walls scabrous with age. He could see a courtyard beyond a window and wooden stairs leading to an upper storey. The floor was tiled and covered with Turkish rugs. The air smelled of frankincense and tobacco. Some-where, in a distant room, someone was moving what sounded like iron pots around.

The woman began to climb the stairs, Daniel following. On the first floor, she turned down a small landing and then entered a room, where she paused in the door-way and beck-oned for Daniel to enter. Hesitantly, Daniel squeezed past her into a small, low-ceilinged room, where a man sat at a table by the window. It was Shemyaza. He did not turn round immediately. He had a glass of tea in front of him and appeared to be looking out at the courtyard, the planes of his face sculpted by mellow light. Daniel paused at the threshold, stunned. "Shem!"

Shemyaza turned then and looked at him. "Hello, Daniel."

Daniel was not altogether surprised, but still felt slightly disoriented to find Shemyaza there. "What's all this about? Where have you been? Who's this female thug?"

"Come in," Shemyaza said. "Sit down. Drink tea."

Daniel walked over to the table. Shem appeared to be relaxed and in good health. What game was this? "Why didn't you contact us? We've been half crazy with worry!"

Shemyaza did not react to Daniel's carping tone. "I have contacted you. That's why you're here. My friend Melandra has been looking for you for some days."

"Was the gun necessary?"

Shemyaza laughed and glanced at the woman, who was now leaning against the closed door. "Gun, Melandra? I hope you haven't been intimidating poor Daniel."

The woman bared her teeth in a predatory grin. "You want me to work for you, but I do the job my way."

Shemyaza shook his head and poured Daniel a glass of tea from a tall brass pot. "Are you ready to work now, Daniel?" He pushed the glass towards Daniel's hands.

Daniel felt dazed. "Work?"

"Yes, you remember. The Chambers of Light? Have you found the church yet?"

Daniel groaned. "Why do you do things to me like this? Why couldn't you just come to the hotel like any normal person?"

"Of course, you do not expect me to answer that," Shemyaza said. "We need to start work tonight. Are the others ready?"

Daniel blinked at him. "There are five of us. We lack one."

"No, that has been attended to. Have you had a good look round St Menas?"

"St Menas?"

"Daniel, you seem half asleep! The church, where we have to perform the opening rite."

Daniel rubbed his eyes. "The Coptic church. No. We were unable to discover the dedication."

Shemyaza expressed his impatience. "Tch! What *have* you been doing?"

"Waiting for you mostly. What else could we do?"

"Daniel, I am disappointed. You were clever enough to bring everyone here, so I would have expected you to have located the church by now." He sighed. "No matter. It shouldn't take long." He gestured at the woman. "Perhaps you could make some enquiries instead?"

Melandra made a languid gesture with one arm. "I'm onto it already." She left the room.

"Efficient but dangerous," Shemyaza said.

"Who is she?"

"The assassin who stalked me in Istanbul."

Daniel couldn't help laughing at the absurdity of the situation. "Shem! What have you done to her, or perhaps I shouldn't ask?"

Shem did not join in with the laughter. "Daniel, there might be complications."

"What do you mean?"

"That woman, Melandra, she works for an organisation dedicated to making sure I'm dead." He raised a hand to silence Daniel's outburst. "No, you don't understand. There is a Grigori faction behind it."

"What?"

"You heard me. Oh Daniel, you won't believe what I've learned, but the truth is there are elements of our people who do not want me to fulfil my destiny. They will try to stop me."

"Can that woman be trusted?"

He shrugged. "She may be unpredictable, but she's furious to discover that she's not working for enemies of the Grigori as she'd been led to believe."

"What do you think your enemies will do?"

"They will use people to obstruct me, as they already have. I don't know if they're aware of the church, but they are certainly behind the threat to bomb the Sphinx. That's what happens, Daniel. They use people's beliefs for their own ends, whether they are Islamic or Christian. People believe they are fighting for their god, but they're not. They're fighting for Grigori, the traditional enemies of their gods."

Daniel drew his hands over his face. This was so much to take in. "We'll need protection, then."

"We have Melandra. As I said, she's quite efficient and happy to be putting her talents to some use now that I've convinced her not to kill me."

"One woman against—what? How many?"

Shemyaza took a sip of tea. "Return to your companions," he said. "We must all go to the church at sunset. Tell Gadreel to bring Qimir's swords with her."

Daniel nodded. "OK. But what if your killer woman can't find the church?"

"She will."

Daniel returned to his hotel, with the promise that the woman, Melandra, would contact him in a couple of hours. Shemyaza told him to make sure the others were ready. He had told Daniel the story of what had happened to him since they were separated, and had introduced him to Penemue and Tiy. Shem's whole attitude seemed to have changed. He seemed more confident and sure about his role, but also more distant and melancholy. It was as if something was bothering him, of which he would not speak.

Although Daniel was glad that Penemue had been found, he could not help but feel slightly annoyed that other players had been brought into the game: Melandra and Tiy. He found it very hard to credit Tiy was actually Shemyaza's mother. As for Penemue, he was a revelation. He still lived in the body that had walked the earth in the days of Eden. He seemed ill at ease in the western-style clothes he wore—desert fatigues— as if his body was made for being draped in long robes. He could speak only in the ancient tongue, which meant he necessarily remained a silent, looming presence.

Back at his hotel, Daniel gritted his teeth before summoning the others to his room and filling them in about all that had happened. As he'd expected, Gadreel and Salamiel seemed put out that only Daniel had been taken to meet Shemyaza, while Pharmaros became jittery at the prospect of coming face to face with him later on. Only Kashday appeared pleased with developments and was clearly eager for the next stage of the game.

While they were still discussing the situation, the phone rang and Daniel answered it. He recognised the drawling American tone straight away. "We have a location, Mr Cranton. It's in Old Cairo, of course, the Coptic quarter. Shemyaza calls this Old Babylon. Do you think you and your crew will be capable of finding St Menas alone?"

Daniel stiffened with irritation. He had the impression that Melandra believed he and his companions to be bumbling idiots, helpless without Shemyaza's guidance. "We'll see you outside in an hour," he said and was about to put down the phone without waiting for her response.

"Not so fast," Melandra snapped, as if sensing he was going to break the connection. "Shemyaza wants you to wait for Penemue. He'll be coming to the church with you. Now, he can't speak English, Cranton, so send someone down to the lobby to wait for him. I'll put him in a cab and he'll be with you within a quarter of an hour. Got that?"

"All right," Daniel said. He felt confused about this development. If Penemue was coming to their hotel, why couldn't Shem accompany him? What was he planning? Daniel put down the phone with a frown on his face.

"What is it?" Salamiel asked.

Daniel shrugged. "Penemue is coming here."

"Alone?"

Daniel nodded. "Yes. Apparently."

Chapter Twenty-Three
The Dark Brotherhood

Cairo, Egypt

Helen and her mother walked the streets of Old Babylon. Lily held her daughter's right hand, although in the other Helen carried the jar containing Met-Met. She had insisted on bringing the scarab with her. "Why here, love?" Lily asked as they strolled down a winding, narrow street. All seemed unusually quiet, as if they had stepped from the bustling chaos of Cairo into an older time. This was a very ancient quarter of the city, the last bastion of the Copts. Mosques were not so prevalent here.

"Met-Met has told me to come here," Helen said, as if the fact was obvious.

"But why?" Lily looked around herself. Would Shemyaza or Daniel step from around a corner? She didn't like this place; it spooked her.

"Met-Met has a job for me," Helen said.

Lily glanced down at her daughter. "Honey, who exactly *is* Met-Met? Why does he tell you to do things?"

"He's my friend," Helen answered. "I can't see him, but I know he looks after me."

"Has he told you what this job is that you have to do?"

Helen shook her head. "Not yet. He's just taking us somewhere."

Helen could not tell her mother how she sensed danger all around. Lily might want them to return to their hotel if she knew about that. Helen was frightened, because to her, the danger felt like a dense black smoke creeping down every alley. These strands of darkness were converging on a single point, and there, she knew, a wonderful brightness would be found. The evil smoke wanted to extinguish this radiance. The light belonged to her. She was part of it and must protect it.

"It'll be dark soon," Lily said, her voice tense. "I think we should go back to the hotel. We can continue this walk tomorrow."

"Not yet," said Helen in a quiet, firm voice.

"Well, here we are," Gadreel said. The group stood before the entrance to St Menas. The church door was situated at the bottom of a short flight of steps. There was no garden around the building, not even a yard. The frontage was unornamented, faced with yellow-painted plaster. Its only external adornment was two pillars encrusted with blue mosaic tiles, on either side of the narrow double doors. A decorated arch curved above the lintel.

"I expected something a little more splendid," Pharmaros said lamely, voicing the thought in all her companions' minds.

Daniel led the way inside. The church itself was cramped and lacked ostentation. Five black pillars ran down each side of the narrow room, framing a simple altar at the far end, below a leaded-glass window. The glass was not coloured, but the coppery light of the sky outside lent an orange hue to the panes. A statue stood to the left of the altar, which upon inspection, the group discovered represented John the Baptist. A statue of Mary riding a donkey, on the right of the altar, was placed near to a high pulpit reached by a flight of wooden steps. Two banks of plain dark wood pews flanked the narrow aisle. The air smelled musty, of old, cheap frankincense. There were no priests, and no worshippers. The place felt deserted.

"Where is he?" Pharmaros asked, turning round in a slow circle.

"Not here," Salamiel said bleakly.

"He will be," Daniel said. "Be patient."

Penemue sat down uneasily on one of the pews. His large frame looked awkward in the narrow seat.

Gadreel had gone to investigate a cast-iron gate to the left of the altar. Her voice echoed slightly. "There are steps here. This must be the crypt." She shook the gate. "But it's locked."

Salamiel and Kashday joined her at the gate and inspected the lock. They would need tools to break it.

"We can't break in," Pharmaros said. "Someone will hear us."

"There doesn't seem to be anyone around," Gadreel said.

Daniel sighed. "Just wait. Shem will come and he will open the gate."

Salamiel laughed coldly. "With the power of his hands, no doubt." He went to sprawl on a pew at the front of the church, with his feet up on the worn wood. "Shall we sing a few hymns to get us in the mood?"

Daniel glanced at him sourly. He sensed the tension in his companions. Pharmaros would be happier fleeing the place; Gadreel was worried Shem would not come; Penemue felt bewildered and nervous having recently been dumped by Shem into twentieth century chaos; while Salamiel thought that what they were doing was a waste of time. Only Kashday seemed confident and calm. Daniel himself felt like a spring about to uncoil abruptly in a confined space. He sensed danger, but not in the church. It was outside, closing in.

Shemyaza and Melandra were walking through Old Babylon, having recently got out of a taxi. Both were dressed completely in black. Shemyaza's hair shone with white fire against his dark shirt. The sun had already begun to sink, but darkness was about an hour away. Before they'd left their lodgings, Shemyaza had given instructions to Tiy. "Go to the Sphinx, mother, and use your inner eye to watch my progress through the chambers."

Tiy had nodded, but with some reluctance. She'd frowned. "Something weighs heavily within you," she'd said. "Have strength, my son."

Shem had nodded. "Yes."

Outside, he had refused to answer Melandra's question as to why he had sent Tiy to the Sphinx. "She does her job," he'd said. "Just do yours. That's all I ask."

"But Giza will be heaving with party-goers," Melandra had argued. "Is that any place to send an old woman alone?"

Shemyaza had smiled to himself. "If I were you, I'd never let Tiy hear you say anything like that."

Now they walked along a street crowded with people and animals and traffic. Dust hung heavily in the air and the sunlight was almost orange. Melandra was sure she could hear the throb of loud music from beyond the city. Bands had been playing on the Giza plateau all day. Since they'd left their lodgings, Melandra had sensed pursuit; faint at first, but now her spine tingled with apprehension. "We are being followed," she said.

Shemyaza nodded. "Keep alert."

"It could be other operatives of the Children of Lamech." Would she have to protect them from someone she already knew?

Shemyaza shook his head. "No. It is the Brethren of the Black Sun."

Melandra had her weapon ready in her bag. She could almost imagine it was alive, eager to claim lives. She felt as if she was walking through a dream. The one she had been sent to kill, whom she'd been told was evil incarnate, walked beside her. He had been a strange companion, distant and silent, brooding upon his destiny. Lately, when he talked, it sounded as if he was uttering the lines from some ancient tragedy. Melandra no longer doubted that he spoke the truth, mainly because of the cordial yet respectful way he acted towards her, and the obvious torment that sometimes smoked from his eyes. She could still not totally disassociate him with the image of Christ, and even now, walking through the antique streets of the oldest part of the city, she felt as if her feet were leading her to Gethsemane. Her feelings were torn. A faint voice from the past, deep within her, questioned her switch of alliance, yet her heart was filled with sympathy for this tall, charismatic man. He seemed so sad, bringing recollections to her of the feelings she had picked up when handling her crucifix at home.

Shemyaza suddenly stopped dead and winced.

"What is it?" she asked.

He shook his head. "They are so...dark." His face had assumed an expression of pain. "Keep moving. The sacred gate is ahead. It was built by a Grigori family many centuries ago and will be a refuge for us."

An electric shudder coursed up Melandra's spine. She could sense the black presences behind them, drawing ever closer. Without her even realising it, the street had become deserted. Their foot-steps echoed, perhaps smothering the sound of pursuit. A strange, ground-hugging mist had begun to seep from every shadowed side alley; perhaps a natural phenomenon from the gullies and culverts of the city's water system. Melandra did not like it, unable to dispel the suspicion that the people following them had conjured the mist as concealment. For a moment, she was filled with doubt. If their pursuers were as terrible as Tiy and Shemyaza had intimated, would a gun be enough to deter them?

There was a wide archway ahead, which spanned the street. It had perhaps once been part of another structure, which had long vanished. Its granite blocks were corroded with age, but there was something imposing about it, something both watchful and meaningful. Melandra and Shemyaza had increased their pace. Melandra felt that if they could just pass beneath the arch, they would be safe. It was an irrational feeling. They were so close now, only feet away. The sun had nearly left the sky.

Then, a tall, dark figure stepped from beneath the shadow of the arch. Shemyaza drew in his breath sharply. Melandra reached for her weapon. There was no doubt in her mind that the person ahead of them represented a severe threat. He was dressed in a long, black leather coat, his short, fair hair swept back from his brow, his face forbidding and emotionless. Melandra shuddered: he looked like a crazed Nazi from an old war movie.

The man made a movement with his hand that suggested he was about to throw something. Melandra reacted quickly and a shot rang out into the twilight. The man uttered a grunt and crumpled forward.

Good shot, girl, Melandra thought to herself. Her self-congratulation was short-lived.

Tall figures were melting out of the shadows on every side, all dressed similarly to the man she had shot. Melandra raised her weapon again, but one of the Brethren flung out his hand. It seemed a bolt of mercurial silver light shot towards her. It struck the gun from her hand. She glanced down and, at her feet, saw a shining silver disk, almost like a CD, but carved with strange, curling patterns. At once, Melandra leapt forward, kicking high. She was trained in half a dozen disciplines of Oriental martial arts. Her body adjusted to the habitual movements, so that she flew with fluid grace towards their assailants. Her training took over. Her feet met solid flesh. Her arms, anticipating every move against her, deflected blows. She felt invulnerable, unconquerable, fulfilling her role as she had been schooled to do,

But then, another of the Dark Brethren threw one of the disks towards her. She could see it coming, shining, shimmering, as if in slow motion. She felt the impact of it, which brought immediate stinging pain. Melandra glanced at her wrist and, in horror, saw that she was bleeding profusely. She clamped her left hand over the wound in an attempt to stem the flow, but it was too deep; the bone laid bare. A quick glance around the street advised her that she and Shemyaza were now surrounded by tall, dark shapes, clad in black leather. Her whole body weakened. They were as good as dead. She had failed him.

"I'm sorry," she whispered. Shemyaza, now standing close behind her, did not answer.

One of their pursuers stepped towards them. His face was as severe as if it was fashioned from painted iron; his eyes were the blue of new steel. "Peverel Othman," he said in a clear, toneless voice.

Shemyaza's body tensed. "You know who I am," he said. "As I know you: Prometheus."

The man's cold, handsome face cracked into a smile. "So, you know one of my names. I am impressed."

"You must let me pass, Prometheus. Do not attempt to obstruct me."

The other laughed. "Alas, we cannot allow you to go any further." His smile faded. "We tolerated Othman, because he was just a directionless mass of havoc energy—quite entertaining. We were prepared to tolerate Shemyaza too, as long as he remained an icon of worship within the Masonic halls of minor, Grigori cabals. But now it appears you want to change things. We are intrigued as to how you intend to do this."

Shemyaza spoke monotonously, as if he was reciting lines from an ancient text. "I have come to the land of my ancestors to put wrong to right. I will open up the Chambers of Light and return to the source of our creation."

The leader of the Black Sun laughed coldly. "How commendable! And just how will you accomplish these things, Anakim? Do you intend to offer a sacrifice, through blood and the fires of hell?"

"My offering is love," Shemyaza answered stonily.

His adversary pantomimed exaggerated concern. "Indeed? Then it seems we really do have a problem. Loving and killing: it's all the same. They both initiate change, and we don't want change to occur. Let's just say we like the world as it is." He raised a hand.

Shemyaza said no more, as if resigned to whatever would happen next. Melandra, dazed beside him, wondered why he had revealed his purpose to these soulless creatures. Couldn't he summon his own power now and destroy his adversaries?

The dark brotherhood moved towards them, from every side. Melandra put her shoulder against Shemyaza's chest, and urged him to retreat, until they were pressed back against the wall of a shuttered house. Her mind was churning with a thousand unconnected thoughts: memories of her childhood; Nathaniel Fox's face; the queen of Babylon; traffic in the city centre.

Prometheus strode towards them, his hands clasped behind his back. His silent companions parted to let him pass between them. Halting directly in front of their captives, he sneered in Melandra's face. "My dear, you, and your incompetent commanders of the Children of Lamech, have inconvenienced us greatly. We dislike dealing with these messy, sordid matters ourselves, but unfortunately your untimely defection has left us no alternative. We are busy people, and traitors have to pay for disrupting our routine."

Melandra felt weak now; her blood pumped out between her numb fingers onto the dirt of the road. An enervating force that poured from the dark brotherhood amplified the effects of her wound. Her legs could no longer support her weight and she sank down to kneel, swaying, before her towering enemy. Tiny, bright motes pulsed before her eyes, but she was still able to see that the Brethren of the Black Sun were all armed; not with guns, or the silvery cutting disks, but with what appeared to be knives or daggers. Perhaps because she was losing consciousness, it seemed to her as if the knives had no real form. They were like black holes in the shape of blades; non-reflecting, made of shadows.

"You, traitress," hissed Prometheus, "have reached the end of your life. You have abandoned your god, so you die in sin. Look forward to hell, little assassin. You will have an eternity to reflect upon the rashness of your apostasy."

The dark figures closed in, their shadow-daggers raised. Their leader stood, hands on hips, appraising Shemyaza with dispassionate eyes. "Few things have the power to destroy you completely, but rest assured these blades will not only end your physical life but annihilate your soul."

Shemyaza did not move. Melandra leaned against his legs now, and it seemed to her as if a torrent of soothing strength flowed out of him into her. Why wasn't he afraid or angry? She wanted to rise up and fight for him, but her strength had gone.

"Helen, I really think we should go back now." Lily's voice had changed from sounding merely tense to fearful. "It's horrible here. We can't stay." The empty streets had closed in around them, watchful and threatening. Dust rose in eddies on the road ahead of them, but there was no wind. They walked through an ochre gloom. The sky, the buildings around them, even the air glowed with a deep, orange tint. No-one lived here or walked here: it seemed no-one ever had.

"Not long now," Helen murmured. She let go of her mother's hand and tilted back her head, as if listening to something.

Lily frowned. "I can't hear anything." She paused. "Helen, listen. There isn't a single, normal sound. No traffic, no people, not even the wind. Even our voices sound muffled. We've got to get out of here."

"Mum, it's all right," Helen said softly. "We're not in danger." She lifted Met-Met's jar before her face and slowly unscrewed the cap.

"What are you doing?" Lily asked in a whisper.

Her daughter glanced up at her with a disturbingly adult expression. "He is in terrible danger," she said. "I have to help him."

"Who's in danger? Where?"

"Shemyaza," Helen said. "He is near to us now. Very near." She removed the lid of the jar completely.

"He's here?" Lily's voice was soft. She appeared to accept Helen's words without argument. Her eyes stared without blinking at the motionless scarab within the jar, as if she expected it to spring to life at any moment and launch itself from confinement.

The scarab did not move, but a sound came out of its container. At first, it was hardly more than a sigh, like scouring sand rubbing against dry grasses, but gradually it changed into a rapid clicking, as if a thousand insects were trapped within the jar and snapping their wing-cases. Met-Met still lay alone in the bottom of the glass, but Lily and Helen could hear an enormous swarm of insects that whirred and chattered its way up in the evening sky. They poured invisibly out the jar, and the noise of their chitinous wings filled the air.

"Fly!" Helen shouted, flinging out her arms. She still held the jar in one hand.

For a moment, Lily saw an amorphous dark cloud hanging over them. Instinctively, she ducked, but then the swarm was speeding away from them over the roofs of the buildings. Lily clutched at her face, staring between her fingers at the burning sky.

With precise movements, Helen carefully recapped the jar, where the body of Met-Met still lay inert, and offered it to Lily to put into her shoulder-bag. "We can go now," she said.

Lily scraped her hands through her hair, swallowed. "Where?" she asked in a hoarse voice. "*Where* can we go?" She knew in her heart they would not be returning to the hotel. Something had begun here, like a spring pushing its way up through the ground. Now, they were caught in its current.

"To the great lion," Helen said and took her mother's hand in her own once more.

"Is Shem there?" Lily asked.

"It is where he wants us to go," Helen answered.

Together they began to retrace their steps through the silent streets.

The Brethren of the Black Sun were so close to their prey now, they were forced to step through the puddle of Melandra's blood. She could not longer tell if her left hand was still clamped around her right wrist and wished, wearily, that it could all be over. If death was to happen, let it be quick. She was prepared to face whatever came after. But these dreadful faces, these cold, inhuman men: she could not tolerate their proximity. They seemed to be advancing in slow motion, relishing the fear and pain they saw in her eyes. Shemyaza was like a statue behind her; she could no longer feel his warmth.

Then, a strange sound, like the rushing of a field of corn, filled Melandra's ears. She blinked, forcing her heavy eyes to focus upon the source of the sound. Was it simply the approach of death, the rustle of his sere robes brushing against the ground? When would the fatal blows fall?

She closed her eyes for a moment, but became aware that movement had ceased around her. Forcing her lids apart, she saw that the Brethren had halted their approach. They had raised their heads to the sky and were sniffing at the air like dogs. They seemed perturbed. Then, Prometheus spoke a rapid phrase in a language she did not recognise. The rushing sound had grown louder. It was no longer the susurration of corn, but something like the whirring of a million chitinous wings. She thought of locusts, a biblical plague. Blinking, she tried to focus on the sky, but could see nothing. The Brethren had begun to slap at their heads and shoulders, as if assailed by invisible insects. Melandra drew in a painful breath. Either her sight was truly fading, or the air had became black and dense, but not with anything that she could actually *see*. She could not describe what she was seeing; it was perceived within the deepest level of her being.

One by one the Brethren fell to the ground, clutching at their throats. A writhing, formless dark mass swarmed all over their bodies, probing with invisible feelers, pushing relentlessly into all orifices. The mouths of the Brethren were stretched into hideous blackening holes as they gasped for breath. Melandra watched them turn blue, their movements become fewer, until they lay motionless on the street around their erstwhile prisoners. Their destruction had taken less than five minutes. A faint, ground level breeze scattered grains of dust over the still, open eyes. Dust gathered in the folds of clothing, between lips, in hair. Melandra imagined that very soon, the attackers would be nothing more than unrecognisable, sand-covered mounds in the street. It seemed as if the desert was prepared to take them already, even here in this back-street of Old Babylon.

Shemyaza uttered a short sigh, leaned down and lifted Melandra to her feet. "Those who hate change should learn that it is always inevitable," he said. "Here ends the Brethren whose legacy has initiated all holy wars throughout human history."

"What happened?" Melandra asked in a slurred voice.

"They were killed," Shemyaza answered simply. "The Kephri beetle will carry their black souls forever beneath its great carapace." He straightened Melandra's injured arm and peered at her wrist where the wound gaped wide. Her skin was covered in sticky blood from her finger-tips to her elbow and her clothes were soaked with it. It pulsed from the wound weakly now.

"I'm dying," she said. "There's nothing you can do. We haven't enough time."

"Hmm." Shemyaza ran one finger over the open wound. Melandra could not feel his touch. She felt no pain at all.

"I don't regret what I've done," she murmured. 'Don't think that. I don't believe that hell is waiting for me."

"No, it's not," Shemyaza said.

To Melandra's dismay, he put his mouth against her wrist. She could feel the smooth hardness of teeth upon her. Was he sucking her blood? She became filled with horror and revulsion and tried to wriggle away. "No!" Her protest was weak.

Shemyaza dropped her arm and transferred his grip to her head. He pulled her towards him, ignoring her feeble struggles. She saw his face loom large in her sight, like a mask. Then his lips were upon hers. She could taste her own blood. And something else. She became aware of an immense void around them, and something she could not describe was shooting towards them; formless light and heat. Her mouth, her throat, then her entire body became filled with it: a sheer energy-filled radiance that poured from Shemyaza' soul, out of his mouth and into her own. She hung limply in his arms, submitting to this weird and shattering kiss. After only a few moments, he released her. She thought she would fall, but strangely her body was quite able to stand.

Shemyaza wiped his mouth and smiled at her. "Forgive my importunity. I had to act quickly."

Melandra frowned. She did not feel weak at all. What had he done to her? She glanced at her wrist and saw the faint line of a scar. Her jaw dropped open. "You have healed me?"

"Take up your bed and walk, Melandra," he answered in a faintly sarcastic tone. "Only don't walk with me. You must go to Tiy at the Sphinx."

"I'm healed!" Melandra said in wonder, still staring at her wrist.

"Yes, you are," Shemyaza answered impatiently. "Melandra, I have to go now."

"What happened?" she asked. "How did those pigs die?"

Shemyaza pulled a face as if their miraculous rescue was of no consequence. "An ally of mine was looking out for us. I have felt her presence for some time, yet I do not know her. All I do know is that she released an ancient power, that of the scarab god, Kephri, which intervened on our behalf."

"Lucky," Melandra answered.

He smiled. "Not luck, but fate. My work is far more important than the intrigues of any Grigori brotherhood. It would never have ended here in futile death, but I'm sorry you were hurt."

For a moment, they stared at one another in silence, then impulsively Melandra reached up and hugged Shemyaza tightly. Very slightly, her wrist tingled as she touched him, as if she'd been stung by a nettle there.

His arms snaked around her and for the briefest of moments, he squeezed her body. "Go now. I have little time." She let him go. "I feel that I failed you."

"No. You are my guardian, but there is nothing to guard me from now. Go to the Sphinx and wait."

"What for? Will you join us there?"

He paused, then stroked her cheek with one finger. "I am always with you."

He walked away then, beneath the arch. Its shadows swallowed him. Melandra watched him go, wondering whether she should follow him discreetly. She picked up her gun from where it had fallen and glanced at her wrist again. No, she would do as he asked.

Melandra headed back towards the centre of Cairo, stepping purposefully over the bodies of the fallen Brethren without looking down.

Chapter Twenty-Four
Love Beyond Death

"He's not coming," Salamiel said. "We've been here half an hour, Daniel."

"He *will* come," Daniel snapped. "Have a little patience for once, will you!"

Gadreel sat down next to the silent Penemue on one of the pews. "Something could have happened to him. How could we know?" She stroked Penemue's arm, who looked at her and smiled. "We should try to break through the gate to the crypt."

"Don't do anything," Daniel said. "Just trust me."

"Trust you!" Salamiel laughed. "You have no idea where Shem is. All you have is your blind faith and endless hope!"

"Oh, just shut it for once, will you!" Daniel snapped. "I'm sick of your sarcasm!"

A voice echoed down the church. "Bickering, bickering! You are like children in a playground."

The entire company scrambled to their feet. A tall figure stood silhouetted in the doorway to the church, limned in tawny light.

"Shem!" Daniel cried, unable to resist glancing triumphantly at Salamiel.

Shem sauntered down the aisle towards them. "Not kept you waiting too long, I hope."

"Not at all," Salamiel drawled. "We've been quite the tourists, enjoying the sights."

Shem walked past them all to Salamiel and draped an arm around his shoulders. "We must get to work. Where's the crypt?"

"Over here," Salamiel said. Together they walked towards the gate.

Daniel felt hurt that Shemyaza had gone to Salamiel rather than himself. Salamiel was the trouble-maker, who asked awkward questions and argued for the sake of it. Why had Shem singled him out for affectionate gestures?

The group assembled around Shemyaza at the gate, Daniel loitering moodily at the rear. Shemyaza examined the lock. "We need the key-keeper to open this."

"There's no-one here," Daniel said.

"Of course there is," Shemyaza replied. "There is always a key-keeper." He pushed through the bewildered group and went to stand hands on hips before the altar.

Daniel was surprised to see that a bent, old priest was standing in the shadows near the pulpit. Had he been there all along, listening to their arguments? Daniel felt a shock course through his body. For the briefest of moments, he was sure that the old man was Mani. Then, the priest took a step forward from the shadows, and Daniel realised he was mistaken.

"I am Shemyaza," Shem announced.

The old man shuffled forward. He was dressed in a long, faded black cassock, his face as brown and wrinkled as a raisin. "I am John," he said, "and I have prepared the way for your coming, Lord." He raised his hands and champed his lips over his toothless gums. When he spoke, his aged voice boomed out with the strength of a fanatic. "The true light that enlightens every man has come into the world and the world was made through him. Yet the world knows him not. From him we will all receive grace and truth."

Shemyaza nodded imperceptibly, faintly smiling. With one giant step, he drew close to the old man and enfolded him in a long-armed embrace. The shabby black figure all but disappeared within Shemyaza's hold.

Nobody spoke. Daniel knew instinctively that John had been waiting in this place a long time for this moment; all his life, as had his father before him. The line of the generations appeared before Daniel's mind's eye: fathers and sons disappearing into infinity. Two thousand years of waiting.

Shem released John from his embrace and stepped back. Daniel thought he could hear a faint sound as of rushing water, accompanied by the beat of hand-drums and ululating cries of tribal women.

"I say to you," Shemyaza murmured, "that the hour has come when all the dead and the living will hear the voice of the fire and of the waters, the light and the darkness." His voice was low, but rang clearly throughout the old building. "For as the father had the light of life, so I, his son, also have light. Do not marvel at this, for the hour of judgement is here."

The exchange had been like a ceremony, played out with ritual responses. Daniel knew now that they were in the right place, and that the entrance to the Chambers of Light lay very close.

John lifted his chin, and took a key from a chain around his waist. "Come, Lord, I will open the gate for you."

Daniel glanced at the statue of John the Baptist. Was it possible?

The old man went slowly to the gate and here spent some minutes fiddling with the key and the lock, but eventually, he turned to the group with a smile and pushed the iron gate open. Shemyaza nodded respectfully to the priest, then led the way down the steps. As Daniel squeezed past John, he looked at the old man. He was still chewing upon nothing, his red-rimmed, rheumy eyes gazing at the rafters overhead, his fingers clasping and unclasping before his chest. It was almost as if he was totally senile, unaware of what was happening around him, and had played his part through instinct alone.

The steps were damp and worn, and led down to an ante-chamber that issued onto two low-ceilinged rooms. The air was moist and foul-smelling. On the right, the group discovered a musty vault that housed a single, unadorned tomb. The floor was submerged beneath half an inch of oily water. They could see an iron gate in the far wall, which appeared to lead to some kind of gully from which water was leaking into the crypt. Gadreel suggested that at some point the gully must have led to the holy Nile, before its course had deviated away from Old Babylon.

Shemyaza looked around this chamber briefly, then ducked back into the ante-chamber. He entered the second room which

lay directly ahead of the steps. Daniel was the first to follow.
His eyes were drawn immediately to a slit in the opposite wall,
where the rays of the evening sun shone through in dim, gilded
beams. They illumined a small room that had a flagged floor
covered in a layer of gritty dust. But at least the room was dry.
Overhead, the ceiling was comprised of enormous, oblong
slabs of stone. In the centre of the chamber lay what appeared to be a well-head, surrounded by a low wall of rough
stones and covered by a black iron grille. Shemyaza walked to
the well and beckoned for the others to draw near.

"This is what we've been looking for," Shemyaza said.

Daniel peered at the well. He could see that it was filled
with dry earth, nearly to the rim of the surrounding wall. A
strong musty smell rose out of it that reminded Daniel of a
long-abandoned house.

Salamiel laughed. "At last: the ceremonial gateway to the
Chambers of Light." He clearly intended it to be a joke.

"That's right," Shemyaza said.

"But..."

Shemyaza silenced Salamiel with a wave of his hand. "Look
at the floor around the well-head. Do you see those rough
slots? There are six of them, and that's where Qimir's swords
will be inserted. I trust you have them with you, Gadreel."

Gadreel nodded. "Yes. But there are seven swords..."

Shemyaza ignored her observation. "I want you all to
sit around the well in a circle, each of you behind one of
the slots." No-one moved. "What are you waiting for?"
He glanced at the window behind him. "We don't have
much time."

The group assembled hesitantly around the well and sat
down as directed.

"Where are you going to sit?" Daniel asked.

Shemyaza did not answer, but gestured for Gadreel to dis-
tribute the swords. She took them carefully from her back-
pack and handed them around the circle to the others.
Shemyaza took the largest sword from her and positioned himself, standing, behind Salamiel.

An air of urgency had come to fill the room, a tense expectation. No-one spoke.

"Place your swords into the ground," Shemyaza said.

Silently, the group obeyed. A couple of the insertion points were blocked by ancient dirt and it required some effort to pierce them with the swords, but eventually, all six blades rose firmly from the ground.

Shemyaza nodded approvingly. "Now, place both your hands upon the pommel of your sword."

Once this was done, he withdrew the key crystal from his pocket and leaned forward to place it upon the centre of the grille covering the well. Then he straightened his spine, staring straight ahead, the seventh sword held upright before his face. Conjuring a halo of golden fire from his hair, the last of the sunlight poured around him and struck the crystal.

The light entered and empowered the stone. Seven laser-like radials, of different colours, spat out from the crystal and struck each of the swords, so that every one of the bearers became bathed in a specific, pure hue of the spectrum. Shemyaza's ray passed right over Salamiel's head. He was enveloped in golden light, while beneath him, Salamiel was wreathed in a brilliant crimson glare. Daniel was enwrapped in green light, Gadreel in violet, Penemue in orange, Pharmaros in indigo and Kashday in blue.

"Whatever happens," Shemyaza said, "do not let go of the swords."

Now, the crystal began to emit seven distinct tones that, in turn, were absorbed by the swords. The blades vibrated in the hands that encircled them.

"Keep your hold firm," Shemyaza said, "and concentrate on directing the energy you are receiving into the ground through the swords. The light around you is *your* colour. The crystal has chosen the sphere of your soul. Flow with it. Use it. Let the light draw substance from your spirit. The guardians of the upper gateway will see only the colours of the heavens."

The resonance of the tones grew louder, until they became a dissonance. The highest note was a shrieking stridency, which was almost ultra-sonic, while the lowest rumbled inaudibly in the chests of the avatars. The effect was extreme, but oddly harmonious.

Daniel's teeth were set on edge by the resonance. He wanted to let go of his sword, but forced himself to keep a grip. Presently, he noticed that the vibration now seemed to have extended beyond the sword, because the ground beneath him had begun to shake. He looked around himself and met the surprised glances of the other avatars. Only Shem seemed unmoved. Plaster flakes sifted down from the walls while, overhead, the massive blocks of stone in the ceiling shook ominously. If even one of them should shake loose, the entire group would be crushed to death. Daniel found that his lips were stretched into a rictus grin. His hands seemed welded to the sword.

The intensity of the crystal lights grew brighter and the hum of the tones reach a painful crescendo that passed beyond the range of sound audible to living ears. Daniel felt as if he was being electrified, as if every atom within his body oscillated to the clamorous frequency.

I can't hold on, he thought. I'm going to burn alive, spontaneously combust.

His muscles were spasming throughout his entire body: it felt like the pulsing tides of a thousand synchronous orgasms. Daniel soared on the overwhelming extremes of terror and ecstasy. When he opened his eyes, his vision was completely obscured by a vibrant green veil of light. Around him, the eyes of his companions had become burning orbs of coloured fire: gold, orange, crimson, violet, indigo, blue. Their mouths, like his, were stretched unnaturally wide to emit soundless cries. Streams of ether poured from their lips, filling the air with a boiling, multi-coloured mist. The sight was terrifying, but peculiarly beautiful. Now, Daniel knew what it was to be truly Grigori. He closed his eyes again and forced himself to flow with the energy, conduct it into the ground.

Gradually, the trembling ground began to settle and the tones started to die down. The tremor lasted only for another minute. After the rumbling had fallen silent, a sound like that of shifting sand hissed out from the well-head. The group opened their eyes. The coloured lights had vanished; the chamber was barely illumined by the dying sunlight.

Shemyaza rubbed his face; he looked exhausted. "You may let go of your swords now."

Daniel tried to release his grip on the pommel but found that his hands were rigid and immobile. Everyone else appeared to be experiencing the same problem.

Shemyaza reached over Salamiel's shoulder and removed the crystal from the well-head. The hold upon the avatars was released, and a powerful last discharge of energy threw them all backwards onto the floor.

Daniel was the first to stand up and nearly fell down again immediately. He felt so dizzy that whenever he tried to walk in one direction he found he was staggering in another.

"Don't worry," Shemyaza said, smiling at Daniel's reeling attempts to walk. "The disorientation will be short-lived." He put his arm around Daniel's shoulders and supported him to the well-head. "Look, our work has been successful."

The soil which had filled the shaft was fast disappearing downwards, as if a plug far below had been removed. Daniel shook his head in wonder. "The vibrations have cleared the shaft."

The other avatars were rising slowly to their feet, brushing dust from their clothes. Like Daniel, they seemed dazed.

Daniel's dizziness had abated now. He pulled away from Shemyaza's arm and leaned on the low wall to peer down into the lightless vertical tunnel. "We haven't got to go down there, have we? There are no hand-holds. How could we manage it?"

"*You* don't have to go down there," Shemyaza replied. "But I do."

Daniel glanced up in surprise. He had envisaged that their journey into the Chambers of Light would involve visualisation. "This is absurd! You can't go down there alone. Surely the journey through the gateway must be astral rather than physical?"

Shemyaza shook his head. "No, the chambers are physical and so is their entrance, although some astral travel is involved. I shall go into them alone."

Salamiel looked over Shemyaza's shoulder. "So, are you just going to jump down there, or should we have brought a rope?"

Shemyaza turned round slowly and stared unblinkingly into Salamiel's eyes. "Neither of those things."

Salamiel pulled a quizzical face. "What, then?"

Shemyaza closed his eyes for a moment, then swallowed. "In order for me to enter the Chambers, all physical life must leave my body."

Salamiel stared at him mutely, while Daniel cried in a shrill voice, "What?"

Salamiel spoke harshly. "More to the point, why?"

"Remember the time of Solomon, when he called upon the knowledge of our race to build his temple."

Salamiel nodded. "You might say I was instrumental in shaping that noble edifice. What of it?"

"At the temple's heart, lay the shrine to the holiest of holies. It contained the altar to the creator, the grand architect. You must remember that any initiates who wished to enter the shrine were required to go completely naked. They were purified in the sacred baths and all hair removed from their bodies. To be in the presence of such power, they had to return to a symbolic natural state. Their souls were laid bare before the source of all. The ritual was about purity."

Salamiel's eyes had taken on a hard, yet knowing expression. "I see..."

"But why do you have to die?" Daniel asked. His voice was high. "Why can't you just go naked into the Chambers?"

Shemyaza turned to Daniel. "The Chambers of Light are the original holiest of holies. Flesh itself must be surrendered before the guardians will allow me passage. When I enter the great crystal at the centre of the complex, I will return to the source itself and cannot take my body with me. My soul will travel the route through the universe: that was the path used by the Renowned Old Ones, all those millennia ago, when they brought the life-giving light to this planet."

"But the Elders had bodies," Daniel said. "Why should you have to surrender yours?"

Shemyaza rubbed his brow. "The way to the stars has been closed down. You know that. The old ways are no longer strong enough to open them up."

"We can't allow you to die," Gadreel said. "Let the Chambers stayed closed and the world carry on as it is."

Shemyaza looked at her with a strangely emotionless expression, although his eyes were wild with feelings beyond mere emotion. His voice sounded hollow. "The light from the Source is greater than any love you might feel for me. And love itself goes beyond life and death."

He's not himself, Daniel thought. It's almost as if he's possessed.

"If you have to die," Pharmaros said timidly, "how will you do it?"

Shemyaza turned his lambent gaze upon her. His voice had become colder, more alien. "The sphere of my solar power must be pierced. It is the only way that my life essence will drain away. If I die by any other means, I could be capable of regeneration."

"Shem," Daniel said gently. "You can't expect one of us to do this thing to you, and Melandra isn't here. I doubt if even she would be able to kill you now anyway. So, if you insist upon this sacrifice, you must accomplish it yourself." He thought he had Shemyaza trapped now. If he was crazy enough to stab himself, the others could act immediately and save him. At this point, Daniel was convinced Shemyaza had lost his mind.

"That's right," Salamiel said. His face bore an expression of cynical incredulity. "Take your own life, Shem. We don't agree with this, and we won't condone it."

Shemyaza's eyes widened fiercely as he stared at Salamiel. "Only you are strong enough to do it, Sal. It must be you."

Daniel uttered a panicked, "No!" which Shemyaza ignored.

Salamiel laughed uneasily. "I don't share your madness. I can't do it."

Shemyaza advanced towards him, until he was mere inches away from Salamiel's face. "You think I am mad, but I am not. You must face what is ordained and inevitable. Look up to the heavens: stop staring at the ground. We are tiny cogs in the vast machine of the universe. We have our parts to play. You know that."

Salamiel shook his head, and backed away. "You can't ask this of me. You can't!"

Shemyaza followed him across the room. "Kill me," he said, in a chilling matter-of-fact manner. "Pierce the sphere of Tiphareth, the solar plexus of my body, with the seventh sword."

For a moment, there was silence. It seemed that Gadreel, Pharmaros, Kashday and Penemue sensed this drama had only three actors, and they were not part of it.

Then Salamiel said simply, "I won't. I can't."

"You can."

Daniel marched across the chamber and put his hands upon Shemyaza's arms. "Shem, wake up! You mustn't do this. It's insane!"

Shemyaza smiled faintly at him. "I am not insane. Don't be selfish, Daniel. You must know in your heart I am right." He picked up the sword from the ground and held it out to Salamiel. "Do it, Sal. Be quick. Don't think about it."

"No!" Daniel snatched the sword from Salamiel's hands. "I won't let you."

Salamiel put his hands over his face and turned away. He looked pitiful; defeated. Shemyaza was a pylon of power before him. "After the deed is done, you must put the crystal key into my hands and cast me into the pit. Then, you must all go to the Sphinx and await the dawn of the new epoch."

Salamiel lowered his hands and spoke in a cracked voice. "Why me, Shem? Why? Are you trying to punish me for questioning your actions?"

Shemyaza shook his head and plucked the sword from Daniel's hands. "No. I have chosen you because you are the strongest of my companions. You always have been."

"Then find somebody stronger," Salamiel snapped.

Shemyaza merely stared at him in silence, as the second ticked by. Salamiel punched the air, and uttered a choked sob. His face crumpled, his eyes leaked tears. The sight made Daniel feel nauseous. He sensed that Salamiel had already accepted that the task would ultimately fall to him. Argument was futile. Daniel took a few steps backwards towards the others, shaking his head in disbelief and horror.

Shemyaza allowed Salamiel to weep for a while, standing before him with folded arms, the sword drooping from one hand. He seemed utterly at peace, accepting of what was to come.

The other avatars looked on in stunned silence. Salamiel, always so strong and flippant, fell to his knees before them, his shoulders shaking. The sight was repulsive, shocking.

Shemyaza hunkered down and placed one hand on Salamiel's shoulder. Salamiel visibly attempted to collect himself, and straightened up, wiping his face aggressively with the heels of his hands.

"Salamiel," Shem murmured. "Why do you weep? In the beginning, didn't you swear to kill me if I strayed one inch from war and revolution?"

Salamiel nodded. "Yes." His voice was a croak. "But it was a long time ago and has no relevance now."

Shemyaza shook his head. "It has. I *have* strayed. Now you must carry out the duty you swore under oath to undertake. The time has come."

"No, it has not!" Salamiel cried. "You haven't strayed, you have led us in strength. You have led us here!" His voice became more subdued. "And besides that, you are my brother and I love you."

Shemyaza's voice also softened. "Then do it with love. It must be done willingly and with the wisdom of my words in your heart." He stood up in the last amber rays of the setting sun that came in through the narrow window. He held out the sword to Salamiel, who stared at it as if in terror for a few moments, but then took the weapon in his hands. His face was ashen.

Shemyaza opened his shirt to bare his torso. "Daniel, come here."

"No!" Daniel's denial was a ragged wail.

"Daniel, if you love me, come take my arms," Shemyaza said. "Hold me firm."

Daniel did not know what reserve of strength or obedience enabled him to stagger up to his beloved master, stand behind him and take hold of his arms. All he knew was that Shemyaza meant to complete this abominable ritual, and ultimately none of them could withstand his power or disobey his word. Daniel felt utterly alone and empty, bereft of gods or faith. He leaned his forehead against Shemyaza's back, his eyes closed tight. He felt that he too must die after this. Now was the end to all for which they'd struggled. The ultimate sacrifice.

"Come; love me, Salamiel. Kill me."

All was utterly still within the chamber. The outside world might not exist. Then, Daniel heard Salamiel utter a cry of rage, pain and blind determination: a cry from the soul. Shemyaza's body was pushed heavily backwards in a sudden jolt and a grunt was expelled from his throat. Daniel held on, but stumbled, so that both he and Shemyaza fell down backwards.

Daniel lay on the dirt floor, dazed, until Penemue came forward and silently lifted the weight from his body. Daniel curled onto his side, into a foetal ball. His fists were bunched before his eyes. His limbs trembled.

"Daniel," he heard Gadreel say in terrible, ragged voice. "It is not over. Get up." Her hands curled around his wrists and attempted to straighten his arms.

Daniel whined like an injured animal and fought her efforts to lift him to his feet. Pharmaros came to help and through joint effort, the two women managed to lift him up. Hanging limply between them, Daniel caught sight of the body at his feet. He expelled a shattering cry that sounded like the lament of a woman who had seen her only child murdered before her.

Shemyaza lay with open eyes, blood pulsing from the horrific wound below his ribs. It was clear the sacred blade had done its work and that already the life force had left him. Salamiel stood like a stooped alabaster statue, the sword hanging from his hands. His eyes were dry, but his face held an expression of horror so deep Daniel imagined that its gaze could petrify the world. Salamiel's shirt and face were spattered with blood, a hideous parody of the crimson light that had recently surrounded him.

"We have to complete his instructions," Gadreel said, swallowing thickly. "Will you help us, Daniel?"

Daniel could neither move nor speak, but only stare at the body on the floor. It didn't seem like Shem any more. It wasn't.

The women left Daniel standing there. Penemue and Kashday assisted them to drag Shemyaza's body to the mouth of the well. Gadreel leaned down and kissed Shemyaza's forehead, then placed the crystal in his hands, curling his fingers around it. "Safe journey, my love," she whispered, and between them, the four pushed the lifeless form over the edge into darkness.

Daniel heard the soft thumps as the body hit the sides of the well on its fall. He thought he was about to pass out, and fell to his knees, but then his stomach turned over and he was vomiting in great spasms onto the floor. Gadreel came back to him and crouched down beside him. She took him in her arms, and rocked him like a child. He could feel her tears raining down onto his face like a deluge.

At the Sphinx, Tiy raised her face and sniffed the air. She and Melandra were pushed up against the left paw of the Sphinx, hemmed in by milling bodies. The atmosphere was that of suppressed hysteria. Discordant, repetitive music filled the night and the acid swathe of laser light. Out on the plain, a solid mass of dancers gyrated in a tribal simplicity to the electronic throb.

"What is it, Tiy?" Melandra asked, glaring at yet another young body that pushed past her. "What can you sense?"

"The seven sorrows," Tiy whispered, her dry fingers curling around Melandra's hands, which were still crusted with the dried blood of her healed wound. "The last is imminent." She looked her age; weak and frail.

"Tiy, can you see Shem?" Melandra cried. "Has he entered the Chambers yet?"

Tiy did not answer, but stiffened abruptly and fell against the younger woman. Melandra eased Tiy to her knees. Had she had a heart attack or a stroke? It seemed that even her milky, blind eyes were full of pain and shock.

"Tiy? Are you all right? What's happened? What is it?"

Tiy felt it so clearly in the wide landscape of her mind and heart. The chaotic sounds and movement around her in reality faded away. All that existed was the agonising thrust of cold, black steel. It pierced her heart. In the terrible numbness that followed, she remembered other times when this had happened: times throughout her life when her beloved son had suffered, felt pain, or had committed the foulest acts of cruelty and hatred. She had felt it then: a sword through her heart. This was the last. The seventh sword.

Melandra watched helplessly, as Tiy threw back her head. The tuneless, constant rhythm of the music around them seemed at once obscene and intrusive. The jostling bodies were mindless, soulless and shallow. Melandra despised them all.

Then, without warning of any kind, the sound system cut out and the great spot-lights and sweeping laser beams popped into darkness. Silence and stillness descended like a white blanket of fog. The pyramids alone remained illuminated, with their own stellar light. The crowd froze, looked around themselves, nervous and scared.

Tiy's fragile body arched in Melandra's hold, and then expelled an unearthly screech, so loud it could be heard across the whole of Giza. The cry seemed endless; the soul-sound of grief and pain. It entered like a dart into the heart of every member of the crowd; young girls in ribbons and lycra; old stalwarts of the festival scene in denim and leather; flamboyant ravers daubed in neon body-paint. Silence and stillness were absolute in the echoing wake of the lament. Not even a child whined in the star-lit darkness. Then Tiy drew in a great breath and screamed, "Pan Medes! Pan Medes! The Great King is dead!"

It was a cry that echoed across Egypt and the Mediterranean. It spiralled around the lofty masts of passing ships and came to rest in the heart of Arcadia itself. The earth shuddered.

Chapter Twenty-Five
Return to the Source

The Chambers of Light

The journey of the soul was not a fall. To Shemyaza, it was like waking up from a dream, for what surrounded him now seemed more real than memory. He stood on the shores of a vast lake between two cyclopean columns of black basalt, and silhouetted against the evening sky, Shemyaza could see an island. Reaching out to either side, he ran his hands up and down the cold stone of the pillars, feeling for any encoded message. The smooth surfaces were adorned with pictograms, more ancient than the earliest Egyptian motifs, incorporating circles, lines and dots. The columns felt real to Shemyaza's touch, even though he was in the astral realm. They delivered a message to him, but not through any carved glyph. A soundless duet boomed through his mind:

"Here in Zep-tepi, the first place: we are the Pillars of Life, of Adam and Eve, Joachim and Boaz. Duality in stone; the foundation. For does not your name, Shemyaza, mean the Pillar?"

Shemyaza gazed out over the lush, fertile landscape, which had once been the land of Khem: a paradise. He stood upon the Giza plateau as it had appeared six aeons ago. Shemyaza stepped between the pillars, initiating the process of returning.

Red rays reflected off the domed roof of a columned temple on the island. He could see it clearly now. History unfolded. The island was the primal mound of creation, and the temple upon it was the first ever to have been built upon the virgin body of Mother Earth. It was the original omphalos of the world. All subsequent sacred omphali had been constructed in its memory: it was the House of the Human Soul. Shemyaza knew that in the time he left behind, the great Sphinx stood in the temple's place, and had done so for six epochs, gazing watchfully upon the changing constellations of each new aeon. Soon, it would gaze upon the stars of Mankind, the House of Aquarius. The consensual soul of humanity that rested in this house would be reborn under the light of those stars. But not yet. First, there would have to be the conception.

He stood upon a narrow wooden jetty, to which a small boat was moored. Shemyaza climbed into the boat and it began to drift swiftly towards the island. Shemyaza gazed into the water. This was the lake where all the spirits that inhabited the earth and sky were forged: the waters of life, the rivers of belief. He was reminded of the silent boat-man of all the underworld myths, who carried the souls of the dead across the waters to judgement.

The boat reached the steps to the temple. Glowing marble disappeared beneath the water, as if made of light. The boat turned itself sideways. Shemyaza climbed out without touching the sacred water; no spirits could reach out for him and suck him down into their dreaming realm.

Shemyaza looked back to the shore he had left. The black columns seemed incongruous, severe against the soft fluttering of foliage. There was nothing between them but a colourless void, for the world beyond had yet to come into being.

Inside, the temple was bare and unadorned, comprised of immense blocks of granite. It was quite dark, because the building faced east, and now the sun set behind it. Shemyaza walked towards the back of the temple, where there was a wide hole in the floor. His feet made no sound and he could not smell or hear anything. He felt calm, already resigned to the fate of possible oblivion. He had been resigned to it for a long time. There was no guarantee that his soul and spirit body would survive the experience ahead of him. The Elders would have left traps and obstacles to prevent intruders from entering the Chambers.

At the edge of the hole, he looked down and saw a flight of wide steps. After a short way, they veered abruptly to the right. Cautiously, Shemyaza began to descend, projecting an astral radiance to light his way. The walls of the stair-well were devoid of paintings or bas-reliefs. This was a functional building, laid bare like his soul and the souls of those who had built it.

The steps swooped down endlessly. Shemyaza had left time behind him, so there was no way of judging how far or how long he descended. His astral radiance lit only the step immediately below him, and even though his limbs moved to his commands, he felt like he was falling. Silence was absolute; his sense of hearing ached with it. He was unsure whether his spirit body would not fragment and diffuse before he reached the bottom of the steps.

The descent ended without him realising it, for now he walked along a horizontal surface. Sparks of coloured light flickered in the air ahead, and he became aware of space around him. He was in a passage-way, constructed of enormous blocks of stone. Again, there was no decoration upon the walls, and by his astral light he saw the passage disappearing into darkness far ahead. Behind him was a blank wall, and overhead, the entrance to a shaft. There was no sign of the steps he had descended. At his feet, lay the crystal key he had found in the Cave of Treasures, shining more brilliantly than it had in the living world. When he picked it up, the crystal's hard surface felt warm and alive in his hands. His astral light intensified, dancing with flecks of crystal colour.

Shemyaza walked along the passageway, which sloped gently downwards. The details of his earthly life blurred in his mind. He felt no weariness, hunger or thirst, even though he'd walked for an eternity.

The passage-way ended at an immense sand-stone door, upon which was carved an image; the first decoration Shemyaza had encountered. It depicted a priest, drawn in the style of Ancient Egyptian art, who held out a ceremonial staff to a winged, lion-headed man. Shemyaza remembered what Tiy had told him about the first guardian of the Chambers. The leonine figure was Cosmocrator, Keeper of the Precessions of the Equinoxes. Between the carved figures, the door was pierced by a purple crystal, about the size of Shemyaza's fist. He leaned down and tried to look through it, but could see nothing but darkness beyond the portal.

Shemyaza held the crystal key up before his face, and projected into it his desire to open the entrance. The key began to hum a low note, which Shemyaza willed into the crystal in the door. Presently, the inlaid stone began to glow with a red light and then to resonate with the sound. The carved figures became warped by moving shadows; they seemed alive. A jewel in Cosmocrator's eye reflected beams of ruby light, as if Shemyaza's intrusion had awoken him.

Shemyaza bowed respectfully. "Cosmocrator, I entreat you to let me pass. I am the spiritual son of those who created you. I am Shemyaza."

The light became vaporous, and Shemyaza could see the spectre of a winged, lion-headed man standing before him; a transparent red image. The wise leonine eyes stared at him sternly, while the tones emitted by the crystal echoed off the walls. Then, so quickly that Shemyaza jumped, the image vanished and the door rolled to the side with a crash.

He stood upon the threshold of a vast, tenebrous chamber. This was the Hall of the Twelve. His body stiffened as his senses struggled to interpret what lay before him. Perspective zoomed out on all sides; he felt as tiny as a seed and his astral light now seemed dim. The hall's ceiling was indistinct in shadow, perhaps a hundred feet overhead. Six columns of highly-polished green stone lined both sides of the chamber; so wide that eight men linking hands would not have formed a circle around one. Beyond the columns, the walls were enormous blocks of a darker green stone, highly polished yet unornamented.

Shemyaza forced himself to take the first step into the hall. It was immense, yet seemed so watchful. He did not want to hear the door crash shut behind him. The hall was sleeping, but alive. He knew that all the columns were hollow and that the twelve initiates of the Chambers had once used them to resonate the sacred tones that had created their empire.

One step. Two. He heard an echo, but it came too late, as if somebody walked furtively behind him. Turning round, he saw no-one, but the door had slid silently shut. Tentatively, Shemyaza ventured further into the hall. He was fascinated by it, drawn to it, yet it terrified him, for he sensed it was the precursor to the immense oblivion of space. Beneath his feet, the ancient flag-stones were covered by a thin film of unmarked sandy dust. He glanced round, and could see his own foot-prints leading back to the door. His astral body had substance in this place.

Tiy had told him that rituals had once taken place in the Hall of the Twelve. The Elders and their philosophy were incomprehensible to a modern mind, even that of a Grigori. Shemyaza visualised the tall, alien forms standing before each of the columns, touching them, invoking their individual tones. It seemed that faint echoes of those hollow notes reverber-ated through his mind, and as he walked further, he sensed ghostly forms drawing nearer.

The twelve walked beside him. The columns seemed to recognise their presence—he sensed a quickening of atten-tion. Perhaps the phantoms were merely memories, emitted by the stone. He could not see the Elders clearly, but sensed their appearance. They were taller than he was, and clad in belted robes of turquoise linen. Their long white hair floated on the air, as if they swam through a sea of ether. Their eyes were an unnatural, cerulean blue, which was the result not simply of pigment but a radiance that filled the entire socket. Their elongated faces looked like masks. Even the pharaoh Akenaten in his wildest excesses of self-representation had looked more human. Shemyaza was not afraid of these ghostly manifestations, for they seemed oblivious of his presence, but their proximity troubled him. It was not revulsion, but simply a strong reaction against the unknown. In the world he knew, he had come to appreciate his special qualities, his divine king-ship, but in this place, he was just a child.

All the pillars had a spectral memory of an Elder con-nected to them, bar one. Halfway down the hall, Shemyaza was drawn to this solitary pylon. It beckoned to him and seemed strangely familiar. Shemyaza placed his left hand onto its glassy surface. Intolerable cold assailed his palm and crept up his arm, and a buzzing vibration coursed through his entire being.

Shemyaza closed his eyes and rested his forehead against the pillar. He could no longer feel the burning cold, and became absorbed in the tonal vibrations that pulsed through the stone. Within them, he could hear a gabble of words and phrases. The words Tehuti-ti and Ku-na-el were whispered over and over again. Shemyaza felt swamped by drowsiness. He wanted to abandon his journey and remain connected to the column for eternity. Its power was *his* power; he felt at one with it. The frequency of its tones had been used to build Kharsag; he just knew it.

Gradually, he became aware of a source of prickling heat somewhere on his body that burned into his communion with the pillar. He forced himself to pull away and saw the crystal key flare brightly within the cage of his right hand fingers. He sensed the urgency of its message and knew he had to move on.

With dragging steps, he went back into the centre of the hall. The ghostly Elders had disappeared now. Perhaps he no longer had the perception to see them.

The end of the hall was very close now. Shemyaza found he had stopped walking and was standing before a black pedestal, upon which rested two spherical crystals of astounding clarity; a small stone, with a hole in its apex, on top of a larger one. The lower crystal had two projections sticking out from either side of it like horns. Beyond the pedestal was another door of black basalt, adorned with carvings of concentric circles, which appeared to be set firmly into the wall. It did not look as if it could be opened. In the centre of the door was a black stone, similar to the one in the portal guarded by Cosmocrator.

Shemyaza extended his hand experimentally over the hole in the upper crystal. At once, the stone emitted a high-pitched tone, which ceased the moment he removed his hand. Instinctively, Shemyaza placed the crystal key into the hole, with its base uppermost. Nothing happened. The crystal spheres remained silent and colourless.

Before the Sphinx, Melandra knelt over the prostrate figure of
Tiy. The old woman lay apparently lifeless upon the dusty
floor of the enclosure. The crowd had drawn back, instinctively giving the two women a wide berth. In the aftermath of
Tiy's unearthly scream, the gathering seemed directionless and
bewildered. Technicians swarmed over the lighting rig and
stage, but as yet whatever had caused the black-out had not
been rectified.

Melandra held Tiy in her lap. The old woman's milky eyes
were open, but it seemed as if they were somehow focused
inwards. Melandra could only offer soft, soothing sounds. She
knew they could not leave this place and if fate had decreed
Tiy should die here, there was nothing they could do to alter
it. At least Melandra could make sure Tiy would not die alone.

Tiy, in fact, was far from death. In a way, she had left her
body, as her whole being had become concentrated on the inner world. The image of her angel son before the black pedestal filled her psychic sight. She too had heard the whispering
voices within the pillar. Now she knew she had to project her
own spirit voice to Shemyaza, who waited at the next gate.

"Say it, my son. Say the words that you heard."

She concentrated hard, willing some part of Shemyaza's
mind to hear her.

"Hush, Tiy, hush," Melandra murmured as the old woman's
frail body flexed in her arms. The mutterings meant nothing
to her. They were in a foreign tongue.

Shemyaza cupped his hand around the upper crystal and focused intently on its core. Knowledge came to him, but he
had lost all memory of his mother, and did not realise it was
her voice who gave him the information he needed.

"Who is Tehuti-ti?" he asked in his mind and directed his
intention to open the door firmly into the spheres. Presently,
the upper crystal began to glow with a golden light. Simultaneously, a ring of the same golden light appeared around the
stone in the door ahead of him. He poured his will into the
crystal, and gradually the light within it transformed into a
blue hue. A blue ring also appeared around the stone in the

door, pushing the golden ring outwards. Finally, the crystal turned red and a red ring appeared on the door. Now, three rings of gold, blue and red light vibrated around the central stone. Shemyaza knew that these circles of light represented sounds manifested as colour. If Shemyaza concentrated upon sound, he could still hear the three tones, but doing so made it difficult for him to perceive the rings. For now, he knew he must focus on the visual image alone.

The black stone in the centre of the door had also begun to glow red. Gradually, this radiance grew stronger, until all the rings merged into one vibrating red disk. The light increased in intensity, until it was glowing pure white.

Shemyaza flexed his stiff fingers away from the upper sphere. Taking a deep breath to summon his strength, he gripped the two horn-like projections on the bottom crystal. With all of his energy, he willed his desire to pass through the door into the crystals.

One moment he was staring at his own hands, the next, his body was flipping over and over through a void. He felt as if he had been turned inside out. A powerful, hungry force had sucked him forward. He was spinning and spiralling: falling. All sense of identity was peeling away from him, and seeds of panic took root in his mind.

Then, abruptly as it had started, the experience was over. He stood in another dark corridor. The door was behind him now; a red glow diminishing in its central stone. He had been projected right through it.

Shemyaza summoned his astral light once more, but found he was unable to illuminate the passageway. Despite the darkness, he could sense its walls, floor and ceiling. He began to walk along it and presently saw another red glow ahead of him. His astral body felt alien and uncomfortable after his passage through the door, almost as if it was losing substance. He must not linger in this place. As he travelled deeper into the Chamber complex, he risked losing his sense of identity completely. His task must be completed as soon as possible, before he lost the memory of why he was here.

After a twenty steps or so, Shemyaza became conscious of a low, deep hum that vibrated the air around him. The sound invaded his being, conjuring greater discomfort. Abruptly, both the red glow ahead and the humming ceased. For a moment, he was suspended in darkness, then the walls of the passageway bloomed with a soft radiance. He could see a door not far in front of him.

Just ahead, two carvings of enormous serpents looped out from the wall. Their bodies were encased within the walls, as if they had been frozen in the act of moving through them, like ghosts. Shemyaza knew that these were guardians, perhaps of a more technological nature than Cosmocrator. Cautiously, he approached them, aware that anything might happen if he acted impulsively. Pausing just in front of them, he extended one hand. At once, a curtain of red light appeared, accompanied by a shrill, harsh tone. Shemyaza winced and quickly withdrew his hand. Immediately, both the red field and the shrieking tone disappeared. The air was filled with a pungent, bitter odour; a residue of the force field. Shemyaza was unsure of what to do. He had left the crystal key behind in the Hall of the Twelve. He could not use it again.

Hesitantly, he extended his hand once more to invoke the field. No matter how hard he pressed against it, the force repelled his being. Maybe he would fail here, a victim of ignorance.

The rigid form of Tiy sprawled in Melandra's lap, barely breathing. The old seeress still watched her son's journey. She could see the serpents that barred his way and, to her, they were very much alive, rippling constantly through the solid stones of the wall. It was obvious to her what Shemyaza must do. The legends of his own notoriety provided the clue.

"Look at the serpents, Shemyaza," she cried in her mind. "They are like you. They *are* you. Remember, you are the serpent in Eden, whom the vengeful God commanded to crawl on his belly in humility."

Shemyaza did not hear these words, but they invaded his instinctive mind. He thought nothing of Eden or temptation, but simply experimented with an idea that had come to him. Keeping the red field in place with one hand, he ran the other slowly down its surface, until he was squatting on the floor. He laughed in surprise, pleased that his wild supposition had been correct. The field did not extend right to the floor. There was a gap. Was it wide enough for him to wriggle under it? He removed his hands and the field disappeared. Then, he lay down on his stomach, facing the door ahead. Slowly, he began to inch forward.

The curtain of light did not appear until the crown of his head had passed between the serpents. Then, it manifested with its shrill scream, and Shemyaza felt as if someone had punched him in the head. He turned his face to the side and kept wriggling. The high-pitched hum filled his being, vibrating so quickly, it made the bones of his astral body itch and ache. His mind felt as if it was under a terrible strain and he was afraid he'd lose consciousness, trapped beneath the force field. But gradually, driven by determination, he slithered forward, flattening himself as much as possible. The pressure on his back felt like intense pins and needles, as if the red energy was cooking his etheric substance. But it was too late to turn back now; he had to keep moving.

He only knew he was through when the infuriating hum ceased abruptly. Pulling his body up into a ball, he rolled over and then knelt up. Behind him, the serpents stared placidly out from the walls. For a while, he could not continue. When he tried to stand up, lights pulsed in front of his eyes and he felt nauseous. Willing these uncomfortable sensations to ease off, he sat with his knees up, his head thrust between them. *This is an astral experience. Fight it!* After a while, he was able to get up without falling over, although he still felt dizzy and sick.

Adjacent to the door ahead of him was another black pedestal supporting two spheres. Shemyaza groaned, unwilling to endure another nightmare journey through a crystal portal. Leaning against the pedestal, he blinked at the door. It took him a moment to realise, with relief, that it did not possess a central passage stone. Perhaps his intention alone would be enough to open this door. Weakly, he gripped the horns projecting from the lower crystal on the pedestal.

I can't do this. I've no energy left. No strength.

But he had to go on. If not, he'd be trapped in this corridor, with no hope of rescue and would remain there until his astral body broke up and dispersed.

You have to try.

He braced himself on splayed legs and arched his spine. With his remaining strength, he projected his will into the crystals, and visualised the door ahead opening up. At first, nothing happened, but then the top crystal began to glow weakly, sporadically. Shemyaza slumped. He felt exhausted.

"Do it, Shem," he said aloud, and heard Salamiel's voice in his mind.

"Don't stray from revolution, brother. Do it; do it now."

Yes! Shemyaza gripped the stone once more and poured his will into it, but it was not enough. He slammed his fists down onto the pedestal, filled with anger.

"What is this?" he cried aloud. "I wouldn't be here if you didn't want me to be. Why all these obstructions and difficulties? Don't tell me love will open this door."

With a cry of rage, he gripped the horns and blasted the crystals with the energy of his emotion. He was sure his mind would burst with the effort, but then it seemed he broke through an invisible barrier. The crystals sang out their tones for him, and a bolt of energy knocked him backwards, although he did not fall. His body was shaking. Something was different. Something…

He became aware of an alien presence around and within him; an unfamiliar personality that haunted the corners of his mind. The etheric temperature had become lower and his body seemed to be moving in a way that was strange to him. He stumbled forward and of its own volition, his body straightened up before the doors. Instinctively, he raised his arms high and a voice issued from his throat. It was not his voice.

"I am Sin-Na-Ru! I am the Opener. Open unto me."

Immediately, and with almost inappropriate slowness, the doors swung gently inwards. At the same time, the alien presence rushed out of him, in a spasm that felt as if his whole body was sneezing violently. Shemyaza did not pause to think about what had just occurred. He hurled himself through the doors before they could swing closed.

Shemyaza lay winded on a hard surface, his eyes squeezed shut. He felt totally spent. Gradually, a deep rhythmic sound seeped into his awareness. It was impossible to classify accurately, as it sounded like a sibilant drum, a deep heartbeat and gravel shifting all at the same time. The pounding became louder, until it filled the whole chamber. Shemyaza opened his eyes.

He was in a trapezoidal room that was wider behind him than ahead. The door through which he'd entered had already closed again. Doors led off to left and right and there was another in the opposite wall. Shemyaza lay down again on his back, with his knees raised. There was time to recuperate now. He would allow himself that. Feelings coursed through him: shock, ecstasy, relief. This was one of the twelve antechambers to the Crystal Chamber itself. Only one more obstacle lay ahead: the door in the opposite wall.

Once he felt rested, he sat up to examine his surroundings. The chamber was lit by an invisible light source and built entirely of the familiar, polished green stone. Its floor was carved with deep concentric grooves, trisected by straight channels that led from the centre of the circles to each of the three doors ahead. Shemyaza recognised them from Tiy's descriptions of the Chambers. The straight furrows were part of a geometric pattern that connected all the ante-chambers with the great, central chamber itself. In the middle of the concentric grooves lay a deep hole, which presumably was once used to accommodate a crystal key, similar to the one he'd left in the Hall of the Twelve. The walls of the ante-chamber were covered in abstract patterns: cubes, oblongs, triangles and dots, which Shemyaza identified as the script of the Elders. The room felt unthinkably ancient, but the patterns and the substance of the walls themselves reminded him of an advanced technology. There was something strangely futuristic about the place.

In the distant past, each ante-chamber would have been used by one of the Twelve as a place to prepare for communication with the source of all creation, which they accessed via the crystal gate in the central room. The Elders had used a process that enabled them to resonate their astral bodies with the sonic vibrations emitted by their key crystals. These astral forms, once freed from the encumbrance of flesh, were able to traverse the grooves cut into the floor, using them as etheric highways. The astral forms were projected along the interconnected lines towards the crystal gate in the central chamber, and there the Elders would enter into its matrix. Neolithic shamans had once learned to use the energy of ley-lines in much the same way, and had travelled in spirit along lines of earth energy that criss-crossed the land. This was one aspect of the Elders' vast knowledge of natural science and technology, which over the millennia had become shrouded in ignorance and lost, remembered only as magic or sorcery

Shemyaza knew that if he succeeded in his task, the science of the Elders would be rediscovered and utilised for the benefit of all. If humanity were able to harness the power of their own natural life-force they would have access to free energy. The implications were enormous. At the very least, the planet would be saved from environmental destruction. And that would only be the beginning. Soon, if all went well, scientists and archaeologists would come to these chambers and embark upon deciphering the Elder script. Perhaps they would learn the secrets of the Chambers and the power that built it. And maybe, with that knowledge, they would see the folly of their narrow-minded beliefs, and learn to initiate change. They might dare to dream; anathema at present to those lords of academe, who clung to what was solid and physical, and understood only by the limited perceptions of the human intellect.

Shemyaza got to his feet, putting aside these ideas for the future. They would remain as dreams if he did not fulfil his destiny. Before he could make a decision about whether to investigate the other ante-chambers or go straight for the heart of the complex, the air became filled with a buzzing noise similar to static electricity. Shemyaza's astral body shivered in alarm. He turned round quickly and found himself face to face with a tall, alien figure that towered over him by at least a foot. Shemyaza instinctively backed away. One of the Elders stood before him, but this was impossible. They had long been dead.

The image shimmered like a badly-tuned TV picture, then appeared to become completely solid. The muscles of the Elder's face rippled with small, subtle movements that conveyed communication. His eyebrows rose and fell, his mouth pursed and stretched, he blinked and twitched the muscles of his cheeks and throat. It was a form of speaking, but without language. Shemyaza understood the Elder completely, almost as if he could hear the words. "I have waited long for the advent of a child of the Twelve. A son of Kharsag has come. I have analysed your etheric substance. It is apt that you are of Ku-na-el's seed."

Shemyaza approached with caution. The Elder had communicated his message and now stood expressionless and utterly without movement. Shemyaza had never beheld such stillness. Like the ghostly forms he had encountered in the Hall of the Twelve, the Elder was dressed in a turquoise robe of thin, shimmering fabric, embroidered with silver thread. Around his neck, he wore a peculiar necklace of golden balls, perhaps a symbol of office. His long white hair fell down over his chest, but apart from that, he appeared to have no body hair at all. His skin was as glossy as polished stone, and his smoking blue eyes gazed upon infinity.

Shemyaza reached out to touch the Elder's robe but before his reaching fingers made contact, communication began again; a strange twitching of features.

"I am the essence of Ish-na-el. You have penetrated to the core of the complex. You that have come: know the history of the Millennia of Eternities."

Shemyaza was unsure of whether the Elder existed in reality or not. "I am Shemyaza," he said slowly.

The Elder's features moved again. "You are the one who has come, and your advent presages the time when the Chambers may be reopened. I am the last of the Twelve. A memory of my image will be placed here to guard this complex. We the Twelve will then return to the Source, but a part of me will be left behind to assist you with your task. It is the duty of my son, Ra-Na-El, to complete the closure of the Chambers, and this he will do, after my word."

Shemyaza still wanted proof that the image before him was interactive. 'Tell me, Ish-na-el, how do you know it is time for the chambers to be reopened?"

The Elder's eyes seemed to fix upon him. "Know this, son of Kharsag. As the seers of your time look into the past, so our eyes have looked into the future. Even as we are forced to close down the complex, we are aware that it will one day be reactivated and used in wisdom. As you stand here, the pole star has revolved through its seven axes six times. Six of the twelve stellar constellations have risen before the eyes of the Watcher, Hor-em-Akhet. The aeons of their influence have come and gone. Now is the time for the constellation of Mankind to rise."

"Ish-na-el, can you hear my words? Do you speak to me?"

Ish-na-el seemed to smile, but perhaps it was just the expression of a word. "Your world is not my world. I no longer exist. I am a projected memory, here merely to grant you knowledge of the word. I can no longer generate sound. Words are lost to me, and the word alone will open the portal. Your spirit body is the comprehension of sound and etheric light. *You* must speak the word of opening. I will accompany you on your journey to come, for by the agency of your spirit, this part of me will return to the Source, whence my brethren have long retired, and there forever remain."

"What happened to you?" Shemyaza asked. "Why did you close the Chambers down?"

"The age of our empire is coming to an end. We have created many empires, and each one of them has ended in destruction. This is the cycle laid down by the will of the Source. We, the Twelve, are not the only council which seeks to govern the evolution of life. The Renowned Old Ones are the keepers of genesis and through us, their creations, they bring evolution to worlds and light from the Source, to the flesh of worldly creatures. But there is an equal and opposite force, whose nature is to stop the process of genesis and to extinguish the life-giving light that comes from the Source. The denizens of this force are known in your tongue as the Star-Spawn of Da'ath. Their names cannot be given to you in our language. Know only that their existence is as fundamental to the multiverse as that of the Renowned Old Ones. In this way, the balance of creation and destruction is maintained. *Our* purpose is only to create. We cannot destroy, and so the Chambers must be preserved and closed. Then we, the Twelve, will disperse our hybrid families out into the world to bring genesis to new cultures."

Shemyaza walked around the Elder, examining him. "What happened to you? Why did your empire end?"

The image of Ish-na-el shimmered briefly, as if he shuddered at the recollection. "One of our Brethren, Ku-na-el, has turned away from acts of creation. He no longer travels with us through the stars to commune with the Source. He no longer brings back the essence of creation, but traverses the land above, recreating himself as a god in the eyes of the humans who dwell there. His shallow hubris has changed the function of these Chambers. One of the Star Spawn of Da'ath has found entry to this world through the crystal gate. Its presence has begun to affect the planet's atmosphere and the earth's crust itself has shifted. This has caused great cataclysms, and we must now close down the complex to preserve the work we have accomplished and seal the gate. Thus, the Star Spawn will be denied entry."

Shemyaza faced the Elder once more. "How did you close the chambers down?"

"The tones of life within the crystal gate have already been silenced. With what remains of our power here, we the Twelve, have created a symbol in stone of the constellation of the lion, which after the final procedures of closure have been completed, will seal the entrance to the Chambers. This great monument to our fall is He Who Watches, who Is Hor-em-Akhet. He will be left in this place to mark the age in which our empire here ended. His function is to watch the precession of the equinoxes. As you stand here, the time has come for Hor-em-Akhet to reveal his secrets to the world, and this process has facilitated the advent of your coming."

"The Sphinx..." Shemyaza said. "Were you responsible for erecting the pyramids as well?"

"We know of these structures. We have seen four aeons into the future and have witnessed their construction. In that

time, an initiate of Thoth, who is Imhotep, will find the gate
of the Cosmocrator and there devise the plans to build three
mighty edifices to map out the stars of Cosmocrator's law."

Shemyaza spoke bleakly. "The stars of Orion. My prison,
my hell and my heaven."

"The edifices of Imhotep will draw from below the remnants of our power in these Chambers. Within the pyramids,
kings and priests will, for but a brief time, be initiated into the
forgotten ways of our law. Ku-na-el seeks to destroy us, and
all our work, but he will fail. This land will remember, and
through those memories the races of the world will dream in
symbols the legacy of our achievements."

Shemyaza frowned. "When I first entered here, you told
me that I was the seed of Ku-na-el. How is that so? If I was,
then surely I would not have been granted entrance."

"He that changed the function of these Chambers must
come to initiate its reversal. You are the son of Anu, who is
the son of Ku-na-el. Throughout the generations of your
blood-line, our fall has been replayed." The Elder paused,
and lifted his hands. "Now come unto me. The history is told.
Speak the word, and together we shall open the crystal gate
once more. We shall traverse the duat back to the centre of
the circle of life."

Shemyaza sighed. "This means, then, I will not return to
life on earth." He had hoped it might be possible and experienced a pang of lonely desolation, glimpsing an eternity of the
emptiness of space, lit by cold stars.

Ish-na-el again seemed to smile. "Fear not, son of Kharsag.
Your province on this world has far from ended. Hor-em-
Akhet will open the way for your return."

Shemyaza saw that the image of Ish-na-el hovered an inch
or so above the floor at the centre of the chamber, directly
over the deeply-cut hole. "I left the key crystal in the Hall of
the Twelve," he said. "What can I use in its place?"

"It is of no consequence," Ish-na-el replied. "Your form is
of sound within light. We need only the word of power to
gain entry into the crystal gate."

Ish-na-el beckoned Shemyaza to draw nearer. "Now, take
unto you the remnants of my image."

Shemyaza walked right up to Ish-na-el and found the Elder lacked solid substance, like a phantom. Standing within the image, he felt the essence of Ish-na-el vibrating all around him, melding with his own being. Once he had absorbed this life-force, he could barely feel the Elder's presence. Standing tall, he faced the closed doors that led to the central chamber and opened his mouth to expel the word of opening in a gust of energy: "Ak-shee!"

At once the doors flew open and Shemyaza felt himself drawn swiftly along the deeply-cut groove in the floor that led out of the chamber. He was an etheric liquid flowing hectically along the stone channel. Propelled into the central chamber, he sped towards the great crystal itself. Its immense and terrifying image burned into his senses. The crystal was conical; a rearing structure that symbolised creative power, far larger than the stone he had entered in the Cornish underworld. Its exterior at first appeared rough and dull, but then a shining bolt of energy preceded Shemyaza's spirit to its core. Its heart began to glow with a rosy light.

Shemyaza was drawn into the stone itself, passing easily through the particles of the matrix. This was almost a familiar feeling, similar to what he'd experienced only five years before in Cornwall. He was suspended within the stone, surrounded by flashing colours of the spectrum. This was where the sensation of familiarity ended.

Shemyaza felt his spirit begin to separate into seven distinct spheres of pure light and energy. They floated and bobbed, each a dazzling spectral colour. Shemyaza's mind was also divided into the spheres. In yellow-gold resided pure awareness; in flaming orange, reasoning; in violet, intuition; in blue, wisdom; in crimson, will; in green, emotion and in indigo, understanding. Shemyaza was suffused with a feeling of comfort: through his seven minds, his brethren were still with him. Ish-na-el's essential presence also remained within and around him, but there was now no communication between them.

Shemyaza became aware that the spheres of his being had begun to oscillate rapidly within the crystal matrix. He could sense once again the seven strident tones that had cleared the entrance shaft to the chambers. The oscillation increased and then, in one shattering wave, Shemyaza's spirit bodies exploded into white light that shimmered with tiny crystal flecks of their original colour. He became one with the crystal and passed through the particles that comprised it, into the spaces between them. The white light had vanished and only blackness enveloped his consciousness.

Shemyaza had passed through the gateway and was now travelling fast. He sensed he was being pulled, but was unable to discern any sense of direction. He could not see any stars, but was aware that he was traversing the duat, which comprised the constellations of Sirius, Orion, Leo and the Hyades.

His awareness had become limitless. He could feel the presence of every atom of matter in the universe, avoiding collision with them through sub-atomic resonance. Space and time itself folded around him. He moved through the eternal, amorphic sea of black matter, which existed in a constant state of flux and mutability.

When the journey ended, the particles that had been Shemyaza had not experienced a sense of the passage of time. He had simply stopped moving, and was no longer aware of the moment when his movement had begun or ended. All that existed was nothingness, without form: a void empty of structured matter, time and life. Then, in the utter neverness, dim red discarnate masses began to form around him. They throbbed with an indescribable energy, pulsating like great jellyfish, hanging in the vastness of this space beyond all stars. Their appearance was amorphic, but Shemyaza sensed they were comprised of the primal substance from which all life derived. He knew then that he had reached the centre of the universe; the point of creation. It was the nucleus of the cosmic pool, from where the concentric ripples of life had surged outwards. The energy beings, who were the inhabitants of this realm, could not communicate with Shemyaza through language, or even through thought. They imbued him with instinctual knowledge, through perpetually emitting the resonance of three tones. In this manner they informed him that they were the Great Architects, the primordial beings of all creation, the source of all gods. The three tones, which Shemyaza had first heard in the Chambers of Light, were their building blocks: a sonic force that through the medium of light created matter itself and transmuted that matter into life. From them, the Renowned Old Ones had issued forth, as cosmic sperm to inseminate with life the barren worlds of the multiverse.

The tones resonated through the discarnate particles of Shemyaza's mind, their vibrations telling him he must become as the Renowned Old Ones. He had only to name the three tones.

Shemyaza extended his senses throughout the multiverse, seeking the names. They existed somewhere, and no realm was denied to him, but he failed to find the knowledge he sought. Then, the presence of Ish-na-el pervaded his being once more. The Elder was leaving him, but in his passing, bestowed to Shemyaza awareness of the names. It was his final gift of creation.

The first tone Shemyaza named Ain; the second Ain Soph; the third Ain Soph Aur. Instantaneously, the blackness became limitless white light. He felt a great sense of coagulation and pressure. Immeasurable heat and sound surrounded him, as all of the particles of his being condensed together.

His form had changed. Now, he was a gigantic, tear-drop shaped creature of light, almost cetaceous in nature. He sped back through the void, and the three primal tones vibrated through him and out of him, in the endless black ocean between the stars. The tones constructed new life and he would bring them back to the world of his own conception.

The crystal gate was waiting, as a womb waits for the fertilising seed. Shemyaza's energy form returned to it, penetrating through the surface shell of its matrix, like the explosion of a crashing meteorite. He buried himself deep inside, burrowing to the centre. The tones still pulsed out of his being, boring into the core of the crystal's energy source. A spark of white light flickered into life there.

At the Sphinx, Tiy still observed the inside of the central chamber. She saw the giant crystal fill completely with blinding white light. She saw the great stone begin to revolve and hum like a spinning top. Rays of light shot out from all over its surface, inundating the lines, grooves and circles carved into the chamber's floor and walls. Soon this light would flood the whole chamber complex and spill out into the world. The soul of Mankind was being reconceived. In time, a golden age would be born. And a new sun would rise in the east to greet the gaze of the watchful Sphinx. Her son. Now Tiy began to weep for his loss.

Chapter Twenty-Six
New Epoch

Helen felt very calm, although she could tell her mother was unnerved by the masses. They had fought their way onto the Giza plateau and had found that once the crowd absorbed them, it was impossible to get out again. The difficulties with the sound system had added tension to an already explosive atmosphere. People seemed excited and full of expectation, but there was a sense that violence might break out at any moment. Egyptian soldiers looked nervous, huddling together in tight knots around their armoured cars, clutching their guns. There was little they could do to control the crowds: there were too many people.

"The authorities shouldn't have allowed this!" Lily said. She lifted Helen in her arms, because no-one seemed to care about trampling over a defenceless child. "Look at them! Mindless, milling around. It's a desecration." She shifted her daughter's weight in her arms. "Thank heavens you're a slight child!" She paused. "Just why are we here, Helen?"

Helen smiled at her mother. "We have to find the others."

"Daniel? Is Daniel here?" Lily could not keep the sudden surge of hope from her voice.

Helen did not answer. She looked up at the shining expanse of the Great Pyramid of Cheops. Its sheer white face looked like a gleaming road leading right up to the stars. Overhead, the constellation of Orion burned brightly in the sky. Helen listened to the haunting tones that whispered softly in her mind: one, two, three.

Lily finally managed to shove her way to the lip of the enclosure and went down towards the great Sphinx. "How will we find anyone here?" she complained. The child was beginning to weigh heavily in her arms.

"There, Mum." Helen pointed towards the left paw of the monument.

By this point, weariness and muscular pain had made Lily quite aggressive. She clasped Helen to her with one hand and roughly pushed people aside with the other. This was Bedlam. "I can't see anyone we know, Hel. Are you sure?"

"Yes Mum. There." She shook her hand in agitation. "*Those* people."

Lily saw two women pressed up against the paw of the Sphinx, although strangely enough, the milling crowd seemed to be giving them a wide berth. Lily walked up to them and gratefully lowered Helen to the ground.

"Hi," she said. "Hope you don't mind us invading your space. My arms were dropping off."

A rather sinister-looking young woman with dark, severely-cut hair sat with an aged crone lolling in her lap. The dark-haired woman did not speak, but glared up at Lily. The older woman looked as if she might be dead. Lily was morbidly intrigued, but didn't like to stare, then noticed the ancient fingers twitching and slivers of white between the fluttering eyelids. "Is she all right? Can we do anything to help?"

The younger woman shook her head belligerently; a gesture which warned, *leave us alone.*

Helen went up to the old woman and put her small hands on the lined face.

"Hel, don't be rude," Lily began, but Helen ignored her and spoke to the dark-haired woman.

"*He's* sent us to you," she said earnestly. "We had to come."

The young woman tore her eyes away from Lily and looked at the child in surprise. Her mouth dropped open. She said, "Shemyaza?"

Helen grinned. "Yes!"

Lily noticed then that the young woman's face was wet with tears; her eyes were reddened. The sight made her stomach turned to ice. She anticipated what came next.

"He's dead," the woman said.

"No!" Helen squealed. "Met-Met told me he was mine!"

Before Lily could take in this information, a squealing, humming sound pealed out over the plateau. Lily winced involuntarily. "What the hell is that?"

"It's all right," Helen told her. "It's the tones. Everyone can hear them now." She turned back to the young woman. "He *can't* be dead. He isn't!"

Lily did not know what Helen meant about 'tones'. She could not take in the fact that Shem might be dead. Who were these two women? What could they know?

Around her, people were looking at one another in alarm. It was clear that, at first, everyone believed they'd heard a shriek of feed-back from the stage, for many of them pantomimed grimaces and stuck their fingers in their ears. Faces broke into smiles for it seemed the music was about to be reinstated. But it quickly became obvious that the unearthly noise was nothing to do with the P.A. It enveloped the entire plateau, becoming louder all the time; a high-pitched, insistent screech. Then, the ground began to shake.

Lily stumbled against her daughter. "It's a bomb! It must be. Oh my god!"

People were becoming hysterical, perhaps sharing Lily's belief in a terrorist attack. The humming was ear-splitting now. Some were affected more greatly than others, and fell to the ground, writhing, desperately trying to cover their ears.

Helen, her face solemn, slowly lifted one hand and pointed towards the pyramids. She did not attempt to speak. A hot wind had arisen, blowing the girl's hair back from her face.

Lily turned. Auroras of blue and gold light hung above the soaring monuments, dancing and wafting like enormous veils in the sky. The pyramids themselves glowed utterly white, capped by brilliant gold.

Deep below, in the Chambers of Light, the crystal gate had ceased its revolutions, having discharged all of its life-force to the land above. Inside the crystal, its substance had transmuted into liquid, which gently bubbled. Within this new, amniotic energy, a foetus hung, tiny as a grain of wheat. Yet its growth was rapid. Now a boy-child was suspended within the stone. His eyes were eyes closed, his beautiful face at peace, dreaming of the world to come. A son of gods was growing there, from seed to man.

Daniel and his companions had left the crypt of St Menas and, following Shemyaza's final instructions, had made their way to the Giza complex. Daniel had not wanted to come, and Gadreel had been forced to drag him physically from the church. He'd wanted to stay there, unsure himself as to why. Perhaps he harboured a spark of hope that Shemyaza might rise up out of the well, as he had clawed his way from the land-slide in Cornwall, five years before. Daniel could not hate Salamiel for what he'd done, aware that he'd had no choice, but neither did he want, at this moment, to be close to Shem's killer. Gadreel, however, had been persistent, and eventually Daniel had given in to her demands.

A hired mini-bus had brought them out of the city, but they'd had to walk for quite a way, owing to the congestion on the roads. Chaos reigned on the Giza plateau. It seemed as if the end of the world had come. Many people were running around and shouting, while others looked paralysed by shock and fear. The avatars were forced to push through hysterical crowds. Around them, a multitude of hands pointed up at the sky. Daniel stared blearily at the aurora of light dancing above the pyramids. He could tell that most of the crowd believed it be a special effect, created purposefully for the party. Those who perhaps guessed the truth stood quietly, gazing at the sky. The pyramids were dazzling beacons of raw, white light, each crowned with a golden sun that illuminated the night. It was a strange and electrifying sight, but none of the avatars felt capable of commenting on it. All were wrapped in cauls of isolated grief, and words did not exist that could express it. Not one of them doubted that Shemyaza's journey into the Chambers was somehow responsible for the phenomena around them. A great change was about to happen, but for them the greatest and most shattering change had already taken place. Shemyaza was dead. It was duty that led them here now. They no longer cared what happened, but there was an urge within them to join the others who, like them, had been Shemyaza's companions: Tiy and Melandra. They all needed to be together at this time.

Daniel concentrated on locating the women, extending his psychic perception over the heads of the frantic crowd. Faintly, he picked up the sound of weeping; sibilant sobs that echoed in his mind. It came directly from the Sphinx enclosure. It was Melandra and Tiy. Strangely, he sensed they were not alone, but accompanied by two other females. These others felt familiar to Daniel's senses, but he could not quite recognise them. There was too much going on around him, and his misery interfered with the clarity of his sight.

"The enclosure," he said to the others. "The women are by the paws of the Sphinx."

A mob of people, all covered in body paint, suddenly surged around them, and the avatars were pushed into one another. "I can't stand much more of this," Pharmaros said. "It's so claustrophobic. Great Anu, if only we could fly over their heads!"

Although Penemue could not understand her words, he clearly read her distress, for he eased himself to the front of their group and with firm but gentle strength, began to push people aside, so that the group could pass through. Silently, he cleared a path for them to the Sphinx enclosure.

Because of his height, Penemue noticed the women first and began to gesture urgently at his companions. Daniel shouldered his way to the front, saw Melandra squatting beside an old woman who was slumped on the ground, then noticed a tall younger woman with auburn hair standing beside them. He cried her name in surprise. "Lily!"

Lily turned, paused for moment, then came loping towards him. She wrapped him in a tight embrace. "Daniel, oh Daniel!" After a few moments, she pulled away from him a little and took his face in her hands. "Is it true, Dan? About Shem?"

Daniel swallowed thickly and nodded. He could not stem the tears that came to his eyes. Lily held him to her fiercely, whispering endearments into his hair; endearments to which, ultimately, he could never respond. "I am here for you, my love, always here."

He could not offer up deep, wrenching sobs of grief, but just an endless river of silent tears.

Penemue, Pharmaros and Gadreel went to kneel beside Tiy and Melandra. They seemed numb, shocked. Helen trotted away from them and joined her mother, clinging to Daniel's knees, her face set in a tight expression.

It seemed that none of them could see, or even sense, the activity around them. They were alone in their bewilderment, abandoned by light, their parts played.

Salamiel and Kashday stood a short distance away, observing the others. Kashday felt that their companions were being hard on Salamiel. They could not speak to him. Kashday himself was at a loss for words, but felt that someone should at least stand at Salamiel's side. He had had the hardest task of all.

Salamiel put a hand on Kashday's shoulder. "There is grief and there is sorrow," he said in a weak approximation of his usual cynical tone, "but there is also reunion."

Kashday reached up and took Salamiel's hand. "Yes," he said. "There is that."

Salamiel shook his head. "No, you don't understand. That young woman crushing Daniel is your daughter. It is Lily."

Kashday stiffened. "Lily...?"

"Yes." Salamiel pushed him forward. "She has her daughter with her. I don't know why or how they're here, but it must be for a reason. For Anu's sake, go to them."

Kashday hesitated for a moment. He could only think that this stranger was Helen Winter's daughter more than his. He had never seen her in the flesh and now, so solid and alive before him, she did not match the child of his imagination. She was a woman, not a girl.

"Kashday," Salamiel said softly, "you must. Let something be salvaged from what we have lost."

Kashday glanced back at his companion, then approached his daughter. He was afraid of her. Would she condemn him for his long absence from her life? Perhaps she did not want a father. Her mother might have said anything to her.

Even though Lily's face was buried in Daniel's hair, she seemed to sense Kashday's presence, for she raised her head as he drew close. Their eyes met. Lily frowned, her expression puzzled, as if she struggled to recapture a memory.

Daniel appeared to become aware of her anxiety, for he pulled away from her. He rubbed his hands wearily over his face, managed a weak smile. "Lily...this is someone you must meet. It is your father, Kashday."

Lily uttered a small sound of shock. "Father?" she said, as if experimenting with the word.

"Yes," Daniel said. "He has been with us, Lil, through everything that happened tonight."

Lily took a few steps towards Kashday, shaking her head. "You have come back," she said. "We thought you were lost."

Kashday nodded. "For a long time. Yes." He paused. "I had not hoped for this."

Lily studied his face for a moment, then closed her eyes and wrapped her arms around him. He could feel her shaking. More tears. She was not like Helen, his lost love, for in his arms she was tall and felt strong. Helen had always seemed physically delicate, a creature to be enwrapped and cherished. He could sense the complexities of Lily's emotions and character; there would be much to learn about her.

"You will come home with us, won't you?" Lily murmured.

And now, at last, Kashday could say, "Yes." In that moment, he knew that the past had released him and that his true life had been given back.

He did not see Lily's daughter come to stand beside them, and only became aware of her when her small but firm voice interrupted their reunion. "Hello, Grandfather."

Kashday glanced down and saw her looking up at him gravely. For a moment, he did not see the face of a child, but the features of an adult woman. It was a face known instinctively by all Grigori: Ishtahar, Shemyaza's lover, priestess of Kharsag. Kashday uttered a sound of surprise and took a step back, but then the image fled and only a dark-haired, pretty little girl stood before him.

"This is Helen," Lily said. "I named her after Mum."

Kashday nodded. There was very little of the grandmother in Helen. She was a Grigori child through and through, knowing in the ways a human woman could never be. He scooped the child up into his arms and pressed her against him. She clung to him like a kitten, smelling faintly of musky earth and cedar wood.

The reunion of Lily and her father had held everyone's attention in the near vicinity. Even strangers had paused to watch. Nobody noticed that, by the paw of the Sphinx, Melandra lowered Tiy gently to the ground and then got to her feet. Her hoarse shout made everyone jump. "Our lord is dead, yet you forget this and smile! How dare you! He's dead! He's dead!"

Eyes turned to look at her, but no-one spoke. Her face looked wild, demented, then her eyes narrowed. "You are all free now, aren't you. He paid the price, gave up his life. All you feel is relief."

For a moment, there was silence, then Salamiel's voice cut like a blade into the stillness. "You don't know what you're talking about. No-one feels relieved, least of all me. It was I who had to kill him."

Melandra stared at him with wide, fierce eyes, then said in a bewildered voice, "*You* killed him? You?"

Salamiel was still spattered with dried blood across his face and neck. It was evidence enough.

"He had no choice," Gadreel said coldly. "Shemyaza ordered him to do it."

Melandra uttered a snarl and spat in Salamiel's face. "Betrayer! Judas! You're not fit to wear his blood."

Salamiel did not flinch, but stood erect, his expression hard. Melandra's spittle gleamed upon his face. "I'll kill you for this!" Melandra growled. "You're dead meat!"

"Quite the little zealot, aren't you," Salamiel said shakily.

Melandra did not reply to this. She bunched her fists and punched Salamiel hard in the chest. He groaned and staggered backwards.

Daniel pushed himself between them and placed his hands on Melandra's arms. "Stop it!" he said in a calm voice. "We've all been through enough."

Melandra turned on him, apparently ready to attack Daniel as well, but before she could take any further action, a baying ululation swept through the crowd on the plateau above.

Instinctively, everyone turned their heads towards the pyramids. The aurora had expanded and now filled the sky with a ghostly image. It seemed to be smoking directly out of the apex of the pyramid of Cheops, drawing substance from the golden light that blazed there. A willow forest of long hair snaked wildly around the apparition's head, netting stars. Its face was as big as the pyramid itself, its features elongated, its eyes burning cauldrons of turquoise fire. It was a star giant, imprinted against the black night sky.

Silence fell upon the gathering on the plateau like the aftermath of a slap on flesh. The gaze of the smouldering eyes above them was hypnotic. They were frozen where they stood, like tiny prey in the shadow of a swaying cobra.

Daniel stared at the image in the sky. He did not feel afraid, nor sense any malevolent intent. He had seen this face before, or one like it. An Elder. "Shem has succeeded," he murmured. "He must have succeeded."

Lily curled her hand through his elbow, shaking her head. "But it's so beautiful," she breathed. "So strange."

Daniel could not tear his eyes away from the Elder's smoking eyes. He felt as if his consciousness was being drawn upwards, right into them. The crowd around him melted away. He was alone. All that existed was the silence of the night and the presence of the Elder.

Daniel's spirit hung before the alien countenance. Its elliptical eyes were a window onto the corners of the world. The apocalypse had come. Daniel saw images of the twelve sites of the sacred crystals around the globe. He witnessed what had happened as midnight had passed across the planet, and what would happen as the hour swept further west.

First, the past. His inner eye looked upon a snow-capped mountain, where a lofty temple hugged the sheer crags. Saffron-robed figures sat cross-legged within it, chanting three repetitive notes. Some of them conjured a ringing chime from bowls of bronze and gold. They were Nying-ma-pa Buddhist monks. Above the pagoda roofs of their temple, the image of an Elder god reared up to fill the sky behind their sacred mountain. Watching, Daniel knew that the mountain had housed a crystal, which had been buried millennia before and had lain dormant since that time. Now, its energy had awoken, and the high lamas prepared for a new cycle of karma. To them, it was the eyes of Pahdma-sam-bava, the oldest lama, that blazed down from the sky. Samsara had ended.

Now, Daniel looked a short time into the future, upon an isolated Greek peninsula, a place where no women ventured. He saw a crumbling monastery that nestled within the woods at the foot of a holy mountain. Within it, black-clad priests prayed incessantly. On the walls, murals of the Second Coming and Revelations shivered with eerie life in the light of candles. As Daniel watched, twelve of the bearded priests rose to their feet and silently left the sanctuary of the chapel. They carried with them a rare jewel of clearest crystal. They knew it as the key to one of the twelve gates of Heaven, and it had been revealed to them within the tomb of their founder.

The priests had read the signs and heeded the omens. Now, as they filed out into the darkness, the sky over the mountain was filled with the countenance of their lord. They averted their eyes, for they feared to look upon his radiance. They would journey to the foot of the mountain to witness his descent. Then a great voice filled their ears and said to them, "Behold, it is done. I am the alpha and omega, the beginning and the end. I am the root and the offspring of El, the bright morning star. To you who have guarded the seventh seal I shall give the waters of life. I shall wipe away every tear from your eyes and death shall be no more, neither shall there be mourning and pain. Go down to the lowlands and find yourselves wives, for the former things have passed away."

Now Daniel's vision sped further into the future, to the slopes of a pointed mountain in Mexico. Many people had gathered there. Astronomers and Ufologists mingled with the surviving remnants of native tribes. Tiny earth-lights whizzed around the dark peak; cherry red, amber and blue. The gaze of a huge phantom in the star-encrusted firmament burned down upon the crowds. Some saw the black, slanted eyes of an alien visitor, while others beheld the burning green fire of the god Quetzalcoatl's return.

Daniel's perception shifted to midnight in England. He saw a gathering of tribal youth who swarmed over the grassy sides of a sacred tor in Somerset. They had come to celebrate the new year, but the beat of drums and the warble of their voices had died away. A vision had appeared that filled the sky: the great earth goddess, her arms extended, her hair aflame.

Nobody moved. The brightly-painted faces of the crowd were transfixed by the apparition. They heard a triad of sweet, female voices that belled out across the mist-girdled land. "All hail the return of the once and future Dragon King, who has supped from the crystal chalice of life."

Images flickered rapidly before Daniel's perception. He saw glimpses of seven other points on the earth, where the spirit of an Elder had been evoked by the summons of a hidden crystal. In every location, all who encountered the vision beheld the harbinger of their hopes, dreams and beliefs. All the sacred deities of the world's civilisation had manifested as the dreaming mind of the world and its peoples had always remembered them.

When midnight struck in whatever part of the world, humanity had held, and would hold, its breath. Even those who had not been drawn to the sacred sites would feel that something momentous was happening. The celebrants of New Year's parties across the globe would invoke the spirit of the new age. It would come as hope, as potential.

Suddenly, Daniel's perception was snatched back to England. He saw the chimneys of High Crag; stark against a clear, cold sky. The French windows that led out to the gardens at the back of the house were open, and sounds of merriment echoed out over the rolling lawns. Enniel Prussoe walked across the frosty grass, arm in arm with a human woman. Daniel recognised her: Emma Manden, his old friend, now mistress of the Pelleth witches. The Pelleth and the Grigori had ever been wary adversaries. Now, Emma threw back her head and stared up at the sky. She laughed. The air was like chilled sparkling wine, the stars fizzing overhead. Neither Enniel nor Emma spoke, but Daniel sensed a peace between them; an impression of coming home, of casting off the past. His heart ached to behold it. He thought of his own family, in the village of Little Moor. So long since he'd seen his father and sister. Thought was transport enough.

There was Verity, his sister, sitting alone in the drawing room of Low Mede, his old home. Daniel felt as if he was sucked into the house. It had hardly changed. Verity sat before a roaring fire, yet rubbed her arms, as if a cold draught had passed over her. She looked older, but more serene.

"Vez," Daniel murmured, but she could not hear him. She held a glass of red wine against her chest.

Daniel didn't want her to be alone, not on this night, but he sensed no other human presence in the house. He knew then that his father was dead. Poor, solitary Verity. He wanted to be with her, comfort her. Then, the door to the drawing-room opened and a tall, dark-haired man came into the room. He was not human, but not Grigori either. A spirit creature in some respects, but also a being of flesh. Verity smiled languorously, turned, and held out a hand to him. He curled up beside her on the sofa, enfolded in her arms. They did not speak, but gazed into the fire together, as if they dreamed of the future. Outside, the church bells rang, chiming in the new era.

Now, Daniel's perception swept up the Thames in London, where an icy wind fretted the surface of the water. He was a bird, skimming between the brightly lit buildings on either bank. His attention came to rest high above the Embankment, by Cleopatra's Needle. He saw two figures standing together, muffled in thick coats and scarves, between the great lions. A man and a woman. It was Aninka Prussoe, who had once been a lover of Peverel Othman's, and Lahash Murkaster, the assassin who'd been sent to Little Moor to kill him. Lahash and Aninka had been estranged the last time Daniel had seen them. He was glad to see they had re-established contact. But were they lovers now? Lahash put one hand inside his coat and withdrew a dark gleaming object. It was his gun, the symbol of his profession. He handed it to Aninka. She held it up towards the stars for a moment, then tossed it out into the dark, shifting waters of the ancient river. Simultaneously, Big Ben began to toll in the new year and across the entire city, a great cheer went up. Fireworks exploded in light above the steeples and the towers. Aninka and Lahash held each other tight before the sacred waters. They too had cast off the past: his need to avenge and kill, her obsession with unrequited love.

Daniel had witnessed glimpses of the lives of people who had been close to him over the last five years. It seemed the millennium had brought promise, hope and reconciliation for them. But there were others, whom Daniel had not yet seen. His mind shied away from touching the sore spots of his past.

Relentlessly, his perception took to the air once more and he was snatched back to Cornwall, not to High Crag, but the cottage that Lily shared with her daughter and brother. Owen Winter. *I do not want to see this,* Daniel thought, sure that there could be no shining road of optimism opening up for Owen. Fighting the vision, Daniel saw the warm lights of the cottage spilling out into the winter countryside. In the distance, he heard the lash of the ocean against serpentine rocks. He was pulled into the kitchen of the cottage, where two people sat at the bare wooden table, a bottle standing open between them. One of them was Owen, Daniel saw that straight away, but the other…It took a moment for recognition to occur. Then he realised it was Taziel Levantine, another of Daniel's past lovers, whom he had spurned to be with Shemyaza. Both Taziel and Owen had felt very bitter towards Daniel; perhaps together they could heal those past hurts. They drank together in silence, as if conversation had dwindled, but their postures were relaxed, their faces content in companionship.

Daniel's perception now swirled up into the heavens once more. It was all so neat, so tidy, he thought. All these endings and new beginnings. He knew that what he'd seen were only visualisations, and therefore perhaps mere approximations of what would happen as the New Year occurred in England. But he also realised that he had been shown something very important. The potential for change was sweeping across the world and, as the bells chimed at midnight, past bitterness and resentment would fade—even if only for a few moments. New alliances, ideas and loves could grow in that fertile soil. In the midst of battle, soldiers would drop their weapons and behold with clear eyes the faces of those they had been ordered to destroy; murderers would pause, blades and guns in hand, above their victims; politicians would consider the hypocrisy of their policies and principles; criminals and delinquents in every country would feel a burden lift from their hearts, leaving in its wake an inexpressible hope; and in the highest cathedrals and churches, bishops and priests would kneel before their altars, pondering their dependency upon

dogma and faith in the unseen. Ordinary people would feel as
if invisible shackles had fallen from their bodies, minds and
hearts. They might liken it to having been asleep all their lives.
Now they were awake and could see the world with fresh, new
eyes. They would be inspired to seek new destinies. Perhaps
somewhere a young man or woman would suddenly have their
own vision of the future and dream some life-changing inven-
tion or political theory. Coincidence might align to let wonderful things happen.

What Daniel saw in his own life, and the lives of those he
knew, was but a small reflection of the greater whole. The
changes in the world would not be immediate or dramatic.
Gods might have appeared in the sky this night, but the phenomenon was fleeting, like the brilliance of a fire-work. What
really mattered was what lived and endured within the hearts
of Grigori and humanity. In the moments of stillness, when
anger lost its power, both races would be given a chance, a
respite from cruel feeling, to really *see* the world and remember
what once it had been. That was Shemyaza's gift and the legacy
of the Chambers of Light.

Now, at Giza, the great pendulum of time swung above
the earth and rolled the midnight hour over into the new millennium. Daniel looked down upon the plateau. He knew
that soon the Elder would be leaving this plane forever and
was granted knowledge of his passing.

Deep within the blackest depths of the oceans, the kings
of the earth sang out in booming, siren voices. Their cry
echoed through every sea, lighting up the darkest caverns.
The ultra-sonic tones of their song called to the spirit that
burned brightly in the sky above Giza. The Elder's form
dispersed in ripples, and travelled like sparkling mist across
the night sky. Faster now, it streamed over the land and the
ocean boiled at its approach. An explosion of sound and
spray succeeded the fusion of salt water and ether; the Elder
had plunged into the waves to join with the wailing song, a
song that shook the world.

Daniel, his perception firmly back in his own body, knew
he had beheld an event that had already taken place in some
parts of the world and waited to take place in others. He

could hardly breathe in the wake of his vision. His eyes were filled with tears of awe. Dimly, he was aware of the voices of his companions calling his name. He realised that Gadreel was shaking him, staring with concern into his face. "It's all right," he murmured.

"It has gone!" Gadreel cried. "It just seemed to break up and vanish."

Daniel looked over her shoulder and saw that the apparition of the Elder had disappeared. The strange luminance had left the pyramids; they were just monuments of stone. The crowd on the plateau had regained the power of movement. Shrieks filled the air, whoops of joy, sobs of fear. People jumped up and down in frenzied excitement, or crouched on the ground in weeping huddles.

Then, the ground began to shake once more.

"What now?" Lily cried. "Is it over? Daniel, what's going to happen to us next?"

Daniel had no answer for her. Surely, now that the power of the Chambers had been released into the world and the last fragments of the Elders had been set free, the phenomena should cease. His flesh went cold. What if the Chambers were collapsing? The entire Giza plateau might be destroyed in an earthquake. All those people! Daniel shuddered in horror and turned to Lily. "We've got to get out of here. All of us!" The ground heaved beneath his feet and he stumbled. People were screaming now and stampeding in all directions. The avatars and their companions were pushed against the wall of the Sphinx enclosure as people tried to scrabble out. Tiy had come back to her senses and was blinking her blind eyes in fear. Melandra held onto her tightly, trying to murmur comfort. Her own face was distorted in a grimace of terror.

An immense rumbling roar filled the air, accompanied by a the sound of splintering rock. The tremors increased and the remaining people in the enclosure fell to the ground. Daniel and his companions were engulfed in a bright, acidic radiance that dazzled their eyes. The great left paw of the Sphinx had begun to rise up, as if on a giant hinge. Slowly, slowly, it reared towards the sky. Dust and stone fell down from it in a choking shower.

"The Chambers!" Daniel cried. "They have opened.!"

The paw had come to rest now, rising vertically into the air in a parody of a salute. Sand sifted down from it in granular streams. Gradually, the tremors died away, until there was stillness.

Daniel jumped to his feet and ran towards the opening that had appeared beneath the paw. His companions followed closely. Light poured out of the tunnel revealed below the monument. A great stone ramp disappeared downwards into its radiance.

Other people around the Sphinx had staggered to their feet and now cautiously approached the opening. Crowds on the plateau had surged towards the lip of the enclosure to see what had happened. The avatars and their companions formed a line at the front of the crowds.

"Shall we go down?" Gadreel asked.

Daniel shook his head. "Not yet." He felt at peace, his heart full of a joyous warmth. Why had he lacked faith? He had been wrong. He should have known.

A shadow formed against the white radiance, the shape of a tall figure who was walking up the ramp towards the opening.

"Who is it?" Pharmaros asked.

Daniel looked at her. "Do you have to ask?" He could wait no longer and stepped into the radiance, holding out his arms. Presently, Shemyaza, reborn and naked, stepped into his embrace.

An ululating wail broke the silence, the sound of women's voices, but no longer singing a lament. All across Giza, women of every faith and creed were united in their beliefs. They sang an instinctive paean. "The king has risen! Long live the king!"

"Shem," Daniel breathed. He could say no more.

Shemyaza held his face in his hands and kissed him. For a moment, they looked into each other's eyes. Daniel was unsure of what he saw in Shemyaza's gaze. He had changed; it was inevitable, but the light of love still burned within him.

"My vizier," Shemyaza said. "I am glad you are here."

His arm around Daniel's shoulder, he walked out of the tunnel and stood before his waiting followers. Daniel stepped away from him. Shemyaza looked inhuman, filled with the Elders' power. His nakedness seemed to enhance his strangeness. All was silent, and Shemyaza looked into the faces of his companions, one by one. Behind them, the crowd stared in uncanny silence, their eyes wide.

Then, an Egyptian soldier pushed his way to the front of the crowd. Everybody tensed, but the man fell to his knees and held out to Shemyaza a rough, army blanket. "You must be cold, master," he said.

Shemyaza thanked the soldier, wrapped himself in the blanket, and spoke. "Lament no more, my faithful company, for I have risen." Then, he smiled. "No more prophecies. The work is done. Come to me, sisters. I need you." As one, Lily, Tiy, Melandra and Gadreel ran towards him and threw their arms around him and one another. Shemyaza laughed and called out above their heads. "Come, Pharmaros, why aren't you with us?"

Pharmaros hesitated only a moment, then smiled to herself and went up to join the huddle. After a few moments, Shemyaza gently eased himself from the women's hold and stepped forward, holding the blanket at his throat. Helen stood alone in front of him and he squatted down before her. For a while, he just stared at her face.

Then Helen reached out and touched his cheek with small fingers. "I thought that you weren't coming back," she said. "I thought I would be alive in the world, like you were, but alone."

Shemyaza ruffled her dark hair. "Ishtahar, little Ishtahar. Of course I came back. I couldn't leave you here alone. Your love brought me back." He kissed her forehead.

Tiy nodded at them, smiling. "You have some growing to do, girl, but it will not be long before you are a woman and will become his bride. You will be the queen of heaven."

Helen smiled shyly and fought to suppress a shy giggle. She was still just a child.

Shemyaza stood up once more and turned to Salamiel. "My brother, will you welcome me?"

Salamiel uttered an agonised sound and turned his face away. "Why are you alive?" he asked in an unsteady voice. "I *murdered* you." Then, he whirled round to face Shemyaza, his red hair flying, yet he spoke in a whisper. "'Love me, Salamiel,' you said. 'Kill me,' you said. And I loved you so much, I did as you asked. Part of me died too in that church, Shem. Now, here you are. Good as new. You mock my pain!"

Shemyaza shook his head and spoke softly. "No, Salamiel, no. What you did was an act of grace. It brought in the new epoch. I had the easier job." He kept his eyes fixed on Salamiel's face and sank to his knees. "Please, Salamiel, don't look on me as the person you destroyed. The world is different now, and so am I. I don't want to play the martyr. You think you murdered me, violated me, but what you did was purify me. The scapegoat of the people is dead now, forever."

Tiy raised her arms and spoke, her cracked voice ringing out over the crowd. "It is accomplished! All your struggles are ended, Salamiel. Do not hold on to them! The salvation of your land and the glory of your people is at hand. If you must weep tears, then weep tears of joy."

Shemyaza suppressed a smile. Then, he lowered his head. "Give me your forgiveness, brother. That's all I ask."

Salamiel looked down upon Shemyaza's bent head. He glanced to the side and caught Daniel's furious eye glaring directly at him. Then he sighed and knelt down before Shemyaza. "Then, I forgive you, brother." He laughed shakily. "Daniel will not forgive me if I don't."

They embraced, and then Shemyaza rose to his feet. He held out his arms and his voice rang out across the sands of Giza. "Gather around me, my brethren. We shall return to the city of Babylon. There our paradise will be regained."

Daniel tucked himself beneath the wing of Shemyaza's arm, and together they led the company out of the enclosure. The crowds parted before them. Some saw Christ pass among them, others saw the god Osiris risen from the Realm of the Dead, while still more welcomed the return of their prophet.

The pyramids stood sentinel against the sky. In the distance, the bells of the Coptic churches pealed in the new year. And from the lofty tower of a mosque, the sound of a muezzin's cry echoed to the east. The last scapegoat had fallen from the mountain.

Storm Constantine Biography

Storm Constantine decided somewhere about fifteen years ago that life should be more exciting than a backroom 9 to 5 for a local charity, and decided to do something about it. With one of the luckiest breaks into publishing (a tale still rare enough in SF to be dined out on) she started her career as a writer with the *Wraeththu* trilogy, published by MacDonald Orbit, about a post-human race of androgyne hermaphrodites coming to terms with themselves and their new world. Ten years later she is currently in the middle of her third trilogy, for Penguin. In a way, everything in between, over some thirteen novels and numerous short stories, can be seen as leading almost inevitably to this point: Storm's long fascination with angels, mythology, the recurrent themes of magic and sexuality, secret knowledge, dark and charismatic figures on the edge of society and outside convention. But this is not merely coming full circle. Each book in its way, from the SF cyber-paganism of *Hermetech*, the threatened elohim of *Burying the Shadow*, the structural nested story games in *Calenture*, and the enigmatic revolutionary messiah of *Sign for the Sacred*, illuminate different facets of a body of work that is unmistakably 'Storm Constantine'.

Who is Storm Constantine? She lives in the Midlands with as many cats as she has published books, in a house that looks entirely conventional until you step inside, and houses a library of Pre-Raphaelite art and esoteric reference books that you would cheerfully kill (or at least lightly maim) for.

A sense of style, in appearance as much as on the page, that would drop jaws at Storm's early appearances at SF conventions. Black clad, in a million silver bangles, with spiky hair and exotic makeup, the Constantine entourage would turn heads in astonishment, and not a little envy amongst the regulars of SF fandom.

Here was Showtime.

The appearance is a little less flamboyant now (though she still takes *ages* to get ready to go anywhere) but can still evoke a spontaneous hug for a stunned waitress in a US bar who recently asked for her ID.

She is a born, almost compulsive storyteller. She has numerous short stories in anthologies, magazines and fanzines and small press publications. And you don't get rich by doing the last two; at most you might get a couple of complimentary copies. So why? Because Storm is a fan too. She found SF fandom at the same time she started writing, and never left (you never really do). Which is why her current project, *Visionary Tongue*, is a writers' workshop fanzine that grew out of her involvement in teaching creative writing classes. And its third issue boasts some seriously fine writing, and almost a dozen SF and fantasy authors on a volunteer editorial board that any professional publication would be jealous of. Because you can always give something back, and you can never run out of stories.

The Complete Constantine
A Storm Constantine Bibliography

Novels, Novellas, Full Length Non-Fiction and Short Story Collections

The Enchantments of Flesh and Spirit
(1987 Macdonald h/b. 1988 Futura p/b. 1990 TOR p/b USA 1996 Heyne p/b Germany as Der Zauber von Fleisch und Geist)

The Bewitchments of Love and Hate
(1988 Macdonald h/b. 1988 Futura p/b. 1990 TOR p/b USA 1996 Heyne p/b Germany as Im Bann von Liebe und Hass)

The Fulfilments of Fate and Desire
(1989 Drunken Dragon Press h/b. 1989 Orbit p/b. 1991 TOR p/b USA 1996 Heyne p/b Germany as Die Erfullung von Schicksal und Begehren)

The Monstrous Regiment
(1990 Orbit t/p/b. 1991 Orbit p/b)

Hermetech
(1991 Headline h/b, t/p/b. 1991 Headline p/b. 1993 Heyne p/b Germany)

Aleph
(1991 Orbit t/p/b)

Burying the Shadow
(1992 Headline h/b, t/p/b; 1992 Headline p/b; 1995 Heyne p/b Germany as 'Schattengraber')

Sign for the Sacred
(1993 Headline h/b, t/p/b. 1993 Headline p/b)

Wraeththu
(Omnibus: The Enchantments of Flesh and Spirit, Bewitchments of Love and Hate, Fulfilments of Fate and Desire)
(1993 TOR t/p/b)

Calenture
(1994 Headline h/b. 1994 Headline p/b)

Stalking Tender Prey
(1995 p/b Creed/Signet; 1998 p/b Meisha Merlin, USA)

Scenting Hallowed Blood
(1996 p/b Signet; 1999 p/b (1999 Meisha Merlin, USA)

Three Heralds of the Storm
'Such a Nice Girl', 'How Enlightenment..' & 'Last Come Assimilation' (1997 p/b Meisha-Merlin, USA, 1997)

Stealing Sacred Fire
(1997 p/b Signet; forthcoming 2000 Meisha Merlin, USA)

The Inward Revolution
(with Deborah Benstead)
Non-fiction esoteric psychology, (1998 Warner, UK)

Thin Air
(1999 Warner p/b)

The Thorn Boy
(1999 novella, p/b, Eidolon Press, Australia)

The Oracle Lips
(1999 short story collection: The Vitreous Suzerain; Of a Cat, But Her Skin; Sweet Bruising Skin; Heir to a Tendency; Remedy of the Bane; The Time She Became; Curse of the Snake; Panquilia in the Ruins; Candle Magic; Blue Flame of a Candle; By the River of If Only…; Immaculate; The Rust Islands; Fire Born; Nocturne; As It Flows to the Sea; The Oracle Lips; The Deliveress; God Be With You; Angel of the Hate Wind; The Feet, They Dance; Return to Gehenna; A Change of Season; The Seduction of Angels (poem), Stark Press, USA, h/b)

Sea Dragon Heir
(book one of the Magravandias Chronicles)
(1999, h/b Gollancz UK; (forthcoming 1999, TOR, USA)

Bast and Sekhmet: Eyes of Ra
With Eloise Coquio
(1999 (forthcoming) non-fiction book on the feline deities of Ancient Egypt; Robert Hale, h/b)

The Crown of Silence
(book two of the Magravandias Chronicles)
(2000, forthcoming, Gollancz h/b UK; TOR, p/b USA)

Short Stories (Published)

By the River of If Only…	1988 Paragenesis/1991 Fear, January (Wraeththu story) UK
So What's Forever?	1989 GM Magazine, Vol 1 #7 Mar. UK
God Be With You	1989 GM Magazine, Vol 2 #4 Dec. UK
They Hunt….	1989 Drabble Project #1 UK
The Pleasure Giver Taken	1989 Zenith 1 (anthology), Sphere, UK
As it Flows to the Sea	1990 Tarot Tales (anthology), Legend, UK

Last Come Assimilation	1990 Digital Dreams (anthology), NEL, UK
The Time She Became	1990 Zenith 2 (anthology), Sphere, UK
Did You Ever See Oysters Walking Down the Stairs?	1990 More Tales from the Forbidden Planet (anth), UK
The Heart of Fairen D'eath	1990 Weird Tales, USA
Lacrymata	1990 Deathwing, Warhammer anthology, Games Workshop, UK
The Vitreous Suzerain	1991 The Gate Magazine (#2), UK
The College Spirit	1991 Temps (anthology), Penguin/Roc, UK
Immaculate	1991 New Worlds (anthology) Gollancz (Nominated for BSFA award 1992) UK
The Deliveress	1992 Villains (anthology), Penguin/Roc, UK
Poisoning the Sea	1992 Dedalus Book of Femme Fatales, UK
A Change of Season	1992 The Weerde (anthology), Penguin/Roc (Inspiration for novel **Stalking Tender Prey**) UK
How Enlightenment Came to the Tower	1992 Scheherazade magazine (#2), UK
Priest of Hands	1992 Interzone magazine (#58) (Used in novel **Calenture**), UK
The Law of Being	1992 Eurotemps (anthology), Penguin/Roc, UK
The Preservation	1992 REM magazine (#2), UK
An Elemental Tale	1992 Inception (limited edition chapbook), UK
Built on Blood	1992 Interzone magazine (#64), UK

The Green Calling	1993 Interzone magazine (#73), UK
Sweet Bruising Skin	1994 Black Thorn, White Rose (anth) AvoNova Morrow USA
Candle Magic	1994 Blue Motel: Narrow Houses III (anthology), Little Brown UK
Blue Flame of a Candle	1995 Tombs: Tales Beyond the Crypt (anth) White Wolf USA
Return to Gehenna	1996 Dante's Disciples, (anth) White Wolf USA
An Old Passion	1996 Festival of the Imagination programme, Aust.
Remedy of the Bane	1996 Realms of Fantasy mag., USA (August)
Dancer for the World's Death	1996 Inception chapbook, UK
Kiss Booties Night Night	1996 Cybersex, (anthology) ed. Richard G Jones, Robinson UK
Fire Born	1996 Science Fiction Age magazine, USA (October)
Of a Cat, but her Skin...	1996 Twists of the Tale, (anthology), ed. Ellen Datlow, Dell, USA
Angel of the Hate Wind	1997 Destination Unknown (anth), ed P Crowther White Wolf, USA
The Rust Islands	1997 Interzone magazine, UK
Such a Nice Girl	1997 'Three Heralds of the Storm' chapbook, Meisha Merlin, USA
The Oracle Lips	1998 Fortune Tellers (anth) ed. L Schimel, USA
Prelude	1998 Mage: The Sorcerer's Crusade, White Wolf USA
My Lady of the Hearth	1998 Sirens and other daemon lovers (anth.) ed E Datlow and T Windling, Harper Prism, USA

Paragenesis	1998 Crow anthology, ed. E Kramer & J O'Barr, USA
Night's Damozel	1998 (with Eloise Coquio), Interzone, UK
Curse of the Snake	1999 The Oracle Lips collection, Stark House, USA
Nocturne: The Twilight Community	1999 The Oracle Lips collection, Stark House, USA
Panquilia in the Ruins	1999 The Oracle Lips collection, Stark House, USA
Heir to a Tendency	1999 The Oracle Lips collection, Stark House, USA
The Feet, They Dance	1999 The Oracle Lips collection, Stark House, USA

Short Stories & Novellas (Unpublished)

True Destiny of the Heir of Emiraldra, The	1987
Spinning for Gold	1987
Germ of Life, The	1988
Time Beginning at Break of Day	1988
The Face of Sekt	1999

Short Story Reprints

Last Come Assimilation	1991 Digital Dreams (Hebrew translation) Opus Ltd, Israel
Immaculate	1994 Cyberpunk, (Italian trans.) Editrice Nord, Italy
Poisoning the Sea	1994 Das Grosse Lesebuch der Femme Fatale (German trans), Goldmann (Germany) as 'Gift-ins Meer giessen'

Immaculate	1995 The End of Century SF Masterpieces (Japanese trans.) Kinokuniya Co Ltd, Japan
Immaculate	1995 Women of Wonder: The Contemporary years (anthology)Harcourt, Brace & Co (USA)
Immaculate	1995 Tahtivaeltaja magazine, (Finnish translation) Finland
Sweet Bruising Skin	1996 Black Thorn, White Rose (anthology) Signet (UK)
Candle Magic	1996 Blue Motel: Narrow Houses 3 anth, White Wolf, USA
As it Flows to the Sea	1996 Tarot Tales (anthology) Ace Books, USA
How Enlightenment Came to the Tower	1997 'Three Heralds of the Storm', Meisha Merlin, US
Last Come Assimilation	1997 'Three Heralds of the Storm', Meisha Merlin, US
Such a Nice Girl	1997 Dark Terrors 3, ed. S Jones & D Sutton,Gollancz, UK
Of a Cat, But Her Skin	1997 Best New Horror 8, Robinson, UK & Bantam USA
Of a Cat, But Her Skin	(forthcoming) Czechoslovakian ed. of Twists of the Tale
The Vitreous Suzerain	1999 The Oracle Lips collection, Stark House, USA
Of a Cat, But Her Skin	1999 The Oracle Lips collection, Stark House, USA
Sweet Bruising Skin	1999 The Oracle Lips collection, Stark House, USA
Remedy of the Bane	1999 The Oracle Lips collection, Stark House, USA
The Time She Became	1999 The Oracle Lips collection, Stark House, USA

Candle Magic	1999 The Oracle Lips collection, Stark House, USA
Blue Flame of a Candle	1999 The Oracle Lips collection, Stark House, USA
By the River of If Only...	1999 The Oracle Lips collection, Stark House, USA
Immaculate	1999 The Oracle Lips collection, Stark House, USA
The Rust Islands	1999 The Oracle Lips collection, Stark House, USA
Fire Born	1999 The Oracle Lips collection, Stark House, USA
As It Flows to the Sea	1999 The Oracle Lips collection, Stark House, USA
The Oracle Lips	1999 The Oracle Lips collection, Stark House, USA
The Deliveress	1999 The Oracle Lips collection, Stark House, USA
God Be With You	1999 The Oracle Lips collection, Stark House, USA
Angel of the Hate Wind	1999 The Oracle Lips collection, Stark House, USA
Return to Gehenna	1999 The Oracle Lips collection, Stark House, USA
A Change of Season	1999 The Oracle Lips collection, Stark House, USA

Articles & Features

Sex and Chaos	1991 Fear magazine (neo-paganism)
A Man's Gotta Do...	1992 Siren magazine (Interview with Carl McCoy)
Ghostriders	1992 Siren magazine (Interview with ENDG)
Icke Can See Clearly Now	1992 Siren magazine (Interview with Creaming Jesus)

Over the Edge	1992 Gamesman magazine (column)
Storm Warning	1992 Gamesman magazine (column)
Storm in a Pint Pot	1992 Gamesman magazine (column)
When the Angels Came	1992 Novacon 22 booklet
Tales of the Nefilim	1992 Watchman II magazine (Nefilim info service)
The Death of Traditional Fantasy	1993 Concatenation magazine
The Everness Kiss	1993 Twisted Souls magazine (vampire article)
The Feast of Fiction	1993 Legacy magazine
Revelations	1993 Nephilim biography on 'Revelations' l.p. sleeve
The Beast Breaks Free	1993 Watchman III magazine (Nefilim info. service)
Introduction to Pat Cadigan's short story collection	1993 Dirty Work (collection) Mark Zeising, USA
Introduction to Pete Crowther anthology	1994 Heaven Sent (anthology) DAW, (USA1995 Heaven Sent (anthology) Penguin, UK
Roots of a Writer	1996 Dark Horizons magazine, BFS, UK
Photo and quote	1996 The Faces of Fantasy, Patti Perret, TOR, USA
Wraeththu Dream	1996 The Tiger Garden: a Book of Writers' Dreams, ed. N Royle, Serpents Tail

Poems

In the Dark   1991 Now We Are Sick (h/bk
                                    collection) DreamHaven
                                    Books, (USA) (1994 Pbk ed)
Colurastes   1995 Collection, Inception
Ishtahar's Confession   1995 Visionary Tongue 1 zine
                                    (as Eden Crane) U
The Gift of Flight   1995 Visionary Tongue 1 zine
                                    (as Eden Crane) UK
The Seduction of Angels   1999 The Oracle Lips collec-
                                    tion, Stark House, USA

Rick Berry Biography

Rick Berry is an award winning oil painter, draftsman, and a pioneer in new media; in 1984 he created the world's first digital cover illustration for a work of fiction, William Gibson's *Neuromancer*.

He left school at age 17 to begin a career in underground comics. After hitching east to Boston from Colorado, he shifted his artistic focus to books, film, and fine art. He has produced hundreds of illustrations for books, magazines, games, and comics. In 1991 *Communications Arts* showcased four of Berry's seven oil paintings in Peter Straub's *Mrs. God*.

Past distinctions include: *Gold Award*, editorial, Spectrum Art Annual; *Best Book Cover*, 9th Annual *Publish* Design Contest; *Artist Guest of Honor* at The 1997 World Horror Convention in Niagara Falls. Selected works are included in this year's Computer Art & Design Annual, From *Print Magazine*, in Society of Illustrators' traveling exhibition—*Illustration: Past, Present, and Future* and *The Digital Show*, Museum of Illustration, NYC, in *The History of Science Fiction Art* by Vincent DiFate, Penguin Art Books; and he is the featured artist in OMNI Magazine's *Dark Echo* world wide web literary site.

Berry has an abiding interest in collaborative work, and, in 1993 , joined with Phil Hale to produce *Double Memory*, an 110 page art book. William Gibson wrote of their book: "...Nervy, pervy, and utterly assured, their work haunts with the disturbing intensity of half-remembered dreams."

Berry and Gibson worked together again in 1995 when Braid Media Arts (Berry, Darrel Anderson, and Gene Bodio) designed and executed the CGI cyberspace climax of Tristar Productions' film (now on video) *Johnny Mnemonic*. The sequence was featured in SIGGRAPH's animation review, 1996.

Barry's early experience in the print production trenches of comics has evolved into specialty editions design work and sent him to some interesting places. (He was flown to Hong Kong in 1993 to supervise presses and advise the Chinese on current electronic press capabilities...*in english*.)

His fine art work can be seen in galleries internationally and on the world wide web, (http://www.braid.com)

Barry teaches *Digital Art: A Collaborative Approach* at Tufts University, as well as conduction lectures and workshops at colleges and corporations nationally on the nature of creativity.

Rick Berry

**Come check out our web site
for details on these
Meisha Merlin authors!**

Kevin J. Anderson
Robin Wayne Bailey
Edo van Belkom
Janet Berliner
Storm Constantine
Diane Duane
Sylvia Engdahl
Jim Grimsley
George Guthridge
Keith Hartman
Beth Hilgartner
P. C. Hodgell
Tanya Huff
Janet Kagan
Caitlin R. Kiernan
Lee Killough
George R. R. Martin

Lee Martindale
Jack McDevitt
Sharon Lee & Steve Miller
James A. Moore
Adam Niswander
Andre Norton
Jody Lynn Nye
Selina Rosen
Kristine Kathryn Rusch
Pamela Sargent
Michael Scott
S. P. Somtow
Allen Steele
Mark Tiedeman
Freda Warrington

http://www.MeishaMerlin.com